'There's a mesmerising, transcendent reverence for love and the land in Hannah Kent's exquisitely wrought novel . . . Passionate and poetic, *Devotion* is a slow burn of a novel, full of grace and emotional gravitas'
Daily Mail

'With an extraordinarily daring twist halfway through its narrative *Devotion* is a remarkable novel, an almost visionary celebration of the death-defying power of the women's love'
The Sunday Times, Historical Fiction Book of the Month

'[Hanne and Thea's] story is an elegy, freighted with loss and longing'
The Guardian

'The poetry of the landscape had, for me, a Whitmanesque sensibility. A mighty impassioned cry to love and the land'
Sarah Winman, author of *Still Life*

'*Devotion* is rare and exquisite, both beautiful and muscular in its portrayal of love found and denied. It's a story of love as a radical act, and a celebration of place and persistence. As we've come to expect from Kent, this is masterful storytelling with pull-no-punches stakes'
Kiran Millwood Hargrave, author of *The Mercies*

'*Devotion* is utterly original. A glorious, heartbreaking love story of infinite beauty'
Heather Rose, author of *The Museum of Modern Love*

'A superb novel. A fantastic merging of exquisite lyrical writing and page-turning adventure. *Devotion* had me constantly surprised, always entertained, and ultimately deeply moved: it deserves to be a glittering success'
Emma Stonex, *Sunday Times* bestselling author of *The Lamplighters*

'Full of magic and adventure. I fell in love with language again reading it. So beautiful and so raw'　　　Evie Wyld, author of *The Bass Rock*

'A tale of the refiguring might of faithful hearts; of love that sustains and love that ruins; of exile and dominion'　　　*The Sydney Morning Herald*

Devotion

Hannah Kent is an author and screenwriter. Her first novel, *Burial Rites*, has been translated into over thirty languages and was shortlisted for the Women's Prize for Fiction, the *Guardian* First Book Award and the International IMPAC Dublin Literary Award. In Australia it won the ABIA Literary Fiction Book of the Year and the Indie Awards Debut Fiction Book of the Year, amongst others. Her second novel, *The Good People*, has also been translated into many languages and was shortlisted for the Walter Scott Prize. *Devotion*, her third novel, was longlisted for the Dublin Literary Award.

ALSO BY HANNAH KENT

Burial Rites
The Good People

Hannah Kent

DEVOTION

PICADOR

First published 2021 by Pan Macmillan Australia Pty Ltd, Sydney

This paperback edition published 2023 by Picador
an imprint of Pan Macmillan
The Smithson, 6 Briset Street, London EC1M 5NR
EU representative: Macmillan Publishers Ireland Ltd, 1st Floor,
The Liffey Trust Centre, 117–126 Sheriff Street Upper,
Dublin 1, D01 YC43
Associated companies throughout the world
www.panmacmillan.com

ISBN 978-1-5098-6388-4

Pan Macmillan acknowledges the Traditional Custodians of country throughout Australia
and their connections to lands, waters and communities. We pay our respect to Elders past
and present and extend that respect to all Aboriginal and Torres Strait Islander peoples today.
We honour more than sixty thousand years of storytelling, art and culture.

1 3 5 7 9 8 6 4 2

A CIP catalogue record for this book is available from the British Library.

Printed and bound by CPI Group (UK) Ltd, Croydon, CR0 4YY

For Heidi

ACKNOWLEDGEMENT OF COUNTRY

This novel was written on the unceded, sovereign lands of the Peramangk and Kaurna nations, and I would like to pay my respects to their Elders past and present. I acknowledge First Nations peoples and recognise and honour their spiritual connection to Country, community and culture, not least the sharing of story across time and generations.

Sei getreu bis an den Tod, so will ich dir die Krone des Lebens geben.

OFFENBARUNG 2:10

Be thou faithful unto death, and I will give thee a crown of life.

REVELATION 2:10

~

Ich habe dich einen kleinen Augenblick verlassen; aber mit großer Barmherzigkeit will ich dich sammeln.

JESAJA 54:7

For a small moment I have forsaken thee, but with great mercies will I gather thee.

ISAIAH 54:7

~

Love is your last chance. There is really nothing else on earth to keep you there.

LOUIS ARAGON,
quoted by Patrick White in *A Fringe of Leaves*

~

THE
FIRST
DAY

my heart is a hand reaching

Thea, there is no line in your palm I have not traced, no knuckle cracked unheard, and the blue of your eyes is the coffin-lining of the world. I would they sing psalms to you and the down upon your thighs, and the eyelashes that have fallen to the fields you have worked. I would they lay boughs upon knees bent to the soil-hum of any place you have rested upon. Thea, if love were a thing, it would be the sinew of a hand stretched in anticipation of grasping. See, my hands, they reach for you. My heart is a hand reaching.

testimony of love

It is time, I think, to tell my story.

In this moment, as the sun stretches its burnished hands upon the world, I feel myself finally pulling apart with time. Something is coming and I feel surrender approaching. A gentle giving-in.

I am not afraid. Not now. I've seen enough to know that fear scrapes feeling from hearts and I have no desire to scour mine down to bare and trembling muscle. Still, after what has happened, in this moment of honey-light, the air a censer of eucalyptus, I wonder how many days remain to me and whether, if I pass out of existence without testament, something necessary will be lost.

I could not remain with her. I think – and the thought lathes a yawning hole of grief within me – that it is over. I think I have already seen her face for the last time. That is what is hard. That is what has brought me up here amongst the trees. And now, one of these days, I will be gone.

Perhaps that is why I want to bear witness. I feel it as an urgency within my body. If I rest my fingers against my mouth, I feel my lips move in readiness to speak.

The light is rising. The wind rises. I lift my face to the sun as it fills the world.

If I testify, no one will hear me. Is a story unheard a story diminished? I cannot believe that. The wind may hear me, perhaps. The wind may yet carry my voice down to the valley, might press it against the ear of a child who will one day wonder at deeper mysteries, the inheritance of miracles. I can be satisfied with that.

The testimony of love is the backbone of the universe. It is the taproot from which all stories spring.

Listen, wind. Here is my small filament.

BEFORE

federschleissen

One night, years ago, in the autumn of 1836, I was lying under the walnut tree in my family's orchard, listening to the tapping of raindrops sliding from leaves to soil. I heard them as a muted concord of bells. The trunk drummed black, the sky was chanting low cloud and I was bathed in hymns of water. Somewhere, beneath it all, I could hear my father calling my name. I stayed where I was. The wind scattered droplets upon my face. The damp soaked through my clothes.

'Hanne!'

I closed my eyes. For the past two evenings, and this night too, my mother had been at the Radtkes' house for a *Federschleissen*, and I was determined to make the most of my freedom. I had escaped outside as soon as she had left. I was fourteen, nearly fifteen, and not yet used to the burdens of womanhood and its inert domestic companions of needle and thread, bucket and cloth. Our cottage with its low ceiling and cramped rooms suffocated me. I missed the livingness of things.

'Hanne!'

The walnut tree was singing to me. *Stay.*

'Hanne.'

A different voice this time, louder. I opened my eyes and saw my brother, Matthias, looking down at me with a bemused expression, lantern in hand. The tree's song subsided.

'What does he want?' I asked, shielding my eyes from the glare of the light.

'If you go inside now, he won't see you. He's looking for you in the lane.' Matthias set the lantern on the ground and helped me to my feet, and together we walked through the orchard, heady with the smell of rain on loam and fallen leaves, to the mud of the yard. I could make out the pale bulk of our pig in the dark of her sty. She lifted her head to look at us as I turned the doorknob.

'Are you coming in?' I asked Matthias.

'No. I'm to bed,' he said, nodding towards the side of the house where the ladder led to the loft. He hesitated. 'Were you listening again?'

'It's better at night.'

'What could you hear this time?' he asked. He was eye-bright in the glow of the lantern.

'Singing,' I said. 'Like the tree was singing to the water and the rain was singing to the earth.'

Matthias nodded. 'You'd best get in. Goodnight, then,' he said, and he moved off into the dark.

As I pulled the door shut behind me, Papa appeared in the corridor, holding a candle. He paused, frowning with his good eye.

'Hello, Papa.'

'Where have you been, Hanne?'

'Getting ready for bed,' I said, easing my feet out of my clogs.

'But you weren't in your room.'

'No, I had to . . .' I flicked a thumb in the vague direction of our outhouse.

My father lifted a hand to guard the flicker of the candle flame. 'Put your shoes back on. I need you to fetch Mutter home.'

'Why?'

'It's late.'

'She's been late the past two nights.'

'*Ja*, exactly. Too late.' He turned and headed towards the kitchen, the candlelight throwing his silhouette against the walls of the corridor. 'Go get her,' he muttered over his shoulder. 'Bring her home.'

The night had cleared and deepened into delicious cold. At that hour in the village, everything smelled of pickled pork and kitchen fire. I walked a little down the lane and then, when I was sure my father would not see me, turned into our neighbours' allotment so that I might walk beside the fields. I passed close by the Pasches' cottage, bending over to avoid being seen through the window by Elder Christian Pasche, who I could hear at prayer within. I pictured his bald head shining in the firelight as he intoned over his Bible, his sons, Hans, Hermann and Georg, slumped and drowsy at the table. The *Federschleissen* was being held for Elder Pasche's second bride, a narrow-eyed woman called Rosina with terrible breath and a mole on her forearm that she scratched at during services. Rosina was closer in age to Hans than his father, but as she and Christian were both dour and humourless, the match was generally agreed to be a good one. 'They will be able to spend many wonderful evenings not laughing together,' my mother had commented on hearing the news.

I pulled off my headscarf to feel the air against my neck. In the clear light of the rising moon, the shorn rye fields seemed soft and melancholy, the forest upon the eastern rise the only interruption in the otherwise flat, silvered horizon of pasture, field and marsh. Only the spire of the church – locked now – steepled into the sky. Everything else was dull and low-lying, a patchwork of farm ground, whitewash and wood shingle. I had lived in Kay my whole life. I could have paced out each house, orchard and field in pitch-darkness.

I could hear the sound of women's laughter as I left the fields and turned north towards the Radtkes' yard. The back door was ajar, offering a glimpse of lamplight and shifting shadows. As I paused by the henhouse to gather my braids back under my headscarf, there was a quiet cough from the side of the building, and I saw Elder Samuel Radtke sitting on his chopping block by the woodpile, smoking his pipe in the dark. He nodded at me.

'Came by the fields, did you? Good night for it.'

'Sorry,' I stammered.

'She's put me out for the night. Dog's inside, though.' He chuckled. 'Go on in. They've been at it for hours.' Samuel puffed on his pipe and gestured for me to enter, just as the women burst out in a new wave of mirth.

Inside the women were squeezed shoulder to shoulder around the large kitchen table, cackling hard while their fingers stripped feathers and stuffed the down into clay jars for the new Frau Pasche's wedding quilt. It took me several moments before I picked out my mother from their midst. She was laughing and, unused to seeing her smile, I was struck anew by her beauty – the painful, astonishing certainty of it. As a child I had not minded when people remarked upon our difference, or had wondered aloud why Matthias, my twin, and not I had inherited her full top lip, her dark eyes and hair. But now, as several heads turned in my direction, I felt again the silent, inevitable comparison and wanted to hide. Here she is, the cuckoo born to a songbird. The odd, unbeautiful daughter.

Mutter Scheck, her round little glasses smudged with fingerprints, nudged Mama. 'Look, Johanne – your little Johanne is here to herd you home.'

Mama glanced up at me. 'No, you've come too early! I'm not ready.' Her voice was high and girlish. The women laughed again and I smiled, my throat suddenly, inexplicably, tight with tears.

'Papa sent me.'

'What does he want? A bedtime story? Your papa can wait.'

Mutter Scheck snorted.

I noticed then that Henriette and Elizabeth Volkmann were sitting with Christiana Radtke and something in me buckled. I had not been invited. Christiana coloured and the girls smiled at me with tight lips. I wanted to disappear.

Elize Geschke patted the space beside her at the edge of the kitchen table, sweeping the bench free of stray stripped quills. 'Here, Hanne. Come and sit with me.'

I lifted my too-long legs up and over the bench, avoiding the guarded looks from Christiana and Henriette from across the room, as Elize squeezed my shoulder and offered me her glass. They were drinking sweet wine. Mama nodded and I took a sip. Elize was only three years older than me but, newly married to Reinhardt Geschke, she belonged to a different circle of women. She rubbed my back as I spluttered on the wine and I wondered how she could bear to have me sit next to her, plain and awkward as I was.

Elize pities you, I thought. She saw Christiana look over and knows you have been left out. She's being kind.

I set the glass carefully back on the table.

'Why don't you help while you wait for your mama?' Elize reached into the goose down, piled like snow, and placed a handful of plucked feathers in front of me. Copying the others, I tore the fluff from the stem, stuffing it into the jar in front of Elize. Magdalena Radtke's sharp eyes were on me, making sure, no doubt, that I was stripping the feathers properly.

There was a brief, companionable silence as twenty pairs of hands busied themselves in union. Elize leaned against me in gentle reassurance.

'So,' announced Rosina from her position at the head of the table. 'The new family up in the cottage. What do we think of them?'

Magdalena cleared her throat. 'I have heard that his wife is a Wend.'

Eleonore Volkmann raised her thick eyebrows. 'If she has married a German, she is German.'

'Well,' continued Magdalena, 'you would hope so. And yet, when I caught a glimpse of them, the wife had the headdress on. You know' – she waved a plump hand above her head – 'that strange-looking, horned thing.'

Elize noticed my confusion and leaned closer. 'Newcomers to Kay,' she whispered. 'We were talking about them earlier. A family, renting the forester's cottage.'

I knew the building she spoke of. It was a ramshackle one-roomed cabin that stood in front of the dark wall of pines at the village border. No one had lived there for some time and the cottage had started to list towards the trees. Sometimes, from a certain distance, it looked as though the house and the forest had begun to reach towards one another. I often walked that way to collect kindling and would sometimes stop and think how wonderful it was that, emptied of people, a building would inevitably reach for the elements that made it. Clay, wood, earth, grass. Disintegration as reunion.

'Will they worship with us?' asked my mother.

'My husband says yes,' replied Emile Pfeiffer, who lived close to the forest. She pulled off her headscarf to scratch her head, grey hairs threaded through the brown. 'Herr Eichenwald asked him about services. His wife seems friendly. Quite forthright. She told us she was a midwife.'

'We lived in a Wendish village when I was a child,' Elize said softly. 'They were very kind to us. They told wonderful stories.'

'Demons and the *Wassermann*,' Magdalena interrupted.

'The *Wassermann*?' asked Christiana.

'A little fish man who lives in a pond and drowns people,' Elize murmured. 'It's a children's story.'

Christiana pulled a face at Henriette, who laughed.

Mutter Scheck piped up in her corner. 'And are there any children?'

'A young woman,' answered Emile. 'Same age as these girls. But no others.'

'Imagine, a midwife and only one child yourself. Pity.' Magdalena clicked her tongue against her teeth.

'Did you meet her – the daughter?' asked Christiana. 'What is her name?'

Emile retied her headscarf. 'She didn't tell us. Her mother did all the talking. But I expect they'll introduce themselves at worship. You and Henriette and Elizabeth can meet her then, make friends with her.'

Elize nudged me with her elbow. 'And you, Hanne.'

I felt my mother glance at me and wondered what she was thinking. Hopeful, perhaps, that I would finally make a friend. That I would become a part of things. She nodded in approval as my fingers stripped the feathers, and I returned her smile, but inwardly I felt my stomach drop, imagining another girl welcomed into Christiana's fold while I remained steadfastly on the outer.

I was forever nature's child.

It is probably best to say this now.

I sought out solitude. Happiness was playing in the whir of grass at the uncultivated edges of our village, listening to the ticking of insects, or plunging my feet into fresh snow until my stockings grew wet and my toes numb. Occasionally, in a spirit of contrition after some misdemeanour and knowing it would please my mother, I would run in the road with the children of the other Old Lutherans. There had been some fun in throwing stones and hanging upside down in trees with the boys, but my brothers' friends did not enjoy being beaten in their races by a long-legged girl, and their sisters had always confounded me. Even as a young child I had felt that girls forsook on whim and offered only inconstant friendship. Allegiances seemed to shift from day to day like sandbanks in a riverbed and, inevitably, I found myself run aground. Better to befriend a blanket of moss, the slip-quick of fish dart. Never was the love I poured into the river refused.

But I was no longer a child, with a child's freedoms. Common chores and the expectations of the congregation had thrust me back into the company of girls I had known my whole life, but whom I did not understand, for all I recognised their faces. Christiana, Henriette and Elizabeth all seemed to accept and perform their early womanhood with an ease that rendered me fiercely jealous. Their bodies were soft, like mine, but they seemed contained where I was long-boned and sprawling. They were small and neat, and their faces had shed childish plumpness and become youthful simulacra of their mothers'. I had Mama's name only. I did not even have the good fortune of resembling Papa, although I alone received his height, which amused him. Christiana, Henriette and Elizabeth knew what to say at which occasion, how to make everyone laugh or smile, how to please their parents and themselves. They came together in a dance I did not know the steps to: I was separate even when in their midst. On the few occasions I had revealed something of my true self, seeking communion or recognition, I had been met with wide-eyed confusion or outright scorn. My interests were not theirs. Another girl my age in the village would be yet one more reminder that I was ill-made.

How do they know how to be? I remember wondering as I ripped feathers that night. How does anyone know how to be?

Mama and I stayed at the Radtkes' well past midnight, helping to clean up the room. Christiana and I swept the floor of discarded quills and washed the glasses and plates, while Mama and Magdalena stuffed the collected down into calico bags.

'Did you know she's a witch?' Christiana whispered under her breath.

'What? Who?' My face grew hot.

'That Wendish woman they were talking about. Frau Eichenwald.' Christiana glanced at me, her face solemn, dark hair escaping from under her headscarf. 'They're all heathens at heart, the Wends. Very superstitious. Mama told me they believe in unholy things.'

'Like what?'

'Like summoning demons to do your bidding.'

I stared at her. 'How?'

Christiana rubbed her mouth where a small puff of down had stuck to her bottom lip. 'How should I know? I'm no *Hexe*.'

'No, I know. I just wondered . . .' I reached out without thinking and gently unstuck the feather from Christiana's lip. She stared down at my fingers.

'Your hands smell horrible. Did you slop Hulda before you came?'

'No.'

Christiana wiped her mouth where I had touched it. 'Can you please watch where you're putting your fingers? They're all greasy.'

'Sorry.'

'Never mind.'

'Christiana, I don't understand why a witch would want to go to church. Emile said the family wish to attend services.'

'Oh, I don't know, Hanne. Here, I'll do it.' She took the glass and the cloth from me. Her expression was sly. 'I'm just saying, don't be surprised if your beloved pig drops down dead.' She placed the glass on the shelf, then faced me. 'Wouldn't want you to lose your best friend.'

The tears I had suppressed all night sprang to my eyes and I turned away, pretending to pick up stray feathers from the table.

'Goodness, Hanne! I'm only teasing!' Christiana patted me on the back. 'You don't have to cry.'

'I'm not crying.' I clenched my teeth together. I want to go home, I thought, sitting down. Please, Mama. Hurry up. I just want to go home.

Christiana sat next to me on the bench. 'Look, I would have asked you, you know,' she said softly. 'But I thought you wouldn't like it. You don't like this sort of thing, do you?'

Her hand was still patting my back. I wanted to push it away.

'No,' I said. 'Not much.'

The sky was clear and loud with stars as we walked home. I heard them keening as Mama wound her arm in mine.

'A wonderful evening, Hanne,' she said, taking a deep breath. 'A tonic for the soul.'

'Do you mean the wine?' Her breath was heavy with it.

Mama pretended to cuff my ear. 'No, friendship.' She paused. 'What? Are my lips stained?'

'Yes. The top one.'

Mama scrubbed hard at her lip with a corner of her apron. 'Is that better?'

'Yes.'

'Ah. A wonderful night. I'm glad you came. Oh, look, a rabbit.'

I kicked my shoe against the stones in the road and the rabbit skittered away.

Mama looked askance at me. 'What's wrong with you?'

'Nothing.'

We walked on. It was cold.

'I wasn't invited to the *Federschleissen*,' I said eventually. 'Other girls were there.'

Mama sighed. 'I didn't know you wanted to go.'

'It's not that. It's about being asked.'

'Hanne . . .' Mama leaned her head on my shoulder. 'Maybe if you put a little more effort in.'

'I do.'

'No, you don't. You prefer your own company and you never want to come with me to visit Christiana and the Radtkes when I suggest it.'

'Frau Radtke doesn't like me. She always gives me these suspicious little looks.'

'Hanne, Magdalena has nine people under her roof. I very much doubt she has the time to think anything of you at all.'

I was silent.

'Christiana is a lovely, modest young woman. If you were friendlier with her, I am sure she would welcome your company.'

'She doesn't like me either.'

'Nonsense.'

'She doesn't! She teased me.' I held my hand to Mama's nose. 'Do I smell?'

'No.'

'Christiana told me I did. That I smelled! She hates me.'

'Hanne, stop.' Mama drew away from me, dropping my arm. 'Stop this self-pity. You're spoiling what has been a lovely evening for me.'

We arrived home. As soon as we turned off the lane, my father opened the door.

'I thought I asked you to fetch your mother,' he said to me.

'Yes, well, she's here now,' I replied, walking straight past him through the black kitchen and its row of hooks, strung with *Wurst*, to my bedroom off the corridor.

My mother's voice was soft behind my back. 'Leave her, Heinrich. She's in a foul mood.'

I lay awake that night until I heard the persistent rumble of my father's snores, and then I climbed out my window and found the outdoor ladder to the loft.

Matthias was sleeping. I nudged his leg with my foot, my head bent against the low, sloped ceiling.

He didn't move.

I crouched and shook his arm.

He sat bolt upright. 'What is it? What's happened?'

'Nothing,' I whispered. 'I just wanted to see you.'

Matthias rubbed his eyes and lay back on his pillow. 'I thought something was wrong. I thought there was a fire. I was dreaming of a fire.'

'Can I get in? It's freezing.'

Matthias silently lifted his blanket and I got in.

'What's the matter?' he whispered.

'I don't know.'

'Can't sleep?'

'No.'

He turned his back to me and I drew close to him, breathing in the smell of the outside world on his skin. Cut grass and horses and earth.

'Are you sad about Gottlob?'

I didn't say anything.

'Sometimes I dream about him,' Matthias whispered. 'I dream that he's sitting just there, at the end of the bed, watching me sleep.'

'Do you talk to him?'

'No. He just sits there. Once he told me he was hungry.' He paused. 'You know what I thought of today?'

'What?'

'Remember when Otto stood on Gottlob's foot and his toe went all black?'

I smiled. 'Oh, that was disgusting.'

'And then the nail fell off and he wouldn't shut up about it. Remember how he went on and on, until Mama made him bury it and sing a funeral dirge?' Matthias began to laugh. I pulled him close.

'I thought I'd forget everything.' His laughter subsided. 'I thought I'd forget, but all I do is remember. I wish they'd talk about him more. They act as though we never had a brother.'

I rubbed my cheek against Matthias's back. 'Me too.' His body felt strange to me. Stronger than I remembered. Muscled from harder, longer labour. 'Matthias, do you ever think there must be something wrong with you?'

My brother rolled over. I felt his hand on my shoulder, the pressure of his thumb. 'What did Mama say to you?'

'Nothing.'

Matthias was quiet. 'No. I don't think there is anything wrong with me. Except this.' He tapped the gap between his front teeth. 'And I don't think there's anything wrong with you either, Hanne. Except . . . you know.'

'What?'

'You are clumsy. And you steal the blanket.'

I rolled my eyes.

'They love us,' Matthias whispered eventually. 'I think they've just forgotten how to show it.'

I settled my head on Matthias's shoulder and the next thing I knew it was morning, Papa was bellowing Matthias's name, and Mama's head appeared in the hatch to the loft. Her expression when she saw me in my brother's bed was odd.

*

'What were you doing?' Mama asked me later as we prepared the midday meal.

'What?'

'This morning.'

'You mean, why was I in the loft?' I cut slices of *Mettwurst*.

'Hm.'

'Oh. I couldn't sleep.'

Mama hesitated. 'It's not appropriate that you go to him.'

'We slept in the same bed when we were little. Matthias calms me. He's my brother.'

'You're not little anymore, Hanne. You're a woman.'

I groaned aloud.

Mama placed the steaming plate of potatoes down on the table then abruptly left the room, footsteps loud on the stairs. A few minutes later she returned with a full bucket and set it at my feet. Water glimmered pink over swathes of suspended rags, and I realised, with horror, that they were the soiled cloths I had left to soak in the cellar.

I looked up at her, appalled.

'You know what these mean?'

'Mama . . .' I glanced at the front door, anxious Papa or Matthias would come in and see them there.

'Hanne.' Mama's voice was calm. Insistent. 'These mean you are a woman.'

'Yes, I know.' My mouth was dry with shame.

'The time has come to farewell childish things. God is preparing your body so that it might be blessed with children, and so you, too, must prepare yourself for the other blessings of womanhood.'

I stared at the floor, face crimson, mortified.

'A home of your own, Hanne. Marriage.'

I bent down to pick up the bucket, but my mother quickly reached out and took my wrist. Her hands were damp.

'Now is the time to renew your faith in and submission to Christ,' Mama said, her voice low and urgent. 'God has created a place for you and a role for you, and now that you are grown, you must learn to fulfil it. It is one thing for a girl to come home smelling of . . . of weeds and river mud . . .'

I tried to wrest my hand from her, but her grip was firm.

'Hanne, I haven't finished. It is one thing for a little girl to share a bed with her little brother' – she inclined her head, eyes seeking out my own – 'another for a woman.'

I let my hand go limp in hers and stared down at the bucket of bloody water, willing myself not to cry. My pulse jumped in my fingertips. I wanted to run from the room. I wanted to run into the forest and never come back.

Mama suddenly pulled my head towards her, kissing it so hard I felt the press of her teeth beyond her lips. 'Do you understand me?'

'Yes,' I whispered.

She nodded at the bucket. 'You can put it back now.'

It is hard to remember these moments with my mother. I wish I knew then what I know now. That Mama's withholding from me was not a sign that she disliked me or suspected me flawed, as I believed at the time, but a sign of a fear she could not articulate. She was afraid to declare her love for me: she did not want to tempt fate by it. Since I have had a child, in my own way, I understand the terror a mother feels at the prospect of loss, and how easily superstition creeps into the smallest of gestures.

If I bless you every night, you will remain here.

If I keep your teeth, no harm will come to you.

If I do not praise you, I will not attract the sweep of a scythe that takes the best, the sweetest, the most loved.

There have been times when I have ached over things that have not happened to him but could. Might still. If I could divine his future in the entrails of animals, there would not be a living thing left ungutted.

Understanding, though, is cold comfort when it comes long after the opportunity for amends has passed. I see now that Mama wished for me a life like her own, and that she truly believed I would only find it – acceptance, motherhood, fulfilment – through subservience to Christ and convention and husband. It is not true, of course. I know now that marriage is no assurance of safety, that adherence to convention can estrange the soul from the spirit. But at the time I did not fathom any of this. I was a girl shrouded in a curtain of unknowing. I believed she was ashamed of me, that she thought me dirty, and the disquiet I already felt within myself was affirmed and deepened.

In bed that night, I spent hours running my fingers over my face, wondering if I had a face at all.

I remember feeling that I was mostly made of nothing. That, in my case, to grow into a woman was to disappear. I missed being a child, free and wild and at one with my body. I missed lifting arms against the push of spring winds and feeling, just for a moment, for a breath, that I might be lifted, that I might be swept ecstatically into flight.

I remember feeling so unseen I thought I might die. I yearned to be touched, simply to know that I was there.

Strange that, after everything that has happened, even as, years later, I teeter on the edge of it all here under a southern sun, I find myself with those same longings. The difference is that, at that time, I was dormant.

Then.

And then. And then and then and then.

The seed split. The shroud tore.

girl in the fog

Word spread quickly about the newcomers to Kay.

Friedrich Eichenwald was a cooper and a Lutheran of the old faith, as we all were. He had told Daniel Pfeiffer, Emile's husband, that they had moved to Kay to live amongst fellow believers and because he had sold their house and most of their possessions. It was a story familiar to many of us. A few years earlier, around the time that the church bell had been surrendered and Pastor Flügel forced into hiding, assistance had been sought from sympathetic benefactors. Excited at the prospect of a new life in Russia or America, many had sold their worldly goods to help pay for passage. But the King refused to issue permits and passports at the eleventh hour and many families were unable to buy back their belongings. Some who had sold houses and farmland found themselves homeless, with only dwindling savings to their name. Herr Eichenwald, it seemed, was one of these unfortunates. The forester's cottage, in its dilapidation, was all he could afford to rent.

When the virtuous reasons for the newcomers' presence was made known, my father was swift to welcome them to our congregation.

'You should go and speak with Herr Eichenwald's wife,' he said to Mama at breakfast, a few days after the *Federschleissen*. 'I want them to know that they are amongst friends. Take them some food this afternoon. Take Hanne along with you.' He nodded towards me, took another bite of his bread.

Mama sucked in her upper lip. 'Would that be wise?'

Papa looked up at her, chewing. 'What do you mean?'

'Magdalena mentioned the wife is a Wend.'

'What is wrong with the Wendish?' Papa licked his finger and dabbed crumbs from the worn surface of the table. 'God's grace is for all.'

'I have heard she is a little different.'

Matthias raised his eyebrows at me from across the table, cheeks full.

Eine Hexe, I mouthed.

He went cross-eyed. I fought a laugh.

'What?' Mama spun to face me. 'What is funny?'

'She speaks German,' Papa continued. 'She is married to a German. She and her husband have suffered for their faith. The same faith they share with us, Johanne.' He lifted his eyes from his breakfast and looked from Mama to me. 'They have a daughter her age.'

'Why do I have to go?' I asked.

'To be friendly,' Papa said, reaching for the loaf.

'I already have friends,' I said.

'You were very recently complaining to me that you don't,' Mama said quietly, passing my father the breadknife. 'Trees are not friends, Hanne.'

I stood up so quickly my chair tipped over.

'If you're storming off outside, you can feed the pig while you're at it,' Mama said, eyes fixed on the table in front of her.

Eyes pricking with tears, I righted my chair and fetched the slop pail. I could feel Matthias trying to send me a look of sympathy and solidarity as I left the room for the back door, but I knew that if I looked at him I would cry.

I threw the slops into the trough then lingered by the sty, leaning over the post and scratching Hulda behind the ears until my nails were nice and black. She grunted happily, pushing her snout up against my forearm for more. I hoisted my skirt and climbed over the rail to rub the length of her spine.

'I wish I were a pig,' I told her.

The sow pressed hard against my thigh. Her eyelashes were so long.

'Food and sun and some mud to roll in. Then a good, swift death.' I drew my dirty nail across my throat, wondering what the knife would feel like. Would it be painful? Would it feel like an emptying-out, all that blood flooding forth? I never liked to see the way the blood dripped into the open mouths of the pigs once they were hoisted, the fall of it from snout to bucket.

'Planning murder, are you?'

I looked up and saw Hans Pasche standing on the lower rail of the fence behind the sty, watching me with amusement.

'What?'

Hans pulled a finger across his throat, copying me.

Heat rose in my cheeks. 'I didn't know you were there.'

Hans leaned over and Hulda obediently went to him. He gave her an enthusiastic slap on the haunches. 'I wish I were a pig too, sometimes,' he said.

'You don't need to tease me.'

Hans looked up at me. 'I'm not. Lots of food, no work to do. Sleep as much as you like.' Hulda turned around and, grunting with satisfaction, let herself be stroked by him. 'Lots of sunshine and fresh air.'

'She likes you,' I said.

'Well, I like her.' Hans hoisted himself up onto the top rail of the fence and sat there for a moment, looking at me. 'I saw you the other night.' He pointed to our walnut tree in the orchard beyond. 'What are you doing when you lie there?'

'Nothing,' I said.

'Is it a thinking spot?'

'I'm not doing anything,' I muttered.

'You gave me a fright, you know,' Hans said. 'I went out to the barn and saw the white of your apron. You were so still I thought you were dead.' He blanched as soon as the words were out of his mouth. 'I mean . . . not like Gottlob. I didn't . . .'

'Never mind.'

Hans stepped along the rail over to me. 'I have my own thinking spots.'

I leaned away from him. 'Do you? What do you think about?'

'Whatever I like. Leaving this place, mainly.' Hans glanced up. 'Oh. Your mother is watching.' Placing a hand on the top rail, he launched himself up and over the fence, landing with two feet on the other side. 'Goodbye, little pig.'

'Hans Pasche is turning into a fine man,' Mama said as we walked along the lane through the village. 'Don't you think? Elder Pasche has high expectations of him.'

'Elder Pasche has high expectations of everyone.'

Mama nodded.

'I hear him shouting at Hans and Georg sometimes.'

'That isn't our concern.'

'He beats them too, you know.'

'Papa smacked you when you were naughty.'

'Only when I was a child, and only because you made him,' I said. 'Elder Pasche uses a rod. I saw him flogging Georg in the yard. I told Papa, but he said, "Foolishness is bound in the heart of a child. The rod of correction shall drive it far from him."'

'That isn't your business, Hanne.' Mama glanced at me as we

turned off the lane into the fallow ground that lay before the pines. 'What did he want with you, before? Hans?'

I passed the basket of eggs and cheese and sausage from one hand to the other, wiping my sweaty palm against my dress. 'He was just talking.'

'Talking about what?'

I shrugged. 'Nothing.'

'Tell me.'

I sighed. 'He overheard me saying that I wished I were a pig. How lovely it would be to eat and lie in mud all day. Become nice and fat.'

Mama's face fell. 'Oh, Hanne . . .' She stopped and looked at me, eyes full of disappointment. 'Really? You said that?'

'So?'

Words seemed to fail her. 'Hanne . . . You have to stop this kind of thing. If you are to be married . . . Oh my goodness, look at the state of your nails! Did you not think to wash before we left?'

'What? Why are you talking about marriage? What has Papa said?'

Mama lifted a hand against her eyes to block the screel of afternoon sun. 'Hanne, you have to think of what is expected of you. If you want a home of your own one day, you might start taking a little more care with yourself.'

My voice was small in my mouth. 'Mama . . .'

'You are pretending you are still a child. Saying odd things to Hans Pasche. And you were filthy at the *Federschleissen*, like you'd been rolling around in dirt. People notice these things. They talk.'

I opened my mouth to reply but Mama held out a hand, and I saw that we were already at the forest edge. A blond-haired man was sitting on his heels outside the old cottage woodshed, tools in hand, a halo of staves behind his head. He stood and greeted my mother.

'Good morning.'

'Morning,' my mother replied. 'Herr Eichenwald?' She gestured to the basket I held. 'I've come to welcome your wife.'

He smiled at us, flipping the adze he held and catching it again. 'Go on up to the house.'

Mama nodded at me. 'Wipe your hands on the underside of your apron.'

As we approached the cottage, I could smell baking bread and wood smoke. A broad-shouldered woman stepped through the door into the autumn sunlight, shaking flour from a cloth. She was wearing a white Wendish headdress, the material tight against the nape of her neck. It brought out the blue of her eyes, her high cheekbones, skin browned by sun. She saw us and waved.

'Frau Eichenwald?' My mother's voice was formal.

The woman nodded. '*Ja.*'

'I am Johanne Nussbaum. This is my daughter. We want to welcome you to Kay.'

The woman's forehead was high and smooth. She smiled with all her teeth. 'That's kind of you. Please, call me Anna Maria.'

Mama nudged me and I stepped forwards, offering the basket of food. She accepted it, looking me up and down. I had expected the new woman to be timorous and appreciative, given what I had heard about the Eichenwalds' poverty and precarious circumstances, but Anna Maria seemed to be neither of these things. The hem of her dress was short; it did not slip lower than her knees. I glanced at her legs. They were bare, calves muscled.

'And what's your name, Fräulein?'

'Johanne. But everyone calls me Hanne.'

'You may have seen my son, also,' Mama offered. 'Matthias.'

There was an awkward silence as we stood, wondering what to say next. I could hear the sunshine ringing like a blow to the ear.

Mama shifted her weight. 'Well, we won't interrupt you . . .'

'No, please, I forget myself.' Anna Maria beamed. 'Come inside for some cake. A drink.'

It was cool inside the cottage, a little smoky. I noticed Mama take in the few pieces of furniture in the room, noting what kind of house Anna Maria kept, and was relieved to see that the hearth was swept and all was neat. Our own cottage was humble – little more than a kitchen and two small bedrooms with the loft above and cellar beneath – but Mama ensured we both scrubbed and dusted it with fearful assiduity. She could be contemptuous of women who did not attend to their homes.

Anna Maria set the basket down on a table beneath the window. Several bowls, each covered with a floured cloth, were sitting in the narrow strip of sun that fell through the glass. She motioned for us to sit down and took out three cups.

'I have a daughter your age,' Anna Maria said, smiling at me. She set pungent cups of vinegar water on the table, then cut slices of *Streuselkuchen* from a fresh slab.

'Is she home?' Mama asked.

Anna Maria shook her head. 'Gathering wood.' She pointed to the fireplace. 'The pull is not strong. We need a lot of fuel to get it going nice and hot.'

'I could send my husband over to see to it? The chimney looks like it needs a little mortar.'

'No, it's fine,' Anna Maria replied, sitting down with us. 'Friedrich will fix it.'

I bit into a large slice of *Streuselkuchen*. It was delicious.

'Good?' Anna Maria watched me chew. 'Have more,' she said, as soon as I had swallowed. She pushed the plate towards me.

'What is your daughter's name?' asked Mama. She glanced down at the cake crumbs spilling into my lap.

'Thea,' Anna Maria said, mouth full. 'Well, Dorothea. But we call her Thea.'

Thea. I ran the name over my tongue.

'She'll be glad to know there are other girls her age to talk with here,' Anna Maria continued. 'Perhaps you two will be friends?'

I looked at Mama and swallowed. 'I don't have any friends.'

There was silence. Mama stared at the floor. I felt an awful heat creep up my neck.

Anna Maria considered me with warm curiosity. 'Well. Neither does Thea,' she said eventually, lifting the cake back to her mouth.

Mama smiled. 'Well, that is to be expected. You've only just arrived here from . . .?'

Anna Maria shook the crumbs from her apron onto the floor. 'Krosno Odrzańskie.' She winked at me. It was the first time I heard the Slav in her tongue. 'Crossen.'

'And is that where you are from?'

'I grew up in Schleife. And no. Thea, she' – the Wend turned to me and sat back in her chair, hands folded over her stomach – 'well, she dances to her own music. Much like you, Hanne, I think.'

Mama shifted in her chair. 'We do not believe in dancing here.'

Anna Maria reached for her vinegar water. 'Of course.'

Mama and I walked back home in silence. My heart was beating hard.

'Do you think that woman *is* different?' The words rushed out of me with a strange breathlessness. I wanted to say that I had felt seen by Anna Maria in a way that made me feel valuable. She seemed interested in me.

My mother flapped her hand at me. 'She is very nice.'

'She's more than that,' I said. 'She seems –'

'Nice is enough for any woman,' Mama interrupted, and that was the end of the conversation.

I remember that in the days after our meeting I kept Anna Maria's words on my tongue like a sacrament.

Thea dances to her own music.

The words, intimating desire of the body, thrilled me. I had never danced before, had never seen anyone dancing, and did not know, truly, what it might look like in any conventional sense. But I did understand the impulse. In my childhood I had heard the fields thrumming with life and my body wanted to move in time with the pulse of seeds. As I grew older, some hymns filled me with a longing to sing with more than my voice; to envelop the harmony with my body. But back then I also believed my parents when they warned me that this was a yearning of the flesh which, like all such yearnings, could lead to distance from God. They told me this after church one day when Emile and Daniel Pfeiffer had apologised to the congregation for indecency. Someone had seen them dancing at a cousin's wedding, and the pastor had been told.

It is hard to believe now, seeing from this height the valley's crops and early vines squeaking into green and the chimney smoke spiralling into this glory of a day, that there was a time when the ground was unploughed. When the nights were adorned with firelight and the sharp echo of sticks clapping out footfall. I wonder what song this place sang then, when the people listening to it had not yet been moved on.

The Peramangk were the first people I ever saw dancing. Back, back, after my first winter here, when they came down into the valley from their settlements on higher ground, a large fire was seen at the edges of the land the surveyor had marked out for pasturage and singing travelled through the valley. The music was unlike anything I had heard before. It threaded itself under my skin until I felt sewn through with sound, and then it pulled me to its source. There was no one to see me go; the villagers did not leave their beds in deep night. As I drew closer to the fire, I saw that there were men dancing in its light, and the beauty and urgency of their movement was everything I had imagined dancing might be, their bodies shaped and held by a music that was closer to the sound I heard coming from the earth than any hymn of my homeland.

Now this valley is emptied of such things. The song of it has been laid over with discordance.

That I had danced more. That I had danced with her.

These are the regrets that plague me now.

I grew distracted about the house. A week of heavy rain made me restless and clumsy. Eggs were broken, milk poured over the floor instead of the pan, the gate left open, dirt tracked through the house. Mama despaired at my mistakes, and any attempt to reconcile after our arguments somehow ended up in greater hostility, such as when she offered to comb my hair one night after a day of bickering. It was a chore she knew I hated.

'I wish I had your hair,' I told her, as she pulled up a stool behind me and took the comb from my fingers.

'You should be grateful for the hair God gave you.'

'I wish I could cut it all off.'

Mama said nothing, but I felt a sudden, rough yank of the comb.

'You're hurting me.'

'You're welcome to do it yourself.'

I winced as the teeth dragged along my scalp. 'I wish I had Matthias's hair and he had mine. I'm so sick of being ugly.'

Without a word Mama went outside. She returned minutes later with my father's iron shears and, before I realised what she was doing, took a lock of my hair and cut it close to the skull.

I spun around in horror.

'I shall rid you of what you hate so much,' she said. 'Sit back. I'll get the rest.'

I got up and ran to my bedroom, hand to my head, and cried for an hour.

When Mama eventually came to sit on my bed and told me that the next morning I should go to the forest to gather mushrooms, I was so furious I did not recognise it as the apology it must have been: she was giving me the opportunity to spend the better part of a morning wandering alone in nature. I believed only that she wished me out of the house.

I set out just past daybreak. The entire forest was shrouded in a thick fog that yawned in white, refusing to lift, and everything was still and muffled. Water dripped from branches and my skirt grew damp as I kneeled and, blade in hand, searched for telltale mounds lifting the carpet of needles. I breathed lung-deep, imagined that I exhaled dust. The relief of the forest was exquisite.

Suddenly I heard stick-break, the cracking of wood, and someone appeared out of the fog.

She was an apparition walking between hazy columns of trees, her outline growing clearer as she walked. It seemed, for one small moment, that we were underwater. I saw her breath stream as she heaved a crooked weight of kindling; I saw her through the cloud of my own breath and held it, the better to see her.

She looked up and, seeing me watching her, stopped.

I exhaled.

The air hung with water. Held its own breath as we regarded one another.

The girl freed a hand from her bundle of sticks. I watched as she raised it, uncertain, then lifted my own palm.

'I thought you were a ghost,' she said. Her voice was low. Unsteady.

'I thought you were too.'

'You scared me.' She hoisted the bundle of kindling onto her hip and approached me through the fog. 'I'm Thea.'

I remembered myself. 'Hanne.'

The mist between us thinned as she drew closer. Her face was round, smooth-cheeked, and I saw that her hair was white-blonde, her eyebrows fairer than her skin. It looked, not unpleasantly, as though she had been dusted with flour.

Against the silence of the forest, her footsteps upon the twigs and needles sounded impossibly loud.

'You're not, then?' She continued walking until she was standing an arm's length away. I could see that her eyelashes were translucent, surrounding eyes that were deeply blue. Fathomless blue, winter's blue.

'What?' Water dripped from the tree above me and fell inside my collar. Trickled down my back.

She smiled. 'A ghost.'

I noticed then that, while her front teeth were small and neat, those next to them stuck out at an angle. It gave her a hungry, slightly wolfish look.

'No. I don't think so. Unless I died in my sleep.'

'Maybe both of us died in our sleep, and here we are, two ghosts. Telling each other we're alive.'

I laughed. For a moment I wondered if there could be truth in what she said. The mist had thickened, and with her white hair it looked as though she might suddenly be absorbed into the cloud about us.

Pain licked across my hand. I had unthinkingly closed my palm across my blade.

Thea placed her load of kindling on the ground and picked up the knife I had dropped, fingers careful around the handle. 'Have you hurt yourself?'

'Not much.'

She peered at my palm, creased with blood. 'You should probably go home and wash it. Dress it with a little honey.' She smiled at me. 'At least I know you're telling the truth.'

'What do you mean?'

'Ghosts don't bleed.' She stooped to bundle up her sticks again.

'How do I know *you're* not a ghost?' I asked.

'You don't.' That smile again, lip catching on pointed tooth. 'Pleased to have met you, Hanne. I hope your hand heals quickly.'

She walked on. I watched her disappear into the white.

The next time I saw her was at worship.

The elders of Kay had continued to hold services in the forest after the church was locked, although not every Sunday. Communion was only held on clouded nights, or, if it was clear, under a small sliver of moon. Attending families were asked to take different paths into the forest so as not to arouse suspicion. Hymns were sung through the nose.

On this night it was Papa's turn, as an elder, to hold the lay service. The single lantern had already been lit and the men and women were standing in their separate groups. Mama pulled me with her into the cluster of waiting women, tight smile on her face, as my father cleared his throat, looking, like any disfigured man with a Bible in hand, rather unsettling. There was a low murmur and, while at first I thought it was the kind of muted approbation reserved for latecomers, I soon realised that the Eichenwalds were there amongst us, and that this was the reason for flutterings of interest. It had been many months since anyone had joined our dissenting group of worshippers.

As Papa commenced the prayer meeting – lamenting, as always, the absence of the persecuted pastor and comparing our congregation to the early Christians, facing down the Union Church as lion's maw – Anna Maria turned around and nodded at me. Then she gently nudged the person standing next to her.

It was the girl from the forest.

Thea.

She wore a headdress in her mother's fashion, but it was lazily done, and in the darkness I saw white hair escaping from its bindings. Thea looked over her shoulder and her eyes met mine. She held my gaze for a long moment, then, as my father began his sermon, turned back around.

'I was born in Harthe,' Papa was saying. 'And in Harthe, because everything was done according to tradition and custom, the Son of God had become customary.'

I glanced over at Matthias and saw him already looking at me from the corner of his eye, mouth twitching. This was a favourite story of our father's, one he frequently folded into sermons around the table. We could have recited it by heart.

'This is how I grew up,' Papa continued. 'God was attended to on a Sunday in the same manner my mother scrubbed clothes on a Monday. A chore. The words of the preachers made no impact upon me. I forgot them as soon as I walked out of the church door! And so, I was dead inside. I spent many years without any true spiritual life. Yes, I learned the word of God. But . . .'

He lifted his hand and, stepping over to where Matthias stood, as though he knew he had been laughing at him, poked my brother in the temple. 'I learned it here . . . not *here*.' The finger travelled to Matthias's chest and prodded him in the sternum.

'But the Lord did not forsake me. He waited until I became a man and married. He waited until I was nineteen years old and then! He filled this eye with darkness.'

My father took the lantern from Elder Radtke and raised it next to his ear so that everyone could better see the left eye that marred his otherwise handsome face, the pupil listing to the side. Papa lifted his drooping eyelid with a finger to demonstrate its unfocused, wayward slant.

'At first I thought I was overtired. But when weeks passed and I saw nothing but gloom, I turned my anger upon God.' Papa closed his hand into a fist and shook it at the forest canopy. 'How dare He do this to me!

'Then one night I dreamed I was standing in my orchard. All around me the trees were dead and dying. Fruit was rotting on the ground. I was despairing at the loss and destruction when an angel appeared. *Ja, ein Engelwesen!* He touched this eye, then – gone. Vanished. I turned to look for him, and I saw that the orchard was not dying at all. The branches were heavy with golden apples. Silver pears. Every leaf shone with the brilliance of emeralds. *Ja*, the orchard was alive with glory.'

'Amen,' muttered someone from the standing rows of men.

I peered over and saw Christian Pasche's bald head nodding in approval. Hans stood next to him, face impassive.

'I woke knowing that I had been blessed,' Papa continued. 'I woke knowing that the power of the Holy Spirit had attended me as I slept, that this affliction was from God. As I had been blinded, so my spiritual eye had been opened. I was convicted of my sins and for the first time in my life I stepped onto the path of righteousness. While my eye had become dead to this world, it had come alive to the next. *Lobe den Herrn in seinem Heiligtum!* Praise the Lord in His sanctuary.'

'Amen,' muttered Christian Pasche again. 'Amen.'

'This eye' – Papa pointed to it with reverence – 'this eye has seen what has been prepared for those who serve our Almighty Lord. It cannot be swayed by the meddling of an earthly king. For this eye sees what is waiting for the faithful. It has seen Heaven.'

I sang clear and bright that night. Blinded in the dark, hushed, my body prickled to the world in a way it had not done since I was a child. The smell of pine needles and the curved fingernail of light above made me feel so joyfully alive that I was filled with gratitude to God for the verity of my being. I was exultant; I reconciled divinity with the smell of sap, imagined the Lord's mansion as a wilderness. The sound of my voice against the mother tongue of pines swum around me until I could see eternal life forever under a canopy of trees, angels appearing like perfect circles of pine cap mushrooms, glistening wet, anointing my fingers with saffron milk.

What I feel now is eternal in its feeling, and so I cannot remember these first meetings without the presence of love. Thea's neck, pale hair escaping, as my father declared Heaven's certainty, remains with me to this day. Why have I remembered this if I was not, even then in my youth and innocence, already buckled with unconscious hope? When I think of Thea turning around and holding my eye, my rib cage, even now, fills with light.

What I would not give to have her, again and again, turning to me in the dark?

holy

The day after service threatened snow. I could smell it in the air and hear its weighted murmur. It filled my head so that I became distracted, dropping one thing after another as I cleared the breakfast table. I imagined the slow descent of snowflakes upon the shorn fields and envied my father and Matthias for being outside, witness to the moment they fell.

I was not expecting the knock at the door.

Mama and I looked at each other. Most women in the village simply called out before they entered, mouths already resuming whatever conversation was last interrupted by work, babies, prayer or mealtimes.

The knock came again.

Wiping her hands, Mama went to the door and opened it. I heard low voices, saw a deep red headscarf against the lane beyond and the heavy sky, then Mama called for me.

Thea stood on the flagstone bundled against the cold, clutching the basket that had held the gift of cheese, eggs and sausage we had delivered to her mother.

'Hello,' she said. 'I've come to return this.'

'You must be Fräulein Eichenwald,' Mama said. I noticed she was staring at Thea's light hair. Next to the unquestionable beauty of my mother, most other women seemed dull, but in that moment I thought Thea the more striking of the two. Her asymmetry was made starker, her strangeness more rare, more precious.

Thea's smile faded a little. 'May I come in?' she asked. *'Es ist kalt.'*

Mama remembered herself then and held the door open, as Thea stamped the mud from her work clogs and stepped inside, pushing the scarf off her head. We smiled at each other, unsure of what to say next. I felt a blush creeping up my jawline.

My mother peered inside the basket as Thea handed it to her. 'What's this?' She removed a small clay pot.

'It's a gift from my mother,' Thea explained. 'For Hanne's cut.'

'What cut?' Mama glanced at me, brow furrowed.

I brought my hands to my face to cool the heat of my cheeks. 'I nicked myself with the knife when I was mushrooming.'

'Where?'

'On my palm.'

'Show me.'

I held out my hand and Mama examined the slight wound.

'You didn't tell me you'd hurt yourself.'

'It doesn't hurt.'

'It's deep. You could get an infection.'

'The salve will help,' Thea suggested.

Mama nodded, letting my hand drop to my side. 'So you two have met?' She set the pot on the table a little too hard. 'Hanne, why don't you offer Thea something to eat?'

'Oh, I only came to return the basket. But thank you.'

'Why don't you walk Thea back home then, Hanne?'

Thea looked at me. Smiled. Again, the teeth barbed on the lips. Red headscarf on that strange hair. Blood in the snow.

She waited as I wrapped myself in a shawl against the weather, then followed me through the door, nodding to my mother on the way out.

'Give my thanks to Frau Eichenwald,' Mama said. Her eyes found mine. *Be friendly*, she mouthed, and then shut the door firmly.

The winter air outside was a whip-crack.

'I'm sorry.'

Thea glanced across at me. 'What for?'

'I don't know. Saying the wrong thing.'

'You didn't say anything at all.' Thea reached out and took my wrist, gently unfolding my clenched fingers. Her hands were cool, firm. 'How is your cut?'

'Better, thank you.'

'Your mother seemed cross about it.'

I eased my wrist from her fingers. 'She is cross about everything I do.'

Thea raised a pale eyebrow. 'Why? What do you do?'

'I wish I knew.'

She nodded, wrinkling her nose.

We walked up the lane. The sky above us was a low, thick yellow, the horizon a bruise. I could see my father and brother in the field beyond the orchard, repairing a broken fence.

Thea followed my line of sight. 'Who is that?' she asked.

'My father and my brother,' I replied. 'My twin.'

'Oh, do you look the same?'

'No,' I said. 'Everyone thinks I'm his older sister. Because I'm tall.'

Thea nodded. 'You are,' she said, but there was no judgement in her voice. She agreed simply because it was true.

I felt my spine uncurl.

'You have a lovely voice, you know,' she said suddenly. 'I mean, I heard you sing at service. It is very clear and true. You've been blessed with a gift.'

I stared at her. No one had ever praised my voice before. No one had ever praised *me* before; it was not my parents' habit to praise anyone or anything but the Lord.

'I love to sing,' I said.

'Yes, so do I,' Thea replied. 'Music is freedom, don't you think? Sometimes, when I sing, I feel my soul lift up out of myself. Do you ever feel like that? Mama once told me that when we sing together, our hearts beat in time.' Thea laughed abruptly and wiped her nose on her sleeve.

I slowed in the lane. I knew exactly what she meant. 'Do you . . .' I hesitated. I wanted to tell her how even the dourest hymns lifted me out of my inwardness, relieved me of the sense of weight I felt, the burden of being.

'What?' Thea stopped walking and faced me. She brought her fingertips to her mouth and breathed on them. She wasn't wearing mittens.

'Can I ask you a question?'

'Of course.'

'Do you ever hear sounds?'

'What do you mean?'

'Trees and . . . and things,' I stuttered.

Thea frowned. 'Blowing in the wind?'

'No. Well, yes, that, but also voices coming from them. Like singing.'

I waited for Thea to suppress a laugh. But instead she took a step towards me. 'Human voices?' she asked quietly.

'No. No, it's not like that. Not like human voices. It's a little like when someone is whispering and you can't make out the words, but you feel that if you leaned in, it would suddenly make sense.'

'Noises.'

'Not noises. Sounds. Like singing. Crying, sometimes. Music.' The words rushed from me then, pouring out as though from a wellspring. I told Thea that I could hear the high pitch of swarming sunlight in an open field. That the sound of snow falling was like chimes. I told her that I hated the silence of the house in the daytime, that it felt dead, that the only living thing seemed to be the fire in its grate. I told her that I loved to be outside, because that was where the world sang to me.

'You think I'm mad,' I said, when Thea had not spoken for some moments. She was looking at me intently. 'I'm not mad.'

'Have you told anyone else you can hear these things? Have you always heard them?'

'Always,' I said. 'I thought it was normal. Matthias, my brother, he knows. He believes me. My mother thinks I'm making it up.'

Thea nodded. We walked on, lifting our scarves up over our mouths against the cold.

'Maybe that is why you sing so well,' Thea said eventually, pulling the wool from her face. 'You hear things other people can't.'

'Please don't say anything to anyone. I don't know why I brought it up.'

'Can I tell my mother?' Thea asked. 'She hears things too, in her way.'

I nodded, relieved at her acceptance of me, of my oddity.

'I know why you brought it up,' Thea added.

I waited for her to go on but she said nothing more, only slid her arm around my elbow and pulled me into her side. I was surprised by her warmth.

We walked in silence. It grew colder still, and as we left the lane and crested the rise towards the forest, walking through the fallow field, it began to snow. Heavy flakes caused the meadow around us to disappear. The thick air whirred; it was impossibly beautiful. The pines at the edge of the forest gathered a hem of white before our eyes.

Thea stopped and tilted her head to the sky. I watched as she let the snow light upon her cheeks and chin. It dissolved in the heat of her skin.

'It feels like a blessing,' she said, eyes closed. 'What does it sound like, Hanne?'

I lifted my face, felt the snow settle on it. I knew what she meant. 'Holy,' I replied. 'It sounds holy.'

We stood and let the snow cover our lips and gather in the corners of our eyes. It pealed down around us like the ringing of bells, and we were anointed together, blessed over and over.

Back then, I thought my loneliness came from being too much in the house, in feeling an obligation to become someone I knew I was not. After all this time, I know that I was lonely not just because I wanted to be seen and understood, but because I also wanted to offer understanding.

To find a home for the love within me.

I knew what it was like to feel strange and solitary. How well I was placed, then, to befriend the friendless. My heart was ready to be unfolded and afflicted.

'Did you thank Frau Eichenwald for the salve?' my mother asked that night, as she set out a cold supper.

'Yes,' I said, looking up as my brother came into the kitchen, face still damp from the washbasin. He sank into a chair. 'Do you want milk?' I asked him.

'What are they like then?' asked Matthias, accepting the pitcher from me. 'I saw you walking up to the cottage with the new girl.'

'Thea,' I said.

He looked at me over the edge of his glass as he drank. 'You like her?' he asked.

I nodded.

'Matthias, wipe your mouth,' Mama muttered.

Matthias pretended he couldn't hear her. 'You seem different.'

'Different how?' I asked.

'Wipe your mouth.' Mama threw a cloth at him and it landed on his head.

Matthias left it there, grinning at me, milk on his lip. 'Happier,' he said as Mama snatched the cloth off his hair and began scrubbing his mouth herself.

Papa stepped into the room and sat down at the head of the table. 'Don't baby him, Johanne,' he muttered.

Matthias laughed as Mama threw her hands into the air.

'Hanne was just telling me about the Eichenwalds,' my brother said, refilling his glass. 'She likes their daughter.'

Papa nodded. 'Herr Eichenwald is passionate in his disavowal of a common service book. We spoke about the changes to sacramental rites after service yesterday.'

'Frau Eichenwald invited me to dinner,' I said, as Mama sat down, setting a plate filled with smoked ham on the table.

'When?'

'Next Sunday.'

Mama reached for my father's plate and began piling it with meat and cheese. 'I don't think so, Hanne.'

'Why not?'

'Their ways are different from ours.'

'Friedrich Eichenwald is as ardent for Christ as we are,' Papa said. He held Mama's eye as she handed him his meal. 'You can spare her, can't you, Mutter?'

*

The following weekend I trudged through the weather to the forester's cottage, arriving windblown and short of breath. Thea threw open the door as soon as I raised my hand to knock and quickly ushered me inside.

'You have to tell Mama what you told me,' she said immediately, pulling out a chair for me at their table, already set for the midday meal. I could smell garlic and frying onions. 'About the world singing to you.'

Anna Maria turned from where she was kneeling by the fireplace, a black kettle steaming over the embers. 'It seems you have a gift, Hanne.' She rose and kissed me on the cheek in welcome, her face flushed from the heat of the fire.

I fought the urge to rub my cheek. I was unused to affection. 'I don't know if it's a gift,' I stammered. 'My mother thinks it is childish.'

Anna Maria exchanged a swift look with her daughter. Thea gently pushed me into the chair and then sat in the one next to it, tucking her legs under her. I waited for Anna Maria to correct her as my mother would have done, to sigh and ask that she sit properly, but the Wend didn't seem to mind.

'What does it sound like today?' Thea asked.

I hesitated, looking to the Wend who stood, a half-smile on her face, waiting for me to speak. 'Well, the cold . . . the cold sounds like a gasping. Like a voice singing on the in-breath. And the trees are saying things through gritted teeth.' I looked at the empty plate in front of me. 'It changes.'

Anna Maria sat down opposite me and, placing her elbows on the table, rested her chin on her hands. 'Do you ever hear them talk to you? Plants, I mean.'

I nodded. 'Sometimes I can make out words. Not very often.' I glanced sideways to Thea. 'I don't really talk about it.'

The Wend's gaze was unrelenting. I felt as though my skin would lift from my body. 'You don't have to tell us what you hear,' she said, eyes not moving from my face, 'if it is not for us to know.'

'I would like to know,' Thea said, leaning over the table and helping herself to a slice of bread.

Anna Maria pushed the plate out of the reach of her daughter. 'Wait for grace.'

Thea peered towards the door. 'Where's Papa?'

'He'll be in when he's ready. You can wait. Tell us about yourself, Hanne. Have you always lived in Kay?'

I nodded. 'Yes, I was born here.'

'And are most families Lutherans of the old faith?'

'Most. Some families do not attend our services. They keep to themselves.' I accepted a glass of water from Thea and took a sip. 'I think they go to the Union church in Skampe.'

'But they don't report the rest of us? Surely they know we are not *Evangelisch*.'

I carefully set the glass back on the table. 'When the soldiers first came, lots of people believed Herr Pfitzer was responsible. He lives in the last house on the western side of the village. They thought he was the one who wrote to the commissioner and informed him about Pastor Flügel.' I glanced at Thea, cleared my throat. 'Our congregation does not speak to him or his daughters.'

'The girls with the dimples?' asked Thea, prodding her own cheek. 'The littlest has a harelip.'

'Oh, no, those are the Volkmann sisters. Henriette, Elizabeth and Karoline. Karoline has the harelip. They would have been at worship in the forest, but they were unwell, I think.'

Anna Maria nodded. 'Tell me, who is the woman with the' – she paused and then assumed a look of rigid severity and tapped herself on the chest – 'with the large bust? Dark hair.'

'The woman who kept looking at us during services?' Thea asked her.

Anna Maria nodded.

'I think you mean Magdalena Radtke. She has five children. A daughter our age and four younger. Elder Radtke's parents live with them too.'

Anna Maria raised her eyebrows. 'I meant to introduce myself, but she left very quickly.'

For a moment I wondered if Anna Maria knew of the rumours discussed at the *Federschleissen*. I pictured Christiana's face as we cleaned, the whispered '*Hexe*'.

'What's her daughter's name? The one our age?' Thea was asking.

'Christiana,' I muttered.

'What is she like?'

The room suddenly felt very warm. I could feel sweat prickle across my brow and undid the shawl I had tucked into my skirt.

'You don't like her,' Thea said quietly, narrowing her eyes at me.

I laughed, embarrassed. 'I didn't say that.'

Thea smiled. 'You didn't need to.'

Just then the door opened and the winter weather swept in with Thea's father, who apologised for the draught as he heaved the door shut against the wind. He collapsed into the chair next to Anna Maria and took his hat off his head, nodding at me in greeting. 'Smells good,' he said.

'This is Hanne,' Thea told him.

'Yes, I know. Thank you for joining us,' he said. He accepted a cup of water from Thea and drained it.

'I'm starving,' Thea said.

Anna Maria pushed her chair back. 'I hope you're hungry.'

*

As we ate *Pellkartoffeln* with herbs, pickled cabbage and thick turnip soup with dumplings, the Eichenwalds asked me more questions about Kay and its inhabitants. They did not seem to mind that, embarrassed to find myself the centre of attention, I dropped cabbage on my lap, nor did they remark on the fact that my cheeks kept flaming red, even though I felt them burn. Anna Maria told me that she had some experience in healing, as well as midwifery, and wanted to know who might be receptive to herbal treatments. I told her about Magdalena Radtke's suspicion of homeopathy and Eleonore Volkmann's digestive complaints, that Mutter Scheck considered herself a competent herbalist but that, as she had outlived three husbands, no one knew whether to trust her skill. ('It all depends,' Matthias said to me once, 'on whether she treated herself or her husbands.')

'I don't know about the others,' I said, blowing on my soup. 'If anyone suffers a complaint here, they generally keep it to themselves.'

'Would your father like his eye treated?' Anna Maria asked.

I hesitated. 'He doesn't see it as a complaint.'

Anna Maria sat back in her chair. 'The angel.'

'Yes,' I nodded. 'His holy eye.'

Friedrich reached for another slice of bread, smiling at Thea as she passed him the butter. 'Daniel Pfeiffer told me that Kay is a stronghold of dissenters. That your own father was fined for refusing to allow Matthias instruction in state doctrine.'

'Yes, fifty thaler.'

Friedrich paused, spoon held in mid-air. 'That much?'

'He sold Mama's wedding dress to pay it,' I said.

There was silence around the table. I noticed Anna Maria exchange a look with her husband and remembered, suddenly, the sodden handkerchiefs I'd found balled up in the laundry the night of Papa's announcement. I had never seen my mother cry, but I wondered then, sitting at the Eichenwalds' table, if she must sometimes. She had never said a word about the loss of the dress.

To break the silence, I told Friedrich that most of the men in Kay had been fined or arrested. The congregation, already stitched together in an embroidery of need and solidarity, had puckered closer under persecution. 'Now, if someone is fined, we all make a contribution to pay it.' I realised I was running my finger around my bowl, savouring the last of the soup, and looked up at him, horrified.

Friedrich dismissed my look with a casual wave of his hand. 'She'd be offended if you didn't,' he said, and Anna Maria beamed.

Thea dropped her spoon and did the same with her bowl, smiling at me with her finger between her teeth. 'There is no shame in appetite,' she said, and both of her parents nodded.

When Thea walked me home that afternoon, her arm in mine, she asked if I would show her the village.

'There isn't much to see,' I said.

'You can show me who lives where,' she replied.

We had reached the lane. Being a day of rest, there were no men working in the fields, and Kay was even quieter than usual. Only smoke drifting silently from chimneys indicated that people were home.

'Well, this house belongs to the Pfeiffers,' I said, nodding to a small, one-windowed cottage, the path to the front door pitted with puddles.

'Oh yes, I met them with Mama. They have two daughters.'

'Yes. And that house there . . .' I pointed, and Thea strained her neck to follow my line of sight. 'See the larger house there, with the goat staked in front? That's Elder Gottfried Fröhlich's house. He's also a shoemaker.' It had started to snow. I unwound my arm from

Thea's and pulled my headscarf down on my forehead. 'I should go home,' I said.

'Why? There's at least another hour of daylight.'

When I didn't respond, Thea took my arm again and pulled me onwards. 'Who lives there?'

'Reinhardt Geschke and his new wife, Elize. And his father, Traugott. Wheelwrights by trade.'

We walked on into the heart of the village, where the cottages crowded the lane, narrow fingers of land spilling out behind.

'That's your house over there, isn't it?' asked Thea. 'Is that your pig?'

I nodded.

She leaned closer to me and whispered, 'And who's that?'

'Where?'

Thea nodded to the Pasches' cottage and I saw Hans standing in the yard, carrying a milk pail. He raised his free hand in greeting as we passed.

'That's Hans Pasche,' I told Thea. 'Elder Pasche's son.'

'I thought Elder Pasche was not yet married?'

'Rosina will be his second wife. Hans's mother died.'

'Thirsty?' Hans called out to us, lifting the pail. I could see steam lift from it in the cold air.

Thea laughed and shook her head.

I was about to stop and farewell her there, in the lane, when I saw Magdalena and Christiana come around the far corner of my house. Without thinking, I veered sideways into the Pasches' yard, dragging Thea with me.

'What are you doing?' she asked.

'Shh.'

Hans stared at us in surprise as I pulled Thea into the Pasches' barn.

'Hanne?' Thea stumbled in the gloom.

I put a finger to my lips and peered out just in time to see Magdalena and Christiana stop on the swept flagstone and stamp the snow from their shoes. I ducked back around as Christiana glanced up, eyes sweeping the yard, and heard her call out a greeting to Hans.

'It's the Radtkes,' I whispered, turning around.

Thea rested a hand on the flank of the Pasches' cow and raised her eyebrows.

Hans stepped into the barn then and set the pail on the floor. 'She's gone inside your house now, if that's who you're hiding from, Hanne.'

'Hello,' Thea said, lifting her chapped fingers into the air. 'I'm Thea.'

Hans nodded, glancing between us. 'Hans.'

'I don't want her to see me,' I mumbled.

'Christiana?'

'I didn't realise they were visiting.'

The three of us stood together for an awkward moment. Thea ran her hand over the cow and smiled at Hans. 'She's lovely,' she said.

Hans beamed. 'She's a bit sad, poor thing.'

'Oh?'

'My father just sold her calf.' He scratched the cow behind the ears and pressed his own forehead to hers.

'Sorry, Hans,' I said. 'Forget we were here.'

Hans shrugged, head still against the cow. 'Don't worry about it. I hide in here all the time.'

'I knew at once you didn't like her,' Thea said, as we walked along the fence line that separated the Pasches' land from my father's. It was snowing heavily, white slowly covering the dun of the bare fields.

'I never said that,' I said. 'She just . . .' I hesitated, wondering how to explain that I yearned for Christiana's approval and yet hated to be in her company. 'She makes me feel . . . I don't know. As though I am nothing.' I took a deep breath. Cold air flooded my lungs.

Thea blew on her fingers and shrugged. 'She sounds awful.' We were standing in the Pasches' rye field, snow catching on the stubble of the ground. 'Where should we go?'

'I can show you the other houses. Or I can take you to the river. It's a bit cold.'

Thea shook her head. 'Take me there.'

I turned and saw she was pointing to the church spire, empty sky showing where the bell used to hang.

'It's locked,' I said.

'Take me anyway.'

It is strange to think of that old church in Kay now that I am surrounded by sunlight and birdsong and the rustle of gum leaves. It seems a dead thing, in my memory. Even before it was locked, I remember it as dark and cold, as having nothing to do with God. I never mourned the church when it was forbidden to us – the forest was the more magnificent cathedral – and I never understood my father when, in a rare mood of despondency, he would reminisce about Sunday mornings of worship held there, the sound of voices echoing off the ceiling, still blue and gilt from an earlier life of Catholicism.

No doubt the church in Kay is in use again. I pity the faithful who attend it. Why do men bother with churches at all when instead they might make cathedrals out of sky and water?

Better a chorus of birds than a choir. Better an altar of leaves. Baptise me in rainfall and crown me with sunrise. If I am still, somehow, God's child, let me find grace in the mysteries of bat-shriek and honeycomb.

Thea and I stepped through the graves, wooden crosses tilting in the frozen ground in various attitudes of age, and reached the heavy doors of the church. The varnish was peeling, snow sticking to the wrought iron spidering out from the boards. A heavy chain was looped through the handles.

Thea lay her hands flat on the doors and turned to me. 'Shall we go inside?'

I pointed to the chain.

'Here.' Thea cast about to make sure no one was coming past, then pushed her shoulder against the door. After some resistance, the doors groaned apart, the chain jolting tight. Cold air reached us from within, smelling of stone and dust.

Thea glanced down. 'Do you think you could squeeze in the gap?'

'No.'

'Try.'

I bent down and poked my head into the space. 'Don't let go now,' I called out to Thea. 'That door will crush my neck.'

'Hurry up then,' I heard Thea say.

I wriggled in further, turning sideways to squeeze my shoulders painfully past the wooden edge, and managed to haul myself forwards, my clogs falling off my feet. For a moment I lay prostrate in the aisle, eyes raised to the altar, before the door creaked closed behind me and the light was extinguished.

'Thea?' I stood and felt my way to the door, pressed my ear against the boards. The awful thought that she had left me in there, had trapped me as some kind of trick, dropped through my stomach. 'Thea?!'

Silence, and then I heard her voice, muffled, on the other side. 'Pull the handle!' A fist, thumping.

I found the iron grip and yanked with all my strength. The door eased open again, daylight striped across the wooden pews, and I saw Thea's red headscarf appear in the gap. I stood to one side as she wriggled in on her stomach.

'You can close it now,' she said, rising to her feet, grinning.

'No, it's pitch-dark when it's shut.'

Thea looked up and noticed the boards covering the windows, then took off a wooden clog and jammed it in the doorway. I let go. Dust rose in the narrow belt of daylight.

'I can't believe we're in here,' I whispered.

'Why not?'

'It's ... sacred.'

Thea walked down the aisle towards the altar, outstretched fingers brushing over the backs of the pews. 'Sacredness is in the gathering of believers who come around God's word,' she said, voice echoing. 'Wherever that may be. Not in a building.' She turned around. 'What happened to this place?' she asked.

'The commissioner came a few years ago,' I whispered. 'We all stood in front of the door and sang hymns until he left. But then he sent soldiers to come and arrest Pastor Flügel. My father and the other elders barred the way and read scripture to them while the pastor fled.' I shivered, remembering my father's mouth, wide with the word of God, the horses' nostrils flaring inches away.

'Did that work?'

'No. They broke through. When they realised the pastor had gone, they let their horses shit in here. I remember cleaning it up afterwards, all the women singing hymns.' I sat down in a pew on the women's side. 'Now, whenever I hear *"Ein feste Burg ist unser Gott"*, I smell manure.'

Thea sat down next to me.

'They came back,' I added. 'They came searching for Pastor Flügel and ransacked homes. Then they arrested people and chained the doors of the church.'

We were silent a moment.

'Do you hear anything in here?' she asked. 'Singing?'

I shook my head. 'Only outside.'

The snow on Thea's headscarf was melting. She took it off and shook the water from it, then balled it in her lap. In the low light her hair seemed to glow. 'You know what you said about Christiana earlier?' she murmured.

'Mm.'

Thea leaned against me in the pew. 'Well, I don't think you're nothing.'

Blood rushed to my face. 'Thank you,' I whispered.

We stayed in that church abandoned to dust and mice droppings, talking in hushed voices, finding empty swallow nests and tracing our fingers over the engravings in the dry baptismal font, until the light began to dim. When I suggested to Thea that she ought to go to ensure she could return home before nightfall, she went to the door and bent down to retrieve her clog.

She looked up at me, alarmed. 'I can hear voices.'

I froze.

'Quick,' she said, pulling her shoe free. 'Close it.'

I pushed the door shut and the church collapsed into darkness. Sinking to the floor, I felt Thea find my hand and hold it, hardly daring to breathe. From the other side of the door came the faint suggestion of women's conversation.

'Did you see who it was?' I asked, bending my mouth to Thea's ear.

'Yes,' she breathed. 'The Radtkes. Probably coming back from your house.'

We waited in silence. In the thick darkness I was aware only of the fading murmur of voices outside, Thea's fingers entwined with mine and then, when we could no longer hear anything, when we creaked the door ajar and glanced out, faces pressed cheek to cheek, our bodies seizing with laughter and relief.

giblets and bacon

Thea and I fell into friendship like rain to the ground, like stones into water.

At their insistence, I began to eat at the Eichenwalds' every Sunday, occasionally calling in on Saturdays too. Anna Maria had a gift for cooking that made my own mother's offerings seem dismal; for all that the Wend would shout at her badly drawing chimney, slipping from German into Slav in her frustration, she worked magic with her three-legged oven bowl. On Saturdays, her baking days, she would lower round after round of smooth dough into its iron belly, carefully covering the heavy lid with embers each time. The dark loaves of bread she turned out smelled glorious, crusts crackling as they cooled. When I asked what her secret was, Anna Maria told me that she let the dough rise in her bed the night before, that a sleeping body offered the best temperature for yeast to ferment. The following Sunday, when I told her I'd suggested to Mama that she might improve her rye loaves by sleeping with them, Anna Maria shrieked with laughter.

'What did she say?'

'She told me to mind my mouth.'

Anna Maria wiped tears from her eyes. 'Oh, I do hope she tries it. I love the thought of Johanne Nussbaum sharing a pillow with a dough bin.'

Thea's home was a happy place to be, for all the winter winds breached the cottage walls and the roof leaked. Friedrich Eichenwald was a quiet man, content with his work and his family, and Anna Maria swept me up in the expansive love she showed her daughter. Theirs was a place of ready laughter, and while at first I found the family's affection for one another odd and uncomfortable to behold, I soon could not help but compare my own parents unfavourably to the Eichenwalds. Anna Maria embraced me more than my own mother did, and when I heard Friedrich talk with his daughter, I wished that my own father would show the same interest in me, would speak to me of his own accord and not through the borrowed word of God. At home, the family table had become less a place of fellowship than a pulpit for my father's denunciation of the Union Church and despair at the ever-shrinking possibility of religious freedom. His earthly sight seemed levelled only at his fields, our animals. Mama never placed her hand on Papa's neck as she served him his dinner. Papa never commented on Mama's beauty, though it was there, remarkable and singular, every hour of the day. They worked within their own spheres, remote and distinct from one another. Papa spoke of Mama as his helpmeet and he only ever called her Mutter. Friedrich referred to his wife by her name. He uttered it like an affirmation.

Matthias, ever my comfort, offered moments of light amidst the endless labour and criticism. During the week I lived for the rare hours when we might be in each other's company: I relished his kicks under the table, the green bean tucked in his upper lip when he thought Mama wasn't looking. But his days were spent in my father's dominion and I was trapped in my mother's.

'Sometimes I wonder if I was born into the wrong family,' I told Thea one afternoon as we sat in front of Anna Maria's hearth, bare feet extended towards the embers.

'Why?' She was drowsy. I could hear it in her voice.

I hesitated. I knew that Thea thought all marriages were like her parents': hands finding one another across tables or in passing, a constant homing of fingers. She never hesitated to wrap her arms about me in affection, and it was difficult for me to articulate the joy I felt each time she hugged me. I was no longer a child picked up by my father or permitted to crawl into my twin's bed. My mother's unpredictable kisses did not satisfy the longing I had to be touched, to be recognised as worthy of touch. I wanted to tell Thea that I was often so hungry for another body to acknowledge my own that I sometimes felt the weight of her arm slung around my shoulder long after I went home. Her cool fingers between my own left my skin burning. I wanted to tell her that sometimes I woke in the night convinced her hand was still in mine.

'Your family does not ignore the body,' I said eventually.

Thea rested her head on my shoulder.

Despite her initial trepidation, Mama tolerated my weekly absences from home in a way she had not since I was a child. Other than occasionally quipping that if I loved Anna Maria's *Sauergurken* so much I should just live there and save her the effort of setting my place at the table, she held her tongue and said nothing when I continually came home late on Sunday evenings, face flushed with cold, as long as I was back in time to milk the cows with Matthias – the one day I was able to share the chore with him.

'Do you think Mama is relieved to be rid of me?' I asked Matthias one night. I had returned home from the Eichenwalds' earlier than usual and had felt, immediately, that Mama was displeased to see me.

Matthias turned and opened his mouth, and I attempted to squirt milk into it. We both laughed as it hit him in the eye.

'Do you even care?' Matthias replied, wiping his face on his shirt-sleeve. 'You don't have to sit and listen to Papa complaining about Calvinists all day.'

'She can't wait to marry me off and get me out of the house,' I muttered.

'Hanne, I doubt it's you. She's happy for me to head off with Hans, when Elder Pasche allows him to go. Perhaps she just likes the time to herself.' He reached out and took my pail of milk, hooking it onto the yoke across his shoulders. 'You're lucky Thea never has to sit and study sermons to keep the Sabbath. Think of how Hans suffers.'

It never occurred to me that Mama might have been preoccupied with her own affairs until, one morning in late January, I found her hunched over in the orchard, a mess in the frost and one arm gripping the bare branches of an apple tree for support. She did not know I was there until I placed my hand on her shoulder. She was shaking.

Mama allowed me to help her into the house and ease her into a chair, even as she told me she was fine, that she had just had a funny turn. Even in the days following, when she stopped eating and heaved at the fatty smell of frying *Leberwurst*, she refused to admit she was unwell.

That Sunday I chose to remain home in order to look after her.

'You would tell me, wouldn't you?' I asked, after a day of watching her run outside to throw up in the snow. 'If you were truly sick?' I was washing the dishes and, when Mama did not reply, I stood up from the pan of hot water and wrapped my arms around her middle.

Mama gently steered me back towards my chore. 'Hanne, what I need now is a little rest and nothing more. A little space.' She picked up her plate and scraped the uneaten food into Hulda's pail.

I hovered at her side. 'You could speak to Anna Maria. She makes all her own balms and medicines.'

'Does she just?'

'Yes. If you tell me what is wrong, she might teach me how I could cure you.'

Mama sighed and reached past me to pick up Matthias's empty cup. 'I would prefer you just did what I asked of you rather than dirty the kitchen making balms.'

'I only stopped to ask you how you are,' I insisted.

'And I have told you that it is nothing.'

'Mama . . .'

'Truly, Hanne, if you are not going to clean, please just get out of my way.'

I was relieved when, by the end of February, Mama's nausea eased and the colour returned to her face. It was only when I returned to the Eichenwalds' cottage and gave them the reason for my absence that Anna Maria explained to me that my mother may have been pregnant and, if so, had lost the baby to miscarriage.

I was angry then that Mama had let my fears grow wild and tangled. Angry that she had not shared with me this hopeful, miraculous thing. When I returned home that evening, I cornered her in the cellar and asked her why she had lied to me.

'It was my own concern,' Mama said.

I sat down on the steps and watched her open a crock. The smell of fermenting vegetables was thick in the air. 'Are you sad?' I asked her eventually.

'I trust in the Lord with all my heart and lean not on my own understanding,' Mama muttered, ladling pickled cabbage into a shallow dish. 'In all ways I submit to Him, for He will make my path straight.' She handed me the *Sauerkraut*. 'Go set the table.'

'Mama?'

'Yes, Hanne?'

I stared down at the cabbage. 'Do you remember when I was a child and I couldn't sleep, and you would let me sit with you in front of the fire while you sewed?'

Mama did not look at me, but I saw her hands pause in their work. 'I remember,' she said.

'I miss that sometimes.'

I turned to go. I did not want to give her an opportunity to wound me with derision or with yet another reminder that I was grown. But before I placed my foot on the stair, I felt Mama catch my elbow and turn me back to face her.

'Hanne . . .' She held my arm in her hands, as though I might run from her. 'Would you like to sew with me tonight? Just us,' she added, and there was something so tender and conciliatory in her request that I could not refuse.

That night, Mama waited until Matthias and Papa had retired to bed and then set two chairs in front of the fire. 'I'm going to teach you how to whitework,' she said, giving me a rare smile. 'That way you can begin preparing your hope chest.'

My heart sank. 'A hope chest?'

'For when you are married. Whitework is lovely on a tablecloth. A christening gown. Bed linen.'

I was silent as Mama chalked a pattern onto fabric so I might practise. 'Try this to begin with,' she said. 'Here, thread your own needle.'

'I don't know why you are so determined I marry,' I said.

'Oh, Hanne.'

'I thought you wanted to spend time with me tonight.'

'I do.'

'No, you just want me to sew up things for a hope chest so you can be rid of me.'

My mother sighed. 'It is not about getting rid of you.'

'Why else do you keep talking about it?!'

Mama hesitated, then placed a hand on my knee. 'Hanne, I need you to listen to me. Your future will be uncertain without the security of marriage.'

I opened my mouth to argue with her, but her face was gentle and searching.

'Women who do not marry do not have children of their own,' she said softly. 'They must live with family, who must then provide for them. If they have family, that is. Take Rosina, for example. Her parents died. But when she marries Elder Christian she will be certain of a future. Of safety. A family and a roof over her head.'

'What would happen to Rosina if she wasn't marrying Christian?' I asked.

'She'd marry someone else.'

'But what if no one wanted to marry her?'

Mama sat back in her chair and licked her thread. 'There is always a man in need of a helpmeet.'

'But, Mama, what if she married someone but she did not love him?' I paused. 'Does Rosina love Elder Pasche?'

'Hanne, that is a private affair.'

'I just –'

'Love comes. In time she will love him.'

There was something in her voice that made my skull prickle. I looked at her, hair sleek and shiny from vinegar wash, eyes black against the darkness of her clothes. 'Did you love Papa when you married him?'

Mama took a deep breath and blew it out, top lip pursing. 'All wives must love their husbands. All husbands love their wives.'

'But sometimes you can't help not loving something. Like giblets and bacon.'

Mama smiled. 'You love giblets and bacon.'

'But what if I didn't?'

'Then you would love the children the giblets and bacon gave you.' She tapped my hand holding the needle. 'Begin.'

The year opened out into a blowy, blossomed spring. Petals fluttered to rest against doorways and walls, and I noticed bees hovering about the tight-budded flowers. A season of humming.

Mama began to run outside in the mornings, hand to mouth, and when I found her bent over, spitting into the new grass, I thought I knew the cause. Remembering our conversation in the cellar, I never asked her outright if I could expect a sibling. Still, Thea, as a midwife's daughter, had an older woman's understanding of these things, and she told me what I might do to ease my mother's nausea. Mama did not refuse the small cups of mint tea or the dry slices of bread I brought her. She might have guessed that I had learned a thing or two at the Eichenwalds'.

Anna Maria had started to attend to some of the women in the area as a midwife, and those who had seen her work agreed that she was capable and calm and worthy. Rumour also had it that she was often already on the road when someone set out to fetch her. She would meet them on the lane, basket in hand. No one other than Christiana and Magdalena Radtke ever suggested out loud that she was a *Hexe* – there was no question that the family had suffered for their faith, and what witch would gladly suffer for Christ? – but it became known that Anna Maria had a preternatural ability to know when a woman was in labour. I was a little afraid to ask Thea about it. Thea, too, sometimes had an uncanny way about her, a way of guessing at my thoughts. Once she answered a question before I had the opportunity to ask it aloud. When I pointed out that I hadn't spoken, she seemed a little taken aback. 'Yes, you did, I heard you.'

'I didn't say a word.'

Anna Maria interjected, throwing flour upon the table in a steady arc. 'You two are old friends recently met, I think.' She smiled at me, handed over a wrapped cloth. 'Take this to Johanne. It's blood sausage, to fortify her.'

Mama gave birth one year after the quiet loss of the unmentioned, unnamed child. She sent me for Anna Maria at midnight, bracing herself against the doorframe to my room, face licked with sweat.

Sure enough, as I ran towards the pine forest, breathless and clumsy, I saw the Wend's headdress bobbing in the dark before me. She grinned at me as we met in the field and told me to wait for Thea, who was following behind.

When Thea approached, carrying a heavy basket, I ran to help her and together we returned to my home. Matthias had not woken from his bunk in the loft – nothing but Papa's shouted summons would wake him in those days – but my father was up, sitting at the bare kitchen table as my mother's groaning – and Anna Maria's calm tones of reassurance – issued from behind their closed bedroom door. He nodded at Thea as she entered, stood then sat again, built up the fire and lit his pipe before knocking it out against the mantel. He pulled on his boots and headed outside.

Thea held out her scarf to the hearth to dry it and smiled at me over her shoulder. 'He's worried for her,' she said.

I sat down on the floor in front of the fire and held my knees to my chest. 'Papa is never worried. He says that the worried lack faith.'

'He is worried. Of course he is.' She sat down beside me, eyes reflecting the flames before us. 'People here believe that they are born with a fixed reservoir of blood in their bodies. Maybe your father thinks childbirth will lower the stores.'

I turned to her. 'You mean that's not true?'

Thea wrinkled her nose at me. 'If it were true, how do you account for the fact that men and women die at a similar age?'

I blushed then. Thea noticed and laughed. 'You look so uncomfortable.'

'I don't understand how you can talk so easily about these things.'

'It's natural. You need not be ashamed.' She picked up the poker and broke a log into embers. 'Mama told me it was a sign of a gift. The power of creation.'

I hugged my knees closer to my chest and stared at the fire. 'The first thing Mama said, when it happened to me, was how to wash and dry my cloths so that no one would ever see.'

'Oh, Hanne.'

To my embarrassment, I felt my chin tremble. Don't cry, I told myself. Not now.

'Hanne? What is it?'

'It's nothing,' I said, but tears had filled my eyes. In the periphery of my blurred vision I was aware of Thea staring at me. I bent my face into my knees and breathed into my skirt, still damp from snow.

The familiar weight of Thea's hand was on my shoulder. 'Hanne?'

I pressed my eyes harder into my kneecaps until I saw lights flicker amidst the dark.

'I didn't mean to upset you.'

'No, I know.' I wiped my face with my hands. 'It's just . . . Gottlob.'

Thea shook her head, confused.

'Gottlob. My brother.' I closed my eyes. 'I had an older brother. He's dead now.'

Thea was silent. 'You've never told me.'

'No. I'm sorry. I suppose I should have . . .' I took a deep, shud-dering breath. 'I mean, everyone here knows and I . . . Anyway, I was reminded of him.' I gave her a small smile. 'It was at his funeral that, you know . . . At the churchyard. I was wearing Eleonore Volkmann's dress. Mama had to scrub the blood from it.'

'Hanne.' Thea looked aghast. 'That's awful.'

'Yes,' I agreed. 'It was awful.'

'What happened to him?'

The door opened then, and Thea and I turned to see Matthias entering the kitchen, arms full of firewood, face bruised with sleep. He peered down the corridor and then at us.

'Has she . . .?' he asked.

I shook my head.

My brother stacked the logs against the wall then joined us by the fireside, sitting cross-legged. He smiled at Thea and smoothed his hair against his skull, then winced as a heavy groan issued from the bedroom.

Thea reached across me and tapped Matthias lightly on the arm. 'Hanne just told me about Gottlob.' She shook her head. 'I'm so sorry.'

Matthias glanced at me, the gap in his teeth visible through his parted lips. 'She didn't know?'

I shook my head.

'Our parents never talk about him either.' He shrugged.

'Do you want to?' asked Thea.

'What?'

'Talk about him.'

My twin and I looked at each other.

'How did he die?' Thea prompted.

'He fell from a horse,' Matthias said. 'Three years ago. He was seventeen and he was taking our horse –'

'Otto,' I interrupted.

'– our horse Otto to Skampe. Hans Pasche found him.'

We were silent. Through the walls Anna Maria said something to my mother over and over again, her voice steady and soothing.

'Papa blames himself, I think,' Matthias said quietly.

I looked at him. 'Really?'

Matthias nodded. 'He once told me he wished he'd told Gottlob to hide as well.'

I was silent for a moment. 'I always wondered if Mama felt responsible. She was the one who asked him to ride to Skampe.'

Thea looked confused. 'Why did Gottlob need to hide?'

'Something happened a few days before Gottlob's accident,' I explained. 'It was when the soldiers were searching for Pastor Flügel.'

'They knocked at our door,' Matthias said. 'Mama pushed Hanne and me out the back and told us to stay out of sight. We crawled into the rye field and hid there all day.'

'Later, when Mama called us back inside, we saw that Gottlob had been beaten. When the soldiers had threatened to set the hayrick on fire, to drive out the pastor should he be hiding in there, Gottlob had picked up a pitchfork and the men had set upon him.'

'Papa intervened,' Matthias added. 'They arrested him for disaffection, saying he'd armed his children against the Church's representatives. When Papa asked how, they pointed to Gottlob's pitchfork.'

Thea lifted a hand to her cheek.

'They took Papa to Züllichau,' I said. 'That's why Gottlob was riding Otto to Skampe. Mama sold the horse to a family there to raise the money to free Papa. But later that day Hans Pasche found Otto trotting back towards Kay, riderless.'

From the bedroom sounded a muffled scream. Matthias and I exchanged frightened looks.

'What had happened?' Thea whispered.

'We never really found out,' Matthias said softly. 'Hans found Gottlob lying unconscious in the road a little further on. He rode Otto home and told Elder Pasche, who went with his wagon to retrieve Gottlob.'

I was quiet, remembering how, after Hans had told us what had happened, Mama had run out the door. When Elder Pasche returned, Mama was sitting on the floor of his wagon, Gottlob's head in her lap. The bloodstain in her skirt had been a perfect circle.

Thea was watching me, eyes wide. 'I'm so sorry,' she repeated.

Matthias nodded. He reached for the fire poker and turned it over in his hands.

I wiped my face with my skirt.

Another muffled cry came from the bedroom.

The poker dropped onto the hearth as Matthias rose suddenly and left the room.

Thea and I were quiet for a moment. The cry turned into a constant low groaning that made me feel sick in my stomach.

'Now we'll have a new brother,' I murmured.

'It's a girl. Mama told me.'

'She knows things, doesn't she?' I asked. 'Anna Maria.'

Thea gave a small nod. 'Sometimes. You know, before we moved to Kay, she told me something strange. I didn't understand it until after we met in the fog.'

'What?' I asked. My face felt tight and warm. I pushed myself away from the fire, back into the darkness of the kitchen. 'What did she say?'

'She said I'd meet my ghost.' Thea did not look at me. Her skin glowed in the firelight. 'She says understanding comes to her in riddles, like that. Like poetry.'

'Like when I hear the trees speak.'

'It must be the way of mysteries.'

We fell into silence. Thea shuffled close to me and I felt her like a fire, warmer than anything flickering in the hearth. The groaning intensified, there was a low and guttural cry, then, seconds later, the wail of a newborn child. Thea looked at me, a smile spreading on her face, as footsteps sounded down the corridor and Anna Maria entered the room with the baby in her arms.

'Hanne, hold your sister.' Without waiting for my reply she gently placed the baby, crumpled and waxen and crying, in my arms and then, glancing at Thea with tight lips, returned to the bedroom.

'What's the matter?' I asked Thea. 'Is it Mama?'

'I'm sure she will be well,' Thea said. 'Try not to worry. No, don't get up. My mother has been doing this since she was my age. Here,' she said softly. 'Give her your little finger to suck on.'

I did as she suggested, and Thea smiled at my astonishment. 'She's so strong,' I said, gazing down at the tiny, working mouth. In the quiet I heard Anna Maria's voice sound from the room, low and rhythmic and loud.

'*Ich ging über eine Brücke, Worunter drei Ströme liefen.*'

'What is she doing?' I whispered. 'Why is she talking about a bridge?'

Thea said nothing, only stroked the damp wisp of hair on the baby's head.

'*Der erste hies Gut, Der zweite hies Blut, Der dritte hies Eipipperjahn, Blut du sollst stille Stahl. In Namen Gottes, Javeh.*'

'"Blood you shall be silent"?' I asked, panic striking through me. 'Is Mama bleeding? Thea, what is Anna Maria saying?'

Thea opened her mouth to speak, then closed it again. She gave me a heavy look. 'My mother, she . . .'

The baby broke away from my finger and, mouth wide, chin shaking, began to cry again.

'What is she saying, Thea?' I was on the cusp of tears myself.

'It's like a prayer,' Thea said. She reached for my sister and placed her own finger in the baby's mouth. 'It's like a prayer,' she said again. 'It *is* a prayer. A prayer of healing. In the name of God.'

At that moment Papa and Matthias returned indoors and, seeing Thea holding the child, approached us wide-eyed. Thea offered the baby up to Papa and, as he held her in his arms, I saw that his good eye was filled with tears. He cupped her tiny skull in his hands and looked at me.

'How is Mutter?'

There was the sound of a door opening and a moment later Anna Maria entered the room, wiping blood from her forearms with a balled-up apron that seemed just as red. As my stomach dropped, Anna Maria offered a wide smile, teeth shining in the low light. 'All is well.'

'Johanne?' My father's voice was oddly thin, as though it might snap in half.

Anna Maria nodded. 'She lost some blood, but' – she glanced at Thea – 'I was able to stop it. With the help of the Lord.'

'Praise His name,' said my father, and tears slipped from his cheeks to the crying baby in his arms. 'Praise His name.'

stones into water

I have been thinking about the dead up here. Already the light is growing rich and the sun is sinking below the horizon. Already a day is nearly gone. I think about all the bodies buried with the heads facing east, the better to greet Christ. All the sunsets they are missing.

In the congregation it was customary to give the dead an opportunity for resurrection. Three days for the body to rise, as Jesus's did, and then, when it did not, they made space in the earth and laid the unrisen to rest until the time trumpets sound and all four corners of the world are shaken like a sheet to upend the buried, so that their sins might be tallied and the chosen called home. Home to silver orchards. Holy honey and magdalen milk.

The three days lent a sort of cruelty to Gottlob's passing. Seven weeks of dying in bed and even then he had to wait to be buried. I hardly remember those three days, only that the flowers placed in his coffin by visitors wilted within the hour.

I do remember the seven weeks.

Gottlob never opened his eyes again after he fell. He was insensible to the world. Still, it took him some time to die. Hans took Otto to his new farm in Skampe and my father was released from prison at Züllichau in time for harvest. Without a horse and without Gottlob, harvesting took twice as long, and so Mama and Matthias joined

Papa to bring in the crop. I was suddenly responsible for cooking my family's meals, for washing their clothes and keeping house. When I was not doing these things, Mama made me sit sentry over my elder brother's body.

The curtains were always drawn; I sat in endless half-darkness. I no longer wandered when my chores were completed but remained indoors, changing Gottlob's bedclothes, dribbling gruel into the corners of his mouth, turning his man's body and attending to the sores that erupted on his skin. For weeks I sat next to my dying brother and, as I sat, my own body was altered. In the time it took for Gottlob to die, my own vigour made itself certain. It was as though my physical being, forced to dwell in such close proximity to approaching death, sought to assert its own vitality. As I sat and watched my elder brother's ribs emerge, I felt my own chest swell painful against the stitching of my clothes. My wrists stretched beyond my cuffs. My toes strained against my stockings. Already tall, I grew taller, but where once I was sleek, epicene, utterly at one with my frame, I now felt a fracture between myself and my body. I did not recognise the new weight, the new shapes I felt under my hands or glimpsed in the glass of my mother's framed wedding myrtle. I was suddenly softer than I knew myself to be. My skin smelled different. One night, lying in bed after a long day listening to my brother's lungs lift and fall in awful gurgling slowness, I realised that I now possessed the body of a stranger.

Gottlob died in the early hours of a Tuesday morning, seven weeks after he fell from Otto's great height. I was seated at his side, dozing, bare feet resting on the edge of the bed. The room was lit only by moonlight escaping through the curtains; I had long blown out the candle. In my half-sleep, I realised that I could no longer hear

Gottlob's rattling breath and the awful certainty that he was gone pierced through me. I was immediately awake. I leaned over him. My brother's chest was still.

It seemed impossible, despite his weeks of unconsciousness, that he was gone, and yet it had happened. Gottlob had always seemed much older than me – there were five years between us – and we had not been especially close. Matthias had always been my favourite brother. But in the minutes after Gottlob's death I climbed into the bed and cradled his head and imagined him walking my father's holy orchard.

It was not until the morning of the funeral procession, Gottlob in his coffin and ready for the waiting *Totenbahre*, the bier, that Mama noticed my body fighting my clothes. The buttons were straining at the back of my best dress, my breasts pressing uncomfortably against a panel of material sewn to fit a child. I appeared at breakfast, mortified. Mama took one look at me, quickly stood up from the table and swept me into my bedroom, where she made me undress and try on one of her own dresses. It didn't fit. I sat on her bed in my shift, on the edge of tears, while she went to ask Beate Fröhlich if she could find something suitable amongst the women of the congregation within the hour. Eventually Beate came into the bedroom with an old dress from Eleonore Volkmann, the only woman in Kay who was of my height. There was no time to take it in at the waist and it smelled of mildew, and as Gottlob was returned to God by wagon and service and soil, I felt hot with shame. Shame that my grief for my brother on the day of his burial was so easily usurped by grief at the loss of my child's body.

That afternoon, as the congregation ate in the shelter shed of the cemetery, I felt a new slipperiness between my legs. I sought a private place behind the wall of yews, and there I lifted my dress. My fingers came away bloody. Only then did I cry.

My sister Hermine was a pink, unpleasant baby. My father could not abide her crying at night. He and the other elders of our village had received word from Pastor Flügel, secretly fled to London, that they should renew their petitions and applications for emigration, and the work – requiring much letter writing and intellectual argument – taxed him and left him emotionally and spiritually worn. Mama was anxious he get his sleep, and so Hermine's cot was placed in my room. Every two or three hours I would be roused by her rising wail and would stumble from my bed and pick her up, bouncing her listlessly until Mama came in and fed and settled her. It was expected that I change my sister and bathe her, soothe her and hold her, as well as complete my usual chores, and I grew to deeply resent Hermine's presence, the cloths streaked with mustard shit, the spumy trails of sick down my back. It was no longer easy to visit Thea on my day of rest. When I told Mama that caring for Hermine seemed as much work as any other chore forbidden on a Sunday, she paused, swept Hermine out of my arms and placed her in her little cradle.

'Let us leave her until Monday, then,' she said.

I do not know how she bore the screaming that followed, but she did not touch Hermine. I waited for as long as possible, dark and angry and exhausted, and considered setting out for the forester's cottage, but I did not dare test Mama's stubborn streak and nor could I bear the grating cries of my sister. I picked her up and she rewarded me with a sudden eruption of curdled milk.

*

Deprived of our pastor, it was up to my father to baptise my baby sister. Samuel Radtke had baptised his youngest child, Elizabeth, but word had reached the local authorities and he had been imprisoned for insubordination. We could not afford for Papa to be jailed again, but my father pointed out that the price of delaying Hermine's baptism was a far greater one to pay, and so one warm night my bawling little sister was ceremoniously sprinkled with well water at our kitchen table.

One week later the elders gathered at our house to discuss the matter of Christian and Rosina's wedding, and it was agreed that, out of duty and necessity, my father, again, must perform it in Flügel's absence.

'It matters not that we have no church,' I overheard Christian say. I was in the kitchen, frying bacon for their supper. '"For where two or three are gathered together in my name, there am I in the midst of them." My marriage shall be recognised by the Lord, if not the King.'

There was a murmur of agreement from the table.

'Will we have it in your home?' Samuel Radtke asked him.

'I think so. In the morning. Will you ask your wives to prepare a wedding breakfast?'

The morning of the wedding I arrived with my parents at the Pasches' early, buttoned and bonneted, my feet blistering in a pair of Elder Fröhlich's leather shoes intended originally for my mother. As my father sat with Elder Pasche and discussed whether they ought to risk singing hymns, Mama ushered me through to the barn which, scraped of manure, was to accommodate both the service and wedding breakfast. Magdalena Radtke and Beate Fröhlich were already there, decorating the place with garlands of early wildflowers and branches of spruce.

'Hello, Johanne.' Magdalena nodded to Mama, her hands full of corn poppies. 'We could use your help.'

Mama passed Hermine to me. 'Take her outside will you, Hanne?'

I did as I was told, bouncing my sister against my shoulder, pacing up and down the Pasches' orchard, which was filled with new, green leaves whispering amongst themselves. Underneath the soft sound of the trees, I could hear Christian Pasche's raised voice travel from the cottage's open back door and, a few moments later, saw Hans march out, cheeks red, new-cut hair still damp. He looked as though he were about to hit someone and, not wanting him to see me, I tried to hide behind a peach tree. In my haste, however, I jostled Hermine's head against a twig and she began to cry.

I lifted my hand sheepishly as Hans saw me standing there. He was dressed in his best shirt, but it was unbuttoned at the throat and there was a wild look in his eye.

'Are you all right?' I asked him.

Hans hesitated, then walked up to me. 'Is Matthias here?' he asked. I could feel the anger pouring off him.

'No,' I said, lifting Hermine and nuzzling her with my chin. 'No, he's finishing the animals and then he'll come for the ceremony.'

'Right.' Hans glanced back at the house. 'Did you hear any of that?'

'I heard your father shouting,' I offered. 'But not what he was saying.'

'He's a hypocrite.' Hans crossed his arms over his chest. It unnerved me to see him this way. '"If a man say, I love God, and hateth his brother, he is a liar; for he that loveth not his brother whom he hath seen, how can he love God whom he hath not seen?"'

'Chapter four of 1 John,' I replied.

'Verse twenty.' Hans ran a hand around his neck. 'My father hates me, you know.'

Hermine wailed in my ear. I bounced her harder, giving Hans a look of sympathy. 'My mother doesn't like me much either.'

'See here,' Hans said and, face livid, hands working furiously, he unbuttoned his shirt and showed me a bruise across his ribs.

My mouth fell open. 'Oh,' I said. 'Oh, I don't think . . .'

Hans buttoned his shirt again, cheeks red.

'Hanne?'

I looked past Hans and saw Thea peeling off from the steady stream of people now arriving in the lane beyond the cottage. She lifted her hands in greeting then, checking over her shoulder, slipped down the side of the house and ran towards us. Hans stepped aside as she approached and threw her arms around me, face shining.

'Oh, I haven't seen you for weeks!'

I glanced at Hans over Thea's shoulder. He was standing there, staring at the ground, shirt buttoned to the neck, hands jammed into his pockets.

Thea untangled herself from me and faced him. 'Good morning, Hans,' she said.

'Hello, Thea,' Hans muttered. He nodded to us, then turned and walked away.

'Is he all right?' Thea asked, reaching for Hermine.

'No,' I said. I placed my arm around Thea's shoulders. 'I don't think he is.'

The service was brief that morning. Christian and my father had decided against hymns, and so once the sermon – written by Elder Pasche himself and delivered by my father – was completed and the vows made, the congregation settled around the barn and began to help themselves to the wedding feast: fresh bread, boiled potatoes, *Wurst* and bacon, salads, pickled cucumbers and vegetables. There was beer, too, and as soon as the surrounding hum of conversation had eased away from formal beginnings, rousing into celebration, I left Hermine with my mother to find Thea. I found her watching the younger children climbing the haystacks.

'Having fun?' I asked her.

'Not really,' Thea said, frowning. 'Christiana was asking me odd questions.'

'Really?'

'Yes, about Mama.'

'Do you want to tell me?'

Thea hesitated. 'I'd rather just leave, to be honest.' She leaned closer to me. 'Do you want to go to the river?'

I smiled. Thea placed her hand in mine and, glancing around, pulled me quietly away from the benches of adults eating and talking in the barn and out into the joy of sunlight.

We could hear the river before we saw it, hidden as it was by a thick copse of birch. The familiar murmur of water grew louder as we walked between the slender trunks, tripping occasionally on fallen branches. Thea had kept her hand in mine, and every time I stumbled, she laughed at her failed attempts to keep me upright. 'You're like a newborn foal,' she said. She peered to where the river lay, straining against its banks. 'There's someone there,' she whispered.

'It's Hans,' I replied. Thea and I watched as he bent to the ground, picked something up and hurled it into the water.

'We should leave,' I whispered.

'Has something happened?' Thea asked. 'He seemed upset before. Oh, he's seen us.'

'Hanne?' Hans's voice called out over the sound of water.

Thea tugged at my arm. 'Let's go talk to him.'

Reluctantly, I followed her to the riverbank.

Hans was holding a stone in each hand and his face was red and sweaty, as though he had just run a long way. He wore the same expression I had seen on Matthias when our father, spine and heart Christ-filled, admonished him for falling asleep during the evening sermon: a combination of weariness, shame and anger.

'What are you doing?' I asked him.

Hans shrugged and offered me one of his stones.

I hesitated, then turned and hurled it into the river. The three of us watched as it disappeared into the current.

'Feels good, doesn't it?' Hans asked.

I nodded.

'We can do better than that,' Thea said, and walked to a heavy stone wedged amongst pebbles and mud and grass. She squatted and dug at the sides of the boulder with her fingers.

Hans and I dropped to our knees beside her and together we scraped away the soil at the stone's base, loosening it from the bank.

Breathing hard, we lugged it awkwardly to the water's edge then, together, swung it out as far as we could. As we all let go, I stumbled and fell into the shallows. Thea and Hans waded in and hauled me to the bank, doubled over in laughter, and I felt a surge of happiness that made me want to cry.

We walked back to the Pasches' in the afternoon, sodden, throwing stones at trees. As we approached, however, we could hear no sound of celebration from the barn, and inside there were only a few members of the congregation sitting in tight bunches, talking intently. Reinhardt Geschke looked up and, seeing Hans, beckoned him over. Elize stood and came up to Thea and me.

'What happened to you?' she asked, eyes wide.

'Nothing,' Thea said. 'We were at the river. Hanne fell in and we pulled her out.'

'Where is everyone?' I asked.

Elize glanced back to where Reinhardt and Hans were speaking in hushed voices. 'There has been news. People have gone home to talk it over.'

Thea and I glanced at each other.

'What is it?' Thea asked.

'Go talk to your parents,' Elize told us. 'Go home, girls. You'll catch your death.'

I stepped through the back door of the cottage and found my father, Mama and Matthias seated around the table in silence.

'Where have you been?' asked Papa.

'At the river,' I mumbled.

Mama pushed her chair back, the legs squealing against the boards, and pulled out the wildflowers Thea had threaded in my hair. She flung them onto the fire.

'What is it?' I asked. 'Elize said something's happened.'

'Elize saw you like this?'

I glanced at Matthias, expecting a look of amusement or solidarity, but he was staring at his hands, face blank.

'Papa? What is it?'

'Consent has been given.' My father suddenly gave a great, gasping sob. 'Consent has been given!'

I stood still, not understanding. Hermine began to cry in her cradle on the ground, but it was as though Mama could not hear her. She sank back into her chair.

Papa looked at me and I saw that his good eye was wet with tears.

His smile was broad and pained. 'Praise God, we shall be free, Hanne,' he said. 'We are free to leave.'

I watched as Mama slowly reached for the wrapped rye loaf on the table and held it, as though suddenly bewildered as to what it was there for, what purpose it served. 'It is Russia then?' she asked, voice soft.

Papa shook his head.

'America?'

He reached across the table and took up Mama's free hand. 'A colony where we might make a new life of our own design. Where we may worship freely.'

My voice was a crack in the wall. 'What place?'

'The colony of South Australia.'

Matthias and I stared at each other, mouths open. We had been moulded in the crucible of our village and its allotments, the forest and the river. I had a sudden fear that if we were to leave our home, I would become formless, shapeless.

'Where is that?' my brother asked.

Hermine's crying pitched higher. Mama withdrew her hand from Papa's and picked her up off the floor.

'It is not so far, Matthias,' said Papa. 'Pastor Flügel writes that the journey will take six months.'

'Six months,' Mama murmured. Hermine arched against her, wriggling.

Papa leaned back in his chair. 'God will be with us.'

Mama unbuttoned her blouse and set Hermine to a dark nipple.

'How will we pay for passage?' asked Matthias. He had gone pale. Papa opened his mouth to speak, but my brother continued in a low voice. 'Last time they told us we had permission to leave, you sold nearly everything.'

'Not everything.'

Matthias shook his head. 'Papa, look what happened to the Eichenwalds. What if the King changes his mind again?'

'It will not happen. Matthias, God has rewarded us for our faith, our patience. Our suffering! We will be issued passports.'

Mama prised Hermine off one breast and turned her to the other, saying nothing. Her chest was mapped with blue veins. I tried not to stare at them.

'How will we pay for passage?' I asked.

'Pastor Flügel has made an agreement with a gentleman in London. He has taken pity on our plight. His agent speaks German; it is all being arranged.'

'He will lend us the money?' Mama asked.

Papa turned to her. 'Johanne, this is our chance. This is the Lord's work.'

Matthias had not moved. I was trembling. Hermine spluttered at my mother's breast as Papa rose and fetched his Bible.

My father's reading that night was so long I grew numb in my seat. Such was his joy, which ever manifested in praise of God. He exalted in the scripture, intoning the words at us as though he were painting us with grace.

After prayers, Papa seized his bread and cheese and ate noisily, breathing heavily from his nose in relief from hunger. I could not eat. Neither, I saw, could Matthias. His voice, when he finally spoke again, was empty of feeling. 'So, then. We are going.'

Papa wiped his mouth. 'Praise God.'

'And what of our things here?' I asked.

Papa shook his head, swallowing loudly. 'Tools, we will take. What may fit in a trunk. Maybe two trunks. Everything else, we will sell.'

I looked around the small room. There was little to sell, only the table and its humble offering of crockery, the breadknife whittled thin from years of use. Six hard chairs, the polish on the seats suffering from years of shuffling bottoms. I tried to tally what else might be scraped together from the kitchen and bedrooms. Nothing of true value really; nothing that others would want. Mama's white tablecloth embroidered with red thread. The dried, pressed myrtle crown from her wedding beneath my dead grandmother's needlework proclaiming, 'He who keeps you does not slumber.'

I sat in silence, filled with a growing sense of panic. The door was open to the night. Insects knocked themselves senseless against the hot glass of the lamp.

A colony, I thought. I tried to imagine what it would be like to live in a place so different from Kay. It was like trying to imagine a new colour. Six months on a ship. I had never seen the ocean before. My stomach turned to water at the thought of it.

'Will Pastor Flügel come with us?' Matthias's voice was querulous, oddly high-pitched.

'Yes, he will join us from England, although he mentions in his letter that he may be on another ship. We are waiting to hear from all the families of his congregations to learn how many will be needed. You saw for yourself how the news was received at the Pasches'. Not everyone is willing to leave, despite the freedom promised them. They lack confidence; they have the faith of Thomas.'

It was then that my heart dropped. I had assumed the whole forest congregation would leave. It had not occurred to me that some might wish to remain, even after so many years of oppression.

'Did Herr Eichenwald and his family say they will come?' I asked.

Papa scratched his beard. 'All the elders and their families agreed at once to leave. The Volkmanns and Pfeiffers, also. The Eichenwalds are undecided.'

A terror drove down my spine that lifted me from my seat without conscious thought. My fingers hummed, and I was conscious of swaying, of needing to grip the back of my chair to prevent myself from falling to the floor. Faces turned in my direction. Their features swam together in the low light. The sound of insects hitting the lamp's glass was intolerable.

'Hanne?'

'Excuse me,' I muttered. My feet pulled me to the back door and out into the evening and its cool wonder of air. I stumbled to the orchard and sank down at the base of the walnut tree, its gnarled trunk against my back.

I did not cry. I could not cry. The air rushed in and out of me, but I could not catch a breath of it. I was aware of my dress, still damp and clinging to my body, of Matthias coming out the door and crouching beside me, his hands on my shoulders, wrapping my shawl about me, telling me to breathe when I could not. In time, I stilled; I slowed enough to hear the words he kept whispering to me.

'All will be well,' he was saying. 'All will be well.'

restlessness

It was several days before I was able to walk to the forest and meet with Thea. My hours were not my own and I was forced to wait until an opportunity arose. Eventually there came a morning when Matthias and Papa were busy and Mama had left for a nearby town to sell some of our possessions, taking Hermine with her. As soon as she left, I struck out across the allotments towards the Eichenwalds' cottage, under a summer sky purring with heat.

Thea appeared as I pushed through their front gate, her arms bare to the elbows and sticky with dough. In that moment, about to learn if we would be parted, the sight of her pared me down to nothing more than heartbeat and hope. I could have fallen on my knees.

She nodded at me, face sombre. 'I'll wash. Wait there.'

As I waited, I worked myself up into even greater distress. Thea would remain here in Kay, her family's cottage still issuing its steady stream of smoke, and I would be buried in the bowels of a ship intent on taking me as far away from her as possible. I would be a stranger in a strange land, trapped in an even smaller circle of villagers who knew me too well. I would disappear and Thea would find another friend. I sat down on the grass, trying not to cry. The image of her arm in arm with another girl, someone not so tall, someone greedy for her confidences, burned through me, so that when Thea came out blinking in the sunlight, she recoiled at my expression.

She pulled me up from the sweet-smelling grass and pushed back my headscarf, the better to see my face.

'Please, please tell me you are coming too. Please, Thea.' The words hooked on a whimper.

Thea looked back at the cottage. 'Let's go to the river,' she murmured.

I followed her to the water, unwilling to take my eyes from the back of her head. Thea's braids had loosened, and strands of hair brushed against the collar of her blouse. The tops of her ears glowed pink in the sun.

I was memorising her already.

We reached the river, high against the banks, streaked with current, and I sat next to Thea on a log thick with moss. It was damp from the night's rain and I could feel moisture seeping through my skirts, but I did not move.

Her eyes were round. Solemn.

'I need to know,' I said. 'Are you coming?'

'Hanne . . . I don't know.'

I brought a hand to my chest and rubbed at the soft depression at my throat. I felt as though I might choke. 'I don't want to go if you aren't coming.'

Thea picked at the moss on the trunk, flinging it into the water. 'I heard my parents talking about it when they thought I was asleep.'

'They know there are passports then,' I whispered.

'Yes.'

'You must speak to your father,' I said. 'You must speak to them. Tell them they will be free from oppression.'

'There are different kinds of oppression. He is worried that, if permission is revoked again, we will not be able to withstand the loss.'

'Tell him that there is someone, some man, some gentleman, who is loaning money for passage to anyone who asks for it. And then he will have land and you can all work it and your father can pay back the debt. That is what we will all be doing. We will all be free.'

Thea stared at the river. 'But none of us has seen this place. And the journey is long. It's dangerous.'

I pressed harder at my throat. My fingers slid over bone, stemmed a rising knot of tears. 'You don't want to leave.'

Thea closed her eyes and rested her forehead against my shoulder. She smelled of bread and something else, something uniquely her. Warm skin and linen washed in vinegar. Baked apples. I pressed my cheek against her hair.

'Thea?'

'Mm.'

'I would follow you anywhere.' The words rushed out of me in a sob.

Thea did not reply, and in that moment I felt winded with shame. I knew that to leave Thea would rend a tear in my side and I did not know what that meant. I had been gifted with a friend and yet still I was unable to offer friendship as other women. She would not follow me. She would follow her family, as people did, as young women must, and she would pity me for the store of need I felt for her.

There is something wrong with you, I told myself, and I dug my fingers more deeply into the soft tissue at the base of my neck.

Thea pulled my hand away. 'What are you doing?'

I shook my head. I could not speak.

'You have left a mark. You're hurting yourself.'

My voice was strangled. 'I'm sorry.'

'What are you sorry for, Hanne?'

For needing too much. For feeling too much.

I stood up, pressed the backs of my hands against my eyes.

'Hanne?'

I turned and walked away from the river.

'Hanne, please don't go!'

I kept walking.

'Don't go!'

Her voice arrested me like a hand, and I stopped. Thea had risen from the log. She stood facing me. I could not read her expression. The wind blew her hair over her face, and when she lifted a hand to push it out of the way, I saw that her hand was shaking.

I returned. We sat back down. Neither of us said anything. We watched the flow of water.

'Mama is waiting to consult her book,' Thea said quietly. 'She will find out whether our fortune lies here or beyond the sea. She says we cannot afford to lose everything again.'

'What?'

Thea leaned back, mouth twitching. 'Her book will tell her whether we must stay or whether we ought to go.'

'You mean the Bible?'

'No, not that. It's a very powerful text. I can show you. Now, if you like.' Thea glanced at me sidelong. 'No one is home. They won't be back till sundown.'

Thea let me inside the cottage, then shut and barred the door behind us. The room was quiet and oddly still, the dough bin on the floor half filled, the lid propped against the wall. Thea carefully lifted the bread she had been shaping to one side of the table, then wiped down the other, looking up from time to time as though trying to guess at my thoughts.

'Truly, Hanne, the book is holy and precious. It is not a wicked thing.'

I did not know what to say. I did not know what she was talking about.

Thea went to the hearth and, reaching into the back of the chimney with a rag, removed a brick and set it carefully on the floor. She took out another.

'She keeps it in a special hollow here,' Thea explained. 'She has to hide it. Some people do not approve.' She took out a small cloth package, holding it in both hands. I watched her set it on the table.

A chill went through me. I thought of Christiana's words. *She's a witch.* An image of Anna Maria crouched in the ashes of her hearth, wishing ill on others, crossed my mind. It was not something I could reconcile with the woman as I knew her, ruddy-faced and wholesome and ready to laugh.

Thea was studying my reaction. 'Do you want to look?'

I gave a small nod and Thea carefully unfolded the material to reveal a small, worn book bound in pigskin. It did not look magic, only old and well-used.

'Mama told me the books were revealed by Almighty God to Moses on Mount Sinai. That is why it is called *The Sixth and Seventh Books of Moses. Das sechste und siebente Buch Moses.* Mama said that as long as the book is in her possession she will not die.'

'That's impossible,' I whispered.

'It's what she said. She will give this to me one day, and then, when I am ready to die, I will pass it on to my own child.'

'What if you have more than one child?'

'I won't,' she murmured. 'The book will not allow it.'

She opened the cover and I saw, briefly, the title filling the page in ornate text, a six-pointed star beneath. Thea slotted a finger between the pages, turning to the second half of the book. 'This is the seventh book. This is the one she uses most. It's herbal cures, really.'

I peered over Thea's shoulder and saw the heading 'To protect yourself from infection' and, underneath, directions for boiling juniper berries, cloves and mint.

'See?' Thea said, turning the pages. 'Directives for healing. This is what Mama used to treat your mother when she was bleeding out.'

The text continued in thick, gothic writing. 'What is that?' I asked, tapping her on the shoulder. My mouth went dry as I read, 'If you want to harm your enemy, write on a glass plate in ink after sunset: "Your misfortune will fall on your head and your malice will fall on your head!"' Thea let the page fall open, and I continued reading instructions to smoke the glass seven times, to invoke the wrath of someone called Adonay. I stepped away from the table, heart thumping. 'Who is Adonay?' I whispered. 'A demon?'

Thea shook her head. 'Don't worry. It is just another name for the Lord.'

'Really?'

'Yes, of course.'

I stared at her. The house was so quiet. I could hear only the crackle of the fire, my own quickened heartbeat. 'Thea, is your mother a witch?'

Thea looked horrified. 'Look, here is a protection against witches. "*Schutz gegen Hexen*".' She tapped the opposite page to the one I had read, and then pointed to a shadowed corner of the cottage ceiling. A blown eggshell hung from a thread, swaying slightly. I had never noticed it before. 'It's called a "restlessness",' Thea said. 'It drives witches away.'

I nodded, swallowing hard. 'What is in the sixth book?'

Thea bit her lower lip. 'Mama does not let me read that book.'

'Why not?'

'It contains magical seals. Symbols, with words beneath.' She placed her palm over the open text. 'With them one may conjure angels and spirits. Even the dead.'

My skin rose in goosebumps and I felt a sudden, terrible fear that I had stumbled on to something dark and sinful. I lurched towards the door and fumbled with the bar.

'Hanne?'

'I want to get out,' I said. I was vaguely aware of Thea hastily wrapping the book, entreating me to stay, telling me that the book was holy, and then helping me lift the lock so that I was once again in the summer light and its reassurance of birdsong. My chest was so tight I had to kneel in the grass and bring my forehead to the ground. I could feel myself trembling, could hear Thea beside me, feel her hair brushing against my cheek as she pressed her head to mine, telling me again and again that I need not be scared.

'I was afraid too,' she was saying. 'I was afraid, but Mama told me all about it. You know my mother, you know she loves the Almighty, you know she is not a *Hexe*.'

I let Thea lift my head from the ground.

'Really, Hanne. She says she will teach me how to use it one day. For good. Only for good.'

'Why would you show me such a thing?' I asked her.

'Because it is powerful,' Thea said. 'Mama is going to consult it to learn whether we ought to leave, and . . . and I thought . . . I thought maybe we could use it.'

'Use it how?'

Thea opened her mouth, searching for the right words. 'To . . . To ensure that we might remain together.'

I stared at her. 'Is there such a thing in it?'

'I don't know. I thought we could look.' Thea shuffled closer to me on her knees and took my hand. 'I'm sorry if it frightened you.' Her cheeks were high with colour and as she entwined her fingers with mine, I realised she was upset. 'I don't want you to go and leave me here,' she said softly.

We were silent for a long moment. The wind picked up and swept down around us, and I let my hair blow across my face, breathed deeply of the sound that it carried, such a rushing sweetness. The grass around us curved in surrender. *We bend*, it sang. *We bend and bow, breathe upon us.*

'I don't want to use that book,' I said eventually. I stared down at our clasped hands and, for a moment, could not tell my own fingers from hers. 'I don't know it. I don't understand things like that.'

Thea looked up at me. Her eyes were red. 'Maybe we could pray. We could ask God to keep us together.'

'Here?'

'No. In the Lord's house. We could go back to the church.' She took a deep breath. 'Hanne, we need to do something.'

'Not the church,' I said. 'It's dead there.' I remembered the feeling of divinity I had felt under the pines the night my father had preached, when Thea had turned around and looked at me. 'I know where we can go.'

The wind blew us to the forest. Hand in hand, skirts buffeted against our legs, hair stringing out into the air above, we let ourselves be carried to the only cathedral we had known together. As soon as we stepped through the shield of pines, into their soft shadow and quiet green, I felt the holy in the air. The wind could not reach us in there, and the stillness on the forest floor, while the tops of the trees above us rushed, made the space seem protected. Sacred.

We reached the small, circular opening amongst the trees. Sunlight tolled down in its centre, a well of brightness on the thick floor of needles. I led Thea to it and faced her.

'I feel like we ought to have a Bible,' Thea whispered. 'Like in a prayer meeting. Or worship.'

'I know. I feel nervous.'

'You're trembling.'

'I don't know why.'

'Here,' Thea said. She bent and picked up two sticks which she placed on the ground nearby, one across the other. 'This can be the altar.'

'Is this blasphemous?'

'No, we are building a church so that God may come amongst us and hear our prayer.' She hesitated, glancing around us. 'Hanne, what is singing to you?'

'What do you mean?'

'Remember when you said the snow sounded holy? Let's gather all the things here that sound hallowed. We'll build our church from the music you can hear.'

I closed my eyes and listened. The wind was a ribbon of worship around the trees. 'How do we gather the wind?'

'We can raise our palms against it,' Thea suggested.

I nodded. 'The moss,' I added. 'The moss sounds sacred.'

'Really?'

'Yes. And the lichen. It sounds like a note in harmony with everything else.'

I watched as Thea picked up a stone covered with moss and set it next to the crossed sticks. 'What should I do with the lichen?' she asked.

'Maybe we can hold some.'

'What else should we do?' she asked softly.

'I think we should kneel here, with the sun on our heads,' I said.

We knelt, facing one another, the altar next to us. The ground was soft. I could smell resin and conifer. Thea passed me a scratching of lichen and I held it in my left palm and raised my right hand to the air. Bible of breath. Thea did the same.

We closed our eyes.

'Dear God,' said Thea. 'We pray that you hear us.'

The trees creaked above us. A pine cone fell from a height.

'We yearn for our freedom,' I added. 'We pray that we will not be parted from one another.'

'Please, dear Lord, let us stay together. No matter what happens.'

I felt Thea take the lichen from my hand and thread her fingers through my own. Somewhere above the forest canopy came the cry of a goshawk. Pine needles shivered in the shadows. Roots pushed into deeper soils.

'Please, dear God,' I whispered. 'May we be with each other always.'

'Yes,' breathed Thea. 'We pray this in Jesus's name. Amen.'

I opened my eyes and saw that Thea was no longer bending her head in prayer but was looking at me intently.

For one strange moment I felt that I was on the verge of something important and that, if she did not look away, something rare and precious would happen. Branches would suddenly, noiselessly erupt into flame. Birds would fall out of the sky. Milk would run down the trunks of trees.

She closed her eyes. '"And all things, whatsoever ye shall ask in prayer, believing, ye shall receive."'

We walked to the river from the forest in silence, both of us lost in thought. My head ached; I felt as though days had passed since I had pushed past Thea's front gate.

'Do you think it will be enough?' I asked her when we reached the bank.

'Yes,' Thea said.

'When you know, you must come and tell me. I don't know when I can visit again. I cannot bear to wait. I . . . I feel sick at the thought of it.'

'I will leave you a sign . . .' She cast about her, then picked up a smooth stone from the river's edge. 'This stone. On the sty gate, so you can see it from your bedroom window.'

'If you are coming?'

'Yes.'

'And if . . .' I paused. 'If God will not allow us to remain together . . .'

Thea leaned towards me. 'It won't happen.'

'But if it does?'

'I'll leave something else. I'll tie my headscarf at the same place.'

I took the stone from her, felt the comfort of its weight. 'And then I will know.'

We fell back into silence, passing the river stone back and forth between us.

'You will come, won't you? You will leave a sign telling me if we are to remain together? In this new place . . . this new life . . .'

Thea rested against me. I could feel her breath against my neck and felt rather than heard her response. 'Yes.'

I could not fall asleep that night. My body took up my mind's anxiety and I could not keep still, rolling in my blanket until my bedclothes were twisted, fingers worrying at a hole in the mattress until husks spilled out across the sheet. Hermine, perhaps sensing my restlessness, woke often, and when my mother came in to feed her, she placed a hand across my forehead and asked if I was unwell.

'No,' I said.

'You feel warm.'

I leaned into her palm. Part of me wanted to confide in her, but I had the feeling that she already knew of my distress and did not entirely understand it.

'You picked at your dinner.'

'I wasn't hungry.'

Mama sighed in the darkness over the sound of Hermine swallowing. 'It is a great change,' she said. 'It is natural to be nervous about the new life that awaits us.' She paused. 'And the journey, too. So long.'

She pulled her hand away to adjust my sister and I lay down, my legs pressed against her warmth. When Hermine fell asleep and Mama carefully laid her in the crib, her hand sought out my forehead once more. I breathed in the smell of baby, of sleep and the caraway seeds that had studded our evening's bread.

'Come sew with me,' she said. 'We can have some milk.' When I hesitated she bent down and kissed me. 'Have faith,' she whispered. 'For nothing will be impossible with God.'

That night, relieved to have something else to focus on, I finished the last details on a tablecloth. I shook it out across my lap, noting how the beauty of the pattern only revealed itself at an intimate distance. 'There is something secretive about whitework,' I murmured.

Mama shook her head. 'No, not secretive. Modest.'

'Why else embroider white thread upon white cloth?'

Mama scraped the ash back into the fire with her clog. 'It befits the godly woman,' she said.

We were cocooned against the darkness of the house by the orb of our lamp, absorbed in our work and our thoughts.

'Thea is like whitework,' I mused.

'How so?' asked Mama. 'Because of the colour of her hair?'

'Because you have to draw close to notice her beauty,' I said. 'She has little flowers around each pupil, little yellow petals, but the rest of her eye is blue.'

Mama said nothing. When I glanced up, she was giving me a peculiar, searching look.

'Have you noticed?' I asked.

'No,' she said, eyes returning to the work in her lap.

I remember wanting to say more to my mama. I wanted to tell her that there was a small freckle on the side of Thea's index finger, quite hidden from view. That she had a scar under her ear. I knew it was a burn, a splash of hot oil. I remember realising, in that moment, that I wanted to tell Mama all the strange, small things I found pleasing about Thea, and simultaneously understanding in some deep, unexamined way that I must never tell her, that I must hold these tiny things under my tongue and keep them to myself. I did not know what it meant that I had noticed the deep beds of her fingernails, the downy hair that always escaped at her neck. But I knew it meant something. Why else did I stop myself?

I know what it means now.

Thea was as a chink of light in a curtain. When I put my eye to her, the world beyond blazed.

When I finally fell into sleep that night, I dreamed of clothing. Christening gowns and embroidered collars and blouses. Sunday shirts and stockings and aprons, all strewn over our orchard, across the shingles, in the lane. I dreamed I wandered the empty village, wondering at it all. There was no one left, everyone had gone. They had gone to seek new freedoms, and these clothes belonged to them. It was a graveyard of garments. I made my way to the sty across from my bedroom and saw, with a sinking heart, a great pile heaped across its gate. I pulled the clothing off, at first gently, one piece at a time, and then in a great hurry until, finally, under them all, I found Thea's headscarf knotted neatly around the top rail. As I untied it, a lock of pale hair fell into my palm and, just as quickly, was swept away by the wind.

I woke suddenly, my throat tight, chaff and husks from the torn mattress sticking to my hands. My bedsheets were tangled about me. It was morning; the light was grey and thin. I got out of bed and looked out the window.

There, perfectly balanced upon the gate post to the sty, was Thea's river stone.

the kiss

Summer was truly upon us, each day longer than the last. All living things wrung the worth from every hour of daylight: trees twitched with leaf, wildflowers wrestled heads clear of uncut grass. No one bothered to cut down the dandelions and sow thistles that grew tall against fences. There was an understanding amongst the departing families that arrangements must be made as soon as possible so that we could leave before the ground shifted once more. The very real possibility that the passports would be revoked, permission rescinded on a whim, licked the days with urgency. Thea and I saw each other only at worship in the forest. It felt like coming up for breath after a week of drowning in chores.

Papa gave notice and a new family was found to take over our lease. I walked in the orchard and when I saw the growing fruit, I thought to myself, I will not be here when these pears bend the branches. The rye and ripe fruit and oats will all be cut and threshed and plucked by different hands, different families. We will be gone. We will be on the sea when the stalks fatten with grain.

Lists began to circulate amongst our congregation. Market days were flooded with families selling their laying hens and furniture. Mama and I began to make the trip weekly, selling what we could and returning with seeds, leather for boots and other necessities such as needles and sewing cotton. Christian Pasche had received further correspondence from Pastor Flügel, as well as letters from the agent of the Englishman financing the journey, and took it upon himself to remind all families of what must be procured and packed, and the woe awaiting those who did not bring sufficient belladonna, bed linen, adze heads and knife blades. Cloth and dry biscuits, bitters and brandy, scythes and saw teeth. It was not uncommon for us to step out in the morning and find him talking to Papa over the fence, loudly reciting all the items the pastor had recommended. Matthias and I took to imitating him under our breath.

'And gold teeth and thimbles and nail scissors.'

'*Ja*, do not be forgetting the nail scissors.'

'And toothpicks. And match heads.'

'And pickled pork and India ink.'

'Or was that pickled ink and India pork?'

'Bring both, just to be safe either way.'

When Thea's father was tasked with building many of the necessary shipping chests, I volunteered to make the journey back and forth to the forester's cottage with payment and instructions on behalf of our neighbours. Mama rolled her eyes when I told her, but nonetheless allowed me to help Thea deliver the heavy trunks to the homes in the village. We hauled them between us on their rope handles and talked breathlessly of preparations for the journey and the life that awaited us beyond. We were excited and unsettled: it was the first time in our lives that our days were not guided by seasons. Winter occupations, such as the unpicking and mending of clothes, were done in sunny doorways. Pigs that ought, by right, to have lived until autumn were snuffed in the fragrant dusk so that families might add to their ship supplies of cured foodstuffs and soap.

My own father made a summons for a *Schweineschlachten* soon after his announcement that we would leave. I was no stranger to pig slaughter, but I loved sweet-natured Hulda, who had given us several litters of piglets, and I did not want to be a part of her death.

'Say it is your time,' Thea urged me. We were lugging a chest down the slope to the village, the smell of fresh-planed wood lifting between us.

I was still unused to her speaking of such things so openly. I didn't know what to say.

'They won't risk you making the *Wurst* go bad,' she said. 'Truly. It's what I do.'

'Doesn't your mother know you are lying?' I ventured.

'I don't care if she does. I cannot bear it.'

We set the chest down on the grass and sat on its lid to rest. For a while we said nothing, only caught our breath, wiped our sweating palms against our knees. The day was wide-bellied with sky.

'It's the squeal,' Thea said eventually. 'I can't stand to hear them squeal. As much as I know it is inevitable, as much as I know . . .' She shook her head. 'There is something broken-hearted in their cry. I hate it. Oh, even the thought of it! I hate to see them die and know it, and cry for themselves.' She attempted a laugh. 'It's awful.'

'You have a soft heart.'

Her wolfish smile. 'I can wring a chicken's neck. My heart can't be that soft.'

'But chickens don't cry.'

'No.'

'And it happens quick for chickens. Just a snap.'

'A crick of bone and they're gone.'

'Mm. But a pig . . .'

Thea took a deep breath. 'A pig knows you have betrayed it.'

'Not soft-hearted, then,' I murmured. 'Pure-hearted.'

Thea stood and pulled me to my feet. 'Anyway,' she said. 'Leave some cloths swimming in a bucket and your mother will not ask questions.'

I did as she suggested, and although Mama made her frustration known, I heard her explain to Papa that I would not be helping.

When the hour came to stick Hulda, I made my excuses and crawled into bed and covered my ears with my hands. The waiting was unbearable. I closed my eyes and thought of Thea and imagined her hiding in her own bed, eyes scrunched tight, and pictured her eyelashes upon her cheek. I wondered if Anna Maria made her whip the pig's blood as my mama usually did, until it stopped stringing together and was ready for cooking. Then I thought of Thea talking of my 'time', and how relieved I was to be reminded that she, too, had such a thing, and that my bleeding was not unnatural, was not a symptom of some deep error within me as I had first suspected but was, as Mama had told me, common to all women who might bear a child. It was then that, despite the blanket over my head and my hands over my ears, I heard the commotion of the catch in the sty and, a few minutes later, the shrill, shrieking panic.

During the next two weeks I fell asleep upon a pillow that smelled of smoke, to the sounds of my mother damping the fire and adjusting the height of the hanging sausages. My dreams were filled with meat.

Night is unfurling herself now. The wind has picked up and clouds have blown in over the rising moon. It is growing dark. Through the trees I can make out lights winking across the valley floor. I imagine that I alone remain outside at this hour. Everyone must be at their dinner or prayers now. I picture open Bibles, scrubbed hands, steam issuing from plates of cabbage and potato.

It has been a long time since I held a Bible. Scripture I once knew by heart has become adulterated with my own words so that it speaks to a truth I know more keenly. But if I close my eyes, I can still feel the weight of my family's black book in my hands. I can picture my name and birthdate written in the back cover in my father's lopsided handwriting. Proof I entered the world, even if it was to eventually salt the tongues of the apostles with poetry to my own taste.

Our Bible was my father's lodestone. He cherished it like nothing else in our home. Of course, I can remember it, not only in my mind but in my body. The texture of its feather-light pages against my moistened fingertip. The softness of its leather against my palm. A crux, a key, an anchor. Without my father's devotion to that Bible I would not be here. Without that Bible, nothing would have happened. I would not be in the cold wind, knees bent to my chest, sitting on this carpet of gum leaves and possum droppings, if it wasn't for that pumping, papered heart of God.

The final weeks before we departed were an exhausting dance between anticipation and dread, excitement and fear. I remember the constant packing, unpacking and repacking of belongings; the careful placement of axes and irons and drivers, configurations of boots and leather, folding cloth in such a way as to fill all available space, picking over seeds. I remember the whittling down of all we owned to those precious trunks, the home gutted and made strange. Most of all I remember feeling on the cusp of something, as though I were rounding a bend, about to see the horizon before me. As though I was being drawn up and up from a dark bank of sleep, about to wake, about to breathe.

I know what it was, of course, now.

The night before we were to leave, I found Mama sitting on the doorstep of our empty home, her head leaning against the frame and her eyes to the sky. I had waited for her to go to bed with Papa, had listened to the low murmur of their conversation from my room and, when silence fell, had assumed they slept. But when I closed my bedroom door and crept down the corridor in my bare feet, I saw her silhouetted in the open doorway.

With her dark hair loose and the moonlight bright upon her skin, Mama seemed younger than I knew her to be and I was struck with the uneasy thought that she had not always been my mother. She had existed before I was born, had lived years I knew nothing about. Had I been part of her then? Had I somehow lived in her flesh, lived her life? I so rarely had the opportunity to look at her without her noticing. In the day the brown dart of her eyes was constant and aimed forever on me and Matthias and Hermine. It was wearisome. If ever I yearned to look at her deeply – out of love or curiosity – she would frown me away or ask me if she had ash on her face or tell me it was rude to stare.

'Mama?'

She startled. 'Hanne. What are you doing out of bed?'

'You look very beautiful, sitting there.'

Mama raised an eyebrow, but a hand went to the hair lying on her shoulders and something in her eased. She patted the space next to her on the doorstep. I sat.

'Is Hermine awake?'

I shook my head. 'I couldn't sleep.'

Mama gave me an odd look. 'You're dressed.'

'We're leaving so early, I thought I'd sleep in my clothes.' It was a lie, but Mama didn't seem to doubt me. She turned back to the night, which was mild and tranquil. All was suspended in moonlight, and the crops of growing wheat and rye looked altered and strange. I shifted closer to the warmth of her body. The rare stillness of her was irresistible.

'The stars will be different.' Mama gestured out towards the horizon.

'What?'

'In this south of Australia.'

'That is impossible.'

Mama shrugged. 'So says Rosina. Elder Pasche knows these things.'

'Is that why you are out here? Saying goodbye to the stars?'

'Well, yes. I am saying a farewell.' Mama sighed.

I looked up at the clear sky. It seemed impossible that we would not see the stars' familiar pattern again.

'You don't want to go, do you?'

Mama didn't respond. We both watched an owl fly over a neighbouring house. It disappeared into the shadows and we heard a scuffle. A squeak.

'You and Matthias were born on a night like this.'

'Our birthday is in December.'

'Colder, yes. But quiet. Clear.' She took a deep breath. 'Lots of stars.'

'They must have sung us out.'

She sighed. Amusement tinged with annoyance. 'The stars?'

'No? You can't hear them?' I blew gently in her ear. 'What about now?'

Mama pulled away from me, a rare smile on her face, and closed her eyes. She was listening.

I heard them as I always had. A faint and faraway singing that was not so much music as a crying-out. A single note of longing.

'Johanne?'

Mama's eyes opened. The stars were silent.

My father stood behind us in the dark of the bare kitchen, sleepy-eyed, rubbing his beard. 'There you are. I thought I heard little mice in the kitchen.'

'Mama is saying goodbye to the stars,' I ventured.

'Is she?' Papa placed a heavy hand on my head. I imagined the dirt ingrained in the pads of his fingers. 'Then that is Mama's business. Go back to bed, Hanne. We leave at dawn. God bless you.'

Irritated, I got up and made my way down the corridor in half-darkness, reaching out to place a steadying hand on furniture that was no longer there. At the door to my bedroom, I looked back towards the kitchen and saw that my father sat next to Mama on the doorstep, their heads bent together under moonlight. I could not tell if they were praying or talking.

Then I entered the bedroom, placed my pillow under my blanket and climbed out the open window.

It did not take me long to reach the pine forest under such a brilliant sky, although once I had stepped under the canopy it took some moments for my eyes to adjust. Thea was already waiting for me in the clearing. Her white hair was uncovered and it seemed to glow against the shadowed sentry of trees behind her. At the sound of my footfall on the carpet of needles she spun around and ran at me, eyes wide and arms outstretched. I caught her and we both laughed, then shushed each other, then laughed again.

'I thought you weren't coming,' Thea whispered. 'I've been waiting so long I was about to go back home.'

'I'm sorry,' I breathed. 'Mama was awake and caught me leaving.'

'She caught you?'

'I told her I couldn't sleep and pretended to go back to bed. Then I squeezed out the window.' I grasped her shoulder. She looked otherworldly in the moonlight. 'I'm so glad you stayed.'

The tendons in her shoulder slackened under the weight of my hand.

'What if she checks on you, to see if you are asleep?'

'She won't. Hermine is in her bed tonight. They sold her cradle.' I hesitated. 'What if your parents wake?'

Thea shrugged. 'They were both snoring. They're so tired from all the preparations. I fell asleep too. I would have slept through and forgotten to come, but I had a nightmare and woke up.' She shivered. 'It was awful.'

'Tell me about it.' I pointed at the ground. 'Let's sit down, shall we? It seems quite dry.'

We sank to the forest floor. The smell of resin rose over us.

'I was in the ship,' she said, 'and it was on fire. I was burning in my bed. My hair was on fire. My nails were melting over my fingertips.' Thea reached for a pine cone and began prising the seeds out. 'There was screaming all around me, and I was unable to move or cry out. Ash was falling into my eyes.'

I could picture it. The sound of a ship splintering. Flames creeping along the beams. A bonfire upon a howl of water.

She threw the pine cone, watched it scuttle along the forest floor. 'My last thought was, let me die before I drown. Then I woke. My heart was pounding. I had to pat the blankets to make sure they weren't smouldering. Had to make certain I was not in the ship. Not dying.'

'Where was I?' I asked. The moon was so bright I could see the crease from her pillow against the side of her face. A slight pucker on the soft round of her cheek.

Thea gave me a long look. 'I don't want to say.'

'Was I there?'

She nodded.

'What was I doing?'

'You were dead beside me.'

I lowered myself down onto the forest floor and lay on my back, staring up to where the highest branches of the pines tilted at the moon, where the stars cried out in all their pincered light. There was a moment of silence. I heard Thea lie down beside me.

'I was so relieved when I woke,' Thea whispered. 'It felt as though I had been returned to life. It felt like a gift.'

'It is a gift. Look, it's so bright.'

'I remembered then that you'd asked me to meet you here, and I could hardly believe it. One minute I was burning alive and you were lost to me, and the next I was awake and walking to meet you.' Her voice was soft. 'A reprieve.'

The smell of sap thickened. I imagined us caught up in amber.

'I know I should be frightened by the dream, but I was just so happy to wake and know that I was alive. That you were alive.'

I turned my head so that I faced her. I could feel the heat of her arm against my own and it lifted the hairs upon my neck.

Thea laughed. 'It was just a dream.'

We smiled at each other, then turned back to the sky, tattered with light.

'Why did you want to come here?' Thea whispered.

'I wanted to say goodbye.'

'To the forest?'

'Mm.'

Thea sighed. I felt her head rest against my own and the forest seemed to shudder at the sweetness of it. The soil depressed beneath us. I imagined we might fall into a web of outstretched hands, outstretched roots, become part of the forest, sprout mushrooms and home ants. Bones becoming one long exhalation of earth.

'I can't quite believe we are leaving.'

'We will never see this place again.'

Thea smelled of vinegar and smoke and her own skin. I leaned into her side and was surprised to feel my eyes quicken with tears.

Thea propped herself up on one elbow and looked down at me.

Her face was in shadow but her pale hair, wound in a braided crown about her head, was lit with the moon.

'You have a halo,' I whispered.

Her stare was deep.

I felt my breath catch. 'What is it?'

She kissed me, then.

Her mouth was warm and soft and sweet, and in the brief moment when her lips pressed against my own, my heart leaped with perfect understanding, perfect recognition. It melted with the heat of her, was sealed under a new covenant.

The forest was still. The trees guarded us.

Thea pulled away, eyes wide. Said nothing. She was trembling violently. I could hear her teeth chatter. It wasn't cold.

Neither of us said anything.

Eventually I reached up and touched her shoulder and gently pulled her back down to the soil. She lay still beside me, staring into the canopy. If it weren't for the rise and fall of her chest, the tremor of her body, she might have been dead.

We lay there for years. The moon waxed and waned over us, and our hair knitted into the forest floor. Our open palms grew skins of moss.

'Goodbye, trees,' I whispered finally, to say something. To say anything. 'Goodbye, bark and moss and birds. Goodbye, Kay.'

Thea said nothing. She was a fire burning into my side.

'Goodbye, moon. Goodbye, stars. We will remember you.'

'Remember us.' Thea's voice was a rustle of leaves.

'Yes. Remember us.'

I did not sleep that night. As each hour passed, I remembered and felt again the pressure of Thea's mouth on mine, and the immediate answer of my own body. The yes, this, sweeping through me like breath, like water, like the spirit of God. And then, again and again, the remembrance of Thea's expression of disbelief and something else. Hunger. Revelation.

I did not know what it meant and I was afraid to ask.

I thought of Thea's dream. The burning flesh. Beams alight.

Let us burn together, I prayed. If that is what is coming, let us burn together.

song on the river

Blackbirds announced the dawn as fatigue finally pressed upon me. The room was still dark. I heard Papa's heavy tread down the corridor, his knocking on the beams to wake Matthias in the loft, and thought again of Thea, of her mouth on mine.

I was awake. I was older than the sea.

Early morning light crept across the wall as we broke our fast in the bare kitchen, gathered around the table that Papa had built inside the room, too large to be removed. Papa was excited, talking of the journey ahead as a blessed adventure. I said nothing, hoping to sit unnoticed, unspoken to, so that I might let my thoughts wander back to the forest. At one point, Mama narrowed her eyes at me and pulled a pine needle from my hair. She pointed it at my face like a knife, like a question, but said nothing. I crammed bread into my mouth, pressed my hips against the table's edge. I knew she could not guess at what I had done, what I was thinking about, but my cheeks coloured anyway.

Outside the morning was dew-heavy, cold and fresh. The lane through Kay was filled with village families, some with wagons to carry their trunks, others with handcarts. I could not see Thea and her parents, but the road was thick with people, and I guessed that they would join the end of the procession, their being so removed from the centre of the village.

'This is it then,' said Papa. He pulled Matthias and me to his side. 'Today marks a new life. We cast off our chains and are freed from our suffering.' He squeezed our shoulders. "'For so is the will of God, that with well doing ye may put to silence the ignorance of foolish men: as free, and not using your liberty for a cloke of maliciousness, but as the servants of God.'" He breathed deeply. 'We shall live as free men.'

We stood a moment in the bustle, watching as everyone said goodbye to those who had chosen to remain behind, who felt their bodies too frail for the journey or who had embroidered themselves too closely into Kay and could not bear to burst their stitches and leave, frayed and unattached. I watched as Magdalena Radtke threw her arms around her sparrow-boned mother. She cried silently, her whole body shaking. The old woman stood there, patiently bearing the weight of her hefty daughter, the lace fringe of her bonnet trembling under Magdalena's sobs. 'Go in God's grace,' she said. 'I will see you in glory.' The five Radtke children watched on from their wagon, faces twitching, until little Franz suddenly leaped over the side and ran to his grandmother, wrapping his arms around her legs and burying his face in her apron. The other children followed suit, and soon I could not see their grandmother at all, so enveloped was she in the clinging limbs of her family. Only Samuel Radtke watched on, reins in hand, digging at his front teeth with a thumbnail.

'It's time,' he said eventually. No one paid him any attention.

Most of the women had tears in their eyes. Amalie Schultze was crying the hardest, tears dripping down her chin onto the red and bawling face of her baby niece. At the Pasches' wedding I had over-heard Henriette Volkmann tell Christiana in a giddy whisper that the baby was actually Amalie's, born a bastard five villages over. 'And how could her sister have had another baby eight months after her first?' Henriette had muttered, chin cocked in disbelief. The thought had made me feel uncomfortable and hot. I watched as Amalie's father gently prised the infant out of his daughter's arms. Amalie wiped her eyes and stood quite still. She had stopped weeping. She stared at the swaddled baby then, suddenly, slapped herself across the cheek. I jumped. No one did anything. She slapped herself again, and then suddenly Mutter Scheck was there, her arm around Amalie, guiding her into the crowd where the first wagons had started to pull away into the lane.

'Well, Heinrich. It's time. Are you sure you want to take these little urchins with you?' I felt a hand tug at my earlobe and turned to see Uncle Ludwig, my father's younger brother, grinning at me, teeth clamped around his pipe. He had come from Harthe to help us travel. Papa had promised him our wagon for his efforts.

I rubbed my ear and did not return his smile. There was no sign of Thea or her parents, and I could not summon even false good humour.

'Matthias,' I murmured, grabbing my brother's coat sleeve. 'Thea is not here.'

Matthias looked about us. 'Hold on,' he said. Climbing the wooden spokes of the wagon wheel, he stood on the driver's bench and scanned the crowd. He frowned, shaking his head. 'Maybe they have already left?'

'Matthias.' Papa beckoned my brother down. His shirt was damp with sweat from hoisting our trunks into the wagon. 'Let us sing a song of praise,' he said. Taking a deep breath he began to sing '*Nun danket alle Gott*' in a voice so loud I had to draw away. Heads turned. And then I heard Matthias reluctantly join his voice to my father's, and beyond his thin and unsteady harmonies I heard other voices enter the silence. The hymn rose up into the air about us. It had been a long time since anyone had dared to worship so openly.

We walked to Tschicherzig as the morning softened into sun, leaving nothing behind but footprints and the trailing notes of hymn after hymn. Papa sat on the wagon next to Uncle Ludwig, singing in his deep, rich voice, smoke from Uncle's pipe lifting behind. Matthias and I walked side by side, saving our breath for the journey. I couldn't help but look over my shoulder every few minutes. Thea and her parents were nowhere to be seen, even as the crowd thinned out along the road.

Perhaps they overslept, I thought to myself. Or perhaps they made an early start and are ahead of us, as Matthias said. Still, a sickening feeling grew in my stomach. My eyes felt sandy, my limbs cumbersome and ill-jointed.

I thought again of the kiss. Touched my fingertips to my mouth again and again.

Matthias nudged me, nodding towards Mama, who sat amidst the trunks in our wagon, bonneted, dress open. Hermine was snuffling at her breast and batting her in the face. 'She hasn't said a word since we left,' he murmured. 'Hanne, look. She's going to cry.'

I looked. Mama was staring at the village diminishing behind us, eyes wet, gaze fixed on the church steeple winking in the sunlight beyond the bobbing crowd of hats and bonnets and scarves.

'I don't think I've ever seen her cry,' Matthias said quietly.

'She was up in the night. Saying goodbye to the stars.'

'That doesn't sound like her.'

I looked back along the stream of people behind us. Nowhere. I couldn't see her anywhere.

'Hanne? In what direction was she looking?'

'Just out towards the rye fields.'

'The old church?'

'I suppose so.'

Matthias pushed back the brim of his hat and raised his eyebrows. I stared at the hair darkening his top lip. It seemed unfair to me that we were to be cleaved from one another so thoroughly by adulthood, that I would not be able to grow the same beard as him, that I would take up my woman's face and he his man's.

'She was farewelling our brother,' he said, and I knew immediately that he was right. 'We are leaving Gottlob behind.'

I glanced again at Mama. Her eyes pierced the horizon. 'Gottlob is with Christ,' I said.

Matthias nodded. 'But we are leaving his bones in the ground.' He placed his hand in his pocket and took out a small, stoppered bottle.

'What's this, then?'

'Soil,' Matthias replied. 'I took it from his grave.' He put the bottle back in his pocket. 'So that our brother can come with us.'

My heart rushed with love and I suddenly had a yearning to tell him about sneaking out of the window and meeting Thea in the forest. I wondered, briefly, if he had ever been kissed. But I said nothing. Both of us had always known, intuitively, that there were parts of us best left hidden. The moment in the forest was mine alone. I wrapped myself around the kiss, like a shell around a nut, keeping it sweet, keeping it safe.

The road was stirred into dust under the wagons. Some of the poorer men, like Daniel Pfeiffer, had tied a trunk to his back. His hat was dark with sweat. Emile carried their younger daughter on her hip, and their eldest, Elsa, pushed a handcart with a second trunk in it. Little Anna Pfeiffer kept copying her father's grunts as the road keeled uphill, and I could see their shoulders shake in laughter, despite their exhaustion. The families of Elder Pasche and Fröhlich the shoemaker swarmed together behind our wagon, Hans nodding miserably as Rosina chastised him for forgetting something or other. Traugott Geschke, Reinhardt and Elize, now round with child, sat in their own wagon, singing before us.

More families joined as we passed through the busy outskirts of Züllichau, and as the breeze lifted, leaves nodding in hedgerows, I saw that we were attracting the attention of the district. Onlookers gathered by the roadside to stare. An old woman and her daughter, both holding squalling children, shouted out blessings and well wishes to my mother, who nodded, unsmiling. Two men rested against a rail, pointing and laughing to themselves. Girls my age unbended from seedlings in vegetable gardens, eyes squinting.

Papa and Uncle Ludwig stopped to load Mutter Scheck's and Amalie's trunks into our wagon when their handcart broke, and Elizabeth Radtke, whimpering and writhing against Magdalena, was handed up to Mama, whereupon she stopped crying to stare at Hermine, open-mouthed, until Hermine poked her in the ear. Mutter Scheck arranged herself between our luggage and cast an appraising eye over those who had joined us. There was now a thick and steady flow of people headed towards Tschicherzig.

'Brethren from Rentschen and Nickern,' she nodded, fussing at her nostrils with a handkerchief and briefly examining its contents. Matthias and I exchanged appalled looks.

'Krummendorf, too, perhaps,' murmured Amalie. She was walking next to me, puffy-eyed but no longer weeping.

I didn't care. It could have been Schönborn or Rissen or Schwiebus or any other place in Kreis Züllichau; they were all the same in the black of their clothes, in their farmers' shoulders, in the whispered arguments that could be heard in the dying notes of '*Lasset die Kindlein zu mir kommen*' – the child's shoe already lost, the forgotten water bag. They had been fined and harassed and driven from worship just as we had been. Hundreds of people with a growing thirst in their mouths, all destined to be packed into ships for some place we could not even picture in our minds. They were all fellow pilgrims and I did not care for any of them. Nowhere could I see Thea or her parents. I needed to see her. I needed to make certain that our prayer had bound us together. I needed to make sure that our faith had been rewarded.

*

The Oder River was glass, smooth and wide and bright under the unclouded sun, but the air was filled with crying.

Pastor Flügel had told elders from his various congregations to hire barges to take everyone to Hamburg, but there was some confusion as to how the families would be divided up, and it took hours before the names were announced and the trunks and luggage unpacked from the wagons and placed on board. Matthias and I sat against one of the wagon wheels as we waited, pulling splinters of painted wood from the spokes and jabbing each other in the arm.

'Are you all right?' asked Matthias. 'You're quiet.'

'I haven't seen her at all.'

'Do you know if they let go of their lease?'

I stared at him. 'I don't know. Oh, I wish all the women would stop crying. They sound like cats.'

Matthias laughed, then winced as a sliver of wood pierced deep under his nail. '*Verdammt.*'

'You'll get an infection.'

'It's bleeding.'

'Here.' I picked up his thumb and, setting his nail between my teeth, tore it off to the quick.

'What are you doing?'

'I'll suck it out.' I placed the edge of his thumb between my lips. 'Ugh, your hands taste horrible.' I sobered immediately, remembering Christiana's words to me the night of the *Federschleissen*. I could see Christiana sitting with her sister Elizabeth sleeping on her lap. She was undoing the toddler's braids and combing her fingers through the matted hair.

Mama stepped around the side of the wagon, surprising us. She stared at me.

Matthias spoke first. 'I have a splinter.'

'Not anymore.' I picked the tiny piece of wood off my tongue and held it up to Mama.

'Get up. It's time to leave.' She hesitated, as if about to say something more, then turned away.

Matthias helped me to my feet. 'Thank you,' he whispered. 'I would have hated to die of a splinter before we got there.'

I shoved him away from me. The uneasiness that had come upon me at our mother's look and Christiana's remembered words continued as we waited for our turn to board. I was clumsy. I had dirty hands. If Mama did not approve of me biting my brother's nail, I did not dare to think of what she would say if I told her what Thea had done. I suddenly felt hot and unhappy, as though I were a dry leaf waiting to be smoked by the Devil. As the flow of people pushed me down the bank to the gangway, I glanced down to the shallows and the thought that I might never touch soil again passed through me. I thought of Thea's dream and felt as though she might be right, that something bad was coming for us, something we would not be able to escape, and the crying that had resumed all around me solidified my fear into certainty. Everywhere, loved ones riven. I stood there, unable to move, until Mutter Scheck gave me a sharp poke between the shoulder blades with her bony finger and I was forced forwards into my father's waiting hands.

Christian Pasche delivered a farewell address to those who remained on the bank once we had all boarded the barges.

I could not speak. On tiptoes, neck craning, I tried to find Thea in the crowd. I examined the faces lining the boats surrounding our own. She was nowhere to be seen. As Elder Pasche's sermon continued, his voice oddly loud in the still air, I was struck with the awful feeling that Thea remained in Kay. That was why she had kissed me. She had known she was staying but had not been able to tell me; she had known it would break my heart. I remembered her body shaking next to mine.

Thea was not there. I would never see her again.

Everything in my body revolted against the thought. I could not leave her.

Pressed tightly against my parents, I held my hands against my ears to mute the sound of sobbing and began forcing my way forwards to the gangway.

Mama swung Hermine onto her hip and grabbed my wrist. 'What are you doing? Stop that. People are looking.'

'I can't go,' I whispered.

'Stop it.'

'No. Thea isn't here.'

'Hanne!'

She pulled me back and I began to cry. Mama stared at me, despairing. But then I saw tears in her own eyes and, a moment later, felt her fingers release my wrist. Matthias took my other hand, secretly, his shoulder pressed hard against my own so that no one might see.

'I thought the Eichenwalds were coming?' he whispered to Mama, eyes fixed on Elder Pasche.

Mama said nothing.

He squeezed my hand.

We were finally released from prayer with a resounding amen. Clouds came in from the west as the anchors were weighed and the boats began to move away from the bank. Someone screamed – a stifled shriek that pierced the low dissonance of farewell. I could see the diminishing figure of Uncle Ludwig upon our wagon, waving his hat in great arcs, and stole a glance at my father to see if he were upset. His one working eye was closed: he was still praying. The other, ajar, glimmered darkly with God.

A single female voice lifted into the air from a nearby barge, singing a hymn of praise. I could not see who sang, but her voice was frayed and earnest and pained.

'Commit whatever grieves thee, into the gracious hands of Him who never leaves thee . . .'

Other voices joined hers, smoothing the faltering notes.

'Who Heaven and earth commands, who points the clouds their courses, whom winds and waves obey . . .'

Everyone joined in and song soared about me. Tears flowed down my cheeks. I pulled my hand from my brother's and opened my throat and sang as loud as I could, as though I were pouring myself out into the air, as though I were making an offering of myself at an altar of sky.

'He will direct thy footsteps and find for thee a way.'

I felt the purity of my voice before I heard it, was aware of faces turning and looking approvingly at me. I sang as though my voice were a ribbon, as though it were something I might later find my way home by.

The hymn ended. Someone briefly placed a hand on my shoulder as an elderly man led into 'Where'er I Go, Whate'er my Task'. We stared at the crowd on the bank, their voices fading as we sailed downriver.

'Hanne!'

My name, faint and faraway, as though I had imagined it.

Again. A cry under the swelling harmony that surrounded us. A beautiful punctuation.

I could not see her, but she was there, on one of the boats. She had heard me sing.

One more time, as the cloud darkened over us and it looked like it might rain after all.

'Hanne!'

My name in her mouth.

*

ard. 'It is not far. The barges will
hem until the ship –'
s. There, amongst the movement of
. She was walking towards me, lumi-
f waiting barrels and dry goods, the
I did not care about. I forgot myself.
ace torn wide by a smile I could not
out of my body, was beating so hard I
wrapped her arms about me, pulled me
y, before releasing me just as quickly, as
though I was flame.

g. We were breathless from running. We
I remember I raised my hand to my chest
response she placed her palm upon hers.
g oaths. Affirming something we did not

urg, suffering a wearying refrain of abuse from
thers who wished to hear the novelty of our
news came that our ship was almost ready for

d us the final stretch of the Elbe to Altona and
ith our trunks. A sympathetic shipping agent let
y warehouse a few streets back from the harbour,
, after prayer, we were informed that the *Kristi* was
h a half-year's provisions and that we would soon
come on board. It was decided that Elder Pasche

It took us three weeks to reach Hamburg, along canals of water so shallow that all able-bodied men were regularly forced to disembark and pull the barges with ropes from shore, and through mountains where lockmen asked questions of our journey, and those who were sympathetic gave us beer and bread and those who were not jeered and called us fanatics. At Crossen we passed under a bridge filled with so many sightseers, the police arrived to keep the peace.

Each day I searched for Thea's face upon the decks of the other boats, and while I did not see her, I saw Friedrich once, hauling a barge over a sandbank, and it was enough.

Every day on our boat, Papa or Elder Pasche or Elder Radtke led prayers and lay services, and every evening we sang as the sun set and the horizon flushed pink, mirrored upon the river. We sang like birds at daybreak and nightfall in exaltation of ever-changing light, and all about us was river and sky and the sympathetic croaking of frogs, the euphoric diving of ducks. The further we travelled from Kay, the more my ears pricked to unfamiliar sounds. The whine of reeds, the slap of sun on water that cowered from the heat and shrank from banks that smelled of mud and rotting feathers. I sang as loudly as I dared, knowing that Thea might hear me. I sang to the music I heard; God felt close to me. I forgot the trepidation I had felt on boarding the barges.

It was rare for us all to spend so much time in each other's company and I sensed that my parents, always wearied by work, were grateful to sit and watch the changing landscape. Even Mama grew lighter in spirit. She brushed out my hair and sang to Hermine, and once I saw her twitch with suppressed laughter when my brother, boyhood swinging a last blow, squeaked his way through 'Our God is a Mighty Fortress'.

Weeks passed. We entered the Spree and then the Elbe, leaving Prussia. The waters changed. And then one morning we woke and emerged on deck to see masts and rigging rising bare and brutish against the sky like a forest in winter, the bargemen already hauling our trunks onto the docks.

The ships at anchor in Hamburg were enormous. Black and looming against the grey morning, sailors and wharfmen crawling like ants all over them, bale hooks in hand. My stomach lurched at the sight of their bulk, at the smell of the harbour, which was salt and smoke and fish and waste. Not many of us had ever been to a city so large and we huddled together and waited for someone to take us somewhere.

The morning turned warm and hazy. We became thirsty. Every now and then someone would begin singing, and heads would turn to watch as all of us joined in, dry-tongued choir as we were.

By noon, those who still had money left to buy fresh food and drink went in search of it, while others decided to stretch their legs and take in the sights of the great city: the buildings three storeys and higher, the bridges and the swarms of people about their business. But Mama was firm. We were all to stay with our trunks, to wait for direction. And so we sat on the docks and I picked at my sunburn and watched the gulls and the oarsmen in their small boats. The water seemed an ugly, greasy thing.

'Is this salt water? When does it become the sea?' I asked Papa.

He took off his hat and ran a hand through his hair, eye skirting the wharf, flicking to the Kay elders who were in intense discussion together. There was a man approaching them, clasping a sheaf of papers.

'Papa?'

He suddenly marched towards the churchmen. They admitted him into their circle, dark coats and hats clustered together like a thundercloud, nodding at the stranger, fingers pointing.

'Mama,' Matthias said quietly, 'what if they do not have the passports? What if they don't have a ship to take us?'

would meet the captain as spokesperson, to ensure all was ready. We watched a sailor row him out, their small boat soon dwarfed by the ship that would be our home for the next six months.

Mama shivered next to me, bouncing Hermine in her arms. All the women from Kay stood together, arms crossed over their stomachs, eyes wide at the sight.

'It's so black,' Elize muttered.

Magdalena Radtke glanced at her, and then cast her worried gaze at my mother. 'It looks like a coffin, Johanne.'

Mama raised her eyebrows. 'As long as it floats.'

'If God is not merciful to us, we shall be buried in the water.'

Eleonore Volkmann lifted a hand to her forehead and squinted against the light. 'Look, they're bringing more supplies out to it now. I wonder what's in those barrels?'

Elize shrugged. 'Pork. Flour. Water. Herrings, someone said.'

'Herrings? I've never eaten a herring in my life,' said Magdalena.

'Ah well. We may eat stranger things yet.' Eleonore sighed. 'Best start with herrings.'

It seemed impossible that we might need so many hundreds of barrels, that such a great hulking ship would not sink under their weight.

'What if we run out of things to eat before we get there?' Rosina asked.

A familiar voice murmured into my ear, 'We can cook the children.'

I turned and saw Hans standing next to me, brown eyes smiling.

'Stop it, Hans,' muttered Rosina.

'Good,' I whispered, turning back to the ship. 'They can start with Hermine.'

'I heard that,' my mother said.

*

We were rowed out to the ship in handfuls, assisted onto the top deck by courteous sailors who shouldered our belongings with ease. A tall, clean-shaven man stood watching us as we boarded, hands folded behind his back.

'That is the captain,' whispered Matthias.

We stared at him, a little awed. This was the man who would take us over the great seas in nothing but a pile of timber. I wondered at how he knew to do such a thing. 'He looks clever,' I said. Matthias nodded. We bowed our heads as we passed him.

When all of us stood upon the deck, hushed and nervous at the height of the masts, the great symphony of ropes and rolled sail above us, the captain cleared his throat and opened his arms wide in greeting.

'Welcome.' His voice was a foghorn against the resonance of water and wood, the shouts of the sailors bringing further provisions on board. 'I am Captain Olsen and it will be my pleasure to bring you to your new home in Adelaide.'

There was a sudden burst of clapping. The captain smiled, bowing his head. He told us a little of what we might expect from the crew, who numbered less than twenty, and then gestured to a man who stood behind him, deep-set eyes shadowed by thick eyebrows. He did not smile, but stepped forwards and looked down over us, Adam's apple bobbing over his neckcloth.

'This is Dr Meissner,' the captain continued. 'He has been appointed your medical officer and will accompany you on this voyage. As the doctor has been charged with your welfare, he will assign you into messes for meals and cleaning. Dr Meissner is also to be regarded as the authority in all things immediately relevant to your personal conduct, health and wellbeing, and will advise you on what you have been rationed, where you may sleep and all other daily administrations that will ensure an orderly and peaceable voyage.

Unless anyone has any immediate concerns they wish to bring to my attention on behalf of the passengers, Dr Meissner will show you to your quarters below deck.'

At this, Christian Pasche raised his hand. 'We thank you, Captain Olsen. This is a momentous day for us. We leave a place of oppression and tyranny for a land where we might freely worship and pay our debt of love to God by glorifying His name. Captain, would you do us the honour of leading us in the Lord's Prayer?'

Captain Olsen bent his head and obliged. His voice was deep and pleasant, but it quickly grew faint as a brisk wind sprang up, sweeping his words from the deck and pulling them out along the river. The ropes creaked above us. I opened one eye and saw the sailors with heads bowed, lips murmuring. Ruffled skirts. Hair blown across foreheads.

The prayer blew out to the ocean ahead of us, blessing the air and waters we would travel through, light and tumbling. A bird to make sure of land.

a bolt of black cloth

Sometimes I wonder if I will hear it again, my voice as it was on that day we boarded the *Kristi*. Surely somewhere that prayer taken up by the wind is still blowing. Somewhere I am still praying. Maybe that is what I am listening for up here in the darkness of the bush: my own sweet voice rushing back at me, offering consolation. Conviction.

Amen. Amen. Amen.

Below, in the valley, the lights are slowly pinching out. I imagine the women in the cottages laying down the clothes they are mending and finally going to bed, letting their fires go out in a way they never did back in the villages where they were born. The night is cool, but not cold. The wind is a bow scraping on the stars.

I will not sleep tonight. I was never someone who fell asleep easily, and now sleep seems gone from me in the same way as so much else. There was a time when wakefulness wound my thoughts into wire. But there is much to love about the night, if you know how to surrender to it.

It took some time for my eyes to become accustomed to the gloom once I had stepped down the hatch to the tween deck. I was bumped by Amalie Schultze coming down behind me on the stair and so groped my way forwards, a hand on Matthias's shoulder, until my eyes adapted to the low light and I saw the place we were to eat and sleep for the long months of our journey.

It was a long, narrow confinement, the upper beams only a short distance above the tallest of the company. A wooden trestle table extended throughout, benches nailed firmly to the boards beneath it, and on either side of the table, beyond walkways, were wooden berths, one row above another, abutting both sides of the ship. Small lights glowered in heavy, black lanterns.

It was close. The air was already warm and stale with bodies and breathing.

'Goodness,' Amalie murmured. 'How will we all fit?'

I heard Hermine's familiar wail rise up to my left, where Mama stood peering into a berth, prodding the bare mattress. People kept coming down the stairs and there was soon too little space to move freely. I felt a jab in my side as Hans tried to manoeuvre three large bags through the crowd. He shot me a look of apology as Rosina shouted instructions at him from behind.

'Silence, please!' Dr Meissner had his arms extended above his head.

There was a scuffle as Traugott Geschke slipped and fell down the hatch, knocking a young girl to the floor. She started crying, rubbing her head where she had hit it upon the corner of a berth, and several babies started up in sympathy. My heart was racing. There were too many of us, it was too crowded, and still people continued climbing down the hatchway, stumbling over one another, over luggage. There were exclamations of indignation, of disappointment. Arguments broke out.

'Silence!'

I looked up. Samuel Radtke had climbed on top of the trestle table, head stooped under the low beam. An unlit lantern smacked him in the ear.

'Brothers! Please, stop. Pay attention to the good doctor.' He extended a hand to Meissner, offering to haul him onto the table. The doctor accepted reluctantly.

'Listen!' His voice was stern. 'You heard the captain! As your doctor I have command over you for the duration of this journey. You are to conduct yourselves with propriety at all times. All of you are to keep your living quarters in good order, and if I ask you to complete additional cleaning or to stow your belongings in a particular way, you shall do so. You shall do so without question! You must obey my directions in all things, but particularly' – a low murmuring had broken out and the doctor raised his voice in annoyance – 'particularly in regards to rations, of which there are a finite supply!' He waited for silence before continuing. 'There are twenty-seven barrels apiece of pork and beef, and sixteen of herrings. Cooks shall be designated from amongst your messes, but no barrel nor hogshead shall be opened without my prior consent, and I shall issue instructions as to when these foodstuffs may be eaten with rice, peas or beans.'

The doctor went on, explaining the consequences for drunkenness, for unruliness, for untidiness, until I began to wonder if he did not hold some prejudice against us, or whether he had suffered through previous journeys with the worst of humankind. I could see the elders bristle as the list of offences continued.

When Meissner had finally run out of possible misdemeanours and their consequences, he pointed out the small kitchens, the barrels of drinking water, the water closet for the use of women and children in the main company and one for the single women in their own roped-off quarter. The small lamps, he instructed, were to be extinguished with utmost strictness at ten o'clock every night and during every instance of severe weather. Finally, sensing the growing irritation swelling from the crowd of passengers, he raised a rolled slip of paper and pointed it to the waiting bunks. 'Berths have been assigned to each family.'

'Finally,' Matthias whispered. 'I thought we'd reach the colony before he stopped.'

'There shall be two persons to each bunk,' continued the doctor. 'If you have an infant –'

There was an outcry of disbelief. Surely it was a mistake. The bunks were narrow even for a single man.

'Quiet!' He stomped his foot upon the table. Everyone hushed, taken aback by the sudden display of temper. Meissner cleared his throat. 'If you have an infant, a box will be provided for the end of the bunk. The carpenter will fix it in place.

'All unaccompanied single men will be confined to the stern and single young women will be placed together in the bow with a chaperone.' He pointed to the foremost area. 'Families will be summoned by name and directed to their berths. Under no circumstances may you change berth without my prior permission. Once assigned, you may store belongings under the lower bunks. Hooks have been provided for those passengers with an upper berth.'

'How will we fit all our things in that small space?' shouted Gottfried Volkmann. He pointed to one of the berths. 'How will I fit in such a small bed?' He slapped his round stomach. 'One big wave and my little wife will be squished. Yes, she will be a pancake.' There was a burble of tense laughter. Eleonore Volkmann, taller than her husband, rolled her eyes.

'You'd think they'd arrange the bunks fore to aft,' whispered Matthias. 'We shall all be rocked like babies in a cradle.'

'I am not an unreasonable man,' answered the doctor. 'Some alterations may be required, as I have already stated. But let us stick to what has been arranged before we discern who is discontented.'

One by one he began to announce the names of all the families on board, allowing Samuel Radtke to direct them to the bunks. The bare sleeping quarters soon looked even more cramped and chaotic as women unpacked bedding, flapping sheets and hanging them between the berths in anxious attempts at privacy.

'Eichenwald! Friedrich!'

My heart leaped at the name. I watched as Thea's father raised his hand. The doctor didn't look up from his documents but waved a hand in the air. 'Friedrich and Anna Maria Eichenwald, lower berth fourteen. Your daughter...' He glanced up, eyes catching sight of Thea. 'Your daughter in the bow.'

I watched as Anna Maria frowned. The white of her headdress glowed in the gloom. 'But she has her parents here,' she said.

'Excuse me, Herr –'

'Dr Meissner.'

Friedrich cleared his throat. 'Dr Meissner, we are here to accompany our daughter.'

The doctor shook his head. 'You are an odd number. Husband and wife to berth fourteen. Dorothea Eichenwald to the bow.' He glanced up at Thea then nodded towards the berths at the front of the ship, separated from the rest of the bunks by a curtain already half ripped off its cord.

Thea glanced at me before kissing her mother and picking her way through the crowd. I watched as she lifted the rope and moved along the empty berths, before sinking onto a lower bunk in the farthest corner. She shrugged at me. I returned her smile, but my heart was a fist.

The names were ceaseless. The air grew warmer. Word spread that there were nearly two hundred souls on board, but only eighty berths. We watched as they filled.

'Nussbaum! Heinrich!'

My father stepped forwards, raising his hand.

The doctor gestured to his left. 'Heinrich and Matthias Nussbaum, upper berth here. Wife, daughter and infant, lower berth. Pfeiffer, Daniel!'

Samuel Radtke indicated the two bunks allocated to my family. 'Ask the carpenter to fit a box for Hermine,' he said. He glanced at me and smiled apologetically. 'Shame you are so tall, Hanne.'

'Where is the carpenter?' asked Mama.

'On deck. Don't worry, there are days yet before we set sail into rougher seas. There will be time.'

I waited until he had returned to the doctor's side before turning to Mama. 'How am I going to fit if Hermine's cot will be fixed to our bunk? My ankles will be dangling over her head!'

'You'll have to put up with it, Hanne.'

'Can't she just sleep with us? Between us? Then I will have room to –'

'No, Hanne. Hermine will need some protection. The boat will rock on the open sea.'

'Perhaps I could join Thea. In the bow, I mean.'

My mother said nothing.

I sat down on the berth. The mattress was thin and I tried to imagine sleeping there for six months, legs tucked up around me. I heard the creaking of wood above my head as my father climbed onto the upper berth.

'Johanne?' he called out.

'How is it?' asked my mother.

'They haven't given us a lot of room.'

Matthias stepped up onto our bunk, gripping the struts like a ladder, to peer overhead. 'You look like you're in a coffin, Papa.'

Mama slapped at his shins. 'Don't talk like that. Here, come help. You can hang your father's things on his hook.' She placed Hermine on the mattress and began to pull out clothes.

I noticed that Reinhardt and Elize Geschke had been assigned the lower bunk next to me and my mother. Elize, breathing hard, gave me an apologetic look as she pinned a sheet into the wood to serve as a partition between us. 'It's the baby,' she said. 'She keeps me awake. You'll be glad for this!' The light from the open hatch cast her into silhouette against the cloth. I watched her shadow fuss at its corners.

'How do you know it's a girl?' I asked.

'Anna Maria,' her voice whispered from behind the partition. There was a pause, and then the sheet was pulled to the side and Elize's face appeared in the gap. 'Don't tell anyone I said so,' she said.

'Why not?' I whispered. But Elize had disappeared, the sheet dropped between us.

With the cloth hoisted, I could no longer see Thea in the bow, although I heard the doctor assign Amalie and then Henriette to its quarters after Mutter Scheck was named as chaperone and agreed to serve as the girls' guardian throughout the journey. Others, too, were sent to the bow – names I didn't recognise. Women from Tschicherzig, I assumed.

The eight members of the Radtke family were assigned to four bunks on the other side of ours: Samuel and Magdalena on a lower berth immediately to my right, Samuel's elderly parents on the lower berth next to theirs, with four children in the bunks above. I crawled out of the berth I was to share with Mama at the sound of Christiana quietly exclaiming.

She glanced down at me from her bed.

'Who are you sharing with?' I asked.

The round face of tiny Luise Radtke appeared over the edge, smiling. 'Me.'

I smiled at Luise but felt a little spark of anger at the injustice of my having to share with Mama and Hermine, when Christiana only had the small body of her sister to put up with. Magdalena was making room for Elizabeth in the berth she would share with Samuel. Elizabeth was crying, skin pink and damp.

'Don't fall out and hurt yourself,' I said to Christiana, my voice as flat as I dared.

She frowned.

'Do you think we'll be forced to stay here in our bunks most of the time?' I glanced across to where Mutter Scheck was drawing the curtain across the bow.

Christiana sniffed. 'Papa says that we will be permitted on deck when the weather is fine. But where else is there to go?' She looked around the crowded quarters. 'It's not so bad,' she added.

'The air is very close down here,' I said.

Christiana smoothed her hair back into her bonnet. 'God only asks of us what we may bear.'

No sooner had each family been assigned a place to sleep and store belongings than the freighter came into the hatch and whistled loudly to attract everyone's attention. In the brief halting of conversation, he explained that twenty-five chests of clothing would need to be returned and left behind.

There was an immediate clamour of protestation.

'They will be sent after you!' he cried. When no one paused to listen to him, he slammed his fist against the nearest bunk. 'Stop! Listen! No one is stealing your things. There is simply not enough room and Captain Olsen has ordered that twenty-five chests be removed and sent after you in the next ship going to your destination.'

'And how long will that be?' cried Elder Radtke.

'Captain's orders!' said the freighter. 'Take it up with him.'

He started to climb back out on deck, then hesitated, wiping his brow with his sleeve. He gestured to the crowds of us standing in the thoroughfares between berths and table, shoulder to shoulder, belongings still piled upon the long trestle meant for meals. 'It is a long journey,' he said kindly. 'Do not make your passage more uncomfortable than it needs to be.'

Mama was rigid, her face pale. 'But we have so little as it is.'

Papa bent low and whispered to her, 'Johanne, we are not leaving the trunk here. Only delaying its passage.' He looked up as Christian Pasche clasped him on the shoulder, face red.

'Come with me to speak to the captain,' he said. 'We've a right to our belongings on arrival.'

Papa nodded. We watched them push through to the hatchway.

Mama closed her eyes for a long time. 'They would make us leave even that.' She pointed to the floor, to the trunks stowed in the hold under our feet.

Papa and Elder Pasche were not long. They returned, followed by several sailors who set to work opening the hold.

'The twenty-five chests must be sent back,' Papa said. 'There is simply not enough room. We wanted to ask him if we could store some belongings on deck, but it is full too. There are sixty-five barrels for water alone. Hogsheads of vinegar, beer. It all must be stored in the open as the hold is already full.'

I thought of ropes breaking, barrels rolling in a storm, wood splintering.

'But there is good news,' Papa added. 'Captain Olsen is not an unreasonable man. He has given his permission for us to store things in whatever sensible place we might find as well as on the hooks and under the berths.' He rose from his seat. 'Christian and I will spread the word. The twenty-five families with the greatest number of trunks below will have to send one back, but we may go through them first and remove things that we cannot do without. You may have your earthly belongings, Johanne.'

Silence fell below as many of the adults, anxious to part with as little as possible, sorted through the chests once more. As Papa would not be parted from his tools – 'Or what will I build our house with?' he asked as I pulled out his adze heads, already divorced from their handles to save room – it fell to Mama to decide what must be left behind. I took out items and presented them to her as she fed Hermine, waiting for her to nod or shake her head. Clothes. Pins. Some silverware.

'This could be sent later,' I said, taking out a bolt of black cloth. 'What is it for, anyway?'

Mama passed Hermine to her other breast. 'I bought it for you,' she said, and gave me a sudden, warm smile.

'For me?'

'It is for your wedding dress.'

I snorted. 'What?'

Mama said nothing. Her smile faded a little.

'I'm only sixteen, Mama. It can be sent on later. If at all,' I added under my breath.

'You'll be seventeen this year.'

'Well, I won't be getting married this year.'

'I was sixteen when I married your father.' She gave me a look with such an edge to it I felt like I'd been cut. 'Put it under the mattress.'

I did as she said reluctantly, thinking that, if Mama was called away by Papa or one of the other women, I might have an opportunity to quickly pull the cloth back out and shove it into the chest that would be returning to the docks. The idea of sleeping on the material that would clothe me on my wedding day filled me with uneasiness.

But Mama did not shift from her seat, and the chest was nailed down by Papa before my eyes.

At dusk the captain sent word that we might be permitted to return to the upper deck. The hustle of the harbour had quieted, and stillness had fallen over the ships at dock and the buildings beyond the wharf. The sky in the west was the colour of a peach, and as I stood on the boards, breathing deeply, I thought I could hear the river beneath the ship pushing to the horizon, eager current running hopeful to the light.

The anxiety of unpacking and hastily fashioning living spaces in the ill-lit confines of steerage dissipated like vapour in the open air. A peace settled as we stood on the deck, so crowded with barrels that many of the men and boys had to clamber over them to find a place to stand for evening services. My eyes sought out Thea and, like a needle drawn ever north, I found her. As though my glance held the weight of touch, her eyes met mine. She smiled and I felt it pull through my spine like a thread.

The sky glowed as we prayed together on the deck. My father had asked to perform the service, and his voice was like a net cast out over us. It held us in the quiet.

'We have not been led to this action by a desire to see a foreign part of the world, nor by the vain desire for riches, but it is belief in You alone, O God, and Your holy word that has made it necessary for us to take this step. And so lead us to a place in Your creation, where we can live and preach Your holy word in its truth and purity.'

I felt pure in that moment. I felt possibility crest beneath me, pushing me forwards into the world, and I thrilled at the uncertainty that awaited. Anything might happen.

*

That night we slept on the ship. The carpenter had not yet fashioned a crib for Hermine so she lay between Mama and me, little arms jerking into my chest. I remained awake, my head on my arm, listening to the murmurs of families behind their partitions. The boards of the upper berths complained as people turned in them. There was coughing. Rapid footsteps of women directing children to the water closet or scraping buckets out from underneath berths, and then the drumming sound of piss. Elizabeth Radtke was still crying. I heard Magdalena sit up, ask her mother-in-law for a wet cloth.

Later, when most seemed asleep, my face grew warm when I heard Elize Geschke sigh behind her curtain and quietly ask Reinhardt to stretch her cramping feet. It seemed impossible that I would hear such a thing, and yet I had. I was suddenly as privy to their intimacy as a spider on the wall. A ghost in the doorway.

The ship seemed a living thing to me. It was unlike sleeping on the barges, where everything felt temporary and open and free. The *Kristi* carried not only the weight of our bodies, our belongings, but the weight of something heavier, something living and soulful. Timelessness and temporality together, somehow, knotted in the cord of the wood. It feels like a forest, I thought. And I wondered at the boards above me and the trees that had been felled and skinned and offered up to the saw. I wondered what would happen to the trees I had loved.

The safety lamp in the main hatchway was extinguished and the darkness seemed absolute. I raised my hand to my face and, unable to see my fingers, placed them on my cheek. I touched my nose, my lips, and as I did so, my body again remembered Thea's mouth upon my own and I realised that it had not been a kiss of farewell.

I wondered what Thea was thinking in her berth. Was she forced to share with Amalie, who might be still crying over the child who was not her child, or was Henriette Volkmann lying there instead?

I thought of Henriette, her narrow face sleeping peacefully next to Thea's in the bunk. The image of the two of them lying so closely together woke something in me, brought upon me a kind of longing belied with dread.

I thought then, for some reason, of the bolt of cloth I lay upon: the wedding dress yet uncut, but nonetheless waiting for me. Crouching under the mattress like a dark flag of a country not yet known. It dawned on me that my future husband was likely resting in a berth in this same close space I lay in. And if not on this boat, then on one of the others filled with Old Lutherans, also sailing for the colony. I imagined myself dressed in black, hair bound with myrtle, head bent under the weight of vows and my hands taken up by a man's hands. I imagined myself lying not next to my mother, as I was then, but beside the unfamiliar terrain of a stranger's body, and in my imagining I saw skin and sinew thread from his body to mine, so that we were as one flesh. That would be it, then, I thought. I would be tied to him by tissue and cuticle and hair. Forever buried in the bodily tapestry of marriage. The thought filled me with panic.

broken beds

Deep night now. The witching hours. The lonely hours.

There is an art to wakefulness at this time, when those around you sleep. All that is diminished with daylight – regret, sorrow and fear – can press on your chest until it is impossible to breathe. Uneasy thoughts can pin you to your bed if you are not careful. The weight of them can sink you into the soil until you feel that you are being buried alive.

When I feel the earth give way around my body under the weight of a troubled mind, I let go. I surrender. I think of all the bones charged to the earth's tender care, and I imagine my own held in her gentle hands. I imagine the peace of that, of being claimed by such beauty and benevolence, and I let the wind take all my sorrow. I give my fear to the ground, I give my regret to the water.

Disintegration as reunion. Ashes to ashes.

The moon rose before I was there to see it. The moon will rise when I am gone again. I yield to that.

A few days later a steamer towed the *Kristi* from the city, and the ship made quick work of the Elbe, hampered only by the ill health of Elizabeth Radtke. All of us soon learned that the little girl was suffering from fever – I was woken by her cries at night, as well as

Magdalena's brittle requests for drinking water from the barrel by the long table. One night I woke to a flurry of raised voices and, listening, recognised Anna Maria's. There was a brief silence and then I heard the Wend exhale sharply out of her nose. 'You know where I am if you change your mind,' she whispered.

Magdalena Radtke's voice was a lash in the dark. 'I will do no such thing.'

I waited, ears pricked for more, but heard only the sound of footsteps walking away and, in the quiet that followed, a sudden, stifled sob.

A few hours later I woke again and heard Christiana, Franz and Luise praying in whispers, then the swift, booted steps of Samuel Radtke coming down from the cabin with Dr Meissner. There was a soft conference of voices and I heard the sound of a spoon scraping against glass. The doctor left shortly afterwards.

'Mama,' I whispered.

'Mmm?'

'Mama, what is wrong with Elizabeth?'

My mother did not open her eyes but reached out a hand and touched my shoulder. 'She has a temperature. The journey here has tried her. Go to sleep. She will be better now that the doctor has been.'

But the following morning I woke to the sound of Christiana crying and the captain below decks, speaking with Samuel and Magdalena. They told us the news, ashen-faced. Later that day Elizabeth's body was rowed out and buried on the shore of a place called Juelssand.

The next day another two-year-old died, and as the family waited for the captain to negotiate a place of burial at a town along the river, the mother took a knife and cut off the child's curls. Many of us had just sat down to eat at the long table, and beyond the muted prayers of thanks, we could hear the husband admonish her. The mother seemed indifferent to his hissed reprimands. I looked up over my plate to see her climbing out of a berth, hiding her face in hands filled with the hair of her child.

The deaths of the two children had a sobering effect on the passengers. Captain Olsen, while sympathetic to the grief of the families, did not seem surprised at the early tragedies.

'In the confines of a ship, illness and disease can spread quickly,' he said to us after our usual morning prayers upon the deck. 'I expect us to reach open sea today and it is my fervent wish that no more of you succumb to ill health. We are just over two hundred souls on board and I will do everything within my power to ensure that we remain so for the duration of our passage. But please, you must listen to Dr Meissner and do as he instructs. He will advise you on the best ways to keep your quarters clean and sickness at bay.'

The doctor himself had little to say. When Mama, anxious at our berth's proximity to the Radtkes, asked him what she might do to inure Hermine against the sickness that had taken Elizabeth, she received a brusque response.

'A doctor may not be able to prevent illness, although he may treat it,' Meissner replied, glancing at the Radtkes' bunks. 'If you are anxious, pray. I am afraid that I cannot heal those who are not yet sick.'

Mama said nothing, but after the doctor had left, and when she thought no one was looking, I saw her press her nose to the soft tenderness behind my sister's earlobe and, eyes shut, fiercely breathe her in.

A few hours after the captain's warning, the *Kristi* sailed out of the Elbe and into open waters. We felt the shift in the tween decks. A steady tugging rose to lift and fall, and those who had not secured their belongings saw them roll under berths. There were uncertain smiles as neighbours returned a runaway cup, a wooden clog, a shaving bowl.

Weeks had passed since we had left Kay, and it seemed impossible that, after so many rivers, after such waiting, we were away. The freedom that had been spoken of for so many years seemed, finally, to be within reach. It had shape. People crowded the hatchway, eager to be on deck to witness the shoreline slip away. Matthias and I joined the throng, laughing as the ship moved beneath us.

'The ocean,' Matthias said. His eyes were sparkling.

'The ocean,' I replied. We gripped the steps and clambered out into the wind-slap and exclamations of our fellow passengers.

The deck was crowded; I saw the sea in the air first. The sky was hazy with ocean-breath that kissed my lips, and when I licked them I tasted salt. I squeezed past the people gathered, forcing my way to port side, where my view was clear.

There. The North Sea was before us, churning blue and green, capped with white, and something in me lifted. I was soul-struck by the immensity of ocean. My spirit rose in recognition of its divinity.

'Praise God,' I gasped. 'Praise God.'

In the press of people, someone took my hand. Squeezed it.

Thea.

I looked at her bright face and I knew she was feeling as I felt. To think, if we had remained, we might never have been in such a presence. To see something so ancient. Awed, we looked back at the sea in eye-wide inhalation. We breathed it in together, and with the firm grip of her fingers between my own, I felt time dissolve in the arms of the ocean's brilliant, salted constancy.

In between the ordinariness of my days there have been moments when life offered itself to me as a blade, and if I didn't hold back, if I leaned into it, I felt everything.

The good Lord knows, if I could live any moment of my life over again, it would be that one. Ribs divided, heart devouring the knife-edge of beauty. To see the ocean for the first time, every time. Her hand in mine.

Holy blade that guts us with awe.

We stood on the open deck for an hour. Many prayed – the ocean's magnitude was a sure manifestation of God's sublimity – but it did not take long for euphoria to descend into misery. Not long after the *Kristi* broached open water, seasickness came upon us.

At first the rolling of the deck in harmony with the sea seemed a joy. It was impossible not to laugh at the sight of Elder Pasche listing from side to side like a drunk, and the novel feeling of movement delighted Thea, Matthias and me. But the novelty passed quickly, and it was not long before we noticed several men and women staggering to the gunwales and emptying their stomachs over the side.

The sight of others so violently ill did little to reassure the rest of us who had also started to feel queasy. Matthias left, and a little while later Thea and I agreed to return to our berths to lie down and wait for the feeling to pass. By the time we began our descent down the hatchway, the deck, once so crowded, was deserted, save for sailors glancing at one another with knowing smiles.

I found Mama lying in our bed, her eyes closed, her lips pressed tightly together.

'Where is Hermine?' I asked.

'Matthias has her. I sent him for water.'

The ship suddenly dipped down, and there came a collective groaning from those who had already cloistered themselves in their bunks. I watched as Reinhardt scrambled from his bed, hand over his mouth, and ran barefoot to the water closet, which was occupied. My stomach lurched as he grabbed a bucket from the floor and was sick into it.

With one hand on the table for balance, I staggered along the tipping decks to the water barrels, where several people had lined up for their turn with the dippers. Matthias was hunched in a corner, Hermine in his lap, crying.

'Matthias? Are you unwell?'

He looked up at me, pale and sweating. 'Can you take her?' he asked.

I picked my sister up and sat her on my hip as he hauled himself up the hatchway, then I staggered back to our berth. Mama was miserably blotting at the mattress: she had been sick.

'Look at us,' she said. 'How will we survive six months of this?'

As night descended the seasickness grew worse. No one was spared. It was a nightmare, everyone in steerage lurching to the water closet, to any spare slop bucket. And the smell. I kept thinking I had recovered only to hear another retch and splatter, and my gut heaved again. We were all wretched, and only a few of us managed to make it occasionally to the open deck, in the hope that fresh air would work equilibrium into our legs and stomachs. Again and again, I lurched to the side of the ship to empty my stomach, only to have the sailors shout at me.

'Leeward! Leeward!' they cried, and then, perhaps in pity at my lack of understanding, they explained that all waste must be hurled downwind to avoid soiling the deck and those about me.

Once my stomach had been emptied, leaving me exhausted and shaking, I rested my head on the gunwale and tried to surrender to the heave of the waves. I knew I ought to go back below deck and relieve Mama of Hermine, so that she might be unwell without the added difficulty of a sick and crying baby, but it was cooler on deck, and the idea of stepping down into the dark, smelling as it did, the hot fug of misery, made my throat close upon itself and my stomach roll again. And so I remained on deck, buffeted by sickness and wind and the remonstrations of sailors, until my father called my name and I turned to see his head bobbing up from the hatchway, finger beckoning, holy eye firmly closed.

By ten o'clock that night, all lamps being assiduously extinguished, most of the passengers had fallen into uneasy sleep, weakened by the day's sickness. I lay in my berth next to Mama and Hermine, too feeble to brace myself against the dip and roll of the ship, my body listing back and forth against the hard plank separating my bunk from the Geschkes' and my mother's shoulder. Every now and then an overwhelming desire to vomit overcame me, and I placed my arm over my eyes and concentrated instead on breathing; I did not have the energy to rise.

I must have drifted off, for the next thing I knew, I woke to the crack of wood and a great pain in my foot. Terrified, I sat up in the darkness, knocking my head against something hard. It took me several moments to remember that I was not in my bed at home, but on board the *Kristi*, and yet I could not understand what had happened. It was pitch-black, and although I felt the mattress beneath me, something vast and wooden was pressing upon me, not an inch from my forehead. The ship is sinking, I thought. It is breaking apart. It is as Thea dreamed it would be.

There came the dull glow of a lamp lit somewhere in the steerage, and enough light seeped through for me to see that I was surrounded by beams. The top bunk occupied by my father and brother, as well as the berths on either side of theirs, had partially collapsed onto the lower bunks, pinning my foot as it hung out into the walkway. The planks had stopped only a few inches from my face, caught by the barrier dividing my berth from the Geschkes'.

'Hanne? Are you hurt?'

There was a shuffle and confusion of voices as the plank was lifted off my foot. More lamps were being lit amidst a rising chorus of exclamation, and shadows were thrown as people rose from their sleep. I saw my father's face peer into the bunk.

'Where's Mama?' I could not feel her next to me.

'She is here with me and Matthias. Hermine also. We are all safe. Can you move your foot?'

'I think so.'

'We have sent someone for an iron to pull apart the rest of the planks. The bunk collapsed. It is too heavy for us to lift as a whole. It shouldn't be long now.'

I attempted a smile, although alarm rose in me.

'Good girl. It won't be long.'

I felt Papa's hand reach in and squeeze my undamaged foot.

It took some time for the right tools to be found, not least because many of those searching had to stop to retch and vomit. By the time the nails had been pulled from the broken bunk and the whole mess of wood lifted away, it seemed that every passenger had woken, crowding the walkway as the men examined the construction of their own families' berths. After the final plank was lifted from my face and I was freed, Mama helped me out, limping, and I was finally able to see the extent of the damage. By lamplight I saw that an entire row of upper berths had buckled, swooping down like a wave and finally breaking over the place I had lain.

'Why were you not trapped?' I asked Mama.

'I was unwell. I had stepped out to empty the bucket.'

The tween deck looked chaotic. Splintered wood and bent nails lay heaped upon the central table, and while most of the bunks remained aloft, it was clear that they, too, risked collapse. Most possessions had been hauled out and away from the berths, and children sat upon the bags and sheets and piles of clothes, blinking back into sleep as their parents worked themselves up into a state of quiet indignation and prayerful relief that no one had been killed. Everyone looked pallid, anxious. Knowing that we were at sea now, with no recourse to solid ground, or even adequate space to address the calamity, made the atmosphere fraught.

By the time I had found a space at the table, my injured foot raised on my mother's lap, I noticed that the captain had entered the tween deck to survey the damage, recoiling a little at the smell. He said little, but his lips were thin with anger, and when my father showed him several bent nails gathered in evidence of poor work-manship, he closed his eyes, as if trying to control his frustration. I watched as they spoke to one another, the captain occasionally glancing at my father's spoiled eye before shaking his hand and leaving.

My father picked his way through the crowd and dropped the nails on the bench beside us. They clattered onto the floor as the ship rose and fell.

'Captain Olsen has given us permission to pull apart the beds and rebuild them. He will give us new nails at first light, when they might be sourced with less difficulty.'

Mama's voice was small. 'Where shall we sleep until then?'

Papa ran a hand through his hair. 'We have permission to find space on the upper deck.'

'In the cold and open.'

My father nodded and turned to me. 'Are you badly hurt?'

'No.'

'Good.'

'It could have been her head, Heinrich.'

'Praise God it was not.'

He tapped Matthias on the shoulder and together they began to wrench the nails out of the planks so that no one might be accidentally injured by their exposed ends. I lay along the bench, my head cushioned by Papa's bundle of clothing. For all my foot throbbed, I relished the warmth of my mother's lap beneath it and, when she believed me asleep, her hand gently sweeping its length.

My father spent the following day directing men on how best to repair the berths, growing increasingly frustrated as the hours passed. Matthias explained to me that it was proving useless.

'Papa thinks the ship was not intended to carry emigrants: the berths have just been cobbled together without thought as to how they might bear the weight of sleeping men.'

After prayers at last light, the elders crowded around Dr Meissner and demanded a solution be found. Few wanted to risk nights atop a berth that might suddenly give way, and those who said they would not mind were soon drowned out by those who possessed the lower beds.

'I will not be squashed in my sleep!' exclaimed Gottfried Fröhlich.

'Yes, lives will be endangered,' agreed Papa.

Dr Meissner seemed at a loss as to what might be done. Eventually he admitted that some of the men would have to take turns sleeping on deck amongst the barrels and packing cases.

'And what if the weather is bad?' asked Christian Pasche.

'If the waves are so large as to risk washing you overboard, of course you may return below,' replied the doctor.

'And sleep where?'

The doctor pressed his fingers to the bridge of his nose. 'I imagine if the waves are that large, no one will be sleeping.'

Papa watched as the doctor climbed through the hatchway, returning to his better quarters, then placed a large hand on Elder Pasche's shoulder. 'Come, Christian. Let us manage our own affairs.' He beckoned to the other men from Kay, and together they sat at the table with the passenger list, discussing the best way to divide the available space amongst the families.

I sat upright in the lower bunk, injured foot in front of me, Hermine on my lap. Matthias appeared and handed me a mug of water. 'I've volunteered to sleep on deck,' he said. 'I'll rotate with Traugott Geschke.'

I took a sip. 'Where will you sleep when he is taking his turn above?'

'In the stern with the unmarried men,' Matthias said. 'Papa and Christian decided that men with families have first right to a berth.' He smiled when I pulled a face. 'I don't mind. I can pretend I am a sailor. Hans and Hermann Pasche will be there too. Daniel and Rudolph Simmel.' He lowered his voice. 'Hans is over the moon to get away from his father.'

'Where will Papa sleep?'

Matthias took the empty mug from me. 'With Mama and Hermine.'

I frowned. 'But if Papa is sleeping in this berth, where will I go?' For an instant I imagined that this meant I, too, would be sent to sleep under the stars, and I felt a surge of excitement at the thought. All that light humming down around me.

'The bow.'

'What?'

'The front of the ship. With the unmarried women.' Matthias reached for Hermine. 'There is room there.'

'Oh.'

He gave me an inscrutable smile. 'Perhaps you will bunk with Thea.'

Belongings were once more gone through, separated out. Hans shot me a gleeful look as he dragged his mattress through the walkway, ready for his night's sleep above. I almost envied the boys. Returning below deck after services, the smell of the past few days' sickness had hit me with such force I gagged. What with the catastrophe of the collapsed bunks and their attempted repair, there had been no opportunity to clean the floors of the sour messes in corners. The captain had assured Papa that seasickness did not usually persist for longer than a few days, and that we would all soon be a great deal more comfortable. It was intolerable to imagine otherwise.

Mama, still peakish, sorted my clothing from hers, wished me a good night and delivered me, limping, to a glint-eyed Mutter Scheck. As soon as I stepped into the bow, she whisked the curtain shut behind me.

'You have a rather unwell friend here,' she said, taking me by the shoulder. 'I thought you might jolly her up. Christiana tells me you two are inseparable.'

'Christiana's here?'

Mutter dropped her voice. 'Poor thing. She hasn't stopped crying. But Elizabeth is in glory now. She suffers no longer.'

The floorboards suddenly lifted under our feet. Mutter Scheck steadied herself, then continued forwards. There seemed to be not a touch of illness about her.

'We're a little crowded. Christiana and yourself are here now. Amalie, of course. Elsa Pfeiffer. And a few more girls you won't know, from Klemzig and Tschicherzig. You'll meet them in the morning. I encourage an early bedtime. Easier to bear all this rolling if you're asleep. Of course, if you must lie awake and groan, it would be best if you could do it quietly. Water closet is there. Mind the entryway.' She grimaced. 'Ottilie did not quite make it. We've some cleaning to do.'

I made out several sleeping forms. Blankets thrown over heads. A pale foot sticking out into the walkway.

Mutter Scheck directed me to a berth farthest from the curtain. 'Here you are then. Sleep well. Mind you don't upset that.' She pointed to a slop pail, smelling evilly, swinging on a hook at the outer post, then turned and lurched back to her own bunk near the curtain.

I placed my bag under the berth, then looked in. Thea lay against the dividing rail on her back, eyes shut, one hand gripping the wood, the other arm flung across the mattress.

'Thea?'

Nothing. She was sleeping. Kicking off my clogs I crawled in and, gently moving her arm to her side, lay down beside her. She twitched in her sleep. I gripped the side of the mattress to stop myself from tipping towards her with the movement of the ship, and listened to Mutter Scheck's bedside prayers, the squeak of metal as the lamp was put out. I blinked back the sudden darkness.

My stomach felt tight. I told myself it was because I had not yet become used to the close air beneath decks and the heat of so many bodies in a small space, that I was still afflicted with seasickness. I told myself it would pass and lay still, anxious to remain on my side of the bunk, my body bracing every time the ship lifted, plunged. I did not know how to lie so close to Thea. I did not understand my own agitation.

Hours passed. The ship creaked. There was the sound of laughter from the main body of berths. Someone shushed. I heard the drip of water as the dipper was lifted, the muffled knocking as it was dropped back against the side of the drinking barrel. Sobbing came from a few bunks over. Christiana, I thought. My muscles began to tremble from the exertion of holding myself to the edge of the bed and at last, exhausted, I gave in, and let myself roll against Thea.

She stirred and I felt her lift her arm and place it around me. The weight of it was a balm.

'Hanne?'

Thea was lying on her side, head in the crook of her elbow. I blinked hard, could just make out her face in the low, swinging safety light of the hatchway. It was still night. My pillow was damp. I didn't remember falling asleep.

'What?'

'You were crying.'

'Oh.' I heard Mutter Scheck cough and turn over in her berth. 'Maybe I was dreaming.'

Thea reached out. I felt the gentle touch of her thumb on my cheek. 'Your face is wet.'

I pulled away, felt the beam dividing our berth press against the back of my head. 'Did I wake you?'

'No. The ship woke me. I haven't slept a night through yet.'

'I never sleep well anyway,' I said. 'Even back at home. Ever since my parents separated Matthias and me.'

'You shared a bed?'

'Until we were ten. Mama said that even as babies we would cry all night if put in separate cribs, and so Papa made a cot large enough for the both of us. They gave us separate beds when we grew, but I would always climb out and find Matthias. I'd crawl in next to him, and then get back in my own bed by morning.'

I waited for Thea to say something, but she only smiled, waiting for me to continue. I felt a wave of affection for her then, the way she listened so absolutely.

'For years, we found ways to sleep together. But then he was moved to the loft. I went up there sometimes, but' – I hesitated, feeling a little flush of shame at the memory of Mama's expression – 'Mama found me there and forbade it.'

Thea wriggled closer to me. 'I wish I had a twin.'

I heard Mutter Scheck cough again and raised my head to see if she was awake, but it was too dark to tell.

'She can't hear you,' Thea whispered. 'Everyone's asleep but us. If she heard us talking, we'd know about it.'

I felt her smile in the dark and smiled back at her.

'It must be nice having Matthias. Someone who knows you to your marrow. Someone who loves you as you are.'

'We used to hold hands, too,' I said, my voice more breath than sound. 'As we slept, or when one of us was scared, or simply because we wanted to. But we can't now.'

We listened to the groaning of boards. The whistle of the wind. Someone was snoring loudly in the main steerage quarters. 'Who is that?'

'Probably Eleonore Volkmann.'

I laughed.

'What? She has such large nostrils. Have you noticed how she flares them whenever her husband orders her about? Like a horse.'

'Shh, Henriette will hear you.'

'Henriette has them too. And her sisters. A whole stable of nostrils.'

I snorted and both of us clapped our hands to our mouths.

The ship lurched then. A baby started crying. Thea rolled against me, and even though the ship began to surge and I heard the muted calling of the night watch above us upon the deck, my heart did not beat with fear, but with a pattern of sudden longing I did not understand.

Thea's hand searched for mine in the dark. I threaded my fingers through hers.

'Are you afraid?' I breathed. Her hand was cool in my own.

'No,' she whispered.

'Me neither,' I said.

Her fingers closed tightly about mine. 'I wish you were my twin,' she whispered. 'I wish that I could have known you from birth, that we had all those years together. I wish that we had shared a crib like that.'

'We're sharing one now.'

Her thumb moved over my knuckle.

'I hate that I'm older than you,' Thea whispered.

'Barely. Eighteen days.'

'The saddest eighteen days of my life.'

I could feel her breath against my cheek, and a sudden vision of Thea in the forest, pulling away from me, the feel of her lips still so pronounced upon my own, came flooding back to me.

The ship rolled. We both braced against the force of the wave, and in the swinging of the safety lamp I saw that she was watching me, her eyes lit with something I wanted to ease, something I wanted to answer in my own.

'Maybe, as God did not allow us to enter the world on the same day, He will give us the good grace to leave it together,' I whispered, and immediately felt foolish.

Thea was silent for a long while. The ship's passage eased, the lamp stilled, and her face fell back into shadow. I thought she had closed her eyes, that she had grown drowsy, when I heard her voice, soft and a little raw. 'I hope we do,' she whispered. 'I hope we do.'

born of soil

Days on the ship took on a rhythm. Every morning those who were well enough would rise at seven o'clock and, if the weather allowed, meet amidst the boxes and barrels on the deck for morning services, held on rotation by elders of the various congregations. We sang and prayed, and I liked the way our voices were diluted by the rushing of the ocean around us, the way we were drowned out by a greater, more ancient voice in praise of itself. Hot water for coffee was ready at eight o'clock, and we would eat at the table, which had a lip at its edge to catch any plates that slid. We soon found, however, that it was difficult to eat at all when the ship was pitching. Inevitably our food would end up in our laps or spill across our neighbour's. After breakfast we cleaned dishes and cutlery, drew rations and water, and were informed by Mutter Scheck whether it was our turn to soak salt meat, roast coffee or otherwise clean the compartment. We swilled and scrubbed the floors with sand at least once a week, and more if someone had been sick upon it.

Someone was always sick.

The women in the bow who remained confined to their beds were largely from Tschicherzig, and although Thea and I caught glimpses of these strangers gripping buckets and heard them groaning in the night, we knew them only from what Mutter Scheck intimated to us. Ottilie, who seemed to bring up every meal she attempted, was already widowed at twenty. Another two Johannes, a dressmaker and her cousin, were travelling together. Maria, a girl our age who was close to Ottilie, was orphaned. Christiana, Henriette, Amalie and Elsa we knew.

On fine days Mutter insisted that every able woman drag her mattress and blankets up onto the deck to air them out, allowing us to return them below only after she had brought her nose to the canvas and sniffed, a practice which mortified us, as did her enthusiastic applications of vinegar if the smell was found to be too unpleasant. We were to wash our faces and hands morning and night, and while she did not lean forwards and smell us, she was not above folding down our ears to ensure that we had cleaned thoroughly. We washed in sea water, which left my skin feeling tight and dry. Sometimes, in the light, I could see tidelines of salt ebbed upon Thea's neck and forehead, and knew I had them too.

'Mermaid,' I whispered to her, the first time I saw them on her skin.

'More like salted herring,' she replied.

Mutter Scheck's appraisal and insistence on cleanliness was not limited to our beds and bodies. Our moral scrupulousness was also closely watched. All single women were forbidden from breaching the confines of the bow at night and Mutter Scheck discouraged us from even lurching to the water closet set aside for our use. Instead she issued us with tin chamber-pots that slid under our bunks, and sometimes had to be fetched from the far wall by wriggling under the lower berths on our stomachs. The *Guzunder*, when finally found and filled, was to be emptied into the slop pails secured to the side of the berth by a hook, and all was to be voided and rinsed daily, weather permitting. Any woman who did not securely replace the lid to the slop found herself saddled with the responsibility of emptying it for a week or more, an unenviable task when the ship was rolling. Mutter Scheck inspected our cutlery and plates after washing and made us keep our dishes against the side of the berths. When Henriette complained about their constant rattling, Mutter produced some string to hold them fast, and my father inserted small hooks into the wood from which we might hang our cups, for ease of drying and reaching. Often times, at night, I would watch my and Thea's mugs sway above my head, until sleep finally arrived, and occasionally, during swell, I would be woken by a plummeting handle smacking into the bridge of my nose.

Everything was supervised, rationed, managed. But, as the weeks passed, I saw that Mutter Scheck, while unyielding and particular, was genuinely concerned for our health, even if that concern manifested in a public urging to take aperient pills and eat a little less salt pork and a little more oatmeal. She was affectionate towards us in her own way. Occasionally there were packets left on berths: washing soda for the girl who did not have a spare flannel; a bottle of castor oil for one who did not attend her pail as often as Mutter Scheck believed appropriate. And once, late at night, I saw her lift Ottilie onto her lap, holding her like a baby, so that Maria could swiftly exchange the damp and soiled mattress for an aired one without exposing the sick woman to the indignity of daylight.

Every Sunday Thea and I were visited by our mothers. Mama gave me Hermine in the afternoon so that she might have some respite, and after briefly telling me that everyone was managing as well as they might, she would return to her own berth. Anna Maria, however, liked to sit with Thea and me at the table or on our berth and tell us exactly what had happened since her last visit: the argument Elder Pasche had started with a sailor who spoke directly to Rosina; the rumour that a couple from Klemzig were not actually married; the dolphins she had seen swimming upside down alongside the ship; the great escape of the captain's pig from its crate upon deck and the unease she felt watching Dr Meissner treat those who remained unwell.

'I believe he considers the work beneath him,' she admitted to us one afternoon, absently letting Hermine chew her finger. 'Do you know the man Helbig, from Züllichau?'

Thea and I shook our heads.

'Well, he is very sick. This morning, after an awful night – we could all hear him moaning – the doctor was fetched. He was conferring with the man's wife, and an argument broke out between them. Frau Helbig was very distressed, shouting at the doctor and asking him how her husband was supposed to get better without any medicine. Everyone went quiet at that. Then we all heard Dr Meissner lose his temper and scream at this woman – this poor woman, afraid for her husband's life.'

'What did he say?' Thea asked.

'I shouldn't repeat it.' Anna Maria dropped her voice to a whisper. 'He said, "Do not tell me how to do my work, bloody peasant!" And then, when he realised we had all heard him, he spat on the floor and told us we were all "a pack of dogs".'

'Does he not have any medicine?' The thought that the man entrusted with our wellbeing held us in contempt made me feel deeply uneasy.

'He does. I have seen his chest.' She shook her head. 'I think the truth is that he is a drunkard and that he had forgotten to give Herr Helbig treatment. The door to his cabin was ajar yesterday. I saw him asleep in there, snoring as loud as you like, no matter that it was the afternoon and children sicking up their water below decks.'

Thea inched closer to her mother on the bench. 'Mama, can you help them?'

Anna Maria nodded, lips pressed together. 'I have been treating some for fever.' Looking at Thea, she added, 'I have a little of that remedy in brandy we packed, but everything else is dry and I have trouble accessing the kitchen.' She hesitated. 'There are some who do not like to see me use it for distillations.'

I glanced around the bow and saw Christiana sitting with Henriette on their bunk, showing her a thimble. 'It's my grandmother's,' I heard her say. 'She gave it to me for my hope chest.' Henriette responded by describing the embroidery on a tablecloth.

I turned back to Anna Maria. 'Are you talking about Magdalena Radtke?'

'She is one of them, yes.' The Wend followed my line of sight and, as if she felt her gaze, Christiana looked up, thimble on her index finger. There was no warmth in her face as she stared at Anna Maria.

'Did Magdalena say something, Hanne?' Thea asked.

'I . . . I heard her. The night Elizabeth died.'

Anna Maria placed her palms down on the surface of the table. 'I might have been able to help that child.'

'Mama, perhaps if you assisted the doctor in his ministrations, these people might –'

'I tried, Thea. He took offence. He didn't even do me the honour of replying, only gave me a look of such utter scorn . . .' She took a deep breath. 'As though I haven't birthed a multitude of children, healed those too poor to pay for the quackery of him and his kind.' She sighed. 'It's all right, girls. I will help those who ask for it. Thankfully, there are some who do not share Magdalena's poor opinion of me.'

Thea glanced over to where Ottilie was sleeping in the bunk nearby. 'Mama, Ottilie hasn't been eating. She can't keep anything down. Mutter Scheck sent for Dr Meissner yesterday, but when he came, he didn't give her anything. He told us to watch for fever, but did so without even bringing a hand to her forehead himself.'

Anna Maria shook her head in exasperation.

'He's supposed to make daily rounds, isn't he?' continued Thea. 'To check on the health of all passengers? To ensure cleanliness?

Well, he hardly ever comes into the bow. Ottilie has been unwell since we set out, and he only learned this yesterday. And when he came, Mutter Scheck made the mistake of complaining about the food, and he told her she was welcome to give her rations to those who desired them.'

It was true that the provisions on board were hard to become accustomed to. The largest meal of the day was dinner, held at one o'clock, and usually consisted of salt pork or beef. It was heavy food; it did not sit well with us. At night Thea and I sometimes listed the things we missed. Pears. Sweet peas prised from pods. Raw, shredded cabbage. Sour apples.

As if reading my mind, Anna Maria asked us who had been assigned cook within our mess.

'Christiana,' Thea and I said in unison.

'If all the doctor is going to do is tell us to fumigate with vinegar, I'll see if I can't keep you well with better food,' Anna Maria muttered. 'At the very least I might see if I can't entice the sick girls here to eat a little more.'

Anna Maria had a word with Mutter Scheck that evening, and the following day Christiana was excused from her duties. Our mess's fare improved dramatically. Salt pork baked on ship's biscuit, which soaked up the fat and grew soft and flavoursome. Dumplings cooked in broth. Rice pudding that held the possibility of a rare, submerged prune. If Mutter saw Anna Maria boiling her herbs in the time now permitted to her in the kitchen galley, she never mentioned it to us.

The days grew warmer as we travelled further south, and by the time the *Kristi* passed Madeira, one month after our departure from Altona, the weather was uncomfortably hot. Bible pages wrinkled under damp fingers.

The nights became so muggy it took all my energy just to breathe in and out. Thea was slick with heat next to me. Anna Maria told us that Samuel Radtke had produced some pieces of sealing wax that had melted together.

Mutter Scheck, determined to keep us all from listlessness, produced a number of needles, white thread and cotton. 'No need to waste your time aboard this ship,' she said. 'Think of the life you will lead in the colony. The home you will make. Keep these hours filled now, and you will be grateful you did not succumb to idleness when we arrive.'

For all that I had detested the drudgery of domestic chores at home in Kay, it was a relief to have something to take my mind off the oppressive atmosphere below deck, off the sweat that trickled down my spine and gathered in the small of my back, the smell of bodies and the sound of arguments. The heat shortened tempers, made people less willing to apologise for the inevitable conflicts arising from living in such close quarters. Anna Maria told us that over forty people were now confined to their beds in steerage, suffering from fevers, and that families were anxious. She had taken to smoking their beds with juniper and cloves, having run out of gentian and rhubarb tincture, and that night in bed Thea whispered to me that her mother was also using her book, privately, to make paper seals that might be worn on the bodies of those who were accepting of such things. When she saw my concern, she told me what was written on such seals: 'Spare them all, Adonay, because they are yours. Your unfathomable spirit is in everyone, you who love life.' The words remained on my tongue long after Thea fell into sleep beside me.

Six women from the bow contributed to the number of ill on the ship. At first Mutter Scheck had thought they were taking longer than usual to recover from the woes that had plagued all of us at the beginning of our journey, but when Ottilie began contorting on her bunk, crying with pain, Mutter hastily told the rest of us to spend the remainder of the afternoon on the upper deck, on the condition that we occupied ourselves with sewing.

Thea and I emerged out of the hatchway into a hot and sullen day. The sea was still and, without any waves to clear the waste from the sides of the ship, the smell on deck was nearly as bad as below. There was no wind, the air so thick that breathing felt like an act of conscious will. Before us lay a horizon of water so large my eyes ached.

Thea and I stood to the side, out of the way of the sailors who were cleaning the deck. For some minutes we simply gazed out at the water. It was one thing to know that we were a long way from land, and yet to see only ocean ahead and behind was to understand how truly vulnerable and small we were. It made us quiet, reflective.

We have nothing but sky and each other, I thought.

Thea suddenly seized my shoulder. 'Look,' she said.

There was something moving just under the surface of the sea nearby. Earlier in the week we'd heard about the sighting of more dolphins, but this creature was of a size that belied imagination.

A sailor cried out and other passengers drew nearer, curious.

'A leviathan,' Thea said breathlessly.

Just at that moment, the whale burst through the surface of the sea, dark bulk gleaming, soaring – an impossible flight of weight. It was bigger than anything I had ever seen; my heart stuck to my chest. Thea crushed my arm. People cried out in awe, in terror, as the whale made its arc, made a fool out of the sky, then fell back into the ocean. In the enormous slap and ensuing rush of water I felt my soul briefly lift out of my body, as though, wonder-struck, it had soared into the divine. The whale *was* divine. Waves from its foaming disturbance reached the *Kristi* and rocked the ship as if it were nothing but a cork in a pond.

'Ah, none of us will reach Australia,' Gottfried Fröhlich muttered. 'We will all be put overboard.'

Thea turned and looked at me, eyes brilliant and shining. She did not say anything. Neither did I. We did not have to.

All talk that morning was of the whale. While some, like Thea and me, were awestruck and jubilant, seeing the whale's breaching as a gift, others became Jeremiahs and wondered if the creature's sighting was a sign of some disaster to come.

'They're afraid,' Thea said, eyes following Elder Fröhlich as he spat over the side and made his way back down the hatchway. 'Word has spread that the doctor has asked to put into harbour.' She gave me a heavy look.

'How do you know?' I asked.

'Someone heard him and told some of the men, Papa included. Mama told me. Dr Meissner believes the ship needs to be thoroughly cleaned, that it will provide people with an opportunity to recuperate on shore. The doctor does not have a diagnosis, but Mama says that it is typhus.'

'That is a bad one?'

She nodded. 'But the captain said that as long as his crew remains healthy and there is no lack of food, he cannot warrant putting into harbour.'

'Are you worried?' I asked Thea.

'I don't know. I keep thinking of Ottilie.'

'Mm. But the whale, Thea – doesn't it fill you with hope?'

Thea smiled. She wiped the sweat from her forehead with her sleeve, then leaned against my shoulder and pointed to the cloth in my hands. 'What will this be?'

'A pillow overcover. It will say, *"Schlafe wohl"*. Sleep well. See?

This is the beginning of the first letter. And then, under that, I've also put my initial.'

'Shouldn't it be J for Johanne?'

'No one calls me that.'

'And I suppose you will add your husband's?' she said quietly. 'When you know who he is?'

I stared at her. I had not told Thea about the black cloth lying under my mother's mattress, even though much of the conversation amongst the women was about hope chests. In truth, since joining Thea's berth I had not given much thought to the material brought in readiness for my own marriage. Neither of us contributed to the ongoing talk about weddings and the households they would lead to. Once, when the elder of the other Johannes asked her, Thea mentioned that she knew her mother had packed some things for her to have when she was married, but she had not shared what they were, and Johanne had not asked. We had never spoken of husbands to each other.

Thea was giving me a strange, pale look. 'We will both marry, I suppose,' she said.

I did not reply.

Thea dropped her eyes. I watched her try to thread her needle before taking the cotton and doing it for her.

'Would you make me a pillow overcover?' she asked. Her voice was small. 'When you have finished yours?'

'Won't you want to make your own?'

'I think it will take me the whole of this journey just to finish this handkerchief.' She hesitated. 'Besides, I would like to rest my head on a place your hands have been.'

*

The night after the whale appeared, I dreamed of our trees in Kay. I dreamed I had returned from the colony, had come back to see the walnut tree in our orchard. Years had passed; it was gnarled now, older.

When I placed my hands on the bark, I felt the tree rouse beneath them, as though awakening from a slumber.

You, it said.

'I came back.'

Wind shook the leaves.

I heard you singing, the tree said.

'What was I singing?'

The endless song.

At that I woke, but the feeling of the dream remained with me. I felt deeply reassured, as though my life had already been lived, and it had been good and worthy.

When I rolled over, I saw that Thea was also awake. We drew closer together.

'You were talking in your sleep,' Thea whispered.

'Was I? What was I saying?'

'I don't know. You might have been singing, actually.'

'I was dreaming about our orchard.'

I felt Thea smooth the hair out of my face. 'Like your father's dream? The one about Heaven?'

I lifted my cheek so that it filled her palm. Her hands were cool, grown soft from a lack of labour. 'No.'

The endless song.

'Maybe,' I added. 'Maybe a type of Heaven.'

'Tell me about it.'

So I told Thea about the walnut tree. Not only how it had spoken to me in my dream, but that I had heard it in my waking hours. How I had always thought that anything growing carried its own hymn to creation. All the while Thea stroked my hair in silence.

'I hope that glory is like your dream and not your father's,' she said eventually.

'Why?'

She touched her forehead to mine, and in her closeness came an upswell of something I did not have words to name. 'I think I would miss ordinary apples.' She hesitated. 'Things born of soil.'

I thought of Papa's vision, the shining paradisiacal fruit. In that moment it seemed a frigid wonder.

I wish now that we had had the language to speak of what was unfolding between us in those moments. I wish that, with Thea's hand in my hair, her nearness sounding through me like hallelujah, like fever's refrain, I had allowed myself to consider the possibility of different devotions. That I had considered the weight of a plain ripe pear in hand, the promise of juice down my wrist.

That we had pushed ourselves off the precipice. That, once begun, we could no sooner stop than we could defy gravity.

I wish I had drawn closer to Thea then. Willed her to kiss me. Deeply, so that the whole world turned in revolution.

Our lives were split by light. In the day, we were as we always had been, occupied by chores, distracted by the weather, the heat, by the requests of Mutter Scheck, the unwell women, our mothers. Sometimes we assisted Anna Maria in the kitchen. Boiling rice. Pulling the leaves from dried sprigs of wormwood. We were friends, as we had been, and easy in our friendship.

But at night, when we found ourselves alone in wakefulness,

we would turn and lie close together, our heads on the same pillow, in a way that made me breathless. Once, I felt Thea's hands run over my body in a way that made me tremble, but someone shifted in their bunk and she did not do it again. In the morning I wondered if it had happened at all. We never spoke of it. We never spoke of the forest and what had happened. It was as though we were both asleep, meeting in a common dream.

With only the safety lamp perforating the darkness, our bodies close and the heat all around us, I found myself telling Thea things I had never told anyone. She listened quietly, never seeking to interrupt me or punctuate my thoughts with nods or murmurs. Her silence was attentive and open and it asked nothing from me. My whole life I had been surrounded by those who had, implicitly and openly, with discretion and demand, asked much of me. My parents' love ever manifested as an urging towards improvement: to be more. More prayerful, more contrite, more dutiful. God, too, was related to me only within a context of request. I was never enough as I was. My best self, the self that might be most loved, most accepted, was forever in front of me – a shadow self ahead of me on the path that, no matter how fast I ran, never melded with my person.

The few times I had spoken to Mama about the contradictions and impulses of my heart, my uncertainties, she had responded with directives on how I might abolish them. But Thea never drifted away from my conversation, her mind already formulating a remedy. She just listened. And so, on the ship, I told her everything. How I was afraid my mother did not love me as well as she might. That there was something wrong with me for not crying at Gottlob's funeral. That I had a canker in my heart.

Thea's response to this last secret was something that, even now, even as I lie here with the stars burning holes in the night, warms me. It was a moment of grace that I have held on to in everything that has followed. Even now, even after the great cataclysm, it sustains me.

'Owe no one anything, only love one another: for she who loveth hath fulfilled the covenant.'

Never was scripture so beautifully rendered to my heart.

One night Thea and I were woken by a sudden thump from the foot of our berth. We had been sleeping in each other's arms. We jumped apart.

A voice emerged from the dark. Hoarse. Afraid.

'It's burning.'

Someone was kneeling on the floor, leaning against our bunk.

'Ottilie?' Thea's voice was husked.

In the ghost-light I saw she was right. It was Ottilie, her arms folded tight against her abdomen. Her nose was bleeding. 'Fire, everywhere,' she muttered. 'It's all burning down.'

'What?'

'Burning down,' Ottilie muttered. She seemed not to be aware of her nose; I could hear the patter of blood on our mattress.

'Wake Mutter Scheck,' Thea said, crawling out of the bed. I did as she said and together we all managed to lift Ottilie back to her berth.

'Tip your head back,' Thea said, placing a cloth to Ottilie's face. She looked up at Mutter. 'I don't think she knows where she is.'

'Tell Johann,' Ottilie was saying. Her eyes were closed. 'Please tell him. He must not breathe the smoke.'

'Who's Johann?' I whispered.

Mutter Scheck was grim. 'Her dead husband.' She returned to her berth and began to dress. 'I shall wake the doctor,' she said. 'Don't leave the bow. See if you can get her to drink some water.'

Thea grabbed at Mutter Scheck's wrist. 'Not the doctor. Fetch my mother.'

Mutter Scheck hesitated, looking at Thea with apology. 'I'll fetch the doctor first,' she said gently. 'Then we shall see.'

Dr Meissner bore the rumpled, wide-eyed look of a man trying to rouse himself from inebriation. 'A blood nose, you say?' He kneeled at Ottilie's bedside and Thea and I exchanged a look. He smelled strongly of brandy.

'And a terrible fever,' Mutter Scheck added. She regarded the doctor with consternation. 'She has had a malaise for over two weeks now, Doctor. She has hardly risen from bed.'

'And now this delirium.'

Ottilie began to cry.

'Girls, best you go back to bed now.' Mutter Scheck took the bloodied cloth from Thea's hand and gently flapped her away. 'Dr Meissner and I can manage here.'

We watched the doctor place his ear to Ottilie's chest. The ship suddenly rolled, and he fell sideways. There was the sound of glass breaking.

'Damn it,' he muttered, trying to rise.

Thea bent and picked up a small vial. The top had shattered, spilling white powder. She handed it to Dr Meissner and watched him clumsily pick out shards of glass from the bottle.

'Thank you, Thea,' Mutter Scheck said. She extended a hand to the doctor as he stumbled against the tipping of the swell. 'Go on back to bed.'

*

The next morning, I woke to the sound of Thea scrubbing the foot of our mattress.

'I can't get it out,' she said, looking up. She was crying.

'What? What is it?'

'The blood.'

I looked down at the stained pattern at the foot of our bed. Ottilie's bunk was empty.

'Did your mother come?' I asked. 'I didn't see her.'

Thea shook her head and took something out of her pocket. It was a folded piece of paper. She gave it to me. 'Open it.'

I did so and saw the words Thea had uttered to me weeks earlier, written in Anna Maria's neat print: the invocation of Adonay.

'Magdalena and Rosina found this when they moved Helbig's body,' she said. 'They will tell the pastor when we arrive in the colony.' I glanced across the bow to where Christiana was braiding her hair, determinedly facing away from us.

'He will understand,' I said, kneeling next to Thea. 'He will know Adonay is another name for God.'

Thea flung the wet rag into the bucket. 'I hope so,' she said. 'I hope so.'

The funerals for Ottilie and the man Helbig were held jointly that morning upon deck. The weather remained sultry, the air thick and hot. I noticed that the passengers stood in two groups, Anna Maria in the centre of one, Magdalena in the other.

The deaths of two adults had proven what many had already suspected: there was disease on the ship. The six elders roused the doctor from his cabin and escorted him down to steerage, where they demanded he diagnose the other passengers. At first Dr Meissner refused to confirm that the sickness was anything more than scurvy.

But they pressed him, listing the symptoms they found common amongst the ill. Fevers. Delirium. Headaches and malaise. The children itched. The doctor examined each of the sick passengers as the elders looked on, and by evening prayers, everyone on board knew that it was as Anna Maria had warned: there was typhus on the *Kristi*.

whale

Life on the ship took on a strange intensity. With the bunks already so crowded there was not sufficient space to create a ship's hospital. The sick remained where they were and those who could bear it joined the passengers already sleeping above deck to give more room and air to those below. More would have gone, but the sea had grown rough again, and waves sometimes broke against the boat, sending foam and spray across bedding and blankets. On occasions of very heavy weather, sea water spilling across the deck would reach us in steerage, where it swilled anything loose upon the floor into corners. The humidity remained stifling. Gottfried Volkmann recounted his experiences of typhus in the wars against the French and was shouted down. No one wanted to hear about the smell of the bodies he had seen. Traugott Geschke and Samuel Radtke came to blows as a long-running feud over a bull was reignited, and Papa was forced to come between them and mediate. The doctor, people noticed, was nearly always drunk. He confused passengers, forgot their names. Amalie Schultze nearly took medicine she did not need because he believed her to be a different woman.

Mama had not spent much time with me in the bow, except to hand over or collect Hermine, but after Ottilie and Helbig died, she started taking me aside after prayers on deck, asking how I was, how the other women in the bow were feeling. One afternoon, having spent the whole day in bed, I looked up and saw her standing at the bottom of my berth.

'Anna Maria told me you did not eat breakfast,' she said, gripping the empty upper bunk to steady herself.

I had not realised the Wend had been keeping my mother apprised of my wellbeing, and I wondered whether my mother shared Magdalena's opinions or whether Hermine's birth had convinced her of Anna Maria's skill.

'I'm just resting,' I told her. 'My ankle hurts.' The sea had grown thuggish since midnight and by morning the ship had been pitching with new violence. I had fallen against the side of the trestle when the ship plunged, spraining my ankle and slamming my shins so hard against the bench that I was convinced I had broken bone. The skin had already darkened to a mottled plum.

Mama leaned towards me and placed a hand on my forehead. I noticed her eyes flick to the unwell in their bunks.

'Truly, I am fine. It is just my ankle. I tripped, earlier.'

'No headaches? No pains in your stomach? You feel warm. Where is Thea?'

I shook my head. 'With her mother in the kitchen galley. How is Papa?'

My mother sat down on the berth and smoothed the blankets. 'Your father is stalwart.'

'And Matthias?'

'I have heard he is having a wonderful time being drenched upon deck. He has turned quite wild with the adventure.'

I smiled, but I could see that Mama was worried. She looked back at the hatchway, visible at the side of the half-opened curtain. Sea water was washing down the stairs.

'He will come down if it gets worse than this?' I asked.

She nodded. 'People are talking of lashing themselves to their bunks.'

As if in response to this, the ship lurched and we grabbed each other.

'God in Heaven.'

Mama glanced back at the hatch. 'We shall be swimming soon. All this water.'

'Mama, you're hurting me.'

'What?'

'My arms.'

'Oh.' Mama let go, then lay down beside me. The ship plummeted and she closed her eyes. It was dark below decks, on account of the bad weather, but I could still see that the journey had thinned her face. It made her beauty a little harder, a little more jarring. I let my eyes fill with her, my mother, dark gem.

'You are happy here with the other girls?' She spoke without opening her eyes.

'I am teaching Thea whitework. On calmer days, when we can hold a needle without the threat of taking out our eyes.'

'Mutter Scheck takes good care of you?'

'Yes.'

Mama opened her eyes and, taking my chin in her fingers, turned my face to hers.

'What is it?' I braced myself for warning. For criticism.

Her eyes looked black in the low light. Her gaze unnerved me.

'What?'

'I thank God for you,' she said softly, more to herself than to me.

At that moment there was a cry from the hatchway. Both of us lifted our heads and saw that two people lay on the floor, water washing around them.

Mama sat up. 'Oh no, it's Elize,' she said, and before I could respond she pulled herself out of the berth and rushed towards the main quarters, even as the ship tipped and sent her stumbling sideways through the curtain. She was gone.

*

Thea came into the bow after the lamps had been extinguished. I heard her stagger along the berths then crawl onto our mattress. I lifted the blanket and she lay down next to me.

'Your feet are wet,' I whispered.

'Sorry.'

'Don't be. Here.' I moved closer and placed my own feet over hers to warm them. 'Better?'

'Mm.'

'What hour is it?'

'Midnight.'

'Where have you been? I thought you were in the kitchens.'

'I was. Mama needed someone to try to keep the fire going in all this swell,' Thea said. 'But then Elize fell.'

'I know. How is she?'

'Georg Pasche fell down the hatch ladder and landed on her as she was walking to the water closet. Georg is fine, but Elize went into labour.'

'She's not at term.'

'Five months.' I felt Thea's fingers move absently over the inside of my arm. 'Reinhardt came and found Mama in the kitchens and I went with her to help. That's why I was gone for so long. I helped her deliver the baby.'

'Oh. Thea . . .'

Thea's voice was small in the darkness. 'Elize can hold her in one hand. I've never seen . . .'

'She's alive? She had a girl?'

Thea nodded. 'But she's so small, Hanne,' she whispered. 'I left. Mama and I left, so Elize and Reinhardt . . .' She could not finish the sentence. I wrapped my arm about her and she cried into my shoulder.

*

Reinhardt and Elize named their daughter Esther, for Elize's mother. We learned the next morning that Traugott had christened her minutes before she died. She had lived a full half-hour. The brick they used to weight the shroud was larger than her body.

The elders approached the captain after services, hoping to convince him to heed Dr Meissner's rumoured petition and put in to the next port. We all stood in silence as they spoke to him, watching Olsen listen and nod. He seemed sympathetic. The morning sky was dark grey, the sea capped white by a blustery wind. I felt nervous, as though something was going to happen that I had little power to stop. A freak wave. Mutiny. The ocean was everywhere, restless, unquiet, sounding like a woman in anger.

'What is he saying?' Thea asked me, voice low.

'I can't hear,' I replied. 'It's too windy.'

Mutter Scheck shushed us.

A few minutes later the captain broke away from the elders and addressed us as a group. 'I understand that many of you desire to call at Port de Praia so that the ship might be cleaned of disease and the ill allowed to recover away from its regrettable discomforts.'

There was a general murmuring of agreement.

Olsen assumed a look of deep regret. 'Unfortunately, I cannot assent to lie at anchor for as long as it will take the sick amongst you to recover. The delay would prove expensive. We do not have enough foreign currency on board to pay for the cleaning of the ship.' He said something else, but the wind snatched the words from his mouth.

'What?' Daniel Pfeiffer cried. 'Say again!'

The captain renewed his efforts. 'We have no source of credit on the Cape Verde islands!'

People muttered in dismay. I had not thought of this either.

'I understand that you are disappointed.' Captain Olsen extended his hands in a gesture of apology. 'I understand that many of you are afraid. And so, I would like to console you with the prospect of Brazil. Should the need become greater than it is now, or should my crew become unwell, I will consider Bahia.

'You have my great sympathy,' he continued. 'And I would like to make a gift . . .' Again, his voice was drowned out by the wind, a snapping sail. 'I hope it might lift your spirits.'

'What did he say?' Mutter turned to me, frowning.

'What is lifting our spirits?' called Christian Pasche.

'Louder, please, Captain!'

Captain Olsen gripped the balustrade and roared. 'A pig! I'm giving you the pig!'

None of us had any livestock on the boat, although there were some chickens to provide eggs and fresh meat for the captain, as well as the pig, which we'd been told Olsen kept as a sort of pet, and a goat that bleated piteously every time waves emptied over the deck. Two days later, as soon as the weather had calmed and the pig had been fasted, Mutter Scheck insisted the girls in her charge come up on deck to take part in the occasion of its slaughter.

'A nice pig,' she said to herself as she climbed the hatchway. 'We won't know ourselves.'

The day was hot, with little wind, and in the rare stillness the sounds of people laughing and making as much of the event as possible were earnest and abrasive. Amalie, Christiana, Thea and I stood with three other women on deck, looking on as the young men squabbled in a good-natured way about who ought to be butcher, their fathers and the sailors goading them on.

Papa placed a rope around the pig's neck, holding it still as Hans and Matthias wrenched the nails from its crate and brought one side free.

'He's very strong, isn't he?' Christiana murmured to no one in particular.

'The pig?' I asked.

'I meant Hans,' Christiana answered, rolling her eyes.

Mutter Scheck twitched in disapproval. '*Halt's Maul, so fliegt dir keine Mücke hinein.* Close your mouth, so no mosquitoes will fly in, Christiana.'

The pig was led out of the crate. Everyone cheered and the animal, startled by the sudden noise, immediately lurched starboard, taking Papa by surprise so that he stumbled and was dragged on his knees. People laughed. Papa joined in, letting out a roar as he got back on his feet. He gave the animal a few slaps on its rear. It squealed and the passengers laughed again.

'I feel sick.'

Thea had been very quiet all morning. I saw that she had turned away from the deck and was looking out to sea.

'Really?'

'I want to go below.'

'Thea, Daniel Pfeiffer will do it. They're not going to let the boys fumble it.'

'Please, Hanne.'

I noticed that she was trembling.

'I can't watch.'

Mutter Scheck was enjoying the mirth. I waited until she had stopped guffawing and tapped her on the shoulder.

'What is it, Hanne?' she asked, still smiling.

'Thea is not well.'

Mutter's smile vanished, eyes flitting to Thea, who waited for me, pale-faced, at the hatch entrance. 'Fever?'

'Just a little tired, I think.'

'Are you sure?'

'Yes, I'm sure that's it. I am too. We've slept so little these past days.'

'Go on, then,' she said, her attention already turning back to the pig and its capture. 'Don't leave the bow.'

The pig's frantic squealing quietened as we returned below deck, but Thea was almost crying by the time we crawled back into bed. She clamped her hands over her ears. 'I hate it,' she said. 'I hate it. I can't understand why everyone wants to watch such a thing. Hanne, talk to me. Sing to me. Tell me something.'

'All right.' I took her hand. It was hot and damp. 'Think of the lives we have ahead of us. Imagine what they will be like. We will have to learn English, you know.'

There was a loud rumble of laughter from above, a shrill screeching from the pig.

'Try not to listen,' I said.

'Do you know any English?'

'I know the word for *Wasser*.'

'What is it?'

'It is "water". Matthias taught me. I forget everything else.'

'Tell me more about our lives.'

'We will have our own farms one day,' I said. 'We'll make sure they are side by side. And we will plant orchards. Nut trees. Fruit trees. Vines. Just think, we'll be able to pick all the fruit we could ever want. Our children will play in the grass and climb the branches, and we will pick plums and apples and apricots. There will be fields of grain, too. And we won't ever have to look at the ocean again.'

'Keep going.'

'And you don't have to raise pigs. You can have cows. Chickens. Maybe a horse. A lovely calm horse to breathe on your fingers on cold winter mornings and warm them. Big dark eyes.'

'That sounds nice.'

'We will see each other every day. We will sit next to each other in church. I'll name my daughter for you.'

Thea turned and pulled me into a tight, fierce hug. 'Promise me,' she said.

'Promise what?'

'Promise it will be as you say. Promise you will name your daughter for me.'

'You can be her godmother.'

There was a loud cheering from the deck. The pig was silent.

'I think it is dead now,' I said.

'Thank God.' Thea exhaled. 'Thank God for that.'

The air below decks was soon grey with smoke from the kitchens, viscid with pork fat. There were cheers and salutations over the unexpected meal. Bones sucked clean. Fat chewed on back teeth. Ears crisped to crackle.

Mutter Scheck came into the bow triumphant, holding a plate filled with tender, glistening pink. 'Come, my girls,' she said. 'Come and have your treat!'

I glanced at Thea lying next to me. She shook her head.

'Hanne!' Mutter beckoned to me. 'If you're not quick it will all be gone.'

'I'm not hungry,' I said, and I felt Thea relax next to me.

'Not hungry?' Mutter bustled over and put a greasy hand to my forehead. 'You're quite hot. Thea? You too?' She eyed us appraisingly. 'Some meat might do you good. Give you some strength.'

'Give it to the others,' I said, lying back down. I felt Thea find my hand and hold it.

'Thank you,' she whispered. 'The smell has been giving me a

headache all day. I feel like someone has split my skull with a cleaver.'

'Do you need some water?'

Thea nodded.

I pulled her mug from its hook and crawled out of the berth to the dipper. I could hear men laughing beyond the curtain, my father's voice telling Rudolph Simmel to bring the boys on deck down for their share. Magdalena Radtke's voice urged him to try the trotters. They were her specialty, she was saying.

I filled Thea's mug and returned to her bunk, my stomach growling.

'Everyone's having a lovely time, aren't they?' she murmured, hand over her eyes.

'They do seem a bit happier.' I passed her the water.

Thea wrinkled her nose as she sipped.

'What is it?'

She wiped her mouth on her sleeve. 'Where did you get this from?'

'The water barrel.'

'It doesn't taste right.'

'Really?' I took the mug from her hand and placed my lips where hers had been. It was dead water, whiskered water, and my stomach rose in revulsion. I spat it back into the mug. 'That's disgusting.'

'Are you sure it is from the drinking barrel?'

'Of course.'

'It tastes poisonous.'

'Did you swallow it?'

Thea opened her eyes and stared at me. 'Yes.'

We told Mutter Scheck, who then informed the elders. Only a handful of the water barrels, it turned out, were new barrels. The rest were used and the water, while in store, had absorbed their histories: whiskey, wine, vinegar. There was nothing they could do about it,

Dr Meissner told the elders. They must either wait for rain or put up with the taste – or thirst. He was not responsible for the mistakes of the shipping agent.

Uneasiness and displeasure swept throughout steerage as people repeated the doctor's comments to one another.

Even Mutter Scheck could not hide her contempt. 'The man is an idiot. He tells us to thirst and then orders us to take rations of salt fish.'

Thea's headache persisted into the night and the next day, and I blamed the noxious drinking barrel. I asked Mutter Scheck's permission to go into the main quarters and take water from the open barrels there, and for one and a half days I was able to convince myself that Thea was better for it. But when that barrel was emptied and the next opened, it was worse than the one in the bow.

As days passed and the temperatures grew even warmer, we forgot the taste of purity and blocked our noses by habit. I began to wait until thirst stuck my tongue to the roof of my mouth before picking up the dipper. My stomach swelled. Cramped. I became accustomed to clenching my fists against the narrow walls of the water closet. And I blamed the foul water for Thea's persistent headache. For five days she grew increasingly listless and distracted, until finally her headache was so bad that she could not stop whimpering from the relentless pain of it. Anna Maria came every day and smoked her bed with juniper, offered her the last of her remedies, but I could see the Wend's anxiety at having so little at her disposal.

I tried to comfort Thea. At night I held her hand and stroked her hair and fetched damp cloths for her forehead, but the smell of them was the same as the rancid water and she could not bear it. I stole up the hatchway and asked the nightwatchman for sea water. The salt dried to her white hair. I brushed it out with my fingers as she tried to sleep.

'It won't be long and we'll have fresh water again,' I whispered to her. 'The wells we dig will be filled with clear water. I'll plant a pear over yours to make sure it is sweet.'

The corners of her mouth flickered in an attempted smile.

'It hurts to talk?'

She nodded.

'Rest, then,' I said. 'I'll stay with you.'

'Am I sick?' she asked. 'Am I going to die?'

Panic billowed through me. I felt my gut drop, my mouth slip open, before I remembered myself. 'Of course not,' I said, and I smiled and placed my hand on her forehead. She was fire.

Thea pulled my hand down against her cheek and held it there, searching my face as though she did not believe me. 'This feels like dying.'

'It's just that awful water,' I said. 'As soon as it rains, as soon as we arrive, you'll feel better.'

'Hanne.' Her eyes were a hot blue.

'You're not dying.'

'You won't leave me, will you? Please – stay with me.'

I watched her kiss the crease in the middle of my palm.

'I'm here,' I said. 'I'm not going anywhere.'

'Promise me.'

'I promise.'

As I arrive at it now, the great hinge of my existence, the taste of that foul water creeps back across my tongue and remains with me. It bristles against my throat even now, all these years later, even here, in the valley, the sky pearling with coming dawn.

That night I saw Thea curl like a leaf in flame. I saw the colour go out of her. I saw her turn to ash.

'Hanne.'

I woke to find Thea pallid and filmed with sweat. She did not smell as herself; she was the smell of turning meat. 'Help,' she was saying, eyes closed. 'Help me.'

I woke Mutter Scheck. Anna Maria was sent for and I gave up my space in the berth and moved my things to Ottilie's bunk, which had remained unoccupied since her death. My mouth was dry. I did not dare believe Thea had caught the sickness, even though I had spent the evening feeling the fever in her skin, holding her steady over the bucket. I watched as Mutter Scheck and Anna Maria stood in soft conversation. I could not hear what they were saying, but I thought I heard Anna Maria's voice lift in vexation. At ten o'clock, Christiana silently rose and put out the light, and shortly afterwards I heard Mutter Scheck's prayers as she readied herself for bed. I heard her say Thea's name.

She is not dying, I told myself. She will be well again soon.

I did not sleep that night. I could hear Anna Maria tending to Thea in the gloom, bringing her boiled water and urging her to swallow all of it. I heard a spoon clink against a bottle. Heard the low, private sounds of Thea's body as it rejected anything that promised recovery or sustenance. When the lamps were lit in the morning, they illuminated a grey scene. The Wend, sentry over her daughter, mouth grim.

'Is she better?'

Anna Maria looked up. Her eyes found mine and they were kind and worried. 'Not yet.'

'What is it?' I asked.

'Nervous fever.' Her voice was soft. Full of bruising. 'Typhus.'

'It was just a headache,' I said. My voice was strange to my ears. I did not recognise it. 'Because of the pig.'

Thea groaned in her bed and Anna Maria turned back to her.

'What can I do?' I asked.

'Pray for her,' Anna Maria replied without lifting her eyes off her daughter. She stroked her cheek. 'Pray for her.'

I did not dare leave my berth that day. I prayed again and again, until it felt as though my words were a kind of talisman, as though they were circling about Thea and, as long as I prayed, they would hold her fast to the world.

I did not eat. When night came, I told myself that Thea would feel the weight of my gaze and be calmed by it, protected by it. I prayed, eyes open. *Almighty God*, I implored, *spare her and make her well. Lord, spare her and make her well. Spare her. Spare her.*

I fell asleep eventually, my body betraying my will. And when I woke the tween deck heaved with slow breathing, sleep and creaking. The air was heavy. The light from the hatchway swung with the regular rocking of the ship, and in its glow I saw Anna Maria sitting next to Thea. At first I thought she prayed over her, but when I heard Thea's voice, I saw that Anna Maria held a book in her hands and was pressing it upon her daughter's chest.

'Accept it,' she was saying. 'Accept it.'

Thea was pushing the book away with what remaining strength she had, and when I heard Anna Maria speak again, I could hear tears in her voice.

'Please,' she was saying. 'Please, you must accept it.'

I did not hear Thea's reply, and although I waited, nothing

more was said between them. Anna Maria rose and staggered to the water barrel, and I shut my eyes so that she would not know I had seen her.

I dreamed of water. I dreamed I divined rivers running beneath the ship's boards. I crouched on the floor, one hand outspread and the other gripping a knife. I plunged the blade downwards and the wood of the boards broke apart. Water bubbled up like a wellspring. Fresh, clean water. It sang of snow melt and rock and silent places. I watched it creep along the floor, rising until it lapped against the blankets of the lower berths. I reached out and placed my palm against the surface, and when I looked up, I saw Thea drinking, scooping handfuls to her mouth so that water dripped down her chin and clothes.

'Water of life,' she said, and she reached for me.

And then I fell out of my bed and woke.

It took a few moments for me to understand what was happening. The bow was black-dark and I could hear voices and cries. There was water everywhere, as in my dream, but as the ship tipped and I started to slide across the floor, colliding with something hard, I understood that it was not fresh water, but salt.

I wanted to cry out but the words caught at the back of my throat. I was strangled with fear. I reached out as the ship rolled again, and my hand found an ankle. I heard Christiana shriek.

'Christiana?'

'Hanne?'

Hands found me and helped me up, pulling me into a bed. The mattress was soaked.

'Christiana, is that you? Why is it dark?'

'The safety light has gone out.'

I could hear sea water sluicing the floor. It sounded like the tween deck was flooded and, as the ship fell in another sickening plunge, I heard the water rushing around us, heard the clattering of knives and plates, heard boxes breaking their fastenings, and all of it tipping from berths and nooks and keeping places and sliding across the floor.

'Our Father who art in Heaven . . .' The words were throttled by Christiana's rapid breathing. Children were screaming. I was aware, at the periphery of my fear, of Mutter Scheck calling for calm. Of my own father's voice deep in steerage calling for someone to 'light the damn lamp'. I was aware of my body shaking, of my eyes blindly searching the darkness, looking for something by which I might anchor myself. Where was my bunk? Where was Thea?

Christiana gripped my arm. 'Thy kingdom come . . .'

'Thea!' My voice broke over her name. I tried again, but my throat was barbed and I could not call out. Christiana's nails dug into the crook of my elbow.

A dim light entered the bow. The curtain had been pulled from its rope, and I could see into steerage, where Samuel Radtke gripped the trestle table, one hand closing the safety lamp, its flame rekindled. Water washed about his legs.

'Papa!'

My father was gripping the stairs of the hatchway, beard and hair wet through from the water falling from the upper deck, calling to someone above. Samuel Radtke made his way to him, falling as the ship plunged, then pulling himself back to his feet. Together they were shouting, but I could not hear what they were saying above the roar of the ocean outside and the crashing of water and loose articles upon the floor.

There was a loud crack from without and Christiana screamed and scrabbled at me like the drowning. 'We are being wrecked!'

'I think it was thunder.'

Turning, I saw Anna Maria lying next to Thea, one arm holding her daughter, the other braced against the post of the berth. They were both silent.

Christiana shook me. 'What are they doing?'

I turned and saw that our fathers were standing on the stairs, helping to haul something over the hatchway, assisting the sailors as they nailed down the battens.

Soon the water falling into the tween deck was reduced to a steady dripping, and while the ship was still rolling at terrifying angles, people stopped screaming as they had done when the deck had been in total darkness. The safety lamp was a comfort, even if it showed just how acute the keel of the waves.

Papa approached the bow and nodded to Mutter Scheck, who remained in her berth, quite white, gripping the planks above her head.

'Are you all right?' he called to me, steadying himself as the ship coursed down another wave.

I nodded. My voice had gone.

'It's a squall,' he shouted. 'Just a bad squall. It has taken everyone by surprise, that's all. The scuppers are not draining the ship of all the water.'

It was such a relief to see him after so many weeks of separation, I could not help the tears that sprang to my eyes. I needed to be close to him. When the ship eased upwards, I threw off Christiana and staggered to where he stood. He caught me with his free arm.

'Do you have faith in our mighty God above?' he asked, holding me firm around the shoulders.

I could feel his strength, the warmth of him behind his drenched clothing.

'Hanne, listen to me.' He looked into my face. 'Do you have faith?'

'Yes, Papa, but –'

'Only those who have forsaken their faith need be afraid.' Papa wedged himself against the side of the ship for balance and brought his hand to my cheek. 'Are not five sparrows sold for two pennies? Yet not one of them is forgotten in God's sight.' He was talking quickly, breathlessly. 'But even the hairs of your head are all counted. Do not be afraid. You are of more value than many sparrows.

'Hanne, go back to your bunk and pray, and know that He who sees all has His eye upon you.' And with that he waited until the ship had righted itself and then pushed me back into the gloom of the bow.

The squall lasted all night and continued into the next day. By morning, the air between decks had grown so close I felt light-headed. I lay as still as I was able on Ottilie's bunk, letting my body roll with the movement of the ship, keeping my eyes focused on Thea. I could hear her laboured breathing even over the sound of the elders arguing behind the curtain. My father and Christian Pasche were adamant the hatches remain closed to prevent damage to the stores. Samuel Radtke was afraid the sick would suffocate.

Spare her, I thought. Spare her.

I imagined Thea's lungs, willed them full. Held my breath to take in less air so that she might breathe a little more.

I wondered where Anna Maria had put her book.

Hours passed. It was hell. My vision became starred with creeping darkness, heart pounding through my body so that I felt my flesh pulse with the echoing beat of it, the ricochet of blood. I soon became insensitive to anything other than my struggle to breathe. The heat was a hand over my mouth. We would all die. We would all be smothered. We would drown in air or water.

I was vaguely aware of the captain's voice and the answering cry, 'Have the hatches opened again or we will all suffocate!' before slipping into unconsciousness. My last sight was Thea, white candle-flame in the darkness.

Water from the storm ruined nine sacks of bread. I know this, because it is the last thing I remember clearly before the warp of illness upon my memory.

Mutter Scheck stands at the foot of my berth with a brush. She tells me the storm has ruined some of the supplies. Nine sacks of ship biscuit have turned in the humidity, and it is the captain's orders that passengers go above deck to scrub them of mould so that they might yet be eaten.

I tell her I will rise, or I think I tell her. I am unsure if I have spoken; my mouth is so dry I cannot properly swallow. There is a fist about my throat. I see Mutter look at me, then drop the brush and place a hand on my head.

Her hand is cool, deliciously cool, and when she removes it, I hear myself whimper for the loss of such soothing.

She fetches water. I drink, and feel it come up again, whiskey water, turned water. My pillow is wet. I turn my cheek into it to cool the fire in my skin, to halt the thrumming pulse in my temple.

Mutter leaves. I feel the weight of the brush against my foot.

Nine sacks of bread, I think. Bread of life. Water of life. Flesh and blood, all turned, all ruined.

I remember other things, too, but I cannot know if they happened.

I remember being lifted from my mattress and carried. I remember the pressure of hands under my body and the discomfort of that.

It must have happened. I remember opening my eyes and seeing Thea beside me. They must have moved one or both of us. I know we were placed together. A sick ward? Were there others? I remember only her eyes and the ocean in them and the flare of love I felt knowing she was still there, still alive, still with me.

Mama's hands at my mouth, fingers at my teeth, prising them apart, and the sound of my own voice protesting. I know now she was perhaps hoping to feed me. The smell of broth in my pillow. Pork bones.

Darkness. Lights in places I did not expect them. A man's voice and the hair in his nostrils as he looked upon me. Adam's apple held in check by a neckcloth; the sight of it made me feel as though I were being choked, as though there were pressure upon my own neck.

Heat coming from Thea's body beside me. Sun. Fire. Exploding star.

Lamps lit and extinguished. A terrible thirst. Coarse, grinding hours of darkness that I sweated into, saw shapes emerge from. Figures. Rats running across my neck, biting my lips. Thrashing and screaming for all the rats upon me, hearing my own voice and thinking it was a stranger's, feeling pity for the poor soul screaming.

Anna Maria kissing me on the forehead. The sound of her kissing Thea.

My mother's voice. Her hands around spoon and vial. Words of prayer around me. Fresh cold air spilling across me, the feel of Mama's hands sliding beneath my neck, raising the thick weight of my head, fingertip at my mouth. A spoon upon my tongue, hard edge against my teeth. Liquid. A gritty bitterness.

I swallowed it down.

This is how it happened. There was a storm, and then there wasn't. I was well, and then I wasn't.

There was pain, and then there wasn't.

That I remember with clarity. The sudden absence of pain. Such sweeping relief, such blessed reprieve, I fit my lips around the name of God.

Breath upon me. A swimming light filled with faces. Damp palms of love. Paper tucked against my heart.

'God be praised on high, she will be well. She thanks her Saviour.'

Mama's voice. I understood that she had been weeping. Mama, who never cried.

Leaning into the curve of her hand as though healing might flow from it.

'She thanks her Saviour.'

I remember.

Thea next to me. Eyes shining with the effort of dying. Anna Maria, howling like a wolf, face hidden in her hands. A male voice saying, 'Blessed are the dead that die in the Lord.'

I remember looking at Thea and everything fading from us. The splintered deck and the bowls of water and the mould brushes for the bread and mothers choking on their love. It all faded. There was the ocean pressing hungry against the ship, and there was Thea, and I stared into her eyes and knew deeply, deeply, that we were for each other.

Somewhere, in the wide water below us, I could hear a whale singing.

Thea did not speak, but I knew she did not want to die.

Somehow my hand found hers.

She blinked at me then, pale lashes dipping. Peace washed through her.

The whale song grew louder. I felt the tremble of it through the water. I felt the song strike the ship, felt the wood carry the notes, felt the ripple in the beams until the song reached our bunk. The fibres of the woollen blanket carried the whale cry into my body, and then I was the song. I was the tremble. I was the cry. The whale was in me, inhabited me. My blood turned to songwater and my heart stopped to listen.

Thea's hand in mine.

The whale passed. The music faded.

I waited for my heartbeat.

It did not come again.

THE
SECOND
DAY

AFTER

press of time

Somewhere in the press of time I was caught, and now I remain here, like a flower turned to paper, untethered to the soil.

Still, I am here.

There was nothing in my life that ever offered the possibility of what has come to pass. It was wheat or chaff. Dead wood or living fruit. I grew up believing in my father's holy orchard and its bounty of grace. I believed in hell, mentioned many times by Pastor Flügel. Hell was a bonfire of unfruitful branches. 'And the smoke of their torment goes up, forever and ever.'

But I am not smoke. And while I have suffered torments, they are not the usual dark stitches cast along needles of pious imagination. They are the same simple hungers of my living self. I hunger to be seen. I hunger to touch and be touched. I hunger for love.

Love. If there is any explanation to my ongoingness, it must be that. Love has pinned me to this world, and so I remain.

The sun is rising again. Fire burning back the night.

Here is another day.

albatross

The last moments of my life are remembered as absences. An absence of pain. An absent heartbeat. Relief. Confusion. A waiting for the continuation of my life and the brief and wondrous second when perhaps I knew, even then, that it was over.

Then a soft and absorbing darkness.

I have spent days trying to fit words around that deepening into nothing. Language is a cramped and narrow thing; it cannot hold phenomena. Things of the spirit reach beyond the farthest boundary of words. But the feeling of that darkness remains with me. As though everything that is to happen had already happened. The dormancy of a seed.

I sense it sometimes, in shifting hours such as this one. Even as sunlight spills over the valley below, as it touches the upper branches of these trees and warms their pale trunks to blush, I feel that darkness glimmer at the corner of my vision. It makes me think that soon I will return to its totality. Or, rather, it will come for me, and I will surrender to it. I will give in and curl into the nothing which holds the possibility of everything.

For now, I am here. Hungry and discontent and not at peace, too full of love. For now, I am here to tell this story to the wind in the hope that it might hold it in trust. Perhaps somewhere, at some time, someone will hear my voice and know that even though I am gone, what I felt remains. What we felt for each other.

There was darkness. And then.

And then. And then. And then there was not.

There was a sudden brilliance. An unbearable light. I was scalded by white-lightness, I was in the heart of a flame. I closed my eyes, yet light still came from above and below. I covered my face with my arm.

I had come from a place of calm cessation. Then light came and gave me form.

I could hear the distant slap of water. Sensed taut shadow of sail. My hands were resting on cloth. Sailcloth. I could feel a raised spine of stitches down its centre.

The light subsided and I opened my eyes and saw blue. Saw the ocean, a perfect mirror.

A shadow passed above. Feathers against the sun.

An angel, I thought.

The wings grew larger and memory stirred in me. The powder and the pain and the whale. And Thea.

Where was Thea?

Wings, feathers burning with light.

The cloth beneath my hands. I noticed a crowd, bent-headed. Was she there? Was she there with me?

The wings drew closer, beating against the sky. Rippling it. Cut the light with feathered knives.

Thea?

There was the whisper of turning pages against the sound of wind.

The light paled then and I saw that the angel was an albatross. Wings spread to the wind, crucified to the sun. Holy host of sky.

My father was singing. I blinked into the hymn and saw that I was upon the open deck of the *Kristi*, surrounded by a standing solemnity of passengers. Voices rose. Around me, familiar faces, singing.

I opened my mouth, but before words could meet air, I glanced down and saw that my hands were resting on a body, sailcloth sewn to the chin so that people might say a last farewell.

It was my own face.

You are dreaming, I told myself. This is not possible.

Someone had combed my hair with water. I touched it and felt that it was damp.

This is a dream. You will wake up.

But I did not wake up.

The lips upon the pale face were ajar. I placed a fingertip upon them and was frightened to feel them so cold and ungiving when the hand I extended was alive. I ran my fingers across my own mouth and felt that my skin was warm and soft. I did not understand how I could be standing over my own body when I still inhabited it, familiar and living.

Shock kept me still. I was afraid to do more. I noticed the thread hanging from the last stitch in the sailcloth, the needle at its end, glinting in the sun. Waiting for the end of the hymn.

I did not understand why, knowing it all for a dream, I did not wake up.

I am here, I thought. I am still here.

The hymn faded. A sob interrupted the pause and I turned and saw Magdalena Radtke crying, eyes sunken with tears and her arm entwined with my mother's.

Relief swept through me.

'Mama!' I walked to her, threw my arms around her neck and waited for her to return my embrace.

Nothing.

I stepped back.

Her eyes did not shift to my own.

I pressed my forehead against hers, and I could feel the hair escaping from her bonnet against my skin, but she was looking beyond me at the sailor folding my face into the cloth.

'No, Mama,' I said. 'That's not me. I'm here. Look at me!' My fingers stroked her cheeks. I tried to meet her eyes. 'Look at me!'

She was still, as though a great weight were balanced upon her shoulders and, if she moved, it would topple and crush her.

It was only when the sailor threaded his last stitch through the nose that she turned away. A stitch to make sure of insensibility. Embroidery for the dead who die at sea.

I was afraid and heartsore. I did not understand what was happening.

A nightmare, I thought. It is only a nightmare.

The sailor nodded at my father. Papa placed his heavy hands upon the shroud. Then Matthias – my brother! – came forwards from the men standing shoulder to shoulder and was held steady as he bent to the body. Tears were slipping down his face, and he was letting them fall. I knew my brother. I knew he was ashamed of crying. I recognised those tears as the same he shed for Gottlob, silent and angry. They dripped from his nose and chin as Papa gripped my brother's shoulders and lifted him upright. Matthias broke down. My father gripped the back of his neck, steadied him with a small shake. He stopped crying.

And then, my mother. Arms by her sides. Stone-faced and pale as milk.

Mama stood over the shroud and did not cry.

My father lowered his mouth to her ear; his holy eye slunk sideways to the waiting ocean. He murmured.

Mama shook her head.

Papa nodded at the sailors and they tipped my likeness into the sea. Everyone flinched, waiting for a splash that did not come, that was not heard. I stood on the deck, staring at the place where the shroud had been. My mouth slowly filled with sea water. I spat it out upon the dry boards of the deck and saw that it did not mark them. I fell to my knees. The ocean was pouring through my hair without a drop hitting the wood beneath me. On all fours, I felt myself sink through a cold so complete and encompassing it awed me. I felt the hard corners of bricks at my ankles, felt them drag me down as my arms lifted in weightlessness. Sediment gathered under my tongue.

I vomited silt onto the deck of the *Kristi* as people dispersed about me. I was crying and my tears were the Atlantic, and no one saw me, no one saw that I was drowning on deck. I looked up, eyes blurred with salt water, and saw Eleonore Volkmann returning to the hatchway, holding Hermine. I grabbed at her ankle but she moved past me. She moved through me. I heard my sister cry, and I said her name, and it came out as a small silver fish. I watched it wriggle upon the deck, unregarded by all.

I blacked out. I disappeared from myself. And when I woke, I was tucked between two barrels of herrings. I could smell spoiled fish and I saw that the barrels had been opened and that the salted herrings within had deteriorated, the flesh coming away from the bones.

Several families were standing in the thick air arguing with each other, hands over their mouths against the stench. The doctor stood between them. I waited by the opened barrels for long enough to understand that some were demanding their rations of herrings, while others were determined to keep them for cooler temperatures. Dr Meissner had allowed another barrel to be opened. The herrings were spoiled, and those who had wanted the herrings earlier were red-faced with anger.

'Please,' I said. 'I want to wake up.'

No one heard me. I recognised Gottfried Fröhlich and stepped closer to him as he reached into the barrel, picked out a fragment of fish and flung it at the feet of a sunken-cheeked man from Tschicherzig.

'Herr Fröhlich?'

Spittle flecked his chin as he shouted at the doctor. 'You are a curse upon us!'

'Herr Fröhlich!'

I reached out and touched him. He was in his shirtsleeves, had rolled them back to his elbows, and I could feel the wiry hair damp upon his forearm. I recoiled, expecting him to turn in disapproval, but Herr Fröhlich continued shouting, and when the doctor reached for his shoulder to calm him, he threw him off and strode to the hatchway.

'Herr Fröhlich, please. Please listen to me.'

But I was nothing to him and he did not hear me.

I followed him down the hatchway, my eyes adjusting to the ghost-light of steerage. It was more or less as I remembered it, but there was a greater sense of people having made the best of things. Washing was strung up between the beams. Children played on the floor as men stepped over them, carrying water and kindling for the kitchens.

Herr Fröhlich stormed off to his bunk and I stood, unsure of everything, by the foot of the hatch. What had happened? Was I still ill?

Go back to bed, I told myself. Either you are wandering in a fever and hallucinating, or you are in a nightmare, dreaming that you have died. Go back to bed. Go back to Thea. She is unwell and she needs you. You said you would not leave her.

I walked to the bow, reaching out a hand to push the curtain aside. I saw my hand grasp it. I saw my hand move it, but I also saw in the same moment that the cloth did not move.

It is delirium, I told myself.

Salt water filled the back of my throat as I staggered to our berth. I could see Thea's pale hair spread across the pillow, visible even in the shadows. By the time I reached her, my mouth was filled with the ocean. I pulled myself into the berth and sea water spilled out over the blankets.

I wiped my mouth. I crawled in further, crawled in over her. Thea's eyes were closed; she did not wake. I sat back on my knees and shook her shoulders.

'Thea, wake up.'

Disease had pulled the roundness from her face. She looked like someone who had touched her knuckles to death's door, but she was still alive. The worst had passed for her.

'Thea, something is happening to me.'

She still did not wake.

'Thea, please. You have to help me.'

Mutter Scheck walked past, polishing her glasses on a handkerchief. 'Her fever seems lessened,' she said. 'I think it will break.'

Relief swamped me. And then I turned and realised Mutter was speaking to Anna Maria, who sat on Ottilie's bunk. The last bed I had occupied. The blanket was gone, the mattress stripped. A sick feeling crept through my stomach.

'I thank God,' replied Anna Maria.

'Sleep, if you can,' said Mutter, sitting down next to her. 'I can stay with her in case she wakes.'

'Mutter?' I climbed back out of Thea's berth and approached them.

'No. If she wakes, she will ask.'

'You want to tell her?'

Anna Maria nodded.

They did not look at me. I dropped to my knees in front of them. 'Anna Maria. Mutter Scheck. Please listen to me. Please help me.'

'Would it be best to wait until she is well enough?' asked Mutter Scheck.

The Wend gestured to the bare mattress behind them. 'What do I say? How can I lie to her?'

Mutter patted Anna Maria on the shoulder. 'Well, should you get tired, wake me.'

Her hands rested in her lap. I reached for them, entwined my fingers in hers. I could feel the warmth of them, the strength in them.

'Anna Maria, can you see me? Where is my blanket?'

She shuddered and pulled her hands to her chest.

'I mean it, Frau Eichenwald,' Mutter added. 'It is not just Thea. I know there are other anxieties on your mind.'

Thea's mother did not respond. She was examining her fingers as though there were something on them, as though she had been burned.

'Frau Eichenwald?' Mutter looked at her, concerned. 'What is it?'

'Nothing.'

'Are you all right?'

'Yes, Mutter.' She pressed her fingertips to her mouth and closed her eyes. 'You're right. I'm tired.' She hesitated for a moment, looking around the bow, before returning to her daughter's side. I watched her kiss Thea's forehead and then kneel to pray. But even as she praised the name of Jesus, her eyes travelled around the room. Watchful. Wakeful.

I wanted my brother. Matthias would reassure me as he always had. He would recognise me, explain that my mind was still hot with fever and I had wandered from my sickbed. He would smile at me, and I would feel all my fear and uncertainty melt away.

I climbed up the hatchway, back into the light and the smell of rotting fish. Two sailors were heaving spadefuls of congealed herring overboard, neckcloths tied around their faces. A few passengers looked on, pinching their noses.

Where was Matthias?

I made my way to the other side of the open deck, edging around the supplies and barrels packed together in the centre, and suddenly saw, in a gap between two tall, wooden cases, my brother and Hans. They had wedged themselves into the narrow space and were sitting quietly. Matthias's hand was on his chest, fingers massaging the skin over his heart.

'Matthias,' I said, kneeling in the gap. 'Matthias, it's me.'

My brother started to pound his chest with his fist.

Hans caught Matthias's arm, and though my brother tried to shake him off, tried to keep hitting himself, face mottling in pain and anger, Hans was stronger. 'I know,' he was saying. 'I know.' And then he pulled Matthias close and held him, fiercely, protectively, even as my brother resisted.

I was trembling then.

The fight went out of him. His body went limp. 'What do I do now?' Matthias's voice was muffled against Hans's shoulder.

Hans pushed my brother back against the packing case and held him there by the collar, as though trying to keep him upright. 'You live,' Hans said, and he lowered his head, finding Matthias's gaze and holding it. 'You find a way to live your life.'

Matthias closed his eyes and Hans let go of him.

My tongue was thick in my mouth, my body numb. I did not understand what I was seeing, did not know, truly, what Hans meant. I was not ready to know, and so I returned to the hatchway, descending the stairs in a fugue.

A nightmare, I told myself. This is a nightmare.

The trestle table in the tween deck was being laid for the midday meal by Elizabeth Volkmann, Henriette's sister. A toddler crawled in the walkway at her feet.

'Elizabeth? Can you hear me?'

She did not look up. Plates laid, she turned and walked in the direction of the kitchens, wiping her hands on her apron.

There was a knife on the table. I picked up the blade, and I held it in my palm across the scar left by the wound that Thea had seen bleed and had healed. I pressed down.

Surely, if I dream, this will be the moment I wake, I thought, hands shaking. Surely, the knife will not hurt me.

I felt the sharp edge in a confusion of senses. I pressed harder; I waited for blood. It came, red, as in life. But as I watched it run a slow rivulet down my wrist and arm, it seemed to issue from my skin in a vapour. It vanished from me like smoke rising from a blown candle.

I lifted the knife from my hand and watched as the wound evaporated.

And then I saw that, though I held the blade, it remained on the table.

There was horror in that.

I placed my hand into a pitcher on the table and felt cool water. I pushed it over. The pitcher rolled and spilled an evanescence of liquid, and when I looked, I saw that the real pitcher remained upright.

You have gone mad, I told myself. This is madness. And I sank to my haunches and pressed my face to my knees. My body shook.

And then the toddler who had been upon the floor crawled through me. I saw her plump hands reach for a dangling blanket, and they moved beyond the boundaries of my skin and I felt nothing but a vague discomfort, a pressing.

I let her crawl through me. I sat on the floor and wept in fear and confusion, and I saw my tears lift in vapour as they dropped from my cheeks. I sat there a long time, crying as people moved around me and through me, finding their places at the trestle table, saying grace and eating. I wept and rocked as they murmured, broke bread, swallowed.

I did not rise again until my tears were done, hanging like a cloud over my head. It was five o'clock. I knew this because hot water was called and there was movement from the berths as people rose to drink their tea. I ran my hands over my face, stumbled to the trestle and sat down, and those I knew from Kay blew on their mugs around me. I looked at their faces and said their names, and no one looked at me, no one responded.

I heard someone mention my mother. They were worried about her, they said. I turned and saw Magdalena rise from the bench, saw Elize Geschke pass her a cup. I followed Magdalena as she made her way to my parents' bunk, hopeful uncertainty filling my stomach. Surely, they would recognise me. Surely, if I spoke their names again and again, they would eventually hear my voice.

Mama was on her side, curled around Hermine, who slept against her stomach, mouth open and cheeks red. My mother's eyes were closed.

'Johanne?' Magdalena peered inside the bunk. 'Johanne, would you like some tea? There is sugar in it.'

Mama stirred, attempted a smile. 'No, thank you. I'm resting now.'

Magdalena perched uneasily on the side of the bed. 'It's been three days. I know you're not drinking enough.'

Mama did not respond.

'I'm not leaving until you drink this tea, Johanne.'

Mama rose onto her elbow then and reached for the tea. She took a small sip and winced.

'Too hot?'

'Very sweet.'

'You need the strength.' Magdalena watched Mama with careful eyes. 'All of it.'

I watched Mama drink, her hand held beneath her chin as the liquid spilled. Hermine's face pulled in waking distress, contorting in the silent beginning of a wail. Mama passed the mug back and lay down again.

'Are you going to feed her?' asked Magdalena, nodding at my sister.

'Give her to that woman from Klemzig.'

'Johanne, you need to feed your daughter. Come, now.' I had never heard Magdalena speak so softly, and I realised that she loved my mother. She was trying to be gentle.

'I will feed her soon. I'm just . . .' Mama placed a hand over her face. 'I'm just so tired.'

'Shall I get Heinrich?'

'No, no. He's with the captain. Trying to sort out all this arguing. All this . . .' She waved her fingers in the air. 'This trouble with the doctor.'

I stepped closer. 'Mama? Can you hear me?' My voice sounded small.

Hermine was crying loudly now. People were turning from the trestle to look. I saw them glance at one another.

'Well, then,' Magdalena said, and she set the mug on the floor and picked up my sister. I moved out of the way as she stood, hoisting Hermine on her hip. 'There now, little one. We'll get you fed.'

'Thank you.' Mama spoke from under her hand.

'Rest, then,' said Magdalena. 'If that is what you need. Sleep some. God be with you.'

Hermine's wailing tapered off as Magdalena bustled down the rows of berths and passed her to a ruddy-faced young woman with light-brown hair. I did not recognise her. The woman looked surprised and then, as Magdalena gestured in Mama's direction, sympathetic.

She untied her blouse and set Hermine to her breast. I could see her own baby's chubby leg hanging over the edge of her berth in sleep.

'Mama?' I sat down where Magdalena had been and placed a hand on my mother's shoulder. I could feel her body lift and fall in breath. 'Mama. I'm here. It's Hanne.'

She did not respond.

'Mama?' My voice strained. 'Please. I'm here, Mama. Look at me!' She did not move. I was as air to her.

Anguish made my mind roil so that I could not grasp any single thought, could not think clearly. I returned to the bow. I did not know where else to go.

Anna Maria was asleep in Ottilie's bunk, knees folded into her stomach, mouth open in exhaustion. I climbed in with Thea and eased myself under the blankets.

She stirred, lips moving. 'Stay.'

I sat up, not trusting that I had heard her speak. 'Thea? Are you awake?'

Her eyes were closed.

'What did you say?' I asked.

'Stay.'

Relief lifted in me. I did not imagine it. She knew I was there. 'Thea,' I whispered. 'Thea, Thea!' I drew close to her and remained still, until all I could hear was her heart. I stayed there until I could feel the vibration of that dark pump in my chest, until I could imagine that her heartbeat was my own, and then I kissed her forehead. I did not care who might see me; I kissed her for my own comfort. To keep my own fear at bay.

I remained by Thea's side for the next three days, waiting for her to speak to me again in her sleep. But she did nothing to show she felt me there, and I worried that I had imagined her voice. Anna Maria came every morning and night and wafted burning juniper over her daughter, and each time she studied the corner of the berth as I moved my hands through the smoke, trying to make it curl around my fingers.

'Anna Maria,' I whispered. 'It's Hanne.'

But she did not speak to me, only waved the juniper in my direction with an uncertain look.

I kept waiting to wake from my exile. I kept waiting for Thea to wake. I resumed life as I had lived it before my sickness, and for the next week I followed the grooves worn down by my earlier self and did as I had always done, ignoring all that was strange because to face it would have been unbearable. I was not ready to ask myself why everything had changed. When the other women in the bow woke and prepared themselves for morning services, I followed them above deck and joined my voice to the prayers. I sat down to breakfast and served myself when no one else served me, and although I could see the gruel at the end of my spoon it was like eating shadow. I tasted nothing. I washed my face and braided my hair and tidied my person. I did not know how else to behave; I did not know how else to be. I prayed all the time; my knees became bruised with supplication.

I distracted myself by watching over Thea. I willed her better. I left Anna Maria to bathe her and dribble liquid in the corners of her mouth, but every night I held her as she slept. I kept her in constant sight, in constant thought, and convinced myself that I was healing her through will and prayer alone. Thea slept the body of each hour, but with each passing day the fever weakened. The strength returned to her limbs. She started to make hoarse requests of her mother.

Water.

Always water.

I listened to Anna Maria tell news of the ship to her sleeping daughter. There were daily quarrels about the food, about too much being prepared, or too little. A wind had blown a fine reddish dust across the ship and it had stained the sails brown. The dust was from the deserts of east Africa. Friedrich had gathered some from a pile that had collected at the base of the hatches. Here – here was a vial full of it.

I watched the Wend turn it in her hands. I was lying next to Thea, sharing her pillow.

'Show me.'

I turned. Thea's eyes were open. She was looking at her mother.

Anna Maria startled. 'Thea?'

'Can I see it?'

My heart soared. I lifted myself onto my elbow, leaned over her. Please see me, I thought. Please. *Please.* I know you, of all people, see me.

'How do you feel?' Her mother was fighting tears.

Thea attempted a smile. 'Better. Can I see it?'

Anna Maria closed her eyes, bending her head low until her face was hidden from sight. Her headdress shook.

'Mama?'

'Praise God. Praise God.' Anna Maria's mouth broke open in a wide smile. 'Here! Here you are, you curious girl. He knew you would want to see it. Oh Lord, I thank you.' She helped Thea sit up against her pillow, then, eyes filled with tears, passed her the glass bottle.

I watched Thea turn it over in her hands. 'I'm here too,' I whispered. I was afraid to touch her. I was afraid she would not feel me.

'When was this?' Thea asked her mother. 'When did the desert come?'

'Shortly before we crossed the equator.'

'The equator?'

Anna Maria wiped her eyes and described how Christian Pasche had complained to the captain when the sailors had conducted their Neptune Ceremony, throwing water on all who had not passed into the Southern Hemisphere before. 'He was adamant that they were startling the pregnant women,' Thea's mother told her, laughing. 'Never mind that the women in question were having a lovely time up on deck, throwing buckets as well as the sailors and appreciating such a cooldown!'

'Was Hanne there?'

I was trembling. Sea water rose in my throat.

Anna Maria's smile faded. 'Thea, you remember . . . Hanne was sick,' she said carefully.

No, I thought. No, no.

'She's better,' Thea said, frowning. 'She was here.'

'Here?'

'I saw her. In the night. She was here, lying next to me.'

Anna Maria said nothing. Her brow furrowed.

I felt water soak my braid. It ran in rivulets down my back.

'Thea . . .' Anna Maria stood up from where she had been squatting on her heels. Sat down on the bed next to her daughter.

The hem of my dress lifted, as though suspended in water. I felt weightless, gutted with cold.

Thea shook her head. 'No.'

'Hanne did not get better.' Anna Maria's voice was sombre.

'No.'

'She died in Christ.'

The ocean was thundering in my ears. I could not hear Thea. Water was filling the bow, lifting me off the floor. I saw Thea's face warp in grief, saw the bottle roll off the bed, saw her throw off her mother's hands, but I could not hear what she was saying. My gullet swamped with brine. I lifted my hands to my face and felt the sailor's stitch in my nose.

The water rose to the lamp. The flame went out in foam. Darkness roared around me.

I am dead, I thought.

I am dead.

tell all my bones

The time that followed remains blurred with pain. At some point I kneeled on the floor to pray. I prayed my tongue sore, seeking answers and illumination. If it was true that I had passed out of life, then why did I remain on the boat?

The connective tissue binding the bones of my life – my family, my work, the seasons I grew through – had always been God. Bible as cartilage. Prayer as sinew. I had never doubted that my father spoke truth when he told me that I had been redeemed by Christ's love. Death would bring eternal life in the Lord's Kingdom. In the beginning there was the Word of God and I had never doubted that Word. It was sacrosanct. It had assured me that death would separate my eternal soul from my mortal body until the final day of their reunion; that, if I died in faith, my soul would find sanctuary within the presence of Christ.

Why was I not in such a sanctuary? I had died in faith. I knew nothing but faith. I had never doubted, never sought to untether myself from the Church, never sought the possibility of otherness, other truths.

Again and again my thoughts returned to the vision I had seen against the brilliance of the sun, the holy flight of feathers. Had I been judged and found wanting? I felt again the old fear that I was ill-made, that my deepest self was unworthy. The thought that Jesus's grace had not extended to me, had not covered me at the last as the Word had promised, reduced me to a howl. I prayed for forgiveness. If I could have scraped together assurance of my redemption, I would have done so until my fingers were bloody.

And yet, and yet. Where was the hell promised by Pastor Flügel? If I had been damned, why was I still with those I loved, those I knew to be sanctified by Jesus's blood?

I am unloved and forsaken by God, I thought. I lay on the floor, my cheek hard up against the grit of the boards, sensible only to the wrenching of my soul. Hours passed. Maybe days. I took to prayer again, grasped for God in my desperation. The Psalm of the Cross swept through me, and I heard myself whisper, 'I am poured out like water, and all my bones are out of joint: my heart is like wax . . . I am poured out like water . . .' before the world blurred about me and I was shuddered into darkness.

Dying is unlike living. The smooth running of time is for the beating heart only. The dead stutter. The hands on my clock do not point to numbers but to each other. There have been times since I died that I have suddenly woken as if from a faint and found myself in strange places. I am present, and then something overcomes me and when I regain my consciousness I am elsewhere. So it was, then, as I lay on the floor of a ship that no longer bore my living weight, no longer able to pretend I was anything other than dead. I collapsed out of myself. Time stopped and I stopped with it.

I was raised with the kind of faith that does not doubt. God had been as much a part of me as my own marrow, and when I discovered my bones to be empty, fluting music discordant to anything I had sung in church, my anguish was real. No wonder I could not keep mind and body together in those early days. I was dislocated. My axis was broken.

The understanding I have now, that the world spins on a deeper mystery than anything that might be set into language, was not with me then. Now I know that my mind is too small to hold the spirit. The spirit, I hope, holds me.

I woke later, when it was dark. I was curled on the floor by Thea's bed, body shifting as the ship rolled in steady rhythm. There was the sound of sleeping women around me. A light snore.

Scripture was crawling through my mind, muddled into poetry.

Many sparrows. I may tell all my bones. Be not far from me; for trouble is near and surely goodness and mercy shall follow me. Surely goodness and mercy. Remember, O Lord, thy tender mercies and thy lovingkindnesses. Turn thee unto me and many sparrows.

I rose to my feet and stood beside Thea's bunk. There was enough light to see that Anna Maria was in bed with her, had an arm around her. They were both asleep. Both were still. But I could feel Thea's distress coming off her like mist. I knew that if I touched her face I would find it swollen. Knew that, if the light were brighter, I would see something damaged in it. Fallen tree. Twisted branch.

'Tender mercies,' I whispered, and I brought my hand down until it hovered above her face. I felt the air warmed with her body, its close aura of life. 'Lovingkindnesses,' I said.

I had a sudden, animal panic to be free from my clothes. I undid my apron and undressed quickly, shrugging off my skirt and kicking it under Thea's bed. The relief of standing only in my underwear was immediate. Mutter had long advised us to sleep in our clothes on account of the lack of privacy on board as well as the frequent need to rise in the night if the weather was bad, and I had forgotten how good it felt to remove the weight of wool and cotton and allow my body its full ease of movement. And then, partly because I felt numb with grief and no longer cared, and partly because I was curious, I removed my shift and stared down at my naked body.

It seemed exactly as it had been in life. My hands and arms were still browned from sun, my stomach and chest were milk. Long legs, small breasts, the freckle above my belly button remained. My feet were still hardened from that last spring in Kay; I sat down and examined my heels, thick and callused. But when I raised my arm to my face and tried to breathe in my skin, I smelled nothing but a slight brine, a suggestion of sea. I licked my palm, ran the tip of my tongue along my lifeline. Nothing. I tasted of nothing.

What has changed? I wondered. Will I still burn? Will I freckle in summer and pale in winter? If I am dead and my body gone, will this self I am looking down on, this false embodiment of life, slowly corrupt as my bones turn on the sea floor? Will it remain as old as I am, or had been – almost seventeen summers?

Seventeen summers.

My life was only ever a hand's breadth. Only ever an inhalation.

I needed to see Matthias again, needed to make sure that I was dead to him, too. It seemed an impossibility that we were divided. For the first time in my life, I did not care about minding the rules that had governed me before and had kept us separated. Mutter Scheck had no sway over me anymore. I had spent days in careful imitation of my life since my funeral, and for what? The praise and approval of people who believed me dead?

Nothing matters anymore, I thought.

*

It was a clear night and the sky was loud with stars. The perfect chaos of light amidst the deep and purple night was so extraordinary that I was suddenly lifted above my grief and held by wonder. The sea was flat and it mirrored the sky's glory, bringing the lights down to the horizon so that it seemed the ship was suspended in stars. It sailed through the night air and not ocean at all. Harmonies of light and water.

Tender mercies.

Stepping quietly over sleeping bodies, I found Matthias lying next to Hans and the Simmels, their beds not much more than a pile of blankets amongst the supplies and barrels roped for the final months of the journey. My brother looked beautiful.

I lay down behind him and breathed on his neck. I counted the freckles upon the ridge of his ear and rubbed my face into his hair.

'Matthias, it's Hanne. Your sister.'

He did not stir.

I pinched his upper arm. 'Wake up.'

He felt nothing of me. He heard nothing of me.

It is true then, I thought, and I remembered Matthias thumping his heart with his fist between the packing cases. Water rose at the back of my teeth, but I swallowed it down. I wanted to guard him. I wanted to be soothed.

Matthias smelled good. He smelled familiar. I wrapped my arms around his broad back and breathed him in so that the calm of his closeness surrounded me.

We were together at the beginning of life, I thought. You have known me before I took breath. We shared our mother's pulse.

The night rested its cheek against us and my pain was eased by its peace. No one would discover me sleeping by his side. So many nights I had lain awake in Kay, wishing I might be beside Matthias as we had been in the womb. His absence had unjointed me, had plagued me with wakefulness. If death meant I might finally return to his side, then I would do so. There was no one to forbid me from doing as I liked.

I lay beside Matthias all night, watching the world's slow turning until the stars died in the sea and dawn rose flaming in the east, a bonfire sucking air from sky. The men began to stir as soon as the sun shouldered the horizon, sleeping forms rousing into unkempt beards and coughs and yawning arms. Daniel Simmel rose and stumbled to the edge of the ship to relieve himself, arching his back as an arc of piss flew downwind. He returned to the group behind the barrels, stepping on Hans Pasche's fingers. Hans sat up, tousle-headed, and shot Daniel a dirty look.

'Sorry.' Daniel waved a hand at him in apology. 'Here, toss me my cup, would you?'

Hans flung the mug at his face. I noticed that something had changed in him since our days in Kay. His skin was a deep golden brown, pale lines around his eyes showing days of squint and sun above deck. His hair, too, had yellowed, and he had started to grow a beard, which was patchy and ruddy, and gave him a roguish, off-centred look. I realised that there was nothing of his father about him. None of Elder Pasche's fastidiousness, his gaunt furrows of criticism. Looking at him, watching as he reached into his blankets and gently removed a small black kitten, its tail tipped in white, I realised I had never stopped to think how lonely Hans might have been, raised by a father so caustic in temperament.

Daniel returned, draining his cup. 'Another night with the missus?'

'She keeps me warm.' Hans brought the kitten up to his chest, nuzzled it with his chin.

'Up now, Matthias.' Daniel nudged my brother with his foot, the toe of his boot passing through my body. I felt sick at the strangeness of it.

Matthias grunted and buried his head in his elbow.

'Are you going to take her with you?' asked Daniel.

Hans unfolded a handkerchief and fed the kitten with bacon fat. He smiled as the cat licked grease from his fingertip. 'She belongs to the ship.'

Matthias lifted his head. 'Looks like she belongs to you.'

'Animals always like to be fed.'

'Give us a hold?'

As Matthias sat up and reached for her, her tiny body went rigid with fear. Her eyes grazed over me. My stomach lurched. The cat opened her mouth, needle-teeth bared, and hissed.

'What did you do to her?' Hans asked.

'Nothing!' Matthias exclaimed. 'I haven't touched her.'

She sees me, I thought. She knows I am here. I leaned towards the kitten, staring her full in the face. She did not take her eyes off me. I extended a hand and the creature suddenly spat and fought her way out of Hans's grip by scrambling up and over his neck.

'Ow!' Hans winced. 'Hey, what's the matter?'

She leaped onto the deck and bolted away. Little spots of blood beaded on Hans's neck where the kitten had clawed her way to freedom.

'Guess it didn't like the look of you.' Daniel grinned, taking out his pipe.

Matthias's face fell. 'I guess not,' he said.

Within the hour passengers emerged from tween decks for morning services, but for the first time in my life I did not join in the prayers and singing. I sat away from the congregation as they kneeled, rose again, kneeled once more. If they were devotion's tide, I was rock. I was unmoved. Each assurance of grace felt like a lie.

After prayers my brother wandered to the side of the ship and spent some time staring into the water alone. My heart swelled with affection for him. I wanted to ask him what he was looking for. Was he thinking of me, of my body now absorbed by the ocean? I was unsure how much time had passed since I had died.

Hans approached starboard and joined my brother at the gunwale. He leaned out as far as he was able, lifting his arms wide.

'Do you ever wonder how deep it is?' he asked, eyes staring down, as though he planned to dive.

'Three foot,' murmured Matthias.

Hans snickered.

'Did you find her?' my brother asked.

'Who?'

'The kitten.'

'Not yet. But I will.' He gestured behind him. 'It's not like she has any place to go.'

They both looked back down to where the hull cut through the filmy water. There were dolphins racing alongside the ship, sleek and twisting below the surface.

'Did I ever tell you about when my mother died?' Hans said.

Matthias shook his head. 'No. I don't think I even know what she died of.'

'A weak heart. I was eight.'

'I remember her funeral.' Matthias glanced up. 'It must have been hard for you.'

Hans nodded. 'She had a shirt. This blouse. I remember her holding me when I was a boy. I used to rub the material of it between my fingers. I still think about it all the time.'

Matthias glanced across at him. 'Her shirt?'

'Her holding me.'

They lapsed into silence. I watched as they gazed out at the horizon beyond the greasy, shifting water. Clouds had appeared, banking steadily darker.

'It doesn't go away. The grief,' Hans said eventually. He cleared his throat. 'I liked Hanne a lot. I liked that she was different.'

My brother said nothing. I heard him swallow.

'Different in a good way, I mean. She was fast as a kid, wasn't she? Beat me every time.'

Matthias smiled. 'Everyone beat you.'

Hans reached out and cuffed him on the ear.

'What? It's true.'

'I know.'

They watched the dolphins for a while.

'How do you bear it?' Matthias's voice was quiet. 'The grief, I mean. If it doesn't go away.'

Hans considered this. 'I make room for it somehow.'

'Sometimes I think it will kill me,' Matthias said, and I saw then, in the way his chin trembled, that he had taken my death into himself, that he carried it in his gut.

'I know what that feels like,' replied Hans.

'I don't understand how God could let it happen.' Matthias cleared his throat. 'It's not right.'

Hans squinted up at Matthias. 'No. No, it's not.'

'Do you ever see her?'

'Hanne?'

'Your mother. Do you ever see her? Sitting on your bed. There when you wake up, or before you fall asleep.'

Hans leaned over the gunwale. 'I dream about her sometimes.'

'But does she ever appear to you?'

Hans shook his head. 'You see Hanne?'

Matthias hesitated, his mouth contorting, as though he were trying not to cry. 'No.' He turned back to the sea. 'Gottlob, sometimes.' He breathed in deeply through his nose. 'Out of the corner of my eye.'

Hans nodded. 'I wish my mother did appear to me. I hope she does one day.'

They pulled away from the gunwale and watched Daniel Simmel cut his brother's hair. Rudolph was laughing and pulling a face as the scissors ran close, running his hand across his shorn neck. I leaned down and picked up a tuft of clipped hair, rubbed it between my fingers. Smelled sweat and maleness. Locks of hair drifted along the boards. I raised a hand to my own head, felt the tight coil of my own braids.

'Hey, boys, stop!' A sailor approached them, face dark. He grabbed the scissors in Daniel's hand and pointed out to the horizon where the clouds were amassing. 'You're bringing on bad luck,' the sailor said, and he threw the scissors on the deck.

There was a brief flash in the sky and, as if in reply, the wind stirred. There were rapid movements from the sailors, furling sails.

I ran my fingers through my hair and turned it loose, and there was satisfaction in its weight upon my shoulders, in the way the gathering wind pulled it.

The passengers stood breathing in the cool change. Thunder rumbled. The sailors directed the women below deck, and Daniel pocketed his scissors, face red, as his brother's cut locks flew across the boards and out to sea.

The wind was strong now. It blew my hair across my face. I felt it like a feeding fire. The women obediently retreated to the dark interior of the ship with the elders, while the single men began to assist the sailors and haul their belongings down the hatchway. I waited.

The sky closed in upon the sea.

The storm approached.

The wind wanted to drag me into a dance. To be touched like that!

The feel of the natural world running its hands over me, all violent invitation, was a wild pleasure. The ocean rose. My skin smacked with water lifted from the cresting waves, and I suddenly felt loose and angry and desirous. As the wind pulled my head up into the closed fist of sky, I understood that I need not hide from it. I was free to do as I liked. Unanchored from life, I could be unmoored from fear of its loss.

And so I stayed.

I remember laughing throughout the storm. I was open-mouthed. I climbed the rigging and clung to it like a spider and felt the spume dash across my teeth, felt my hair whip about my skull as if the wind would have me scalped. It could not touch me. The water could not drown me. I swallowed it down. I remember the cold upon my skin, the laceration of salt. The ship groaned, boards creaking, and I imagined passengers below, hands gripping the planks between their bunks, rolling with the waves, praying for safety.

I shook the rigging and curled my toes about the rope and sang to the storm.

'Praise God,' I screamed, 'for He has a wild heart and I am in His image! Praise God, for his angels are birds and their trumpets are filled with fish! Praise God for the wind that blows the skies apart!'

I am done with my dying. I remember thinking that, as the storm filled my lungs. I am done with my dying.

I woke sticky with salt. My cheek pressed against the rope, my hands and feet knotted in the rigging. Undrowned, skin raw only with the cold.

I climbed down and sat in the sun, revelling in my curling hair, its tangles down my back. I felt wayward and mutinous. Around me sailors were busy. I paid them no attention. My whole body thrummed. My eyes stung from the rain and sea water that had harassed them, my skin prickled, and my hands ached from where I had clung to the rope. I did not feel invisible. I felt as though I had fought something and won. As though I had wrestled out a blessing.

I did not braid my hair again that day, but let it remain loose and salt-filled. It was the first stirring of my resistance. I remained in my shift, too, even as I returned below deck. What need of modesty had I, who was seen by no one? I felt ungoverned for the first time in my life.

In the bow, I found Anna Maria and Friedrich telling Thea about my funeral: what hymns were sung, the prayers offered, the sunshine of the morning. Anna Maria told her that services were not the same without my voice. That my family was being strong and making the best of things. Friedrich offered a prayer of such deeply felt gratitude that I shuddered to hear it. I watched him press his fingers together to stop them from shaking as He praised God for keeping their only child with them, as he extolled the Lord with gulping breaths for the great blessing of her recovery.

I sat by Thea's side as she watched him pray. She was dry-eyed, mouth twisting as though she wanted to interrupt him. When he finished, his amen falling from his mouth like a shrugged-off weight, he reached for Thea's hands and held them to his forehead.

'But Hanne did not recover,' Thea said. Her voice was a snapped twig. 'Hanne has not been kept.'

Friedrich looked up, eyes red-rimmed. 'No,' he replied softly. 'The Lord has taken her to be with Him.'

'How can you be sure?' Thea said.

'She died in faith.'

'How can you be sure she has gone at all?'

I rested my head against Thea's.

'What do you mean?' her father asked.

Thea opened her mouth, then closed it again. I noticed Anna Maria frown.

'I saw them tip her body into the sea, Thea,' Friedrich said. 'Let's pray for her.'

I did not want to hear any prayers for the keeping of my soul, not even from Thea's lips. I climbed out past Friedrich and went into the main quarters. Many of the passengers were trying to sop up the water that had fallen below during the storm, wringing out rags in buckets and hanging sodden clothes to dry on lines strung between the useless upper bunks. I ducked under dripping breeches and blouses and found Mama lying in her berth, Hermine propped up between her legs.

'Hello, Mama,' I said. I sat by her side. Touched her beautiful dark hair.

She closed her eyes.

Her stillness frightened me.

'Buh.' Hermine stared at me.

I shifted to the side. Her pupils followed. 'Hermine?'

My sister smiled and shoved her fingers in her mouth, drooling.

I touched her cheek. She swatted me away, then toppled sideways, head colliding with the post. Mama sprang up as Hermine opened her mouth to cry.

'Shall I take her?' Elize Geschke pulled aside the cloth between the berths as Hermine began to bawl in earnest. 'We'll go for a little walk.' She hoisted Hermine up over the dividing plank and sat my sister on her lap. 'Look, Hermine! What is this? A biscuit! Reinhardt, show her the little poppet you made.'

The cloth dropped back down and Mama sank onto the mattress.

'Go to sleep, Mama,' I said. 'I'll watch over you.'

I stroked my mother's hair until she fell asleep that afternoon. I hoped she might feel something tender, even if she could not know its source. Mama had held me at my moment of birth and at my hour of suffering, and I understood that there was a part of my mother that still lay in the soil of Kay, and that now a part of her would remain in the ocean.

'She is with God,' Papa said to Mama later, deep in the night. I saw Mama's dark eyes staring at the ruined upper berth, lips pressing together over and over.

'Johanne?'

'Mm?'

'She is dwelling now in that place where there is no more pain or sorrow, and she shall be the Lord's handmaiden and under His protection.'

'Tell me that is true, Heinrich.'

'It is true.'

'Tell me she is with God.'

'She dwells in glory. She is at rest.'

My mother murmured assent.

The knowledge that my father spoke a lie and was so believing of his own falsehood tore at something deep within my heart. I was not with God. I was with them. Part of me hoped that Papa's canted eye would light upon me and see my form as a contour in the air. A shifting of space. I followed him as he hauled nightsoil to the upper deck, and when he stood at the ship's rail, empty bucket at his feet, looking up at the churning masses of clouds, I threw my arms around his middle. He gave no sign he sensed me there.

'Papa?'

I reached up to angle his eye to my face. I could feel his beard under my palms, could feel his jaw working. There was his blind eye, the glisten between eyelid and lash. Part of me wondered if I might see my own image reflected in this pupil, angel-blessed, seer of Heaven and all unearthly things.

'Look at me. Notice me.' I waited for recognition, and when none came I wondered if his ruined eye truly did see Heaven, and what he had thought when I failed to appear in that holy orchard after my death. Had he lied to my mother about my inhabiting it? Or had he always lied to me?

His holy eye is simply afflicted, I realised, as he stepped through me and moved off towards the hatchway with the empty bucket. He sees nothing but the desires of his own mind.

I never saw Mama cry for me. She had not cried over Gottlob either, and I had thought then that her lack of tears spoke to a ruthless stoicism. I had resented that strength and thought her heart hard. But as I watched her quietly drag herself through the hours, I saw that my mother was possessed by loss. Her blood wailed with it. Her milk dried up and the young, red-cheeked woman from Klemzig became Hermine's wet nurse.

Mama understood me to be gone from her and, in her suffering, I saw evidence of such love. I was awed by its enormity. She had loved me my whole life and she loved me still, but she had no place to put that love and she suffered under its weight.

If only I had known this in my living years.

such a thing happened

The storm shifted something within me. It was an untethering. If my first christening had, with still and sanctified water, welcomed me into the light of the Lord, the ocean that night admitted me into His shadow. I was the baptised dead. If my brief and wondrous life was gone from me, and if all I had now was the freedom to go where I pleased, to watch whom I wanted, then I would do so.

Days passed and I grew wilder with each one. Unbound from the religion of my father, I lived by my own nature. I explored the ship as I would never have been able to in life. I watched Christian and Rosina complain in whispers and remove food from each other's teeth. I noticed Emile Pfeiffer give her daughter the better bread and Beate Fröhlich weep in private at the lice. I examined the long, white sideburns of Samuel Radtke's father, placed my fingertip inside one of Eleonore Volkmann's mammoth nostrils and overheard sailors' vulgarities, which I repeated to myself in delight. Most days I climbed the rigging. Wind in my hair, I gave names to the water. I introduced myself to the sky.

I watched the other women slowly, kindly, distract Mama with requests and chores, pulling her upright with appeals for an extra pair of hands to brush the mould off the biscuits, to advise on the best way to cool a child's heat rash, to suggest an appropriate blessing for commemorative embroidery. 'Best to brush downwind. Don't scratch at it – a damp cloth will soothe. "God's Grace to your green wedding; Go joyfully towards the silver one!'" She ate more. She snickered at Eleonore Volkmann's wry observation that the doctor was playing '*die beleidigte Leberwurst*' – 'the insulted sausage' – and she struck up a curious friendship with the young woman who now nursed Hermine. Her name was Augusta and she had been born in Klemzig only a few years before I came into the world. Her husband, a man called Karl, ten years older, had suffered rather badly throughout the journey from scurvy and had lost a lot of weight, and, to Magdalena's disapproval, I saw Mama bring Anna Maria to his berth to treat his bleeding gums. Hermine found a playmate in their chubby son, Wilhelm, both babies sitting on the floor mouthing things they found discarded under the bunks.

Papa approved of Mama's new friendship. I guessed that he felt relieved his wife had resumed something of her old self. He was now free to resume his duties as elder and representative. I watched a keener edge of religious fervour emerge in my father as he took his place as leader of the people. He gave himself further to God and summoned Him into every decision, from how best to divide bacon to whether to complain to the captain about the water barrels, which were now only good for tea and coffee. It was difficult for people to argue with him when every choice was staked to gospel, and so passengers complied and the small fires of argument between decks were largely extinguished. It helped that Papa put himself last in many ways; he did not eat the bigger portion, and he offered his hands to the dirtiest work. If he had held the esteem of his countrymen in Kay, on the ship my father was respected to the point of veneration. He reminded everyone that the journey would end in such freedom and prosperity as they have never known before, and I sensed a growing excitement spread throughout the congregation with each new day.

It was painful to see my parents mourning me, but it was harder still to see them begin to accommodate that grief and find a place for it within their lives. Their faith assured them that I was in a place of peace, and their certainty of this made my death even more catastrophic to myself. Regret and anger sometimes wormed through me so relentlessly that when Mama and Papa spoke of inanities – the vile rations of salt herring, the sunburn of Gottfried Volkmann – I wanted to rip the boards from the floor. Some days I crawled into any free berth, covered my face and let time make a puddle of me. How much I had taken for granted! I had been so stupid to assume I had years ahead of me, even after seeing Gottlob's own life pinched out. My parents' belief that my death was the will of God broke my heart.

Thea spent most of her time sitting on her berth, ignoring the other girls as they sewed – determinedly, endlessly – for their dowry boxes, flipping through her father's Bible without seeming to read a word. I watched Anna Maria labour in the kitchens, cursing the clay mortar that had begun to break up around the copper pans, trying to conjure something that might tempt her daughter's appetite. Barley with beef. Rice cooked with sugar. Thea raked her spoon through the food and absently licked it clean, but inevitably her meals were left to grow cold.

Mutter Scheck had less patience for Thea's listlessness. She encouraged her to rise from bed and take exercise about the bow, and when she refused, Mutter Scheck seemed at a loss as to what to do next. She was not used to disobedience. One day she flung a shawl on Thea's bed and stood next to it, hands on hips. '*Gott lässt uns wohl sinken, aber nicht ertrinken.* God lets us sink, but not drown. Still, I'm sure He'd appreciate it if you made an effort to swim.'

Thea looked up at her, face expressionless. 'I don't know what you mean.'

'I've heard a whale was seen from deck this morning. You should go. Some fresh air will do you good.'

'I'm quite tired.'

'It need not be long,' Mutter said. She grabbed Henriette by the shoulder as she passed by. 'You too. Go on. Take Thea upstairs and have a little sightsee.'

Henriette showed her the bedsheet she carried. 'I've nearly finished this.'

'Take it up with you.'

Henriette hesitated, looking askance at Thea.

'Really, Mutter Scheck, I would rather stay here,' Thea said.

'No. You're as sallow as anything. Go on. You too, Henriette.' Mutter Scheck picked up the shawl and wrapped it around Thea's shoulders.

I followed Thea and Henriette up the hatchway, blood swelling again in memory of the whale's song that had kept me company in my last moment. I wanted to see the whale. I wanted to sing with it, and for Thea to hear my voice echo its siren song.

The day was grey-mouthed, wide with high cloud. Thea and Henriette stood about in the chill wind for a few minutes, looking out to sea, before a sailor, guessing at what they were after, told them the whale had not been sighted for several hours.

'Should we go back down?' Henriette asked Thea. 'It's cold.'

Thea turned to the ocean. It was dark and choppy, the surface crowded with gulls that swooped and alighted between the waves. 'Don't let me keep you.'

'What was that? Noisy things, aren't they?' Henriette murmured. She glanced at the embroidery in her hand. 'I might just sit and do a little more,' she said, settling herself against a barrel out of the wind. 'The light is better. Oh, you can see all my mistakes.'

Thea pulled the shawl closer about her neck and left Henriette sucking her teeth over the bedsheet. I followed her to the gunwale. Her face was sprung with bones I had never noticed before, edges she did not used to have. She looked older. At the same time, I was reminded again of the beauty I had always seen in her, the way it lay in the hidden details of her body. The small lines in her lips and the sudden, thrilling sharpness of her teeth when she smiled, and the white-lightness of her eyelashes that gave her an ethereality, a startling difference. So much of her beauty, I realised, is adulteration. I watched her as she looked at the circling birds, a small smile emerging at the corner of her lips as they suddenly dived and emerged, all wing-flap and outrage, fighting over some fishy prize. I felt hungry for her imperfections. I lifted my hand and placed a fingertip on the scar under her ear, traced it with my nail.

A plume of water suddenly burst through the surface of the sea. As others exclaimed and came running to port, Thea leaned out over the side of the ship, eyes gleaming. I leaned out with her. I could hear an upswell of music, a keening, louder than anything I had heard in life. I felt my body tremble with it, the pleasure of it.

A whale swam in clear view. Another gust of water erupted from its blowhole as it briefly rose to the surface.

'Henriette,' Thea said, eyes not leaving the cutting water, 'Henriette, come and see.'

'I saw.' Henriette got to her feet and backed away a little.

Thea turned. 'You can't see it from there.'

'Do you think it might upset the ship?'

'No.'

Henriette stepped forwards and peered out to the ocean, eyebrows lowered.

'Here, stand where I am. Can you see it?'

'It's so big.'

Thea grinned at her and jealousy spiked through me. Water from the whale had blown over the ship: a fine mist hung in her hair and her face was damp and beautiful. 'Isn't it wonderful?'

'I don't like to see them so close.' Henriette returned to her sewing.

I noticed Thea's face fall, just a little, and there was satisfaction in that. I knew that she was thinking of me, that I would have loved the whale too. And so I stayed beside her and told her that I was with her, that the whale was all song, weightless mass and gentle power. Its music reverberated through my blood.

The humpback remained within sight of the *Kristi* all morning. Henriette dropped her needle, losing it between the boards, and soon tired. She tried to convince Thea to return downstairs and then, annoyed, left without her. Thea hardly noticed. She stood watching the whale breach again and again, the sight of it filling her like air, like colour.

I leaned into Thea's side. 'This is a blessing.' When she smiled, I pretended it was in answer to my voice, and then I saw her hand reach into her skirt pocket and pull out the pillow overcover I had left unfinished. I had not known she'd been carrying it with her.

Thea ran her hands over the cloth until she found my completed initial amongst the white. She traced the stitches of it with a fingertip, and I tried to remember what it had been like to be touched by her, the pressure of her hands. It seemed miraculous that they had ever held my own.

Such a thing happened to me, I thought. Those hands hold a memory of me.

Thea quickly, furtively brought the initial to her lips and kissed it, and then, leaning over the side of the gunwale, dangled the cloth as though to cast it into the sea.

She waited. The whale breached again, tail slapping the water. I watched the embroidery flap as the wind tried to snatch it from her fingers. Still, Thea did not let go. She began to cry. She cried in a way I had never seen, all at once, as though she could not breathe, as though she was being pulled apart. She brought the whitework back over the side and pressed it to her face, clinging to my initial as though it were a buoy that might keep her afloat.

The whale lifted to the surface. Joyful cluster of barnacle. Steadying. Full of grace.

After the whale, Thea spent more and more time above deck. The sea air swept an appetite back into her stomach, and the roundness returned to her face. Still, I felt compelled to keep watch over Thea in the shifting hours. Every night I sprawled my limbs next to her body until I felt her rest in sleep. Her breathing seemed to fall in harmony with the creaking of the ship, until it seemed as though the boat were lifting and falling by her lungs alone. At dawn, too, I made sure I was by her side so that I was there as she woke. I listened to the sound of her voice as she prayed, her lips puckering over God's name.

It was only in the hours when the lamps were out and Thea's breathing steady, her limbs heavy against my own, that I left her to find my brother above deck.

It was a rare and curious thing to suddenly be able to listen to the conversations of men. As soon as Gottlob died, Matthias had been pulled into the fields and I had been swept into the house. Men were for the outside world of tillage and labour and politics and society, and women were for *Kinder, Küche und Kirche*. Women stood to one side at church, men at the other. I knew as well as any farmer's child what occurred between animals. I knew what was done in order to beget stock and I knew what Gottfried Fröhlich meant when he complained about Samuel Radtke's bull being a 'dry blower'. I also knew that this act was the preserve of marriage, and that the separation of the unmarried was to ensure this remained so.

All of this had made me apprehensive about men. I imagined that they were a little dangerous and, while I could not reconcile this with Matthias, or with Hans, it was partly a desire to see if this was true that kept me coming above deck to sleep amongst them. Fear that I might be found out did not dissipate for weeks. I imagined Mutter Scheck appearing, red-faced and breathless, her little glasses fogged with fear at finding me in their company. I expected alarming discoveries: low language and lower behaviour.

In truth, I warmed to the men above deck in a way I had not expected. Rudolph lay awake each night examining the sky for shooting stars, smoking his brother's pipe and noting the altered constellations in a notebook with a pencil stub. Hans tried endlessly to coax the kitten to his side, leaving little trails of meat and rubbing her skinny belly until she purred herself into sleep. If Matthias ever wept at night, Hans would wake and start wondering aloud about the life that awaited them in the colony. I believed he hoped to distract my brother from his grief, to give him something to look forwards to.

As Maria and the Johannes, Christiana and Henriette had spoken endlessly about weddings and the life that marriage would bring ('nine children,' Christiana had said, 'if God would so bless me'), so Matthias and Hans began to fill their nights talking about rain and soil and when they might strike out on their own. Sometimes they lay awake until the early hours of morning, imagining themselves men of independent means.

'I would like a large farm,' Matthias said one night. 'My own farm.'

'At least you will inherit your father's,' Hans replied. 'Hermann will get Papa's land if Rosina has no sons.'

Matthias shook his head. 'I can't wait that long. I want to work for myself. I want to be the man of my own house. To do things my own way.'

'Then you shall have to marry a widow, perhaps.'

Matthias pulled a face and Hans laughed. 'What? There is no shame in a marriage of convenience.'

'What about you?' my brother asked. 'Will you marry for land?'

Hans was silent. I had expected a smirk or a shove to Matthias's ribs, but Hans lay there, eyes fixed on the firmament, hands behind his head.

Matthias smiled. 'Oh. You have someone in mind.'

Hans turned to my brother. 'I did. But no. Not really. Not now.'

There was a long moment of silence.

'Hanne?'

Hans nodded.

I froze. I had never known Hans thought of me at all, let alone in such a serious manner. The thought of a husband had never filled me with hope or excitement as it did Christiana or Henriette. Rather, my feelings had invariably drifted between dread at belonging so completely to an adult world that promised only more curtailed freedoms, and a vague uneasiness at the prospect of a wedding and all that it would lead to. My thoughts flicked to Elder Radtke's bull and the cows rolling their top lips back, the undignified rising on two legs, the jab with the pizzle.

'Does that make you angry?' asked Hans.

Matthias hesitated. 'Papa would have liked that. He probably would have tried to arrange it.'

'My father, too.'

'I didn't know,' Matthias said. 'You never said anything.'

'You know, she once told me that she could hear water singing underground. We were kids. Nine, maybe. I started teasing her, and she said, "I'll show you," and she started digging. Of course, she didn't find any water, she was just digging with her hands. But three years later Old Hermann came to divine for a new well and he stopped just where Hanne had said. Sweetest water you ever drank.'

I had no memory of such an incident.

Matthias smiled. 'That sounds like her.'

'The thought of her madly scratching at the soil with her nails, like some mad chicken, trying to prove me wrong...'

'She did prove you wrong.'

Hans shrugged. 'I know.'

'Mm. Hanne and Hans. A mouthful.'

'How about you?'

'What do you mean?' Matthias stretched, cricking his neck.

'Any nice widows you have an eye on?' Hans raised his eyebrows and my brother started laughing. 'Maybe Mutter Scheck?'

Matthias picked up his pillow and belted Hans over the head with it.

'Hey!' Daniel raised his head. 'Some of us are trying to sleep.'

Matthias and Hans settled themselves back into bed and soon, after a few fits of ribbing, sleep overwhelmed them.

I was wide awake. My fingers felt thick with blood, my knees jellied. The glow of the night watch's pipe floated orange in the darkness. The night was unclouded, pitted with stars, moonlight pooling in soft echo on the weathered boards. I felt the cold air address my hot cheeks.

Hans, I thought. I might have been married to Hans.

Had my parents known? I agreed with Matthias: Papa would have approved of Hans. Both of my parents had given me an understanding of what they considered important for a successful marriage: faithfulness to God, strength and an ability to work hard. Practical skills. Property. Hans was the son of an elder, just as I was the daughter of one. He seemed strong enough. They would have liked me to marry someone from Kay. Someone they knew.

Hans shifted in his sleep and I looked down at his face, lit by the moon. Christiana had often mentioned that she thought him handsome and so I supposed it for fact. It was true that I liked the way the moonlight lay on his skin, the way it made shadows of the depression in his throat, the corners of his eyes, his temple.

He might have been my husband.

I leaned down over Hans until I could see the flicker of his eyelids, the hairs on his top lip. I pressed my mouth to his.

Nothing. I could sense the give of his lips, feel his breath exhale into my own, but nothing quickened within me and I knew instantly that I was deeply grateful in every coil of my gut that I was dead and would not have to marry him.

To be happy to be dead! What would I have wanted instead? What else could I have hoped for, if not marriage?

The answer came to me in a ghost-beat of my own blood.

I could not lie to such a witness of stars. The thought that I might have been married to Hans unnerved me because I had already given myself to another.

Thea.

I wanted Thea. I still wanted her.

The sudden understanding of that coursed through me and solidified into both shame and exhilaration.

This was what I had sensed in myself. This was what I had wanted. It was an impossibility.

And yet, Thea had kissed me, and I had felt affirmation in my bones and blood and the wick of my soul had caught flame, had burned bright.

Yes, this. Yes, this.

I rose and made my way down the hatchway and into the bow. I found Thea's berth. She was asleep, had tucked her hands up under her chin, and I felt my love for her rise up in me, filling me until I felt steady and sure and ballasted against the world.

It had been one thing to feel without understanding, but it was another to feel love and to know it for what it was.

'Thea.' I said her name for the solace of it. 'Thea, better your face than the face of God. Better your love, better your grace.'

And I wondered if she loved me as I loved her.

I saw it then. The pillow overcover she had almost cast into the sea. In the light of the hatchway lamp, I saw that she had finished the *Schlafe wohl*. And when I picked it up, I saw that next to my initial she had added her own.

There was a time when I wandered in grief. I left the cupped palm of the new village and its familiarity because I felt myself betrayed. That time changed me. I saw things I would never have seen in my lifetime, had I lived. I saw things that I know my own parents will never see, that they may not, to this day, truly know about.

So much of what I encountered in those years was cold and broken. But sometimes I saw things that led to a deeper understanding of myself. Sometimes I stumbled across things that made bonfires of my heart.

I once encountered a love like mine. I had fled to the stringybark forest upon the ranges. It had not been by design. The Tiers, as I knew this place, surrounded the track that led, eventually, to the plains. At the time I was following any path that promised distance. The stringybarks were dense, the ground so steep in places it was impossible to walk down the hillside. A place of shadows, where foresters lived and cut lumber.

Darkness fell and I lost the path. I was not looking where I was going. I stumbled and fell, and moved from tree to tree, trunk to trunk.

When I saw the glow of a small cabin in the forest, I nearly wept for the relief of light. The door was open. I stood in its gap.

Inside there were two men eating supper straight out of a cooking pot. Both were lean and wiry with muscle, and that, together with their youth and the way they ate, hunger bringing their mouths close to the pot's rim, reminded me powerfully of Matthias. I was suddenly buckled with longing for my twin. It was never my habit to stay with strangers. Not even during that time of exodus, when loneliness made me yearn for oblivion, did I decide to linger at bedsides. I watched people, of course I did, but at a distance. But these two men, these two beautiful men, manifested Matthias in my mind in a way that compelled me to stay. I curled up by their fire and watched them finish their meal. One of them, addressed by the other as Tom, washed their cooking pot and spoons, whistling as he did so. He was shorter than his companion, who was slightly rangier, with thick scar tissue across the back of his neck, near his hairline. He had very dark, very beautiful eyes.

'Will you have a drink, Tom?' he asked, getting up from his seat and going to the windowsill, where a bottle stood in the corner. He picked it up. He was missing the tip of his little finger.

The shorter man nodded, turning and smiling as the other approached him, uncorking the bottle. I watched as, instead of pouring a drink in the mugs waiting on the table, the taller man gently brought the neck of the bottle to his friend's mouth. Tom drank and something in the way they looked at each other sounded through me like a bell, so that when the bottle was pulled away and set on the table, and the two men drew closer and kissed, I did not feel anything but recognition. I had not known such things were possible in life. Even when, on the ship, I had understood my feelings for what they truly were, I had not imagined that I would ever see such a thing reflected back to me in the lives of others.

I stood. I remember that. I stood at the sight of it, and although some small part of me waited for shock or disgust, none came. Instead, I was happy. I was happy for them, these two beautiful men, who, pulling apart from one another, shared such an intense look of affection and desire that I was jealous. Tom resumed washing the cooking pot, head turning over his shoulder as the taller one undressed, bringing his shirt over his head and dropping it over the back of his chair. I had never seen a naked man before. I had never seen a naked man undress another man before, and even as I remembered myself at last and moved past them, out into the dark filled with frog sound and the silent rustling fall of bark easing away from trunk and branch, I felt my body ripple with revelation.

I had been clear-eyed about my own feelings for years by then, but I had never known there might be others.

We exist, I thought. And all that night I wondered at the mysteries of such things and, remembering the desire of the men holding each other in the light of their fire, thought of Thea and imagined us in their place.

What might have happened? I wonder this even now. What might have happened had I known of such possibilities in my living years?

It is enough to bring me to my knees.

a long-memoried place

The day we arrived dawned in perfect cerulean, sea and sky the one colour so that to look out at the horizon was to feel unsure of space, of gravity. I had spent the night listening to the ocean's muttering and a new kind of music that occasionally threaded through it. At sunrise I followed the sound up on deck and saw that the *Kristi* was floating through sky. The ocean had lifted hands up around the ship and all was blue, blue, blue. The breeze was fresh, and I stepped up to the bow so that I could feel the air carve around me. I lifted my arms up and closed my eyes and I heard it clearly: a humming that floated on the water like oil, chordal and so old it seemed to hold notes long lost to music. Rock, water, salt, sun, soil, fire. The sound of a long-memoried place remembering itself to time.

We are here, I thought.

The island appeared like a vision from all that water and air. It arrived like a dream, a bruised line so that the elements divided once more. A long slick of not-water, of not-air. Mass. Darkly green and grey. Rock formations still against a backdrop of thick forest. I knew at once that the humming was coming from the island.

My skin shivered. A curious feeling of dissipation swelled in my fingers, in my feet. My hair lifted. It felt, suddenly, that the song of this place was filling me, like sheet lightning fills a sky. There – I felt a stagger of separation from myself. I let go of the mast. Another – as though something much greater than myself had pulled me from my body. The song flooded my mouth, it cracked knuckles, and the feel of it was gratifying and soul-deep.

What is happening? I wondered. The ground fell away from me, my heels rose from the deck.

I am being undone, I thought, and just as I felt I might surrender to the song, might let it shake me apart, I felt myself whole again.

What was that?

The song quieted to a hum. A rising shoreline speaking in tongues.

News spread quickly. As soon as land was called, voices begin to talk excitedly behind me. I heard them rise in volume and multiply and felt the press of passengers at my back, until I could not hear the sound of the land over the cries of celebration.

'We have made it! We are finally here!'

'*Känguru* Island. Look! We will remember this moment for the rest of our lives.'

'We have not yet put into harbour.'

'God provides! Praise His name.'

'The wind is good! We may reach the strait this evening.'

I felt the relief and hope and gratitude of the congregation swell around me until I thought I might weep. Eleonore Volkmann held her clutch of daughters tight to her chest, all of them laughing and dabbing their eyes. Mutter Scheck emerged onto the deck gripping Amalie's arm, and, seeing the island in front of her, made the younger woman polish her glasses on her apron so she might better see 'the promised land'. Samuel Radtke kept lifting the corner of his elbow to his face, wiping his cheeks on his sleeve when he thought no one was looking, and the Simmel brothers were whooping into the wind, hats gripped in their hands.

I heard my papa's voice then, deep and sure and loud, and within moments all the voices around me collapsed into a hymn of praise. As soon as it had finished, another song began. I had never heard the congregation sing like this before; it gave me gooseflesh. Even as the ship passed the island and began to buck in the strait like a horse desperate to shed its rider, heading towards the mainland, the congregation remained on the open deck, pouring their voices into the sky until even the air seemed to glisten with music.

South Australia. It seemed miraculous in its unmoving certainty. I stood on the deck, head full of the sound of my people mingling with the song pouring off the country ahead of us. When I heard Thea's voice rising through the chorale, I made my way through the crowd to find her sitting in Mutter Scheck's huddle of single women, eyes watering from the wind, a broad smile on her face. I kneeled at her feet, laid my head in her lap and closed my eyes. I wanted to memorise the sensation of the full sails driving the ship forwards. I wanted to remember the motion which had accompanied my last days of living. Of living with Thea, of us in the dark. All the love I had felt for her, before I even knew it was love.

'You're here,' I said, looking at the exhilarated faces of the congregation. 'You're free.'

'Amen,' they sang. 'Amen.'

The *Kristi* anchored in the gulf that evening. My father led the service, lifting his hands towards the shoreline and praying as his body was coated in golden light from the setting sun behind us. I climbed the rigging and watched them in their devotions until the sun sank below the water and the world was plunged into a purpling darkness. From my height I could see small lights from the land ahead. I could see my mother kneeling, head covered with her good bonnet. Matthias helped her rise when the prayers were concluded. I imagined my papa smiling at him with his good eye.

I did not go below deck that night, even after the captain

addressed the passengers by lamplight and advised them to set their berths in order. I did not want to be part of the haste towards order and departure. In truth, now that the ship had arrived, I was afraid. Thea was leaving behind everything that might remind her of me. There would be no more pine forest, no path to the cottage, no stone set upon a fence post or snow blessing our faces. She would lie down in new places and that berth in the bow, that little cradle of sickness and midnight whispers, would be forgotten. I would be forgotten. She would walk paths I could never mark with my own footprints; she would walk out and away from the life she had known me in.

I watched the sailors smoke below, their pipes extinguishing into the darkness one by one, soon followed by the lights from the mainland. Hours passed and I did not heed them. I sat amidst the ropes and watched the moon rise and strike loveliness onto the shifting surface of the sea, and I was calmed by it.

What happens now? I wondered, again and again. What happens to me?

Captain Olsen rowed out to the mainland at first light and returned in the evening with news. The anchorage was bad in the bay. The passengers, excited and impatient, crowded the deck, watching Olsen send the first mate and four sailors back into the boat to find the pilot station up the gulf. Two days later, once the water was high enough to allow the pilot to guide the ship safely over the bar, the *Kristi* found the entrance to the harbour and anchored.

I had expected that the ship would immediately be loosed of its passengers and cargo; the journey had been so long. Instead, there seemed to be a strange etiquette of arrival. The captain asked that the passengers return to the tween deck and ensure everything was as clean and neat as possible, and within the hour several sunburned

Englishmen stepped down the hatchway with Captain Olsen following. I climbed up onto the scrubbed trestle table to get a better look as they made their way through the space, peering into the kitchens and bunks.

That night, three sheep were rowed out to the *Kristi*. The passengers laughed to see the woolly faces peering behind the rowing sailors.

'What? More Englishmen?' roared Gottfried Volkmann. The mood was euphoric.

The sheep were hoisted on deck by ropes, bleating in bewilderment, their legs dangling.

'They've been sent for your refreshment,' the captain explained. 'You all made an excellent impression.'

That last night on board the ship stank of mutton fat. People talked until late in the evening, then fell asleep in their clothes, ready for disembarkation in the morning. Neat bags lay ready at the foot of each bunk, and without the usual bunting of drying washing and sheets and belongings, the tween deck looked forlorn and bare. Even the curtain separating the bow from the other quarters had been taken down.

As I sat cross-legged on Thea's bunk, a vision of my body appeared in my mind's eye. Hair suspended in the water like a dark aura. Bubble of air trapped in my eyelashes, fish peering into the whorl of my ear, canvas shroud torn and caught about my legs. Skin milking into nothingness.

I could feel salt stinging my gums as I lay down next to her. Water pearled down my neck, dripped into the blankets. I felt something under my tongue and pulled a fragment of abalone shell from my mouth. It glistened.

'Don't forget me,' I said. And I slipped the shell into Thea's mouth as she slept.

*

There was no wharf at the port. One after another, passengers threw their legs over the side of the *Kristi* and climbed down a rope ladder to where the sailors waited in a small boat, which then was rowed out until the water was waist-height. It was windy and hot – the oarsmen struggled to keep the boat in the channel. Once as close as possible to the firmer ground of the sandhills, the sailors and men climbed out, splashing through the shallows and mud of the marsh, trying not to drop their wives and children and luggage. I lifted my legs over the gunwale and perched on its edge, watching everyone leave in handfuls.

Visions of my body buried at sea kept me clinging to the rail. What would happen if I fell into the water? Would I be drawn back to those turning bones, whittled clean by wave and creatures sucking the flesh from them? How would I follow if I could not swim?

I felt myself tip towards the sea beneath. If I fall, do I disappear? Do I sight God? Do I remain?

There was a ruffle of suppressed laughter on deck and I looked up to see that Magdalena Radtke, who had just been rowed out with her family, was refusing to be carried at all. She had jumped into the water from the boat, skirt and blouse immediately soaking and heavy, pulling her down with every step. She waded to shore, kicking through the shallows, whipping her head behind her as if she could hear the remaining passengers chuckling at her expense. Everyone pretended not to see when she stumbled forwards onto her knees, drenching herself entirely. I watched her haul herself to her feet, wipe the mud off her hands on the shoulders of her jerkin and set off grimly once more.

My father insisted on placing all other families before his own; the sun was blaring in the west by the time he beckoned Mama and Matthias, Hermine sleeping in my brother's arms. The ship's arrivals were a dark mass on the sandhills in the distance. I imagined they were waiting for instruction as to where to go.

When Matthias and Mama were seated in the small boat, belongings at their feet, I left my place on the gunwale and approached the ladder hanging over the side. I peered over the edge and saw my father step carefully from the ladder into the boat, gripping the arm offered by one of the sailors.

'That's all then?' the oarsman asked.

'We are the last,' my father replied. He turned to my mother, face beaming. 'This is it, Johanne. Our life begins anew.'

Go, I thought. Hanne, you must go now. Quickly!

I felt the rope strain against the arches of my feet. Down, down, until the suck and slap of the sea was just below my heels. As I lifted my foot off the rung, shifting my weight for the drop into the boat, the sailor used his oar to push off from the side of the ship. I fell, scrambling at the rope as water rose up about me. Panic set in, hard and flailing, all thrashing fear, until I remembered that I had no need of air, that I could not drown.

The sea pulled me down and I let it. I opened my eyes, saw the silt stirring through the water, felt my feet sink into the softness of the sand and dirt and sediment. I opened my mouth and the water flowed in, warm and full of grit.

I know your taste, it said. *I know the flavour of your bones.*

I struggled to move. I did not know how to swim.

All things come to shore eventually, the water said, mouth accented with marsh. *The shore is made of the dead.* And it filled my throat and darkness took me.

I woke smelling swamp and mud and mangrove, hands filled with reeds. It was night. A strong wind was blowing and sand was stinging my skin. I was on the shoreline. Squinting through the darkness, I stumbled up over the rise of sandhills and saw a cluster of lights in the distance. I headed towards them, leaving the ocean pushing in hungry against the mudflats.

I had thought the lights might indicate a town, but as I grew closer I found only three houses abutting a lane of cracked earth, light escaping under doorways and through gaps in the walls. There were no windows. The snap of canvas behind me made me turn, and I saw a long row of tents on the other side of the track, sand hissing against them. There were no lamps – I wondered whether any could be lit in such a gale – but the moon was full and the wind high enough that any cloud was quickly blown over its surface. I counted thirty tents and crept past each until I heard familiar voices. I dropped to my knees and crawled inside, and found Friedrich, Thea and Anna Maria sitting together in the darkness. There was another family with them too, and as my eyes adjusted, I saw the sleeping forms of Augusta, the wet nurse from Klemzig, her husband Karl and baby Wilhelm. I crept into the farthest corner of the tent.

'Mama, you're scaring me,' Thea was saying.

'Anna Maria, we do not have that option. Our livelihood is tied with our congregation. It is the only means we might be assured of land. Of credit.'

'Shh,' whispered Anna Maria. She jerked her head around, eyes searching the darkness.

'If they go to the pastor –'

'What was that?' she whispered.

'What?'

'Augusta, is that you?'

'Mama, Augusta is asleep.' Thea sounded tired.

'Someone has come in.'

'It's the wind. This place is a desert.' Friedrich's voice, low and soft.

'No . . .' Anna Maria lifted herself up onto her knees and peered in my direction. 'I saw something come in.'

'*Liebling*, it's late. We're all exhausted.'

'Maybe it was an animal.'

I could see the whites of Friedrich's eyes as he rummaged tentatively amongst the canvas bags, the opened trunk. 'There's nothing, Anna Maria.'

Anna Maria did not say anything, but I could hear her breathing, feel her eyes searching the dark. 'Lord protect us,' she whispered. 'I saw something.'

'It's me, Hanne.' My voice sounded strange. 'You don't need to be afraid.'

'You have it safe, don't you, Thea? You packed it.'

Thea's voice was tense. 'It's swaddled in a sheet. In the bag.'

Friedrich placed a steadying hand on his wife's shoulder. 'Come now, get some sleep. We'll talk about it in the morning.'

Thea and her father settled themselves, their breathing deepening into sleep within minutes, but for hours into the night the Wend lay awake, eyes searching the corner of the tent where I sat.

While on the *Kristi* I had heard one of the sailors refer to the harbour as Port Misery, and when I left the Eichenwalds sleeping the next morning and stepped out into bald daylight, I understood why. Stagnant waters lurked around mudflats that varied from mire to grey banks scorched and cracked from a hard sun. The tide had deserted the place, and I could see the *Kristi* stranded in low water some distance away, the trickle creeping in from the river at the harbour mouth doing little to alleviate the reek of its stagnancy.

It was already very warm. At the sound of a cough I looked across the lane to see Elder Fröhlich relieving himself against the trunk of a small, harassed tree. He was sweating hard, rivulets running down his neck and his shirt damp at his back. Passengers were emerging from the squalid little canvas tents, looking about for a place to wash or fuel to cook with. I saw Mama duck out a few tents down, holding Hermine on her hip, her ship's mug in hand. Papa followed her.

'The remainder of the surplus provisions ought to be here by afternoon,' Papa was saying to Matthias, who stepped out behind him. 'We must see to it that they are equally distributed. Remember, the doctor gave some families more rations than others. We must see all is made equal and right.'

'Did he keep a list?'

'Who knows? We shall speak to everyone. Learn who received their full allocations of fish and bacon.'

'People may lie.'

'Then the sin is on them.'

I followed as Matthias and Papa walked down the dunes, feet sinking into the sand. 'Captain Olsen said we might expect Pastor Flügel today. He sent for him at Holdfast Bay. Praise God! He will be able to tell us more.' Papa paused at the edge of the marsh, wrinkling his nose at the stink of the flats, then bent down, scooped a handful of water to rinse his mouth, and spat. 'Has anyone found fresh water here?'

'There is none,' Matthias said. 'Apparently it is all brought by bullock from the river in the town.'

'Adelheid.' Papa scooped another handful of water and washed his face with both hands. He stood a moment, beard dripping. 'Go see if the water barrels were brought ashore yesterday, Matthias. People will be thirsty. They will want to wash the journey from them. Especially once they learn that we may be reunited with our pastor.'

*

The congregation immediately found new zeal and energy at the news of Flügel's expected arrival. I watched as women scrubbed their faces in the filmy waters at the edge of the mud, and Daniel's scissors were passed amongst the men so that beards might be trimmed, nose hairs and runaway eyebrows tidied.

As soon as the travelling party was sighted coming from the Adelaide road, the passengers gathered together in the sun and, swatting the flies from their open mouths, sang one of Pastor Flügel's favourite hymns, *'Nun danket alle Gott'*. I sat in the shade cast by the shanty houses opposite the tents and watched the pastor arrive like Jesus into Jerusalem. Even though I felt brittle and bitter, believing myself to be deserted by the God they were all thanking, I could not help but marvel at the reunion. The last time the congregation had sung with Flügel, the church in Kay had still had its bell and Gottlob had been alive. Now here they were, on the other side of the world, sweating into their heavy clothes under a sky so wide and blue it seemed to devour the earth.

The elders helped Flügel off his horse and there was a great cheer as his boots touched the ground. Flügel lifted his arms up in praise and invited everyone to pray. 'The Lord is great, His mercies have no bounds. Blessed be His holy name!'

The pastor bore evidence of his persecution. I remembered him as stout, but now he was thin, his face lined and whiskers greying. The ridge of his prominent nose was peeling badly, and when he removed his hat to pray I saw that his forehead, too, had become mottled with sun. In life I had always been a little afraid of the pastor, awed by his power. I had not liked to look him in the eye, and I had never spoken to him beyond a few murmurs of assent, even when he had schooled me for confirmation. But dead, and no longer under the weight of his religiosity, I could regard him as a man rather than as Christ's authority on earth. I had never noticed the hair sprouting out of the pastor's ears before, or the purple hollows in the corners of his eyes. His hair was fine and thin and he had a loose neck which wobbled as he spoke, out of time with his words, so that he reminded me of a beady-eyed rooster, wattle jiggling.

Flügel placed his hat back on his head as the congregation murmured, 'Amen,' the broad smile on his face showing a missing incisor. 'There is much to talk about,' he said, shaking hands with the men and nodding at their wives and children. 'Let us spend the day in conference. Let us rejoice at our freedoms and praise His name for so swiftly delivering you to this paradise!'

As soon as Flügel intimated he would speak with each elder from his congregations first, Magdalena pushed her husband in the small of the back, mouth close to his ear. Samuel glanced at her, uneasy. I followed him as he approached the pastor.

'Elder Radtke.' Pastor Flügel gestured to a grey-green tree, the same one I had watched Elder Fröhlich piss under that morning. 'Shall we sit? The English call this particular tree a she-oak. There isn't a great deal of shade, but we might hope for a breeze.'

As soon as they had made themselves comfortable and prayed together, Samuel gave his account of the journey. He spoke of Elizabeth's death, his fear for her soul on account of her christening performed at home, and seemed greatly relieved when Flügel, voice gentle, assured him that Elizabeth was with Christ, in glory.

A little distance away, Magdalena was staring intently at her husband. The pastor noticed. 'Would Frau Radtke like to join us?' he asked.

Samuel shook his head then, changing his mind, called for Magdalena. She made her way over, lips stretched over her teeth, face going red. 'Pastor Flügel. We are overjoyed to see you in such good health.'

'Your husband says you have something you wish to discuss.'

Samuel was staring at the ground, boot toe nudging the sand. Magdalena shot him a look of irritation. 'I don't mean to burden you so soon after our arrival here, Pastor,' she began, eyes flicking back to Flügel, 'but something quite grave, quite concerning, occurred on the journey.' The pastor waited for her to continue, hands on his knees. 'I have reason to believe that a member of our congregation has a book of the occult.'

Pastor Flügel frowned.

'There were some incidents on the ship.' She cleared her throat. 'A paper seal bearing occult symbols was found on the body of a man who perished. I have reason to believe that the seal was placed there by the same person who, against the direction of the ship's surgeon, practised herbalism upon the sick. The same person whom Christiana witnessed pressing a book of the devil on the chest of her dying daughter. The daughter in question was expected to die.' Magdalena glanced across the port to where Anna Maria and Thea were dragging a branch along the ground. 'She made an unusual recovery,' she murmured.

The pastor followed the direction of Magdalena's gaze, hand lifted against the sun. 'You know who this person is?'

'Her, there,' Magdalena said. 'Anna Maria Eichenwald.'

Pastor Flügel nodded. 'I have not met this woman.'

'She is a Wend,' Magdalena elaborated.

'Married to a German, Friedrich – a good man,' Samuel added, eyes still lowered.

'And have you confronted his wife?' the pastor asked. 'Where is the book now?'

Magdalena hesitated. 'I don't know where it is. I presume she's hidden it.'

Pastor Flügel bit his upper lip. 'I will speak to her.' He shook Samuel's hand again. 'Thank you for telling me. Now is the time that we must work to preserve the purity and sanctity of our faith, as we build our community and lay its moral foundations.'

I remained by Flügel's side that afternoon, as he spoke with the head of each family and listened to their concerns and questions. It was hot and unpleasant, but Flügel did not complain nor ask for respite from his congregation, and as much as the reverence shown him troubled me, I saw that his faith and conviction gave them comfort.

Flügel prayed over the passengers who still suffered from scurvy and reassured those who were afraid of the great sum of money owed to Angas, the English benefactor. Several families came to him with new, unanticipated concerns: some had not realised that the land was inhabited by '*Eingeborene*' and, having spent the morning speaking with the occupants of the shanty houses and the sailors, were now afraid of being speared.

'We see much of them at Neu Klemzig,' said the pastor, speaking of the village he had founded. 'The English call them Cowandilla, though they themselves do not use that name. You will see them, but you have little to fear. The greatest threat to our way of life are those who live in a profligate manner. I do not like that Neu Klemzig is so close to Adelaide. I worry for the young amongst us, that they should be so close to places of drunkenness and gambling.'

I knew that my father was anxious to speak to Flügel. He did not let the pastor out of his sight all afternoon, and I imagined that he wanted to learn as much as he could about Neu Klemzig. Papa was a farmer, after all: if he had any earthly appetite in his body, it was lust for good, friable soil. I was surprised, then, when Papa sat beside Flügel in the pitiful shade and spoke not of Neu Klemzig, but of me.

'Pastor, I ask for forgiveness. I hope you will pray for me.'

'What is it, Heinrich?'

Papa turned his hat in his hands. 'My daughter Hanne –
Johanne – died on the journey here.'

'I am sorry.'

I crept closer until I was kneeling by his side. Tears were flowing
from my father's good eye. He wiped them from his face. 'Forgive me.'

'Your grief is understandable.'

'I know that our Lord is just. But there is such . . . anger. There is
such anger in my heart.'

'This is the second child you have lost?'

At this my father broke down and I felt my own chest crack open.
'Papa,' I said. 'Papa!' I wrapped my arms around him.

'Great afflictions are great instruments, Heinrich. They open the
hidden treasures of God's mercies.'

My father nodded, weeping still.

Flügel placed a steadying hand on his shoulder. 'I shall pray for
your daughter.'

'Don't bother,' I snapped. I wanted to bite him on the knuckle.
'I'm right here.'

'Thank you,' Papa said.

'How is Frau Nussbaum?'

'She is well, thank you.'

'And Matthias?'

'Healthy, thanks be to God.'

Pastor Flügel squeezed Papa's shoulder. 'How old is he now?'

'Seventeen. A man.'

Flügel glanced over to where Matthias sat next to Hans, both
laughing at the cat as she chased the flowering head of a reed they
were dragging along the ground.

'There is a great need for labour here,' Flügel said. 'When we
arrived, we were swamped with visitors looking for workmen, farm-
hands. No doubt Matthias will be invited to go out to the stations. You

too, I suspect. Women will be invited to leave and work as servants. Now, I understand that all of you are anxious to repay your debts and avoid further interest, and Matthias, I am sure, will be eager to do his part. But it is my sore hope and prayer that we do not give in to fear of poverty and disband. We cannot disperse. Do not let our young men be tempted by such offers – we cannot know anything of the character of employers, cannot be assured they will permit our people to worship and rest on Sundays. There will be work and opportunity enough when we settle.'

'At Neu Klemzig? Is there land enough there for us?'

I saw the pastor hesitate briefly before he nodded. My father noticed it also.

'I have spoken to the captain,' Papa ventured. He looked uncomfortable, was still wiping his cheeks with the heel of his hand. 'He has advised us to go there and form our own opinion of the land.'

'Yes, go, form your own judgement, Heinrich. But remember, we have all emigrated for the sake of our faith.'

My father smiled. 'Faith. Yes. But, as the captain said, "God has given us bodies as well as souls." He is concerned that the settlement at Neu Klemzig will expose us to hunger and worry.'

Pastor Flügel looked over to where the captain stood, conferring with his first mate. 'It is the land provided to us by Herr Angas. I have secured a loan of twelve hundred sterling so that we at Neu Klemzig might buy cattle.'

'With interest.'

Flügel smiled. 'Ten per cent. "Render unto Caesar . . ."'

'But cattle must be fed. The earth must be able to produce something for us.' Papa lowered his voice. 'The land is not good. Pastor Flügel, we know. We have been warned not to go there. How might we live as an independent community, if we are unable to pay our debts? If we are unable to feed ourselves? Would it not be better for those at Neu Klemzig to remain there, and for us who have come on the *Kristi* to form our own village? We would remain your congregation. You could move between several congregations, several communities. As it was in the old country?'

'As I said, Heinrich, you are welcome to assess the land in question and form your own opinion.' Flügel reached for my father's hand, shaking it firmly. 'I remember your daughter. I shall pray that the Lord eases your suffering.' He pulled my father in closer. '"And God shall wipe away all tears from their eyes; and there shall be no more death, neither sorrow, nor crying, neither shall there be any more pain: for the former things are passed away."'

'Thank you, Pastor.'

A greasy-fingered light was setting across the mudflats when Pastor Flügel approached Anna Maria. She and Thea were cooking rice over an open fire in the sand behind the tents. They looked up at the sight of the pastor squeezing between the canvas walls.

'Good evening,' he said. He gestured to their fire. 'May I sit?'

'It is a pleasure to meet you, Pastor Flügel,' Anna Maria said, dipping her head. 'The congregation of Kay have been exceptionally kind to us.'

The pastor opened his hands in a gesture of appreciation. 'We are pleased to welcome all believers of the true faith. It is one of the reasons I would like to speak to you, Frau Eichenwald.'

I noticed Thea glance at her mother.

'You would like to speak to me?'

'Frau Eichenwald, it has come to my attention that, on the journey here, you engaged in homeopathic medicine. Is that true?'

Anna Maria straightened her back. 'I am a midwife and a healer. There is no shame in that.'

'No, I understand.' Pastor Flügel placed a hand on his chest. 'I, too, put great store by homeopathy. I have benefitted enormously from its wisdom. I recognise, however, that amongst herbal crafts there is variance, and that such things can – if one is not careful – descend into immoral practices.'

Anna Maria did not take her eyes off the pastor. A smile stretched across her face.

'Frau Eichenwald, I will ask you outright, and I urge you to answer in truth. Should your answer be affirmative, it would bring me great joy to pray for you, to hear your confession, and to facilitate steps towards public contrition so that the congregation may trust and commune with you and your family. Grace is for all.'

'What is your question, Pastor Flügel?'

The wind dragged at the flames beneath the pot. Unsteady light shone across Anna Maria's face.

'Do you have in your possession a book of the occult?'

'No.' Anna Maria's answer was swift and sure.

Pastor Flügel paused, blinking, then sat back. 'What do you say to those who believe they saw one in your possession?'

Anna Maria picked up her spoon and stirred the rice, eyebrows raised in an expression of tired forbearance. 'I would ask that they remember the six things the Lord doth hate, yea, seven are an abomination unto him.'

The pastor's mouth twitched in uncertainty as Anna Maria continued, gaze level, spoon stirring. '"A proud look, a lying tongue, and hands that shed innocent blood, a heart that deviseth wicked imagination, feet that be swift in running to mischief, a false witness that speaketh lies, and"' – she smiled at the pastor – '"he that soweth discord amongst brethren."'

'You know your scripture, Frau Eichenwald.'

Anna Maria placed a hand on Thea's back. They looked the

image of each other, mother and daughter, veiled by steam, both looking blue-eyed at the pastor, now rising, already replacing his hat on his head.

'We love the Lord with all our heart, Pastor Flügel. We did not spend six months in the belly of a ship for any other reason.'

the tree

Learning small amounts of English from the bullockies from Adelaide was the only thing that seemed to distract the congregation from the anxiety that soon shivered over the port. After the joy and exhilaration of arrival, there was suddenly little else to do but talk of the terrible soil at Neu Klemzig, debt, and all the things that would need to be bought on credit. It was with visible horror that people learned the exorbitant price of provisions in the colony. Sixpence for ten potatoes. Cucumber seed more than a shilling. Traugott Geschke came back from an exploratory trip into Adelaide white-faced. A pair of bullocks cost more than forty pounds. So, when the captain summoned everyone together and told them he had secured temporary work for them at the port, the news was received with relief. Surely there was no harm in working while they waited? Surely Flügel could not begrudge them the money and occupation? The captain had arranged for unmarried daughters and sons to ferry water from the new spring on the Adelaide road, saving the bullockies the trouble of drawing water from the Torrens, and for married women to work as laundresses. Men would labour in the nearby district and town.

The next day I watched Christiana, Matthias and Hans rig up sledges from she-oak trees and set off inland on the dray track. They returned by midday, dragging heavy casks of water through the sand, promptly sold it all, and set off again so that Magdalena, Emile, Beate, Eleonore and my mother would have water for laundry. I would have followed them – I was interested to see something more of the place than the blasted port – had Thea not been told to remain by her mother. Anna Maria had volunteered to cook for the working families and had insisted Thea stay back to help her, but I could see, in the way she kept her eyes on the women laundering, that she did not trust Magdalena. Having Thea there was the only way to ensure their belongings might never be left unattended.

Strange waiting days, on the cusp of a new life and unable to seize it. A month of dirty handkerchiefs. Four shillings each time my mama scrubbed the English sweat from a shirt, until the skin of her knuckles split when she closed them over the money. Hans and Matthias came with their buckets of water and left again like the tide, endlessly, three times a day or more, until their feet grew as hard as boot soles, and my brother's arms twitched in sleep with remembered weight. A month of splinters from driving posts, ship-soft muscles hardening with hauling and splitting and sawing and lifting. Hans's cat shed the last of her kitten belly and coiled with lean muscle. A month of sun on Thea's face until her cheeks patterned with freckles that I studied until I could have found them in the dark.

And then, a piece of paper held aloft by the captain, a broad smile on his face. Moved by the plight of his passengers, he had negotiated a contract on their behalf. Promises in exchange for debt and industry and interest. Captain Olsen had secured one hundred and fifty acres of land to be rented by those who had come out on the *Kristi*: those from Kay, as well as families from Tschicherzig, Klemzig and Züllichau. They would rent the land as a group; it would be divided into fair and equal portions for each family. The captain had also arranged credit and allowances for a church and school. The debt would be shouldered by them as a collective, a community responsible for each other. Those already settled at Neu Klemzig could choose to remain there or join the new congregation.

German tongues laboured over the names of English landowners, English prices, English measurements, against cries of: 'God will reward you, Captain!' Dutton. MacFarlane. Finnis. 'You are the Lord's messenger!' Poultry. Cattle. Pigs. Surely Flügel would see that this was God's providence? Seven pound sterling an acre. 'Let us prosper under Him. *Möge Gott Sie segnen!*'

The sound of this country is one long sustained note that does not end. It is a humming that holds all the other music of this place in harmony. Every other sound is threaded upon it.

It was at the port that I began to curate new litanies. Between the bullock drivers that rumbled in from Adelaide, the sailors, the merchants, the English come in search of labourers, I found words given to the music I heard against the constant run of the wind amongst the rushes and sand dunes.

She-oak for the tree with long, scaled needles, whistling the wind in a way that made my skin lift.

Magpie lark for the two-shriek calling peep in changing hours.

Salt paperbark for the crooked trees groaning wooded, cupped fruit.

Mangrove, wattle, saltbush.

In the months that came afterwards I learned new words as the congregation did, as they crossed the dusty, ticking plains of Adelaide. I placed them next to one another upon the deeper vibration of this country.

Galah, cockatoo, lorikeet.

Kangaroo, wallaby, possum.

Emu, goanna, quoll.

Now, years later, sitting on the lip of this valley, I can make prayer beads of the trees that crown me, the small living things glimpsed if I am still and silent. Red gum, blue gum, quandong, stringybark. And the birds, ever here, ever singing, a liturgy to govern the hours towards gods of cry and shriek and call.

Kookaburra, magpie, shrike-thrush, wagtail.

Currawong, crow, boobook.

Scripture may no longer roll off my tongue in smooth certainty, but my mouth is still full of spirit. Holy Writ of living things, each one a prayer against the teeth.

The pilgrimage to the promised land took months. No family was able to carry all their possessions at once, and so were forced to trek back and forth, carrying what they could in a day's journey, and then returning the next for another load. Sometimes it took two weeks to complete a distance that would otherwise have taken less than a day.

As the congregation slowly advanced forwards, following the dray tracks of the plains towards the lush blue-green distance of the Mount Lofty Ranges and its promise of cool, I sprawled on my father's handcart, letting my head loll on its hard edge, and studied the sky. I could not fathom such impossible blue. The sky was higher, bigger, a cloudless wonder of vastness. Everything seemed small under its endlessness. Everything would die one day, but the sky would remain, and under such timelessness all time-tied things seemed sweeter for their impermanence. My throat tightened thinking about such things, and I slid myself off the handcart and walked from person to person, running my hands over their hot foreheads in wonder that they existed at all. You are all here, alive, all at once. What miracle, I told them. You will be gone one day. May the sky that has steepled over you hold you in its memory like a spark! I shouted this at Herr Pasche. Even dour-faced Christian seemed to me, in that moment, a marvel of life.

Nature had always been my whetstone, had always made me keener, and after the congregation reached the foothills, I felt myself sharpen to life. The landscape on the ascent to the ranges was unlike anything I had ever seen before. I had thought the pine forest back in Kay a place of divinity, but this country was infinitely more sovereign. Each morning, while it was yet dark, the birds filled the air with singing so that the sun, when it rose, brought light as symphony. The birds were everywhere: hosts of raucous angels, black-bodied, yellow-topped messengers of shrieking delight. Soot-streaked choral masters. Feather-fat kookaburras suddenly, alarmingly, proselytising to the dawn. Even the trees grew in such a way as to welcome the sun to the world. In Prussia canopies were dense and thick. Forest floors were deeply shadowed. Here was a place of lightness. Leaves dappled thin and shiny, fluttered pink, grey, green. I crushed them in my palm and smelled medicine. Healing. Hot, still days dropped branches, all bone-crack, and brought the sounds of bees. Sometimes I smelled honey warming the air. Animals were muscled fur and liquid eyes, or scaly thicknesses, tongues darting. All of it, trees and possums and kangaroos and bright beads of ants circling trunks, veered from stillness to flashing movement in an instant. There was energy here. Rough-softness. Sometimes it rained and, when it stopped, the air was perfume, a clean scent of wet leaf and damp sweetness. I wanted to drink that washed summer air. I imagined it tasted of reprieve.

My father, too, was invigorated by everything he saw. He ran his fingers along the ground and filled his nails with soil. 'God's gifts,' he said, smiling at Matthias. Papa's voice in prayer was the first to interrupt the dark. He scaled the ridges with kingdom-come strides, and remarked aloud upon the extravagance of sunlight, the yawning orange of rock faces, the views that suddenly appeared, paradisiacal, when the trees fell away to vistas that stretched to a shining belt of sea. He wore the hardship of the journey like a hair shirt: the wonder and the deprivation and the physical toll were bringing him closer to God. It was all sanctification.

No one else seemed to find such joy in the journey; the to-and-fro soon became tedious. While the Pasches, Radtkes and Volkmanns had, like my own family, bought small barrows from workers at the port, other families from Kay had no choice but to carry their possessions on their backs, and as the journey grew harder and heat settled into the days, the trail of Old Lutherans thinned. I decided to leave Papa's barrow to walk beside the Eichenwalds, and I soon noticed that some of the women seemed to be avoiding Anna Maria.

They have heard rumours, I thought to myself, watching as Beate Fröhlich ignored Anna Maria's request for help and let the Wend's bottles of dried herbs – fallen from a rip in her canvas bag – roll down the track. Magdalena has troubled them against her.

Whether by design or accident, the Eichenwalds found themselves moving through the gullies and ranges largely alone. They often made camp early and spent the last few hours of daylight examining their surrounds. Friedrich felled trees to examine the wood and Anna Maria, her bag already filled with samphire from the port, picked plants to smell and taste them.

'They dry my mouth out,' Friedrich said one night, chewing some small red berries she had kept.

Anna Maria threw a spoon at him. 'You don't trust me?'

'I like them,' said Thea. She examined one in her fingers. 'Like a cherry, only the stone is on the outside.'

'Topsy-turvy, like everything here,' Friedrich said, spitting the stone into the bush behind them.

I noticed that the Wend had suddenly stilled. 'Friedrich?'

'Hm?'

Anna Maria placed a hand on Thea's knee and I noticed, then, what she had seen. Behind Friedrich, standing a little way off behind the trees, was a group of people regarding them in silence. Three women stood, cloaks draped over their shoulders, with two men and a few small children. Even in the gloaming their bodies shone, hair greased and reddish. I was struck by their upright bearing.

'*Eingeborene*,' Friedrich whispered. He had gone very still and serious. I watched his eyes flick to the small hand axe that sat in the dirt at his feet.

Thea noticed. She shook her head at him, eyes alarmed.

The group calmly looked across at the Eichenwalds before one of the women nodded at the unlit pile of twigs and fallen wood in the centre of the camp. She inclined her head and muttered something to the other women.

It was Anna Maria who moved first.

Eyes not leaving the group, she got up and walked to where she had heaped their belongings for the night. She gave the women a quick smile, hands shuffling in a canvas bag, and then removed a wrapped parcel of ship's biscuit.

'*Brot*,' she said, approaching the group.

One of the women said something in a language I could not understand and glanced down at the biscuit in Anna Maria's hand, then back to the pile of kindling. She did not take it.

'Give them some real bread, Mama,' Thea whispered. She reached for the crust of rice and wheaten bread she had been eating and offered it. The bread hung in the air for a long moment, before one of the other women stepped forwards and, with a few words to Thea, took it. In the twilight I saw that this woman was the same age as Anna Maria, perhaps a little older. With her free hand she reached up and gestured towards Thea's hair. Thea removed her headscarf, and the woman peered at her pale braids, looking back at her companions and making some comment that made the other women smile.

'You can go away now,' Friedrich said. 'Off you go.' He had gone pale. '*Weggehen*.' He motioned them away from the clearing. The smiles vanished and the men stared him down for a few moments before making their way back onto the path.

They do not look at their feet when they walk, I thought.

Thea and Anna Maria stared at Friedrich as he kicked apart the pile of kindling. 'Best not to light a fire tonight.'

'Why?'

'Well, we don't want them to come back, do we? What do you think will happen? Were you planning on giving them the rest of our food?'

'Papa . . .'

'I suppose I was the only one who saw the spears the men were holding?'

'You have an axe.' Thea pointed at it.

Friedrich opened his mouth as if to speak, then thought better of it. He shook his head.

'It was only a matter of time,' Anna Maria said, lips thinning as she stood over her husband. I watched her as she wrapped the ship's biscuit and tucked it back into their bags. 'We saw them on the plains. Did you expect they would make themselves scarce up here? This is their home, too.'

'If it is their home, then why can't they find their own food?'

Anna Maria looked askance at her husband. 'Doubtless they do.'

'But you thought it wise to show them they needn't?'

'Oh, Friedrich, it was a little bread!'

Thea leaned her forehead into the palms of her hands. She glowed like a ghost in the gloom. Night was falling.

'A little bread, and then a lot of bread,' Friedrich continued. 'And then what else?'

Anna Maria glared at him. 'This selfishness does not suit you.'

Friedrich looked as though she had slapped him. 'You call me selfish?'

Thea closed her eyes.

'Yes!' exclaimed Anna Maria.

'I would seek to protect my family.'

'From what? Families such as ours?'

'From starvation!' shouted Friedrich. He stood up, flinging his arms wide to the murmur of bush behind him. 'Do you see where we are? We are in the wilds! Look. Look! All we have is in that little pile. We have no livestock. We have no money.' He counted on his fingers, spittle flying from his mouth. 'No home. All we have is debt!'

'Friedrich, the Lord –'

'Do not dare to talk to me about faith. I am not Heinrich Nussbaum, drunk with God.' Friedrich's chin trembled. 'Our daughter nearly died.'

There was silence.

'I know,' Anna Maria said, anger draining from her voice. 'But the good Lord preserved her.'

'The good Lord, or your witchcraft?'

Anna Maria's hands rose to her mouth.

Friedrich shook his head. He glanced wearily to Thea, the anger fading from him. 'You heard me,' he muttered. 'You and your goddamn book. You think I don't see the way some of the others look at you? Anna Maria, we cannot afford to fall out of the fold. We need this settlement.'

'That book is God-sent.'

'You forced it on her,' Friedrich said.

Anna Maria lowered her hands and stared at her husband, eyes cold. She turned to her daughter. 'You know I did no such thing.'

Thea stood. 'I'm going to sleep now.'

'Did she ask for it? You were creeping about in the middle of the night. Pulling it from your bag, hiding it in your clothes.'

'I hardly wanted others to see me!' Anna Maria protested.

Friedrich tilted his head. 'Why not? If it is such a Christian book.'

'Friedrich . . .'

'I'm going to sleep,' Thea repeated, turning her back on them.

I followed her to the shelter built against a cluster of stringybarks and lay down next to her on the ground with its smells of dry leaf. The first stars could be seen in the gaps between the bark. Faraway keening.

I could hear Anna Maria and Friedrich arguing in the dusk. 'Your father is afraid,' I told Thea. 'Love and fear. The only reasons anyone does anything.'

Thea lifted her hands to her ears.

There was silence, then eventually Anna Maria crawled into the shelter and sat next to Thea. 'I'm sorry you had to hear that,' she said finally.

'Mm.'

She stroked her daughter's arm. 'I didn't force the book onto you. You accepted it. It was your choice.'

I felt Thea hold her breath. Ribs filling with air and held words.

Anna Maria hesitated. 'I had tried everything else. It was the only way I could save your life.'

'At what price?' Thea shrugged off her mother's hand and sat up, head brushing the bark above her. I could feel the anger coming off her.

'What do you mean?'

Thea's voice was strangled. 'You pushed the book onto my chest. You made me accept it.'

'I didn't . . .'

'I was unwell! I was in the grip of a fever. Mama, I was dying and you pushed it on me.'

From somewhere in the cooling forest came a scuffle. Chirrup of insect.

I waited for Anna Maria's apology. None came. The Wend's voice broke through the gloom after a silence, serrated with barely suppressed irritation. 'One day, Thea, you will have a child. And you will love that child so much you would do anything to protect it. You would give your life for it.'

'You didn't give your life for mine.'

'No,' Anna Maria replied, 'but I am saying that you will do anything to keep your child al—'

'You didn't give your life for me. Hanne did.'

Quiet, then. Only pitched cricket pulse as my heart filled with a deep and feral ache.

An owl called into the dark.

'Thea . . .' Anna Maria was careful. 'Thea, Hanne died because she was sick.'

'I was sicker.'

Breathe, I urged her. Breathe.

Thea looked at her mother. 'I should have died. But you gave me your Book of Moses and because of that, because death couldn't touch me, it took Hanne.'

'That's not . . .' Anna Maria sighed. 'No. It doesn't work like that.'

'Really? Because it feels as though that is exactly what happened.'

I shuffled closer behind Thea and wrapped my arms around her, felt the reverberation of her voice in the soft-leanness of her belly.

'I'm sorry you feel that way,' said Anna Maria.

A hurt, broken laugh. 'Do you remember telling me I came so close to death I looked upon the face of God?'

'On the ship?'

'You told me you saw a – a stillness in my chest. Only then I was restored to you. You said it. "You looked upon the face of God."'

'I remember. I thought you had gone. You did go. For a moment.'

'Well, I never saw the face of God.'

'You might not remember such a thing.'

'I saw Hanne's face.' Thea stared her down. 'I looked upon her face.'

'Thea,' I whispered, and tears filled my eyes.

Anna Maria was silent. She looked up to the sloping bark above her. 'I know you miss her.'

I buried my face in Thea's shoulder. She smelled of fatigue and fear and sap.

Thea put a hand to her heart. 'It hurts.'

Anna Maria closed her eyes. 'I know.'

Thea exhaled. 'It hurts so much.' She seemed on a precipice. I thought again of the embroidery fluttering in the wind, dangling above the ocean.

'It is natural that you miss her.'

Thea shook her head. She was clutching her chest as though holding bones together, stilling blood flow. 'She still feels so close. I dream about her every night.'

'What do you dream?'

'Sometimes I dream that we are still in Kay. But more often I dream I wake and Hanne is lying next to me.'

The chambers of my unpumping heart filled with love and sea water.

Anna Maria raised her head, shifted her weight so that she was leaning on her elbow, studying her daughter. 'Do you dream you wake, or do you wake?'

Thea paused. 'What do you mean?'

'I mean, are these dreams, or have you seen Hanne beside you?'

Thea hesitated and I could feel the question pass through her.

'Perhaps you have a shadow.' Anna Maria studied Thea, bending her head to look her in the eyes. 'You know what I mean.'

Thea's eyes were wide in the dark. I found her hand. Squeezed it.

'I feel her everywhere,' she whispered. 'I feel her here.'

'Hanne.'

Thea nodded.

'Here.'

'Yes.'

'In this shelter with us, or in your heart?'

'Both.'

'And does it frighten you?'

Thea shook her head.

'Well then,' said Anna Maria, and she leaned back again, eyes fixed on Thea. 'There have been a few times.'

'What do you mean?' Thea spoke in a whisper.

Anna Maria was silent. 'Someone. A presence, but only when you are with me. At your shoulder. Once, when you were sick and sleeping, I looked at your hand and your knuckles were white, your hand pink, as though someone were squeezing it. I wondered then.'

There was a small smile on Thea's face. 'I dream she holds my hand.'

'Perhaps it is not a dream.'

They both looked down to Thea's hands, which I held still, my fingers tight around her own. I could not hold them tight enough. I squeezed them until my bones ached.

Anna Maria inhaled slowly. 'Do you ever talk to her?'

Thea shook her head.

'Maybe you should. But, Thea, it would not be wise to tell anyone of this. It would be an unkindness for Hanne's family –'

'Of course.'

'– and it will raise suspicions. People will doubt your faith. You know what Magdalena says of me . . .'

Thea nodded.

'You understand?'

'Yes.'

'But you should talk to her. You are not afraid?'

'No. The thought that Hanne . . .'

Tears slid down my face. I leaned forwards and rested my forehead on our entwined fingers, kissed Thea's knuckles. I was trembling.

Anna Maria's eyes did not leave her daughter and I wondered if she guessed then, in that moment, what we had been to each other. I wondered if it filled her with fear or whether Anna Maria, who trailed her fingers in stranger rivers, accepted that there was little she understood, and that not understanding was no reason to be fearful. I have never met anyone who so willingly surrendered to mystery, to things beyond their knowing.

'Well,' Anna Maria said eventually, 'I'd best go speak with your father.'

Thea caught her sleeve as she crawled towards the opening. 'What do I say? To Hanne?'

'Whatever is in your heart, Thea. The dead are drawn to the heart, wellspring of love that it is.'

Thea lay back down after her mother left. I could tell she was listening, was stilling her body to better hear the world around her. She closed her eyes.

I lay down beside her. I placed my ear to her mouth, felt the fluttering of her breath against it.

'Hanne,' she said. Her voice around my name, gentle summons, undid me. I rested my head on her chest, filled my mouth with my balled-up shift and cried silently, feeling the soft reverberation of her beneath me saying over and over, 'I miss you. I miss you.'

I slept with my hands in her hair. She woke in the night, once, and said my name again, and I answered her with her own. She smiled and I wondered if she had heard me. Our names, passing between us in breath.

The next morning rose gently over the ranges. When Thea and Anna Maria left the shelter, they noticed a small grey mound resting in a shallow hole in the dirt, a little charred on one side, and a pile of tubers lying beside their packs.

'Oh goodness,' Anna Maria said, picking up the ball. 'Look, it's burning somehow.'

Thea took it from her mother and blew on it. I saw a little smoke issue, a red flare of live ember. 'It's smouldering. Like incense. What is it? It's too light to be wood.'

'Some kind of fungus?'

Thea's eyes travelled to the kindling scattered by Friedrich the night before. 'They thought we could not light our fire.'

Mother and daughter shared a look.

Friedrich did not touch the tubers. He sat in front of the now-roaring fire, stiff from sleeping in the open. But he did not say anything when Anna Maria and Thea tried them, tentatively at first, and then with relish.

'Are you sure you don't want any, Papa?' Thea asked, holding out the root. 'It's sweet. A little nutty.'

'It's good, Friedrich,' Anna Maria said. 'Not bitter at all.'

Friedrich shook his head. 'I'll have ship's biscuit,' he said.

'Really?' Anna Maria raised her eyebrows. 'You'd rather eat from what little stores we have? Our preserves? When all we have is debt?'

Friedrich hesitated. I could see him bristle at Anna Maria's words, but he could not deny the truth of the matter. He took a root and ate it quickly, eyes closed.

'Good, isn't it?' Thea asked.

Friedrich swallowed.

'Your daughter asked you a question,' Anna Maria murmured.

Friedrich sighed. Then he lifted a hand and gently cupped Thea's cheek. 'It's good,' he said.

'I didn't hear that,' Anna Maria interjected.

Friedrich ran at his wife. I braced myself for violence, closing my eyes, but I heard only a loud shriek of delight, and when I looked again I saw Friedrich had lifted Anna Maria in his arms, was spinning her in the clearing as Thea looked on, chewing and grinning.

'Why did I marry you?' Friedrich was shouting, swinging his wife so that she had to grip onto his shoulders. 'Such a nag and harridan!'

Anna Maria threw her head back and laughed. 'Because you love me,' she said. 'And you know I'm always right.'

From that night onwards, Thea spoke to me. Through the long and upward climb she whispered my name under her breath. Her voice tied me to her. I could not have walked away even if I had wanted to. During the day she stayed close to her parents. Even though there was a faint track to follow, the possibility of becoming lost hung over them on every misty morning, or whenever, in their fatigue, they imagined other tracks, other ways, and found themselves sliding down steep embankments, slippery with leaves. But at night, when

Anna Maria and Friedrich fell asleep, Thea crawled out of their improvised shelter and walked from tree to tree, placing her hands on trunks glowing ghost-white in the dark, fingers tracing coarse bodies of bark. Only then, in her solitude, did she whisper my name into the night air.

'Hanne.'

Saying my name as though she were calling me. As though she were not the moon and I the ocean, tidal with longing, ever turned to her.

'Hanne . . .' She paused. 'I feel you like a knot in my throat.'

I placed my hand on top of hers, splayed my fingers between her knuckles.

'Today there was a fire burning. I smelled the smoke first. There were ashes in the air. I climbed the rise and saw the plume, some flames beneath it. Papa thought it was a wildfire and became anxious – Pastor Flügel's warnings and so on. "The breath of the Lord, like a stream of brimstone . . ." But it was a ring. The fire was burning inwards from all directions. Coming together upon itself. And when we had climbed the next rise and could see again, the fire was out.'

She turned towards a tree and placed her forehead against it. 'Hanne,' she whispered. 'Hanne, that is what I feel like when I think of you. A fire closing in upon itself.'

I did not dare speak for fear of missing a word, a breath, a hesitation.

She closed her eyes, turning her head so that her cheek lay upon the pale trunk. 'Show me,' she whispered. 'Show me you are here.'

I do not know how it happened. Not that first time. I shivered at her voice in the dark. The tree she was touching was smooth, radiant in the moonlight, and all I wanted was for her to rest her hand upon my face as she rested it upon the tree. I wanted to feel her touch me.

The longing grew in me until I felt a strange trembling at the edges of myself, as though I was dissolving into air.

Thea's skin pressed against the tree. The tree. Silver streak soaring into night sky, dripping with leaves still and slender, foaming fragrance into quiet air. I could feel that tree and its deep sinking into soil. I could feel it sending its hum deep under the earth, felt the air between its branches and knew that the tree was not only itself but many others, that the growing of the tree was the growing of everything else around it.

And then *I* was the tree. Rivers of sap rolled through us; I could feel everything we were and everything we would be. Leaves not yet unfurled, blossom capped in gumnut, roots needling moisture from the soil. We were everything that had passed, and we were what would come, the waited-for. Oh, we were waiting. Waiting for fog. Waiting for leaf-drop. Waiting for drip and bird call and waiting for heat and soaring and touching of sky.

I was the tree. It was sharing itself with me.

And somewhere, in the great unbellying of time, we were aware of the pressure of a living thing.

Little pale sapling. Her shiver at all night-shifting and wind-stirring. Breathing against us.

Thea.

I wanted to touch her. I wanted to bend to her.

All living wood, all stem and years ringing the heart of us bent to her breath, bent to her voice, and there was a giving-way, a crack, and as the branch fell, I fell with it. I blacked out and passed out of time.

I was the tree, and then I was not.

When I woke, I was alone, curled on the floor of the bush, moonlight making a mockery of the darkness. I sat up and felt oddly faint, and when I brought my palms to my face they were beaded with sap, blossom threads suspended in sticky trails. My feet ached. I cradled one in my hands and examined the sole. Beneath each toe a whisper of fibre. A tendril of root.

I did not understand it at all. It was a dream. A strange temper. But Thea was gone and around me, broken in several places, was a large branch upending its leaves at head-height.

I ran my hands over the jagged end where it had snapped from the trunk, every splinter sharp with desire.

Voices then, from the dawn unclawing yonder. Thea and her parents dragging their parcels ahead, marvelling still at the near miss. I rose to my feet and ran to the sound of Thea's voice exclaiming, 'A miracle it did not touch me.'

'It would have broken your back.'

'But it did not touch me.'

I reached them as Anna Maria brought her arm around Thea's shoulder. She bent low and said, 'You understand now. The book.'

That day, the sap and fibre upon my body fell away, and if it weren't for that lingering feeling of tree-soar, the otherness of it, the memory of life running through me, I would have wondered if it had happened at all.

For the next three days, as the Eichenwalds climbed ever higher into the hills, I stood at the base of cup gums and tea-trees and native cherries, wattles and blackwoods, and I placed my hands upon their branches and leaves and trunks, and I willed a shaking back into life.

Nothing happened. I couldn't understand it.

I tried wrapping my arms around the white trunks of candle barks. I waited for nights. I asked God to join me to the green-grey fronds of acacia and placed my mouth over beading sap. Nothing.

And then. And then.

One day I stood beside a banksia loud with honeyeaters and nectar. The music lifting from the tree was so joyful, I joined my voice to its singing, and as I sang, I thought of Thea. I yearned for her and I yearned to be absorbed by the banksia, and in the rising key of all the strains of growth, I felt the banksia admit me and we were together. We knew what it was to bud and blossom and eat the light. I felt the birds upon me like a visitation from God.

That is how it happened.

In the valley below, the bell is tolling for sundown. Time to put down tools and shut in the animals returned from pasture. Time to go indoors and breathe heavily of the Bible. The end of another day.

How is it that days keep coming?

I will stay up here and recite my own grace. Gratitude for that first time where I learned what might be possible to me, when I once thought I would be forever shut off from life.

Stringybark, red gum, blue gum, I give thanks. To know what it is like to ache as a root divining water. What it is to hold time's soft circumference within me. Thank you for the pleasure-hunger of that journey next to Thea, when I was able to be her canopy.

beten und arbeiten

It was a red-gold valley, gentle-sloped, and when I first saw it, arriving with the Eichenwalds in the dying days of April, it was bronze with kangaroo grass that caressed the waist. Unlike much of the forest across the ranges, the valley was open country, expansive, interrupted only by immense gum trees that drew the eyes skywards and stretched the throat. They stood in weight with arms raised, bearing the knobbed scars of lost branches, bark peeling from gargantuan trunks that soared, twisting upwards, outwards. Some of the gums stood leafless yet screeched white-raw with cockatoos. Others were hollowed. As I walked beside Thea, following a tributary of the river we had passed earlier, I saw that a family had set up home in one of these trees, canvas strung to extend the shelter. Washing draped over nearby fallen branches, drying. I peered in and saw someone sleeping in bedding laid over heaped grass. A ship's trunk had been turned into a cradle in one corner, the detached lid in use as a table at the entrance, next to a mound of ashes ringed with stones. I placed my hand on the lip of the hollow, on the outside of the trunk. Thought of what it was like to be fleshed with wood, tender-hard and rippled with years.

Not one, but many. Older than old.

'This must be it,' Friedrich said, setting the trunk down on the track and taking the hat from his head. Thea and Anna Maria paused, breathing hard. A flock of parrots burst out of a nearby tree and they smiled at each other.

'We're here, then,' Anna Maria said quietly, taking in the valley. 'A new home.'

Thea swung her burden onto the ground. 'Someone is coming.'

I turned and saw my father wading through the high grass towards the Eichenwalds. My heart leaped to see him, although I was struck by the way his shirt hung from his shoulders.

'Welcome, pilgrims,' my father announced, removing his hat and lifting it in greeting. He wiped his palm on his shirt before shaking Friedrich's hand. I noticed the dirt sunk deep into his nails. 'Welcome to Heiligendorf.' He turned and, fingers to mouth, whistled hard. Soon after, I saw Matthias, followed by Hans, pushing through the grass towards them.

'Here, boys,' Papa called, nodding at the Eichenwalds' belongings. 'Give them a hand, would you?'

Matthias and Hans greeted Friedrich and Anna Maria, smiled at Thea. She seemed as shocked as I was to see how lean they were. I threw my arms around my brother's neck as he stooped to pick up the rope handle on the side of the Eichenwalds' trunk and breathed deeply of him. He looked like Gottlob but smelled as I remembered, of grass and chaff and sweat. I ran a hand down the side of his face, feeling the beginnings of a beard beneath my fingers.

'Hello, Thea.' Hans heaved the other side of the trunk into the air and he and Matthias began carrying it along the track. Papa picked up the bundle from Thea's feet, swinging it onto his shoulder.

Friedrich indicated the nearby campsite. 'How many are here?'

'Most now. The first of us settled a month ago, in March. The heat! You remember? But the day we found this paradise, the creek was still flowing . . . Here, you must see what we prepared.'

The Eichenwalds followed my father, looking about them at the campsites spaced regularly along the track. Papa veered left, heading towards a small shelter slouched under a crooked gum tree. It was scarcely more than a shepherd's hut, made from latticed branches thickened with dried mud and straw.

'What is this then?' asked Anna Maria as she ducked her head under the low entryway. It was dark inside, despite the open doorway and the sunlight coming through gaps in the daub. I looked up and saw that a sheet had been pinned in lieu of a ceiling. Someone had painted it with stars.

Papa set down Thea's bag at the entrance. 'We began work on it as soon as we finished our journey. The day we first arrived, we raised our hands to the sky and thanked the Lord. The Holy Spirit moved amongst us and we agreed that a church must be built as soon as we had collected all our belongings, before the surveyor had even marked out the allotments, before we had built our own shelters.'

Hans glanced up at the bedsheet, then at Thea. Mirth twitched at his mouth.

Papa noticed. 'It's not much at the moment,' he admitted, 'but we shall improve it. Imagine . . .' Papa said, turning to Friedrich and trailing his hand through the air as though presenting a miracle. 'Imagine the spire that will rise here, the bell that will call us to work, will call us to rest and worship!' He seized Friedrich's hand once more. '"Rejoice, ye who act in faith. The Lord shall reward thee."'

'Very fine,' Friedrich said, smiling. He glanced sideways, to his wife. 'Has Pastor Flügel seen it?'

'We've sent word for him to come and dedicate the church. He will move between here and Neu Klemzig every six weeks or so. We must find him a horse so that we do not have to hold all our weddings and funerals at once. The dead do not like to wait.'

Hans grinned at Matthias. 'Neither do the betrothed.'

'It is Sunday tomorrow –' Friedrich began.

'Christian Pasche will deliver the sermon,' my father said, interrupting him.

'My father has delivered all the sermons thus far,' Hans added.

'And did Herr Pasche suggest the name Heiligendorf?' asked Anna Maria.

'That was me,' my father said, finally turning to her. 'A fitting name for a place where all seek to walk in Christ's footsteps. Our holy village.'

Anna Maria smiled without showing her teeth.

Papa turned back to Friedrich. 'I'll fetch the surveyor so that you might draw your lot of land. But first, let us give thanks for your safe arrival.' He waited until all was silent. 'Dearest God, I thank you for giving us this rich and fertile land so that we may prosper and serve you in freedom. "Truly, every good gift and every perfect gift is from above, and cometh down from the Father of lights, with whom is no variableness, neither shadow of turning."'

'Papa, I may turn into a tree at will,' I said and kissed him on his slumped eyelid.

'Amen', said Papa. 'Amen.'

The land rented by the congregation had already been subdivided, the layout of the village drawn up as a *Hufendorf*, a horseshoe of narrow homesteads that surrounded the crooked gum, the wattle-and-daub church and the place for the school that would one day be built. The surveyor, a pleasant man of some education from Züllichau, explained to Friedrich and Anna Maria that each family or married couple in the congregation would receive an equal share of one acre, enough for a house, garden and small farm, and that they would all have access to some communal land for grazing. Each allotment was numbered and corresponded to small folded pieces of paper that the surveyor kept in a chipped milk jug. He had tried to be as equitable as possible in terms of land size, fertility and access to water, he explained, but it was clear from my father's expression that the number Friedrich drew from the jug was one of the better allotments.

'The soil here is unquestionable proof of divine blessing,' Papa said as he led the Eichenwalds to their land. 'Here, this is where you will live. I am just beyond, where all those trees are. Your allotment is already mostly clear.' Papa kneeled down and parted the tall grass with his hands, looking up at Friedrich with his good eye. 'Here is God's providence! Look.' Papa pulled up some of the grass, showing Friedrich the soil beneath. He pinched some with his fingers and spread the rich, dark earth across his palm. 'There is at least three feet of topsoil in some places. Three feet! It makes me pity those who decided to stay on at Neu Klemzig. May God bless them. Trying to grow cabbages out of that gravel pit.' He wiped his hands on his trousers. 'It's soft. Spongy. You can feel the goodness under your feet. God has given us a park. Truly, we have much to thank Him for.'

'Captain Olsen, too,' added Friedrich, bending to the ground to examine the earth.

'Yes, he is the Lord's agent. Wait until you taste the water here.'

'Pure?' asked Friedrich.

My father laughed and threw his hat in the air.

The warmth of the day was fading fast by the time Papa left the Eichenwalds to make camp. I was tempted to follow him, to see Matthias again and Mama and Hermine, but Thea was yawning into her elbow and I was unaccustomed to spending evenings away from her side. I sat cross-legged on the ground and watched while she and her mother lit a fire with the slow-burning fungus and constructed a shelter. Friedrich took advantage of the remaining light to make his own assessment of their land.

'How long will it take us to build a proper home?' Thea asked, carefully storing their belongings in the narrow cleft of a fallen tree trunk.

Anna Maria stepped back from the slanting framework of intertwined branches. 'I think we might pull it apart and start again once we have collected the rest of our luggage from the ridge,' she said, looking at it doubtfully. 'Cut some saplings and dig them into the ground, like others have done. Go cut some of that grass,' she said, handing Thea a scythe blade. 'I'll plug the gaps.' She looked up at the clear sky. 'It feels cold now. Doesn't it feel cold?'

'Mama?'

'I don't know, Thea. There are more important things to attend to for now.'

'Crops.'

Anna Maria nodded towards the bagged wheat seed the surveyor had given them. 'What will alleviate the debt.'

Friedrich returned, his face satisfied. 'We've good access to the creek,' he said, throwing an armful of gathered sticks on the fire. He squinted in the smoke as flames began to crackle through the leaves. 'Heinrich is right. The water and soil are good.'

'Are you happy, Papa?' asked Thea, handing kangaroo grass to Anna Maria.

'Happy? Yes. I think so.' He suddenly turned away from his wife and daughter, working his jaw.

Thea placed the scythe on the ground and wrapped her arms around his waist.

'It's good to be here,' Friedrich said finally. He covered her hands, tight around his stomach, with his own. 'After everything that has happened...' He opened his mouth to say more, but the words seemed to stick in his throat and he could do no more than gasp, 'Yes. Praise God.'

*

That night, Thea did not sleep. Although she closed her eyes, I could tell that she was awake, and when she finally crawled quietly out of the shelter, I followed her. It was a clear night. A moon, yellow as a dog's tooth, rose above the black silhouette of bush on the rise of land beyond the valley.

I could see Thea's breath as vapour. I lifted my fingers to it.

'Hanne,' she said, looking out towards the moon, arms crossed over her body against the chill, 'we would have been neighbours.'

To our left, well within sight, was the small glow of my family's fire.

'I am burning down,' she whispered. 'I am burning down.'

There was the sound of a stick cracking. Thea startled. I saw a figure in the shadows.

'Who's there?'

'Sorry. Sorry, I didn't mean to scare you.'

'Who is it?'

'Hans Pasche.'

'Oh.' The fear went out of Thea's voice as Hans stepped forwards, taking off his hat. 'What are you doing here?'

Hans gestured towards the allotment bordering the other side. 'We're neighbours, you know.'

Thea peered past him to where another campfire could be seen, flames sending sparks into the night.

'There?'

'*Ja*. It's good to see you arrived safely. Are all your things here?'

'Not yet. It might take us a few weeks or so to fetch them.'

Hans nodded. 'So. What are you doing, wandering around in the dark? I heard you talking to yourself.'

'What? No. I couldn't sleep. I'm not the one loitering.'

'Loitering?' Hans feigned offence. He picked up a stick and poked the ash of the Eichenwalds' fire, revealing bright fragments of ember. He cleared his throat. 'Have you seen my cat?'

Thea raised her eyebrows.

Hans blew on the coals. They flared orange, illuminating his face as he smiled up at her. 'You know, black. White patch on her tail. The one the sailor from the *Kristi* gave to me. She's not left my side since.' He narrowed his eyes in mock suspicion. 'Then you arrive and she disappears.'

'You think I stole your cat?'

Hans lowered his voice. 'Don't all witches need a cat?' He paused. 'Christiana Radtke might have mentioned a certain book she saw given to you.'

Thea said nothing. I saw fear twinge through her body.

Hans rose to his feet, hand outstretched. 'Don't worry,' he whispered. 'Your secret is safe with me.' He threw the stick on the fire and watched it smoulder. 'So long as you give me the cat back, I won't tell Flügel about your book.'

Thea glanced back at the dark hut where her parents lay sleeping.

Hans laughed. 'Look at you. You think I'm serious.'

Thea stared at him. 'I don't know what to think.'

'You think I'd care about anything Christiana Radtke said?'

'I have no idea what you think about Christiana Radtke.'

'Not much,' said Hans. He placed his hat back on his head. 'I'm sorry. I didn't mean to tease . . .'

'People are saying things?'

'Oh.' Hans shrugged. 'You know the Radtkes.'

'No.' Thea shook her head. 'No, I don't. They have never been friendly to my family.'

Hans hesitated. 'You shouldn't worry. Pastor Flügel has welcomed you into this congregation. He is the authority here.'

'My mother is not a witch.' Thea paused. 'Nor am I.'

'I know.' Hans's voice was gentle. 'Well, would you let me know if you see her? She did run off this way. But then I found you instead.'

'Yes, well. Sorry to disappoint you.'

Hans smiled and I was struck by the warmth in his face. 'I'm not disappointed,' he said.

Thea nodded and, without saying goodnight, returned to the shelter.

Hans remained by the dying fire, looking at the place Thea had been, then slowly turned and walked off into the dark, looking back every few steps as though he expected to see her still standing there, wrapped in firelight, all uncertainty.

The moon was a hanging gallstone. Salt water trickled out of my nostrils and down my chin.

May arrived and brought the last of the families and their possessions, as well as days of rain that greened the land and washed the air of dust thrown up by the clearing of the valley, already begun in earnest. After the dry heat of summer, it was with a mixture of relief and consternation that the congregation received the change in weather. I spent each night by Thea's side, sitting between the comfort of her warm back and the wall of rough saplings. Some mornings dawned white with frost, and when I tucked myself into the heft and tower of a nearby blue gum I felt the thrill of ice melting upon our leaves.

With each new bright, crisp day, I walked to see my own family. My father prided himself on being the first to wake in the valley. Each morning, after pissing at the base of the same wattle, steam rising from the ground, he bent low at the entryway to his hut and thundered, 'What more has man to do than to labour and to pray without ceasing? Hm? *Beten und arbeiten*. Pray and work!' Mama and Matthias would emerge moments later, faces haggard with want of sleep, Hermine well wrapped and stirring in irritation on my mother's shoulder. After prayers by the dead char of the previous night's fire, Matthias would walk Hermine to Augusta, then return to work. Mama hauled the bag of wedges and sledgehammers from tree to tree for my brother and Papa, sawing smaller branches herself when needed. The grass was scythed short, the smaller wattles and gums felled with axes. The larger red gums took days. I watched Papa and Matthias labour through the hours, digging trenches, cutting as many roots as possible to weaken them. There were three magnificent trees bent together, so tall they seemed to commune with the sky, and each day Papa stared them down while scratching his beard. They stood in the middle of the land he intended for wheat, and I could see that they irritated him in their disruption. I sang my way inside the smaller of the three to watch my father circle below, muttering aloud about ringbarking, fire, while we felt hollows within ourself, filled with the soft turning of furred babies. In the end, the magnitude of the gums seemed to intimidate him, and he let them be, although not without several evenings of vented irritation to my mother about the inequity of his being allocated a section so sat upon by giants.

I was glad my father left the three sister gums alone; I took to keeping sentry within the smallest. Together, we were alive and thrummed with sap. We were scarred with old feeding tracks of termites, heavy with years, pathed with nicks from the claws of creatures who rested within and upon us. The comfort of a sleeping koala nestled in our forks was akin to the weight of a hand upon a weary shoulder. From our height, we felt the congregation burn and dig and scrape the land down. Drizzle kissed us. Smoke fires billowed over us. And always, below, the hypnotic pull and thrust of the saw, the relentless swing of the adze. As the days grew ever shorter and colder, everything smelled of fire and turned earth and the heady, brutal tang of new-felled wood.

At night, again myself, I felt my teeth ache in memory of the bone-deep reverberation of trees hitting the soil and consoled myself by sitting at the Eichenwalds' fire, listening to Thea tell her parents what she had planted from the seeds provided to them. She stored them in paper within her canvas ship's bag, kept dry within the hollow of the trunk next to their campsite. I listened to her recite the names of plants like answers to a catechism.

'Lettuces, green peas, radishes, cabbages. Turnips. Spinach and cress.'

At first light she stalked the rows like a bird, eyes sharp for signs of growth in the soil. When the seeds sprouted, tender miracles of green appearing, she kneeled and gave thanks to God, and even my own disbelieving heart was filled with awe. I sat in the earth beside her as she prayed and I rubbed that giving dirt across her forehead so that the garden would know she belonged to it.

It was strange to see the land so quickly transformed. On Sundays, when the congregation gathered around the humble daub church, Elder Christian turned his Bible to the Book of Joshua, and the bush was compared to the wall of Jericho. God would help them bring it down. I could see the triumph in the shoulders of the men when they were able to finally wrest the more stubborn of trees from the air, and I understood that had I, too, been clearing the soil each day, I would have felt the hot dash of relief in my body when progress was made. But from my deep abiding within heartwood, root and leaf vein, I could more clearly feel that to clear the land was to scar it, and to triumph in that scarring seemed sinister and unholy. I did not sing the praises of felled trees. I did not sing the glory of sown seed potatoes, bags of wheat at one pound a bushel.

I do not praise it now. It has been a long time since I sought out the life flowing in the sapwood of a river red gum, but my memory of it remains acute. I know more now. That is why I no longer do it. I have no desire to sweep the earth clean of trees.

Winter settled in, squatting over the landscape and pissing down more freezing rain until the creek took on a wild, agitated look, creeping up its banks and threatening to flood. Often, after a heavy rain, small groups of '*Eingeborene*' walked through Heiligendorf, looking in the makeshift shelters and observing the clearing of the land, before gathering by the creek to remove fish from traps they set there. They never stayed long and it was presumed by the elders that the valley was not favoured by them. When MacFarlane, one of the landowners who had negotiated the contract, drafted men from the congregation to fence his station, Matthias and Hans returned describing campsites they had seen higher up in the ranges, snug homes of stone and others abutting tree hollows built from branches, bark and leaves.

'Cosy as you like,' Hans said to Thea, visiting one Sunday afternoon. 'Beds with possum skins, all sewn together. Much better than the hovel we're living in.'

'I heard Rosina complaining about it yesterday,' Thea admitted.

'I told my father we ought to spend the time making a better shelter, but no. "Wheat first, a house later."' Hans rolled his eyes. 'Now he asks me why I'm doing so little to keep out the weather.'

'I'm sorry,' Thea murmured.

'That's why I've come,' Hans explained. 'I was wondering if your father might let me take some of those saplings by the border?'

'Ask him yourself,' Thea said. 'You don't need to go through me.'

Hans smiled, and there was something in it that unsettled me.

'I also wanted to give you this.' He handed her a small cat, whittled from wood.

Thea turned it in her hands.

'You can have it, if you like.'

'What good is a false cat to a witch?'

'Keep it,' he said. 'I made it for you.'

Thea did not speak of Hans to her mother. The wooden cat was placed in her canvas bag and not drawn out again, and although I watched her carefully for the flush and self-consciousness that attended Christiana and Henriette when they spoke of marriage and dowry chests and children, Thea seemed unruffled. Still, it wasn't until I walked the track through the village and saw Magdalena Radtke yoked to their family's new cow, Samuel Radtke behind, pipe in one hand and reins in the other, that I was able to distract myself from a lingering sense of discomfort. Christiana, following the plough with a basket of seed potatoes, was so red-faced with embarrassment that I sang myself into the Radtkes' vegetable garden for the joy of it.

Sweet euphoria, to be an onion seedling in well-turned earth. To feel the swelling of our tiny bulb was to feel the universe within.

The valley grew damp with a rising water table and mornings soon brought a chorus of coughing from those who had been unwell on the ship. Passengers whose teeth ran bloody, or who hobbled around on ankles fat with sickness, stopped work altogether. The leftover rations from the ship had dwindled, and there was no *Sauerkraut* left, only rice which was ground and mixed with ever-smaller amounts of wheat flour. Matthias mentioned to Mama that

Augusta's husband was unable to work his own land. I noticed that he began to take a portion of his own breakfast for Wilhelm.

I was not bothered by the cold or frost or rain. If anything, I liked the sharpness of the winter wind on my face and the droplets that flew from the tossed clusters of wet gum leaves. I cupped my hands in the creek and felt the ache driving into my knuckles. But I could see the way the winter rain was worming into the living. They were hungry. Cold. Conversation turned to the chests of winter clothing left behind on the docks at Altona, the woollen stockings and flannel they thought they would not need.

'Who knows if we will ever see them again,' remarked Elize Geschke, filling pails at the creek, voice muffled by the thick scarf she had wound around her head.

'Work makes me warm enough,' said Beate Fröhlich. 'Besides, there is no snow.'

'It's not the cold which bothers Karl, but the wet,' murmured Augusta to my mother. 'He says his bones are paining him, and it is worse when it rains. He's short of breath.' She lowered her voice even further. 'He hasn't passed any water for days. This morning he asked for the pastor.'

Mama nodded. 'I'll come and see him.'

'What about Anna Maria?'

Several of the women glanced up at the name. There was a moment of uneasy silence.

My mother cleared her throat and, though I saw her cheeks rise in colour, her voice when she spoke was calm and sure. 'I'll ask her to come too.'

Beate Fröhlich shook her head, mouth hard.

'Is there something you'd like to say, Beate? Or would you like to come and treat Karl yourself?'

'It's not for me to say anything,' said Beate. 'It's for the pastor.'

'I agree. Let us leave Pastor Flügel to discern what is best for us all.' Mama hooked her pail onto the yoke across her shoulder and made her way back up the muddied creek bank. 'I'll fetch her now, Augusta.'

A child's wail could be heard long before Anna Maria, Thea and my mother arrived at Augusta and Karl's campsite, which was the hollow tree I had peered inside when I first saw the valley. Rain was puddling under the canvas awning, the campfire smoking badly under a black kettle. Wilhelm was sitting up in the ship's chest, bawling, while Karl lay still under a heap of blankets and spare clothing.

'Karl?' Augusta bent under the dripping canvas and called into the tree. 'We've visitors. Anna Maria Eichenwald, Frau Nussbaum. They'd like to see you.'

There was a pause, then Karl, groaning, lifted his head. *'Ein Fest, oder?'* The words wheezed out of him.

Anna Maria crawled into the hollow on her knees. 'Yes, a party. How are you feeling, Karl?'

'I don't think I'm long for this world.'

'Don't say that,' Augusta said. She gestured for Anna Maria to pass her the baby. 'Karl has become morose,' she whispered to Mama.

I crept into the tree on my hands and knees and made my way to Karl's side. He lay on his back as Anna Maria, now leaning over him, gently turned his head one way then the other, and examined his tongue and limbs. When she lifted the blankets, I saw that his feet were so bloated as to be disfigured. The legs of his trousers had been cut at the seams to allow for the swelling.

'How on earth did you walk all the way up the ranges?' Anna Maria exclaimed.

Karl attempted a smile. 'Augusta' – he paused to breathe – 'dragged me. She is a force.'

'You need vinegar,' Anna Maria said gently. 'Some vegetables.' She stretched her neck towards the canvas awning, where Thea was pulling faces at Wilhelm. 'Thea, how are the radishes?'

I heard Thea hesitate. 'Not ready.'

'The tops are up, though?'

'Yes.'

'Go get them.' Anna Maria stroked Karl's hand. 'Some greens will help.'

Karl nodded. Speaking seemed to tire him. 'See she marries again,' he murmured.

Anna Maria shushed him. 'No need for her to marry when she already has a fine husband.'

'Please. I want . . . my son to have a father. How will she survive on her own?'

Anna Maria patted his hand. 'Don't you worry about that now. Rest, and I'll bring you something to eat in a little while.'

'I may not have as long as that,' breathed Karl. 'I see her.'

'Who?'

'The angel.' He pointed to where I sat holding my knees to my chest, resting against the inside of the tree.

Hair lifted on the back of my neck.

Anna Maria was silent. She glanced in my direction. 'You see something?'

Karl nodded.

I leaned forwards, body prickling, mouth dry. 'You see me?'

'She speaks,' he said.

'What is she saying?' Anna Maria's voice was quiet. Careful.

I placed a hand on his leg. Felt it twitch beneath my palm. 'Karl?'

Karl's eyes crinkled into a smile. '*Nun ruhe ich in Gottes Händen.* Now I rest in God's hands.'

I scrambled closer, leaning over his face so that my hair fell onto his forehead. '*Sie sehen mich?!*'

He closed his eyes. 'I see it all,' he said softly, and then he began to cough.

When the fit passed, he lapsed into unconsciousness.

'What is it?' I heard Augusta ask from outside the tree. 'Anna Maria, what is it?'

Thea crawled into the hollow clutching radish tops in her hand, hair misted with rain. She was breathing hard. 'I ran,' she explained to Anna Maria, glancing down at Karl before giving her mother an uncertain look. 'Is he dead?'

Anna Maria gave a little shake of her head. 'Soon,' she whispered.

Augusta's face appeared. 'He's sleeping?'

Anna Maria crawled out from Karl's side. I could hear her directing Augusta away from the tree. 'He might become better,' she was saying. 'But he might not, too. He has been unwell for some time, I think.'

Thea sat still, staring at Karl. She picked up a corner of his blanket and wiped the rain from her face, then gently tucked him in. I saw her look around the hollow. Shiver.

I touched the ends of Thea's brilliant hair, lit with water. Put them to my lips.

Sour wine on the hyssop.

Anna Maria remained with Augusta all afternoon. As they boiled radish tops, I crouched over Karl within the hollow tree and willed him awake. Every time he shifted or groaned, I spoke to him.

'Wake up,' I whispered. 'Wake up.'

But Karl did not rouse back into consciousness. That afternoon his breathing became strangled and Anna Maria gently advised Augusta to summon the elders. I watched the man's chest rise and fall with wet breaths as Papa prayed over and blessed him. I thumped my fist on Karl's heart. 'Wake up. Tell them you see me! Tell my father you see me!'

The rain began to fall in earnest. Wilhelm's cries were drowned out by the sound of the downpour upon the canvas.

They left Karl's body for three days, covered with a sheet that gathered a detritus of unfamiliar flowers and leaves as the congregation paid their respects. I spent every hour of daylight at his body's side, wondering if Karl would reappear as I had. But when the body was finally lowered into the ground beside the church – the first, lonely grave in that cemetery – I remained alone.

If others are here, as I am, we are as unseen to one another as the living. The lonely dead, wishing for ghosts of our own.

hunger

Night is falling now. There is an empty feeling to the land below.

Once I found a coastline and walked the shore for weeks. I remember it as a cold time. The ocean raged against rocks and land; I saw the way salt worked upon the world. I passed a place where river met sea, and there were many people living there who read the country like my father read his Bible: in assurance of its graces and knowledge of how they might be found. I sat at a distance and watched them cook in ovens of stone. There were shell middens there, so old they shared the hum of the land. But some of the faces of the people bore evidence of affliction, and the more time I spent there, the more I saw ugly shepherds of smallpox and violence force an unnatural migration upon these people, away from the country they belonged to.

I spent the nights curled in dunes amidst the grasses. Every morning-come I was covered in sand.

I found a whaling station that smelled of death and disruption, white men missing teeth, their faces greased mean with hunger for seal pelt, and even though the coastline there was a deep love song of granite submitting to time and weather, I felt uneasy. I continued on and later, when the wind blew up from the south, it was a mouth filled with horror and it said dark and urgent things I could not understand, though it raked fear through me. That afternoon, walking along the coast, I saw an Aboriginal woman half in the water and half out of it.

She fled the island, the sea said as it flowed through her hair. *She wanted to return home. We carried her the distance she could not swim.*

I knew nothing of those things when I first came to the valley. I had no understanding of the world.

Night is falling now. I am not gone yet. Here, wind, listen. There is more. There is always more.

On a clear day towards the end of winter, the same day Flügel finally arrived in Heiligendorf, a large group of Peramangk arrived in the valley.

At first, the congregation considered them with a quiet sort of interest. But when, over the next few days, bark huts appeared at the periphery of the allotments, now cleared and dug and sown with wheat, curiosity turned into a kind of mute apprehension. It was clear that they had left the higher campsites, wrongly assumed to be permanent settlements, and intended to remain in the valley around the dwellings of the village.

Milling amongst the congregation after Flügel's first service the next morning, I heard Rudolph Simmel tell Matthias and Hans that he had ventured close to one of the campfires the previous evening, wanting to have a closer look and make some sketches in his notebook. The '*Schwarze*', as he called them, had promptly covered up their coals. 'I suppose,' he said, 'they did not want much to do with me.'

Flügel spent the afternoon visiting the various allotments, listening to the concerns of the various families and nodding approvingly at the piglets and fowls delivered by MacFarlane's men. Mostly he tried to allay the concerns about the debt, hanging over the congregation like a dark cloud, and I soon grew sick enough of wheat talk to leave the pastor alone and return to Thea's side.

As I approached the Eichenwalds' campsite, I noticed a group of Aboriginal women passing in the opposite direction. Anna Maria was watching them walk by, and as I reached their campfire, she stood up and, indicating that Thea should come with her, followed them at a distance. The women, while turning occasionally to look the Wend up and down, did nothing to make her stop but continued about their business, turning off the track and venturing further out into the bush behind the Eichenwalds' allotment. Eventually they paused by a decaying tree and kneeled. Anna Maria peered over them, openly curious, and after glancing at each other, room was made for her to observe their work.

I watched them too. The woman at their centre looked at Thea and, gesturing, indicated a small bulge in the tree and a tiny hole beneath it. Cutting away the wood, she made a hook from a stick and prised something thick and white from the cavity inside.

Anna Maria raised her eyebrows. The woman smiled and tipped the large, slow-writhing grub into the Wend's hand. She indicated that Anna Maria should eat it.

Anna Maria looked uncertain.

'Is it a caterpillar?' Thea whispered.

'Eat,' the woman said in English, encouraging her by bringing her fingers to her lips.

Anna Maria did so, chewing and swallowing quickly.

'What does it taste like?' Thea asked.

'I don't know,' she replied. 'Nutty.'

They watched as more grubs were pulled out.

'*Warum isst du sie nicht?*' asked Anna Maria, bringing her fingers to her mouth. She turned to Thea. 'Why aren't they eating them?'

The woman who had handed her the grub nodded towards a campfire smoking in a clearing beyond the tree.

'I think she prefers to cook them.' Thea turned. 'Cook?' she asked. '*Das Feuer?*'

'Yes. Fire.' The woman nodded again, then pointed at Anna Maria, imitating her bewildered expression. The group burst into easy laughter.

Magdalena and Pastor Flügel were waiting outside the Eichenwalds' shelter when they returned from the bush. Thea spotted the pastor first, his dark sleeves flapping in the wind that had sprung up, one hand on his hat to keep it in place, and touched her mother's elbow.

Anna Maria looked up from the grubs she held in her hands. 'Thea,' she murmured, eyes fixed on Magdalena, 'where is the book?'

Thea stilled, teeth caught on her lip. 'The tree hollow,' she whispered.

'Keep walking,' Anna Maria said. She lifted her arm in greeting. 'Are you sure? It is not in our bags?'

'No, it is wrapped and deep in the dead trunk.'

'God preserve us,' Anna Maria muttered. She took a deep breath and, drawing closer to the campsite, smiled at the visitors. 'Pastor Flügel, we are so pleased to have you come again to minister here. Thank you for your sermon this morning.' She turned and nodded at Magdalena. 'Frau Radtke.'

'What is that in your hand?' Magdalena looked at the grubs in horror.

'The women here have shown me how they might be eaten. Would you like one?' Anna Maria asked.

'Mama . . .' Thea dug a finger into her mother's elbow.

Pastor Flügel stared at the grubs, then sat down on the trunk beside the fire. 'Frau Eichenwald, Frau Radtke has come to me with a complaint.' He took a deep breath. 'She says she has reason to believe you have cursed her vegetable garden.'

Anna Maria laughed out loud. 'What?'

Magdalena's chin quivered. 'Anna Maria, I know we have not always seen eye to eye. It does not give me any joy to cast aspersions. I know that there are many who do the Devil's labour unknowingly. Ignorance –'

'The Devil's labour?'

Magdalena stared at her. 'Christiana saw it. She saw the book.'

Pastor Flügel steepled the tips of his fingers together. 'Frau Eichenwald, Frau Radtke says that she has reason to believe her garden has been cursed.' Anna Maria opened her mouth to protest, but the pastor held up a hand. 'Let me continue. It is true that something has afflicted the Radtkes' vegetables. Possibly something supernatural.'

'They withered overnight.' Magdalena's face morphed from anger to pain. '*Overnight.*'

Anna Maria stared at her. Thea, by her side, was pale. 'Show me,' the Wend said finally.

The garden was dead. Not a living seedling remained in it. The leaves of the mangel-wurzel were limp and yellow, already turning back to earth, the onion seedlings wisped into nothing.

'I don't know what we will do,' Magdalena said. 'What we will eat when our stores are gone.' She was near tears.

Anna Maria turned to her, hand over her mouth. 'Magdalena, I would never do such a thing.'

The pastor gave her a sharp glance. 'Do you know how?'

The Wend lifted a hand to her headdress, frowning. 'No,' she said gently. 'No, of course not.'

'There are false texts that teach a person how to do such a thing. The witches' bible.'

'I do not own a witches' bible.' Anna Maria turned to Thea, mouth set. 'Thea, we have more seeds at home?'

Thea swallowed. 'Yes. Some.'

Anna Maria nodded at Magdalena. 'They are yours,' she said. 'I did not do this. Nor have I any desire to see you or your family starve. Will that satisfy you?'

Magdalena flung a withered mangel-wurzel into the field beyond. 'For now.'

Pastor Flügel walked Anna Maria and Thea back to their campsite. 'Frau Eichenwald,' he began, stopping and facing her as they arrived at the shelter, 'I feel compelled to invite you once more to tell me if you are in possession of such a text as the one purportedly witnessed by Christiana Radtke.'

'I possess no book of the occult.'

Thea sat down on the hollow log, fingers splayed against its greyed wood. She stared at the fire, unblinking.

Pastor Flügel sniffed. 'You are unfamiliar to this congregation.'

'My family and I have been a part of it since we moved to Kay. We have been familiar these past three years.'

'You are unfamiliar, then, to me,' he answered. 'In cases of church discipline, I accord to the letter of our laws. There are three grades of punishment that may apply to all members of my congregations, without respect of person, rank, age or sex. The first is exclusion from the Lord's Supper, an opportunity for self-examination and penitence. The second is appearance before the congregation and confrontation with the sin that has been committed. The third is excommunication and committal to Satan, in the case of a sinner who, though fully convicted of her transgression, obstinately denies and impenitently continues her offence.'

I sat next to Thea and placed my head on her shoulder. I could feel her trembling.

Anna Maria smiled at the pastor. 'I am aware.'

'Good.' Flügel nodded. 'Good. Well, then, I have said what I came to say.'

As spring advanced and the wattles frothed yellow, the watchful silence between the congregation and the first peoples of the country eased into cautious friendliness. Magdalena, Elize, Mama and Amalie, all of whom now received regular laundry work from local English families, found themselves sharing the waterway with the Peramangk women who arrived to catch yabbies crawling from the mud, and they agreed the hot flesh offered to them on the banks of the waterhole was delicious.

Anna Maria continued to follow the same woman who gave her the grubs, and over time she was shown how to find white ant larvae and the better bird eggs to eat. Hans Pasche, who often stopped in at the Eichenwalds' on his way to and from his father's allotment, tried everything the Wend placed before him. I watched Thea laugh as he sucked the nectar from stringybark flowers, and while I was glad they were friendly with one another, I found myself dreading the sight of Hans approaching through the allotments.

'You should come and see something,' he said to Thea one day, interrupting her as she watered her vegetable garden. 'Can you come now?'

I followed behind Thea as Hans, grinning, led her to where Matthias stood at the feet of the three red gums in my parents' allotment, looking upwards, hands over his eyes to shield them from the morning sunlight.

'What is it?' asked Thea.

Hans beckoned her closer and pointed into the canopy. As I drew closer I saw that a Peramangk man, with incredible skill and dexterity, was climbing the tallest of the gums. With no low-hanging branches, he'd cut steps for his feet in the bark with a sharp, pointed stick, and was making more as he climbed higher. Finally, reaching a hollow, he deftly pulled out a possum and killed it with a single blow to the head.

I remembered the feeling of furred warmth turning within my hollows and, as I did so, noticed that the smallest of the gums had yellowed and was unflowering. It looked like it was dying.

Matthias and Hans clapped as the man climbed back down, stepping forwards to admire and examine the tool he had used to scale the gargantuan tree. He showed it to them patiently, speaking in both his mother tongue and in English, while Thea, I noticed, fell back, eyes on the possum that hung from his hand.

'I think he is saying that it can be eaten,' Hans said, turning to Thea.

'It isn't for the fur?' The possum skin cloaks worn by many of the women were familiar sights by then.

'No,' said Hans, glancing back at the man. 'No, it's also food.'

The man cut them some meat and that night Hans stayed to eat it beside the Eichenwalds' fire, nodding enthusiastically as Thea described the scene to her parents. The knowing glance shared between Anna Maria and Friedrich buckled through me like a wave.

'That Hans Pasche cuts a striking figure,' Anna Maria said later that night, watching Hans return to his family's allotment in the twilight. 'Don't you think?'

Thea glanced up from her whitework and followed her mother's gaze into the soft light. She shrugged.

Anna Maria patted her daughter's knee. 'He visits us quite a lot now. Do you ever wonder why?'

'Probably to escape his father,' Thea said, snapping thread between her teeth. 'He works him and his brothers like dogs.'

'Still,' Anna Maria said quietly.

'He likes your cooking. He likes those yams you get from the women.'

'Honestly, Thea.' Anna Maria looked steadily at her daughter, and when Thea did not meet her eyes placed a hand over her sewing.

Thea looked up, exasperated. 'What do you want me to say?'

'He's fond of you.'

I was sitting at Thea's feet, looking up at her, my head resting on her knee, but at these words I stared at the fire like I might throw myself onto the embers. I did not want to see Thea's face. An ache gathered in my gut.

'I . . .' Thea hesitated. I felt tension wire through her body. She pulled her knees together.

'I know it embarrasses you.'

Thea said nothing. Sap ran sticky down the length of a burning branch, hissed into steam.

'You may want to consider your future,' Anna Maria said softly, 'in case his thoughts turn to marriage.'

Thea laughed and then fell abruptly silent. Water issued through my hair. Liquid gathered at the ends of my fingers.

'I don't understand why he would be thinking of such a thing.' Thea's voice was quiet. Strangely empty.

'Well . . .' Anna Maria sighed. 'He is his father's eldest son. He has two brothers. Four men there, on that allotment. In time he'll need to find his own home, his own land.' She hesitated. 'Like you say, Christian works him like a dog.'

I was drowning, next to the campfire. My heart was caught in salted current.

'I don't understand why he visits me . . . for that.'

I heard Anna Maria shuffle closer and turned to see her place an arm around Thea. Maternal love wrapping around a doubting daughter.

'He would be lucky to have you. He knows it too.'

'Why not one of the other girls? Christiana is desperate to be married.'

'You'll have to ask Hans.'

The light around us swam. I lifted my eyes and saw sharks circling in the darkening sky.

There is little doubt in my mind that, had the Peramangk not shown the congregation how to find food, many would have died. That first spring the piglets were growing but not ready for slaughter and the chickens provided by MacFarlane were too young to lay. The wheat was growing on the cleared slopes – my father had been right about the fertility of the soil – but it was still green and not ready for harvest. Much of the ship's biscuit bloomed with the same mould scrubbed from it on the *Kristi*, and bread baked from rice and wheaten flour had become a Sunday treat rather than a staple.

MacFarlane had supplied some of the men with rifles, but the shot frightened more kangaroos, pigeons and ducks than it struck. Only the Aboriginal men, using spears and clubs, or ambushing the animals and driving them into nets, were able to kill enough to feed whole families. The ringing of a rifle never matched the elegance of the snares made from small branches that deftly, quietly, strangled birds in the long grass.

I liked to watch the Peramangk commune with the country. I liked to listen to their language, even if I did not understand it. Over time, however, I noticed that if I drew too close, there were always a few men or women who seemed to grow uncomfortable.

'*Krinkri*,' they would say, and the others would pause in their work and straighten their necks, as though they were aware of being observed. As if they knew I was there, in their number, trying to remember what it was like to hunger.

In early summer I looked up from Thea's side at the morning's campfire to see my mother approaching, Hermine toddling at her side. My sister had grown, and while I still sometimes tried to attract her attention, tickling her feet with rushes from the creek or whispering her name in her ear, she no longer seemed to notice me. She had grown leaner, a little neck emerging from baby fat. I watched her bend clumsily and pick up a fragment of quartz from the ground and flushed with memory from the night of her birth.

Thea, in firelight, hand on mine.

'Good morning,' my mother said to Anna Maria.

'Johanne.'

Mama turned, looking out at Thea's flourishing vegetable patch. 'I was speaking with Eleonore and Emile. They're sending their girls down to Adelaide. Pastor Flügel told Elder Pasche there is a dearth of fresh vegetables amongst the English. The women at Neu Klemzig are now getting two or three shillings a cabbage head. I thought Thea might like to go down with them. You have so much produce already.'

'As the moon swells, plant for above ground. When the moon wanes, plant all for below.'

'When are they leaving?' Thea asked.

Mama sat down at the campfire, pulling Hermine back from the embers. 'Tomorrow evening,' she replied. 'Augusta and Elize are going, too.' She cleared her throat. 'And Christiana Radtke.'

I noticed Thea glance at Anna Maria.

'Thea, if you all leave at midnight, you should reach the plains by morning. Then you can sell the vegetables and return with the money. It will be a full moon and light enough. You can follow the new track through the Tiers.' She lifted Hermine onto her lap as the breeze shifted the smoke into her eyes. 'I was hoping, Thea, that you might take something from my own garden for me. Until I am free to go myself, there being no other . . .' She stopped short, lips pressed together.

Thea looked at Mama and something passed between them.

'Of course you'll go,' Anna Maria said gently. She inclined her head at my mother. 'How are you?'

Mama pulled down her headscarf, passing it to Hermine to play with. 'Things are as good as can be expected. The new cow is yielding excellent milk.' She smiled at Thea. 'I have some butter I would like you to take. Pastor Flügel says it is like gold to the English.'

'And Matthias? How is he?'

Mama raised her eyebrows. 'He is well. The work, this land . . .' She shrugged. 'He thinks he is a man now. He wishes to marry. Start a family.'

My mouth slipped open and I fought a sudden rush of jealousy. Matthias? Already? He has a family. I had been his family. For so long we had shared everything, and for a moment I did not understand why he had not told me this himself.

'Truly?' Anna Maria looked surprised. 'He works hard. I often see him.'

'Thank you. He does.' Mama looked down at Hermine sucking on the headscarf. 'How quickly they grow.'

Matthias, you are leaving me behind. The thought filled me with sadness.

'I think of Hanne all the time,' Thea said quickly. 'I am so sorry. I am so . . .' She brought a hand to her cheek, eyes swimming.

My mother took a deep breath. '"For our light affliction, which is but for a moment, worketh for us a far more exceeding and eternal weight of glory. While we look not at the things which are seen, but at the things which are not seen: for the things which are seen are temporal; but the things which are not seen are eternal." I have been dwelling on this scripture. I pray on it.' Then, as if afraid she had said too much, Mama stood and lifted Hermine onto her hip and left Thea and Anna Maria staring after her.

The next evening I followed Thea like a shadow. The young women were silent as they set out near midnight, neat braids wound over their heads, dark gowns covered with Sunday aprons, bare feet stepping noiselessly on the track.

Each bore a heavy basket or yoke on her back, and as the moon rose vast and orange in the sky, I listened to them breathe, falling in behind Thea as the track narrowed. The girls walked in single file up the slope away from the valley.

It was only when the glow of Heiligendorf's fires were hidden from view and the incline levelled out that the women began to talk.

'Elize?' Henriette tapped her on the shoulder.

'Hm?'

'What's the stick for?'

Elize glanced behind her. 'Reinhardt said we're to be watchful of Tiersmen.' She considered the heavy stick in her hand. 'He made me take it.'

'Tiersmen?'

'Men living in the Tiers. The stringybark forest. He's worked with them, sawing, stripping bark, out on the station, and says some are scoundrels.'

'What do you mean, "scoundrels"?' asked Augusta.

'Convicts from the east. Escaped maybe. Released? I don't know. But he saw one man's back and it bore scars of flogging. He said they gamble and drink and live rough in the forest.'

'You're going to protect us all with a stick, then?' Christiana's voice piped out behind me. I turned and saw her peer into the dark bush on either side of the track. 'Some use that will be.'

'Oh, Reinhardt is just like that. He's protective.'

'God save us,' Augusta muttered.

There was a crack of branch. Henriette yelped.

'Oh, for goodness' sake,' Elize breathed. 'Forget I said anything.'

Silence fell again as the track wound up a rocky incline and the girls took it in turns to help each other up the slope, their burdens threatening to send them off balance.

'Shall we sing?' ventured Elizabeth Volkmann.

'Save that until we're going downhill at least,' replied Elsa Pfeiffer, catching her breath.

'It's too quiet,' Elizabeth replied.

'Well, let's talk, then. Christiana, any news?'

'Why me?'

Elize laughed. 'You know all the stories.'

'No, I don't.'

'Yes, you do,' everyone chorused.

The track widened again and those at the rear ran awkwardly to join Elize, Thea and Henriette at the front.

'I don't,' Christiana protested. 'There's nothing to say. Ask Augusta.'

'What?' Henriette glanced sideways at her friend, frowning. 'What's the matter?'

'*Ja*, Christiana, you make me think you do know some news.'

'Well, it's not *my* news,' Christiana said. 'Go on, Augusta. Tell them.'

The girls slowed. Each head turned to Augusta.

'Well,' she said, glaring at Christiana. 'It isn't really . . . Christiana, you shouldn't have . . .'

Christiana shrugged. She was smiling, but there was a hardness in her mouth.

'You can't say a word.'

'Oh, Augusta, out with it,' exclaimed Elize.

'Matthias Nussbaum and I shall marry.'

The footfall ceased.

I felt my skin tighten. My brother. My twin. This is what my mother had been speaking of. I thought of all the mornings Matthias had left Hermine with Augusta. The small pieces of ship biscuit he had saved for Wilhelm.

'Oh, Augusta.' Elize's voice was warm. She clasped Augusta's fingers.

'Pastor Flügel will read the banns this Sunday, when he returns from Neu Klemzig,' Augusta continued, face sober.

'I didn't know you were sweethearts,' Amalie said.

'We're not.'

The women were silent.

'I mean . . .' Augusta hesitated. 'I mean, what with Karl . . .'

Elize patted her on the shoulder. 'You don't need to explain.'

The women circled Augusta and congratulated her, setting their packs down so that they might embrace. A dark fluke of jealousy wormed in me as Thea gently pressed her lips to Augusta's cheek. 'Go well,' she said gently.

'I know it's soon,' Augusta said to no one in particular.

'It will be good to have someone to help you farm your land. With Karl gone. I mean, you needn't go into service,' Elize reassured her. 'You can stay.'

'Yes . . . That is what Matthias said.'

'And your son.'

'*Ja*, he will need a man to look up to.'

The women shouldered their baskets and continued walking in companionable silence.

'How do you feel?' Thea's voice was a feather in the night.

'Relieved,' Augusta admitted, steadying the yoke on her shoulders. 'The allotment is too much work for me alone.'

'Yes, and now Matthias will live next door to his parents. He shall have much land, combined.'

Augusta shrugged. 'I think of my future, Christiana. As must you.'

In the greying hours before dawn, the women reached a stream in the foothills and paused to rest and soothe their feet in the water. Then, as the sun slipped over the horizon, they walked down into the foothills. The inhabitants were pleased to see them, and although none of the Heiligendorf women spoke English, I was relieved for Thea's sake to see that the prices for their eggs and butter and produce – conveyed by holding up fingers, pointing to coins offered in an open palm – were accepted without question. There were happy exclamations over the fresh vegetables, with even the gruffest speculators eagerly paying a shilling for two carrots, a shilling sixpence for three onions. By mid-morning, the yokes and baskets had been emptied of every item and, under Elize's guidance, the girls exchanged some of the unfamiliar currency for sewing thread and needles and sugar. After tobacco had been found and bought for Gottfried Volkmann – 'He insists upon it,' Henriette apologised – Elize directed them to the brickworks on the banks of the river, where she purchased a small number of bricks.

'They're for the church,' Elize said, passing them two apiece. 'Elder Pasche has asked us to bring some back each time we come here. The pastor suggested it.'

'Small church,' muttered Amalie, hoisting her basket up onto her back.

Elize rolled her eyes. 'In time we will have enough.'

'How many bricks will it take?' asked Elsa Pfeiffer.

Elize shrugged. 'It's not for me to question Pastor Flügel.'

'In the meantime,' Thea mused, weighing the heavy bricks in her hands, 'we stand a better chance against the Tiersmen.'

It wasn't until the girls returned to Heiligendorf that I understood what had happened. What I had done.

As soon as they were all walking down the track into the valley the next day, Magdalena Radtke appeared, sweeping an arm around Christiana. 'Now, he's all right,' she said, casting an inscrutable eye back to where Thea followed behind, 'I don't want you to worry for him, but your father had a very near miss this morning.'

Elize, hearing the last of this, stepped forwards and placed a hand on Magdalena's shoulder. 'Elder Radtke?'

'A tree,' Magdalena spat out. 'A great tree nearly crushed him to death.'

Christiana paused, eyes wide. 'What?'

'By God's grace, it missed him,' her mother said. 'But by inches.'

The girls glanced at each other.

'Which one?' ventured Thea.

Magdalena turned to face her. 'One of the gums on Herr Nussbaum's allotment.'

*

As the women made their way back into the heart of the village and Thea peeled off to her parents' allotment, I could hear the distant rasp of saws ringing out on the air. Thea stopped at the fence line. The smallest of the sister gums had fallen to the earth with such force that its huge branches now lay gouged deep within the wheatfield like an abandoned plough, the root ball lifted high into the air, exposed in a vast, tangled mass of earth. Matthias, Papa, Samuel Radtke and Hans were already at work, sawing the huge trunk into rounds. I noticed my mother hauling smaller branches into a pile, thick with dead leaves, ready to be burned.

My sister gum. The tree I had been. I stood next to Thea and remembered running with rivers of sap. I felt, too, the falling of wood, as though it were a memory held within my own body. A crack upon the earth, a boom that sent birds screeching into the air. I imagined the reverberation in my own bones, felt them splinter into dust.

I had done this.

The broken branch. The dead onion seedlings. And now, the sister gum. As these trees and plants had admitted me and let me join to them, had let me feel again the rush of being and let me swallow light and grow, I had poisoned them with my own lifelessness.

I thought of the banksias and the tea-trees and the stringybarks along the old trail from the plains to the ranges. I had moved from one to another to canopy Thea since the night of the tree, to love her with leaf and blossom and gumnut. Were they all dead now?

I had not known.

pig

Matthias and Augusta were married by Pastor Flügel under the remaining two sister gums on my father's allotment. Stumps and rails from the fallen tree were used in the absence of proper church pews, the men and women separated with an aisle between. I climbed up into a crook in the lowest branch of one of the trees and watched Augusta walk towards my waiting brother in her best black dress, given away by Elder Pasche in the absence of a father. Matthias, I noticed, wore Papa's Sunday trousers, and I smiled to myself imagining my mother hemming them to suit his smaller stature. As Pastor Flügel conducted the long and sombre ceremony, I picked gum leaves and dropped them spiralling down upon the heads of the bride and groom, each a blessing.

May you learn to love her, I thought.

May she learn to love you.

Giblets and bacon.

I pulled apart the fibres of blossom and sprinkled them upon the air. And if you do not love each other, I hope you are happy in the soil she gives you. I hope you are happy, brother.

"'Two are better than one,'" intoned Flügel, "'because they have a good reward for their labour. For if they fall, the one will lift up his fellow: but woe to him that is alone when he falleth; for he hath not another to help him up.'"

Matthias lifted his gaze to the trees towering above him and I saw his gap-toothed smile. A vision of him spitting at me from between his teeth, eyes almost shut from laughing so hard, came back to me, and I had to grip the branch to stop from falling in a sudden welling of love.

I hope you can find happiness with her, brother, I whispered, and my tears, when I tasted them, were salt.

The wedding breakfast was boiled parrots and new potatoes eaten on sheets and blankets spread under the trees. In Kay, even in lean times, wedding feasts had been extravagant. Giblet noodle soup, chicken, goose and duck. Wine and beer and hot plum cake if fruit were in season. Still, Matthias seemed content, sucking parrot meat off tiny bones, Augusta next to him, Wilhelm on her lap. The day was warm. Insects were loud in the wheat. Below me, Gottfried Volkmann held court in a group of men, pipe smoke issuing from his purple lips. 'The track goes right past my door, you know! All these men and their animals on the way to Melbourne and what do they have to drink? Water from the creek. What do they eat? Whatever filthy English food is rolling around in their saddlebags. I would be a fool – no, it would be a disservice to God not to take advantage of such opportunity!'

'But what do you know about coffee shops?'

'Make it fresh and pour it hot!' shouted Gottfried.

'But what if it does not succeed? How will you eat while you try to finally clear your patch?'

Gottfried smiled and pointed to the trees. 'I can spend another year boiling these little noisy parrots. The more I eat the less noisy they will be! These stockmen will be throwing their shillings at me. Have you tasted Eleonore's bread?'

Some of the men rolled their eyes as Gottfried grinned and looked about him. He gestured with his pipe then, raising his eyebrows, and I noticed that he and several other men were watching Hans approach Thea as she kneeled on a blanket next to Henriette.

Something stilled in me. I was sunk in a mire of sudden, dreadful understanding. Then, panicking, I half climbed, half fell to the ground and threw myself down next to Thea just as I heard Hans ask if he might walk with her a little. I wrapped my arms around her middle, pulling her close to me. 'Don't go,' I whispered in her ear.

Henriette nudged Thea with her knee.

'Don't go. Please.' I placed my lips against Thea's earlobe.

Thea picked at the stitches of the blanket's hem, colour creeping up her neck. 'If you like,' she murmured.

'Sorry?' asked Hans. 'Sorry, you speak so quietly today.'

Don't come so close to her, I thought. I was scowling. I felt myself as a blackening in their midst, and as the women smirked at each other, I glared crow-black at Hans until he glanced to where I thunderstormed.

'What is it?' asked Henriette, turning.

'Nothing,' he said.

'She said you're welcome to walk with her,' Henriette announced, slyly squeezing Thea's elbow.

Christiana stared, mouth open.

Hans stood up a little straighter. 'Thank you,' he said. 'I would like that.' He stood for a few more excruciating moments before bowing and stepping backwards, away from the girls exchanging knowing expressions. Henriette gave Thea excited little nudges as she rose and allowed Hans to lead her away from the wedding, down towards the waterhole.

I could not move. I could feel my very being flicker, could feel myself dissipate into the weave of the blanket beneath me, the heat of the sunshine, the dappled shadow of the remaining sister gums behind me. I looked at my body; grass seeds were falling from my hair, my toes were crumbling into soil. My skin flowed with water, and I could feel the slight, white lines of mycelium creep around my knees. I was dissolving into the earth.

I stood, then. I ran after them. I wanted to feel force, needed to feel the hard slap of my feet hitting the ground, arms propelling myself forwards as though I were running from wildfire, as though I were running for my life. I wanted to run the distance of the world and never stop. I wanted distance and oblivion because this was too much, seeing the woman I loved, would bleed for, being drawn into a life I had no place in. How could I guard her at night if she had a husband? I could not sit there and watch him sleep beside her. I could not watch her serve him his dinner, pour his coffee. That would be true suffering, loving Thea as I did while another stepped through life with her. She would forget me. She would be taken up into that woman's life and leave behind all things of her unformed self, all of me and what I was to her.

I stumbled to a stop just before I fell down the bank to the waterhole. I could feel the force of my movement still running up my heels, felt my ankles bleeding, saw the blood lifting off my skin into nothingness.

Hans and Thea stood by the water's edge, staring at the reflection of the sky and canopy. Thea was absently pulling at the tops of reeds as Hans spoke to her, hands deep in his pockets.

'You are a hardworking and respectable girl . . .'

Salt water rose in my throat, tidal through the marrow of my bones.

Hans smiled at Thea uncertainly. 'The land here is good, but it isn't mine. I am a man now. I would like to make my own life. And I will need someone to . . . Well, to manage a home. To . . .' He cleared his throat and took off his hat. 'Thea, I know . . .' He faltered, tried again. 'I know that there are suspicions against your mother. I know that there are some who would see your family lose their place in this congregation. Lose their allotment . . .'

Thea stiffened, lips parting in understanding. I could see she was thinking, see that there was a storm under her skin. I knew her; I knew what her stillness meant.

'Thea, I will be good to you,' he said softly, looking down at the water before them. 'They would not send you away.' He ran a hand through his hair. 'My father is an elder. He . . .' Hans sighed.

Thea glanced at Hans, eyes moving over his face.

'We could be great friends,' he added.

Thea scattered the seeds from the bulrushes into the air. They floated down and settled on the skin of the water. 'Are you asking me to marry you, Hans?'

'Have I made a fool of myself?'

'No.' Thea's voice was so faint I wondered that Hans could hear her at all.

Hans broke into a smile. 'You will?'

Thea hesitated.

I was breaking into pieces. I was being knifed apart. The sea was sweeping in.

Thea nodded.

Hans laughed and dropped his hat, snatching it up just before it rolled into the water. 'We had best get back,' he said, smiling broadly. 'They will wonder where we've gone!'

'In a moment. You go on ahead. I . . .' Thea motioned that he should walk on without her.

'Are you all right?'

'Yes.' Thea smiled at him and I thought that she had never been so beautiful. I was breaking.

Hans left reluctantly, turning and smiling at her and throwing his hat in the air before he rounded the bend and was gone from sight.

Alone, Thea's smile vanished. I stared at her as she studied her shaking fingers. She was trying not to cry.

And then, as I reached for her, sought to hold her to me and find reassurance in her closeness, in the smell of her skin, Thea ran splashing into the water, skirts billowing out with air as she waded in. Her face disappeared below the surface and she emerged again, gasping, chest racked with sobs, wet hair slick across her forehead, surrounded by a distorted reflection of eucalyptus and reed.

I could not tell if she was crying from happiness or sorrow. My own heart was broken.

I walked. I walked away from the waterhole, up past the celebrations and onwards through the wheatfields. I walked until dusk fell, groping my way up the escarpment, away from the village, not knowing where I was going, following only an urgency to move, to flee. I stumbled through the bush beyond Heiligendorf until it was dark, and then I sank to the ground and curled into a ball. My suffering was so acute I felt that I was on the cusp of tearing, as though my skin would rend and my insides come blowing out like feathers. Thea does not love you as you love her, I told myself. Thea does not love you. She does not love you.

And yet, and yet.

Again and again I remembered Thea throwing her arms around me, her laughter making me feel the same as when I saw light glance off a body of water. The sun warm on our shoulders. Hands brown from summer, fingers entwined with my own. Her face before she bent to me in the forest.

She had kissed me.

A sudden memory of Thea in our berth, in the darkness, burned through me. Neither of us speaking, our heads so close together I could feel her breath upon my skin. Thea slowly sliding her finger across my cheek, then her tongue.

'Salt.'

One word whispered, hot and held. In the morning I had woken with my heart racing, wondering if it had happened at all, unable to ask her, the thought of it knotting inside me so that I felt tight and bound and waiting.

Her hands briefly, wondrously upon my body in the darkness of the ship.

I felt betrayed and ashamed and unsure about everything. The thought of her wedded to Hans made me feel utterly forgotten.

Dawn came. I watched sunlight split the land from sky and then, in the corner of my eye, I saw a black creature emerge from behind a blue gum, something wet and feathered in its mouth.

Hans's cat, I thought.

She stared at me, a growl wavering in the back of her throat, before vanishing into the bush.

The ocean rose in my mind. I thought of my bones in that vast coldness, and when the darkness came, I let it take me.

That was the first time I came up here. And now I am here again, waiting for an end.

The summer continued despite my constant, aching grief. While I cried for my own broken heart, the congregation of Heiligendorf filled every damned hour with work. While I spent days singing myself into the scaly leaves of she-oaks for the consolation of keening with the wind, knowing I was harming them but, in my misery, caring not, the mood amongst the congregation lifted.

The cows were giving good quantities of milk and the fields of wheat turned from green to gold. Labour outside the settlement – shearing, laundering, fencing – quietly addressed the collective debt, and soon *Fachwerk* frames of red gum walled with pug replaced the little shelters of saplings. Adzed slabs were turned into tables and chairs, animal pens improved with sod. Matthias began building a home from the wood of the fallen sister gum for himself and Augusta. Wells were dug under the watchful eye of Mutter Scheck, and Samuel Radtke constructed a wagon in the image of the one he had regretfully left behind.

I watched it all, ever in orbit around the one I loved.

Believing a *Schwarzekuchen* a stupid idea in a land so hot, Anna Maria enlisted Thea's help in making an oven and smokehouse outside her back door, cutting curved branches then applying stones and a thick mud plaster before firing it into hardened clay.

'I need to show you these things now,' Anna Maria said to her, scraping out the ash from the burned wood. 'You'll have a home of your own before long. When will Pastor Flügel return?'

'This Friday,' Thea replied, picking fragments of dried mud from her wrists. 'Hans will speak with him then.'

'How are you feeling?'

Thea shrugged.

'You don't talk with me like you used to.'

Thea came up behind her mother and, wrapping her arms around her, laid her head on Anna Maria's back. 'There's nothing to say,' she murmured.

That Friday evening Thea and Hans walked to the church. They lingered by the doorway until Flügel appeared and shook Hans's hand.

'Come in,' he said, turning back inside and seating himself on a chair between the pews. I sat next to Thea, sick to my stomach. She was anxious – I could see it in her jaw, in the way she pressed her feet into the floor – but I still did not know if her nerves spoke to fear or excitement.

The pastor leaned forwards, gaze moving from Hans to Thea. 'You wanted to speak with me?'

Hans cleared his throat. 'Thank you, Pastor. We would like to be married. In the autumn,' he added. 'After harvest.'

Flügel smiled at him. 'You would like to be married. Let us do this with the necessary formalities.' He rose from his chair and took out a sheet of paper, a pen and ink from an inkstand at the side of the room. 'Your full Christian names?'

Hans glanced happily at Thea. 'Hans Reinhardt Pasche.'

'And the bride to be?'

'She is Dorothea Anna Eichenwald.'

I lifted my legs up onto the pew beside Thea.

'The names of your fathers?'

'Her father is Friedrich Eichenwald, and mine is Elder Christian Gottfried Pasche.'

The pastor looked up from his paper. 'Do you both actively, willingly consent to this union?'

'We do,' said Hans.

'Dorothea?'

'I consent.'

'And have you remained chaste?' he asked.

Colour crept up Thea's throat into her cheeks and she stared down at her folded hands. Hans, too, seemed uncomfortable.

I thought of her kissing me in the forest. I thought of the *Kristi*, Thea's tongue tasting the salt of my skin.

Thea gave an almost imperceptible nod.

'And you, son?'

'Yes.'

Flügel hesitated then, giving Thea a careful look. 'If none should object to the banns and you are wed, you must both understand that you will be expected to do as the Church asks of you, to uphold the faith of the congregation.'

'Yes, Pastor,' Hans replied.

'Well, I give you my blessing, and it would be my honour to wed you both.' He sat back in his chair and regarded Thea again. 'My dear, remember: "There is no fear in love; but perfect love casteth out fear: because fear hath torment. He that feareth is not made perfect in love.'"

'Thank you, Pastor Flügel.'

'May the Lord bless you both.'

That Sunday, I lay on the ground outside the church, staring at the clouds streaking the summer sky, listening to the service. When the congregation sat to sing their hymns, I closed my eyes and imagined new words against the harmonies and as I hummed I felt the earth vibrate and my own being shudder with the sound. It was like being pulled apart by time. I was a sheet of paper tearing; I was softening, deliciously, into ash. But the singing ended and I heard the pastor close with prayer. A little delirious, I walked towards the door of the church, left open due to the heat.

Such rows of hatted, bonneted heads. Orderly rows of sunburned necks. All of them looking to Pastor Flügel, rolling his shoulders under his black robes. I could see the skin of his throat pressing hard against his starched white *Bäffchen*.

'A few public announcements,' he said, voice projecting to the back rows. 'There are some whose repayment of the passage money is tardy. These defaulters are to make payment as soon as possible, or make public apology: Herr Pfeiffer and Herr Kirschke.'

I noticed Emile Pfeiffer sink lower in her pew.

'I also announce the banns of marriage between Hans Reinhardt Pasche and Dorothea Anna Eichenwald of Heiligendorf.'

There was a low stirring. I saw Christiana glance at Hans. She looked as though she'd been slapped.

'If any of you know cause or just impediment why these two persons should not be joined together in Holy Matrimony, you are to declare it. This is the first time of asking.'

I stepped into the church and its hush. I was shaking. My bones half-hinged to ligament.

'Yes,' I said. 'I declare that I have cause.'

I walked down the aisle and stood beside Thea. I faced the pastor.

'They cannot be married because we two –'

Flügel smiled. 'Well, then.'

'– we are for each other.' I reached for Thea, and as I did, I heard the sound of the ocean, at first faint, but quickly amplifying to a roar. The light drifting into the church went dark, and I turned just in time to see a wave of water filling the doorway and upending the congregation, knocking the pews forwards in one heaving mass of ocean before it hit me like a wall and I surrendered to its drowning.

I woke by my mother's side, drenched and shivering, seaweed tangled around my legs. I was in my parents' house and Mama was on the floor beside me, kneeling before the opened shipping chest from the *Kristi*. I unwound the seaweed from my feet and pulled myself up on their bed as Mama leaned into the chest and took out the bolt of black material she had intended for my wedding dress. She held it across her lap, her mouth suddenly warped in sorrow.

Even in her solitude she could not permit herself the sound of her own tears.

Then, quite abruptly, Mama pushed herself back to her feet, smoothed her hair with her free hand, then stepped out of the house.

My father was seated by the campfire, the sky cherry-red behind him. He was eating from a bowl balanced on one knee, Hermine seated on the other.

'What do you think, Heinrich?'

Papa looked up from his meal, wiping his beard with the back of his hand. He was silent for a long moment. 'What about Hermine?' He gently rapped his spoon on her nose.

'It will be moth-eaten before she is ready for it.'

'Not for yourself?'

Mama smoothed the wrinkles in the fabric. 'No. Not this.'

I followed Mama to the Eichenwalds' cabin and it was as if Thea was expecting her. The sacking cloth was drawn aside and Thea regarded her for a heavy moment. 'Frau Nussbaum.'

'Take this, Thea.' My mother's voice was clipped. 'For your wedding.'

Thea was sombre. 'I don't know. Are you . . .?'

'I'm sure,' said Mama, handing her the material. 'I wouldn't be here if I wasn't.'

My mother and Thea stood there for a long moment.

'Well then,' said Mama, wiping her hands on her apron. 'I'd best be –'

'I miss her terribly.' Thea pulled the cloth close to her chest and folded her arms about it. 'I hope you know that.'

Mama's lips twitched.

'I wish she were here. I think about her every day and I keep her in my prayers.'

'Well. That is why I thought you might like the cloth.'

'Yes. She told me you had brought it.'

Mama looked down at her empty hands.

'Thank you,' said Thea softly.

Mama stepped forwards and quickly, briskly, kissed Thea hard on the forehead, leaving a red mark. 'Congratulations,' she said, already turning away, the word thrown over her shoulder.

Thea unfolded the black cloth on her parents' bed, smoothing the fabric out over the mattress. I watched her lay down upon it. Against the black of the fabric, she was golden.

'Hanne.'

I drew nearer. She was so beautiful. Already I could imagine her in the black dress, myrtle leaves against the pale smoke of her hair.

'I am to be married,' she whispered.

It was the first time she had spoken to me since she had accepted Hans's proposal.

I climbed onto the bed with her and placed my head next to hers. She turned towards me, our foreheads touching, our bodies mirrored. For one hallowed moment it was as it used to be, the two of us only, the entirety of the universe ending at the periphery of our curled limbs.

The banns were read at the following two services, and each time I declared that it was impossible. I loved Thea. We had already given ourselves to one another, had sealed that covenant, had made witnesses of trees. We have married ourselves, I told the congregation. Ask the forest. Ask the ship lumber. You'll find our signatures in the bruised gills of mushrooms. In the salt air above the sea.

No one said anything. The ocean claimed me each time.

I woke here, where I sit now, in the bush, amongst the scrape of fallen stick and undergrowth. I placed my hands on trees so vast they seemed at once to encompass time itself and, standing under their certain weight, I wept for myself.

They were cragged and beautiful and defiant. *You know nothing*, they said, and they meant it kindly. They were not indifferent.

A few weeks before the wedding, Hans told the Eichenwalds that his father had agreed to slaughter a pig to ensure a decent feast for the congregation. 'The farm is doing well. The days are cool enough now,' Hans said to Friedrich and Anna Maria. 'We've fasted one. We're hoping for tomorrow afternoon, if it does not rain.' He smiled at Thea. 'Please come. All of you. You too, Anna Maria. Rosina complains at a lack of stepdaughters.'

I looked at once to Thea, whose face had taken on a pall.

'Of course,' Anna Maria replied. She smiled at Thea. 'Bacon and *Wurst* and fresh bread and *Sauergurken*. Oh, it will almost be as it was back home.'

Hans grinned. 'No more parrots.'

'No more parrots! Oh, Friedrich, remember the bird with white feathers?'

'*Der Kakadu?*'

'It was like eating string.'

Friedrich gestured at Thea's pale face. 'You know, Hans, Thea doesn't much like a *Schlachtentag*. Hasn't got the stomach for it.'

Hans's face fell.

'It's the squeal,' Thea offered. 'It's –'

'She'll come.' Anna Maria frowned at Thea. 'Tell Rosina we'll help, of course. Thank Elder Christian for his generosity – Thea doesn't mean to be rude.' She nudged her daughter. 'Won't be long before you two will have pigs of your own.'

I lay beside Thea that night, watching her as she stared up into the thatch, following the curve of her eyebrows, tender lines branching out from her eyes. I was trying to imagine her as an old woman, the wrinkled face and white hair.

We will see each other every day of our lives. We will sit next to each other in church.

Thea sighed. 'Hanne?'

I'll name my daughter for you.

I closed my eyes, heartsore.

'Everything feels so wrong.'

'A pig knows you have betrayed it,' I murmured.

Her voice was a hot whisper in the dark. 'It's as though I don't know who I am. There is no one here to remind me who I am.'

'I love you, Thea,' I whispered. 'I know who you are.'

The next day, Elder Pasche greeted the Eichenwalds as they entered the yard, turning from where he was sharpening his knife. 'That's the one,' he said, pointing the blade to a long-bristled fattening pig separated from its fellows. 'Hans!'

Hans emerged from the house followed by Rosina. 'Well then, are we ready?' she asked.

Christian tested the blade on the hairs of his arm. 'Ready,' he muttered.

Rosina passed Anna Maria a whisk and motioned for Thea to come and take the pail by her feet.

Thea did not move. She had drawn away from the sty and looked waxen with dread.

'Thea,' Anna Maria said patiently.

'I feel a little . . .' Thea shook her head at her mother.

'Pick it up,' Anna Maria said.

Thea did so, all the while staring at the pig. A memory of her on the *Kristi* came back to me.

Hanne, talk to me. Sing to me. Tell me something.

I began to hum, then. I let my voice join the song coming to me from the ground – that old, chordal note of earth – and turned from Thea to the creature, whose own piggish sound was lifting off its back like steam. A body hymn to the warmth of hot-bellied brothers, earflap snuffle of mother nipple against wet snout. I hummed it all, and as I did, I felt a scattering. I felt a fluttering within myself. Everything around me blurred except the pig, which was now before me in exceptional clarity. I could see each bristle as it caught the sun, see the tiny pupils widen. The gleam on the snout. It was before me, iridescent, this pig now running, now fleeing. And as I felt myself fade into the air, the pig grew spectacular. I not only saw it, I heard it in a way I had never heard a pig. The hammer-heart of it, yes, but the blood-rushing too, and the gurgle of the empty stomach. I could hear the knocking of gristle and the clap of mud between toes and the air-suck of lungs taking breath. Frightened breaths. For I felt it then, the fear coursing through the pig. It was my own fear, too. It was ours. And suddenly, those small pupils were my own, too, and we saw mud and reaching hands, and felt our heat pushing out against the chill of autumn air.

I was the pig.

We were the pig.

We stopped running. We were a marvel.

We were weight and it was good. The slick of mud upon our

stomach was a cool lick of blessedness. We wanted more. We wanted to loll in it, feel the wet bliss of earth against us. But the smells! We could smell it all. It was humus, fungi in dark places. It was eucalyptus burning spicy under cauldrons of puffing grain. The sun smelled like grass, smelled like living things. Skin and curdled milk – good things! Pap of soured vegetables, human breath, and castings from the worms below us. Smoke. Split rock and clay.

There was laughter and exclamation. Then hands grabbed us and elation rushed me. Hands, human hands! To be touched. It had been so long. And then, tears. Real tears, at the feel of muscled arms around us. I remembered what it was for skin to be addressed with skin, remembered the smallness of my hand in the sturdiness of my papa's, Matthias's shoulder against mine in the wagon. I was so happy to feel the life of another, pressing against our pig self, and I realised I had hungered for this, in death: to feel and be felt. How glorious, the press of flesh.

We looked into the faces of the people about us. They were all so beautiful. Foreheads shining in the soft afternoon light, chests heaving. Hands stroked our side, and pleasure was everywhere. There was Hans. He looked at Thea, smiled and shrugged. We had no reason to run from the touching. We wanted the moment to last forever. I had forgotten how wide men's hands are, the strength in their hard palms. But they were gentle with us. They were glad to catch their breath. Hans took a rope and we felt him knot it about our leg and secure us to the fence. In that moment we believed he did not desire to hurt us.

'Good pig.'

We felt his voice reverberating in his hands. He rubbed our ears and we leaned into him, felt his feet stumble under the surprise of our heft. There was laughter.

'You have the knack, Hans.' Friedrich's voice. 'He's taken a liking to you.'

We were petted, stroked. Quick-bit nails scratched our glorious body. We closed our eyes. This was rapture. To be touched with love and our snout filled with all the livingness of earth. We felt a sudden yearning for milk.

And then something quick and grey. Our head. We were mute. Blur tumble and white-hot shock and quick and sharp at throat and the world swung upside down and our face was covered in hot and red. Iron and gush. Drip. Bucket. The pale flashing of Anna Maria's arms as she began to whisk.

oblivion

I woke and it was night. The soil was damp beneath me. I was in the pen.

The last moment played through me like a dying note of music. Blood dripping over the tip of our snout, and panic. Wide-eyed fear, and then pounding light-headedness. Shallow breath. Then, immolation.

The pig and I, both. Not going, gone. A giving-in.

Such peace. Such absolute surrender.

Around me, in the darkness, my hands found little bristles. Scrapings of what I had felt upon us. Of what had been part of us.

I knew what had happened since I went into the black. I had seen it many times in my living years. Whipped blood, unstrung from clots, in a bowl. The halved head in water upon the kitchen table. Organs separated into wide-mouthed crocks, covered with cloths, protected from flies and dust. The runners lying between layers of salt, cleaned and ready to be used as casings. And the body, headless, gutted, watered. Dried and hung.

There was a creaking, and I turned and saw a large bag swinging from a tree by a rope. The hanging carcass.

The pig was cool and stiff beneath my hands under its covering. It was nothing like what it had felt to be inhabited, all life and smell and movement. I rested my head along the sway of its back, wrapped my arms around its ribs. I was in those ribs too, I thought. I moved them. And I was crying. Crying as if over my own body, and crying, too, for the fact that, for some hours, I had been truly dead, and I knew nothing about anything, and what a relief that had been.

I wanted to die again.

I said it aloud. 'I want to die.' I wanted that rush of death. With Thea wed, there would be nothing for me in a half-life. I should be as this pig, I thought. Dead, until the trumpet sounds and I claw my way back from the bottom of the sea to be judged.

The Eichenwalds returned the next day at dawn, Thea bleary-eyed, her parents excited for the work ahead. The rope was untied, the carcass hefted onto their shoulders. I followed them as they carried it into the house and placed it on the table like a body to be waked, amidst a scraping hymn of knives on whetstone.

Rosina was puffy-eyed, sleeves-rolled. 'Strange creature,' she said, scratching the mole on her arm.

'I always say, nothing wasted but the squeal,' Anna Maria observed.

'Odd, wasn't it? The way it ran up to Hans.'

'No squeal to be wasted.'

'Glad of it,' Thea muttered. 'I hope I never have to hear another pig squeal in my lifetime.'

I left them all to their ordinance of meat.

Outside, Georg and Hermann were lighting the smokehouse. The damp chips of red gum wept such sweet smoke; the tang of them upon the cool dawn air was consolation. The sky was already clear, high. But all I could think about was the moment of dying. And before it, that strange dissolution into the body of another. I could slip into the bark of a tree. Could I now slip into skin, also? And if a tree withered and sickened and perished, would an animal die, too?

The day was tranquil and I let my feet walk me out into the unspoiled bush, passing the Peramangk as they dug in a clearing of yellow flowers, gathering the same tubers Anna Maria had taken a liking to. Two women looked up in my direction, and I wondered if they sensed me there, and quickened my steps to move beyond their gaze. I walked from tree to tree, to rock to earth, placing my hands on the ground and letting the hum of the place soothe me. The longer I stayed still, the more life I saw around me. The tiny movement of leaves as ants trailed amongst them, and birds – birds everywhere. The sky was a chorus. The trees a low and pulsing metronome.

If I had heard the noise of trees and rivers and open fields in Kay, it was nothing to what I now heard, my entire being opened and attentive. I listened to the music spilling from the leaves around me, and then to the smaller sounds of the insects, the koala that stared at me, eyes half lidded, wedged in the fork of a stringybark, the wagtail flit-dancing. If I had sung well in my living years, it was nothing to the harmonies I now sang against the chitting, sprouting, slow-tongue lolling, clawedness resounding, against the steady chant of soil, the murmur of water.

At first there were glimpses. Briefly a butterfly, gravity pulled me after each great uplift of wing. I fought for nothing more than suspension; thought, Flyingisfallingisflying, before I was again upon the ground, fingers soft as dust. I was a cossid grub, and that was hunger. And then, as dusk fell, I remembered again the pig, relived the bright press of life briefly felt, and tried again with a wedge-tail.

An eagle on the wind is an apostle speaking in tongues: Pentecostal, filled with Holy Spirit.

I woke to limp bodies, feathers fanned out in salutation to flight.

*

That autumn, the people of Heiligendorf gathered to slaughter their pigs, and not once did any of those pigs cry out. Each time a slaughter day was announced, I slept with the pig in its snuffle-mud-warmth and shivered into it morning-come. I urged us to go placidly to the knife. Even when the blade bit and we felt panic throb in our pig-heart and we longed to buck and run screaming from what was coming, I throttled the impulse and we leaned into it, and we went quietly. I did not want them to suffer, and I did not want Thea to hear us squeal.

I took a dark liking to sacrificing myself in this way. When all the doomed pigs had been killed, I inhabited unwanted roosters, the occasional goose. I walked into the hands of women and placed my chicken neck between their fingers, closed my eyes for the break. I told myself I stopped the creatures from fear and distress. But that immediate close of death, the blank oblivion – that is what I sought. Oh God, the glory of that brief immolation when I forgot the looming wedding and my own struck heart! It was my panacea against the constant upswelling of love that threatened to suffocate me.

When Anna Maria and Thea sewed the wedding dress in the evenings, moths dancing around their candle, I let the flash of their needles act as a mesmeric until I, too, felt dazzled by the light and mothsong and forgot everything but the euphoria of the flame's brilliance. Oh, that exquisite sizzle. I was a mosquito thirsty for the slap.

Stupidly, I thought that these small, ill-fated returns to life would be hardly noticed. But in the days after each *Schweineschlachten* doorways and kitchen tables filled with quiet marvel that each pig had gone in silence. Soon, no one could speak of anything else. I hovered around the circles of men and women after Sunday services, listening to them remark upon all the ways I had died in the week.

'It's about time we planted a yew tree in the churchyard,' Henriette said, bending low to Christiana.

'What is a yew tree to a witch?' Christiana muttered.

Several nearby women glanced at her.

'You heard me. These are supernatural deaths. Who amongst you ever heard of a pig lifting its neck to the knife? A rooster placing his head on the block at first sight of the axe?'

'It's strange, I'll grant you,' said Elize. 'But what harm is in it?'

'What harm?' Christiana repeated. 'It shows that there are those amongst us who might bewitch. It shows that there are some who have false texts here in this congregation.'

Elize sighed. 'We all know who you are talking of.'

'I saw her give it to Thea!' Christiana said. 'It was a witches' bible.'

'The kind of book you are talking of is an encyclopedia of herbal cures,' Elize interrupted. 'It's not witchcraft.' She flushed as the women turned to stare at her. 'I haven't one myself but . . . my mother's friend, in my youth . . .' She turned to Christiana. 'This is what you're speaking of, isn't it? *The Sixth and Seventh Books of Moses.*'

'It is. And God forgive you and your mother, Elize. The pastor told Mama he has burned copies of that same book. It includes a conversation with the Devil.'

There was an uneasy silence.

'You think Thea Eichenwald has such a book?' asked Emile Pfeiffer.

'She or her mother.' Christiana glanced across to where Hans was speaking to Thea outside the church. 'She witched our garden. If she can enchant creatures, why not any of our number?'

Elize shook her head. 'Christiana, stop. Pastor Flügel spoke with Anna Maria. She denied having such a book.'

'I am no liar,' Christiana replied. She took a deep breath. 'There was a book. It is hidden here, somewhere. And when it is found, the pastor will ensure it is destroyed. There is no room for the Devil in Heiligendorf.'

The following morning, a gentle knocking woke Thea from her bed by the fire. Blanket wrapped around her nightshift, she stood at the door, peering out into the darkness. It was still very early. No one was yet awake.

'Johanne?'

My mother came inside, headscarf tight around her face. She closed the door firmly behind her.

Thea glanced to the door leading to her parents' bedroom. 'Shall I wake Mama? Would you like to sit down?'

'No,' my mother said. 'I've come to see you.'

'Oh.' Thea frowned. 'What hour is it?'

'Early,' Mama said, not taking her scarf off. She leaned against the table's edge and took in the small room. 'A fine home your father has made here,' she said. 'Of course, I imagine you will be going to live with the Pasches before long.'

'Hans has made an outbuilding for us. But his hope is to buy land of his own, once we are married.'

Mama nodded. 'You must ensure you build a chimney.'

Thea was confused.

'With a few loose bricks,' Mama added. She lowered her voice. 'You never know when you might need a hiding place.'

'Frau Nussbaum . . .' Thea pulled at the dry skin on her lip.

'No, you do understand. I know you understand.' Mama's eyes were fixed on Thea. 'When the pastor visits this morning, I am sure he will be pleased to see this fine home your father has built. To examine everything within it.'

'The pastor has returned to Neu Klemzig.'

'No. He hasn't. Pastor Flügel will visit this morning.' My mother tapped her fingers on the table. 'And if you still do not understand, please relay my message to your mother. Although I believe you have received that inheritance.'

Thea blanched.

'Your mother saved my life,' Mama said quietly. 'I believe she tried to save my daughter's. Well . . .' She paused by the door. 'Have you finished the dress?'

'Almost.'

Mama nodded, then let herself out into the cold air. The door closed behind her.

Pastor Flügel announced himself outside the Eichenwalds' cottage at dawn, stepping inside before Anna Maria had time to welcome him in. Thea had not told her of my mother's earlier visit, and so the Wend's surprise at Flügel's intrusion was genuine. And while she tried to hide it, I could see, too, real fear when the pastor told her he had come to search for a book that, by direction of the Lutheran Church, must be burned. Someone had been bewitching animals. Anna Maria sat at the table, trying to catch Thea's eye as the pastor peered under beds, rapped his knuckles on the wall and opened her dough bin and earthenware vats of fermenting vegetables. Thea was a calm surface of innocence, standing patiently in the corner of the room with her hands folded in front of her apron. It wasn't until the pastor had left, rumpled and annoyed, and Anna Maria had spun around to her daughter, face red, that Thea pointed to the dirt floor beneath her feet.

'Fetch the spade,' she said.

Anna Maria clapped her hands together and laughed. 'How did you know to hide it? Clever girl.'

'Johanne Nussbaum warned me.'

'Johanne Nussbaum?' Anna Maria raised her eyebrows. 'When?'

'She came this morning.'

'She surprises me.'

Thea dropped her eyes to the earth floor. 'I nearly threw it on the fire myself.'

'Oh, Thea.'

'I did. I nearly burned it.'

'Why would you do such a thing?'

'I'm sick of the suspicion, Mama. Why else do you think I'm marrying Hans? Why else am I attaching myself to the family of an elder?'

'What?'

'The Pasches are respectable. The Radtkes will be less inclined to level accusations at Hans Pasche's mother-in-law.'

Anna Maria shook her head. 'One day you'll study that God-given book and you'll find the wisdom you need in its pages. Those books are as holy as the five the pastor reads from in the Bible. I never told you to marry Hans.'

Thea lifted her hands in the air. 'I just . . .'

'What?'

'I know. I know that if you hadn't given it to me, Hanne would still be here.'

'You don't know that. Hanne was sick. "Hanne, Hanne." Think of yourself! You – *you* would have died. You looked on the face of God in that ship.'

'Did I?' muttered Thea. 'She has such curly hair.'

'Do not blaspheme,' Anna Maria snapped.

'Do not take Hanne's name in vain.'

'Thea! What has happened to you? You were always such an open child, such a bright and curious girl, and now – now you do not honour me.' Anna Maria stood from her chair. 'Where is your light?

That inner light of yours? You hardly speak to me. You hardly speak at all! And when you do . . .'

'I'm not a child anymore, Mama. And you no longer know what is best for me.'

'A mother always knows what is best for her child.'

'Yes, her child, but I am grown now. I am grown!' Thea ran her palms over her face. 'I do honour you, Mama. If I didn't, your book would be ash.'

Anna Maria stared at her daughter then, nodding grimly to herself, went outside.

Thea sank to her heels against the wall. 'No light.' She gave a sad laugh. 'What a cruel thing to say to someone.'

There is a cave not far from here. I found myself at the mouth of it during those years of wandering, when I did not keep track of days or the changing face of the moon. Inside the cave were ochre paintings that suddenly pulled me into time. I sat and looked at them and time passed and I knew it was passing, but there was give in its direction, there was curve, and days passed like a whirlpool, its distance extended only within, against, beside itself.

There is ochre on the ground here, where I sit. I feel it underfoot, even in the dark. This country is clay country. Ochre country.

That I could draw her face with it. Draw us, mark us in time. We were here. We existed in time. We exist.

The night before her wedding, Thea called me by name.

She was in bed. My head was on the rise and fall of her ribs, my hand filling her upturned palm. It was late. The house was quiet. I was memorising the creases of her elbows, the whorls of her fingers, like a mother tongue I was afraid of forgetting. I was saying goodbye.

'I dreamed about you, Hanne,' she whispered.

I felt rather than heard her voice. It went through me like a song.

'I dreamed we were birds. I felt feather quills shivering out along my skin, and then there was water beneath me. We were flying. Then a sailor shot you out of the sky and you fell into the sea, and I drowned trying to find you. I forgot I could not swim.

'Hanne, I miss you.' I felt her ribs seize with emotion. 'I thought that faith would be enough. I thought the forest . . .' Thea began to cry. I entwined my fingers with hers and waited until she fell asleep. I did not know what to say.

All that night, I composed hymns to the sound of her heart. Hymns that might hold its steady beat in perpetuity, once she was wed and gone from me.

The morning of Thea's wedding, there was a heavy autumn mist on the ground. It was impossible not to think of Thea as I first met her, all those years ago.

Here we are, two ghosts. Telling each other we're alive.

I heard Flügel's handbell calling the congregation to the church as Anna Maria peered through the small window beside the door to the cottage, white headdress crisp and sharply folded. She called out to Thea, dressing in the bedroom. 'I can see Radtke's wagon arriving for Hans. Goodness, you'd best move yourself.'

'Here.'

And there was Thea, standing beside the table, her hair white against the black of her wedding dress, covered with a wreath of green leaves. She looked a sprite. She looked a woman. Sombre and serious. The sight of her filled me with reverence.

'Oh. Thea.'

'I cannot do these buttons.'

Anna Maria slowly walked around her glowing daughter and fastened the high collar. 'You're trembling,' she said.

'I know.'

'Are you nervous?'

'I think I might be sick.' Thea turned, eyes searching her mother's. 'What do you think?'

'I think you look very fine.'

I was a pilgrim before an apparition. In that moment it was impossible not to imagine, however briefly, that Thea was marrying me. I knew that such a thing was an impossibility. I knew that no one ever contemplated such a thing. And yet, for one hallowed heartskip, that moment expanded into a life. Shared bed under two framed myrtle crowns. Skin on skin. Hours of ordinariness and days of rain, and night-walking to the creek, and sun-warmed clothes in arms. More time together than we had ever been allowed. More time. More time.

Anna Maria pulled her daughter into a close embrace and rested her chin upon Thea's head. 'You will be married then.'

The moment passed, and I was only shadow admiring the light.

Silence stretched the length of the room. Anna Maria stepped back, smoothing Thea's hair behind her ears. Her expression shifted.

'You're crying.'

Thea nodded.

'What is it?'

Thea shrugged. Tears spilled out over her cheeks, even as she furiously wiped them away. Salt water. Streams of it. My bones and blood were full of it. I wondered that Thea and Anna Maria couldn't smell the ocean, that they didn't drown in the water creeping across the floor.

'I know I should be happy,' Thea said. 'I am happy, I think. I don't know. I feel as though I have been waiting for something to change. I . . .'

'Oh, Thea.' Anna Maria wrapped her solid arms around her daughter. She was a wall of strength.

Thea's muffled voice issued from the press of clothes and flesh. Anna Maria pulled away.

'What was that?'

Thea wiped her nose on the sleeve of her wedding dress and rested her head against her mother's shoulder. 'I wish Hanne were here.'

I sobbed, then, at the way her voice held my name. I kneeled with my arm across my face, my body shaking, tears oceanic down my skin.

Anna Maria did not respond for what seemed like an eternity. Then, blessedly, a sound that was not my own choked breathing.

'I know you do.'

The Wend stared out the window at the approaching wagon, deep in thought. 'I know.' And she kissed her daughter on her brilliant hair as a knock sounded from without. 'They're here.' She passed Thea a handkerchief and watched as she dabbed at her face.

'Can you tell?'

Anna Maria smiled and gently pinched Thea's cheeks. 'A little colour will help.'

The knock came again.

'Are you ready?'

Thea took a deep, shuddering breath and smoothed down the front of her dress. 'No,' she whispered. And then she opened the door.

*

I followed the wagon to the church, stepping over the trail of manure left in the lane by Samuel Radtke's horse as it walked on. Thea's back was upright, her gaze fixed forwards. Hans, to her right, full of movement. A handful of children kept running along the lane, pulling a length of rope across the way, and only scattering again, laughing, when Hans threw them coins. He was smiling, flipping pennies with his thumb, a small sprig of myrtle in his buttonhole.

I wanted to hate him but I felt nothing so simple. I could hardly feel anything towards him at all. I thought only of myself, broken-boned and weeping water.

'*Vorwärts*.' Elder Samuel clicked to the horse. The children lowered the rope and the wagon lurched up along the lane and turned towards the church. The congregation had already gathered there, summoned by Flügel's bell. I could hear them talking within the walls. A hive of bees.

'Well,' said Samuel Radtke, turning around to face Hans and Thea. 'We're here.' He winked at them both.

Hans glanced at Thea and raised his eyebrows. Then Christian Pasche came out of the church and helped them both out of the wagon. Hans was sweating. I could see the glisten upon his forehead. Thea seemed to be in a world of her own. She followed Hans and Christian to the church door, but just before she entered, she turned and looked behind her, as if looking for something. Someone.

'Thea,' I said, voice broken. 'Thea, I'm still here.'

Thea frowned and took something from her lips. She paused, looking down at her hand.

'Dorothea?'

Christian Pasche inclined his head to the open door where Hans was waiting.

Thea stepped quickly towards her bridegroom. Then the two of them entered the church to the mournful sound of 'Jesus Lead Thou On'. The door closed and, suddenly, I was quite alone.

The horse whickered softly at its hitching post. I reached a hand to it, but the animal flattened its ears and took a few sudden sidesteps. The sound of the congregation singing came from within the church.

'If the way be drear, if the foe be near, let not faithless fears o'ertake us, let not faith and hope forsake us . . .'

I walked to where Thea had paused by the doorway.

'For, through many a woe, to our home we go . . .'

I could hear her voice against the greater drone of the congregation. A little husky, a little strained.

'When we seek relief from long-felt grief, when temptations come alluring, make us patient and enduring. Show us that bright shore where we weep no more.'

Before I could summon the strength to walk away, I pushed the door open.

Hans and Thea sat in matching wedding chairs at the end of the aisle. I walked towards them as the congregation sang the last mournful verse of the hymn, Flügel facing his flock, eyes shifting across every face. By the time the hymn was finished, I was standing in front of her.

Thea gleamed in the low light of the church. She sat very still, straight-backed, her hands folded in her lap, bareheaded except for her myrtle crown. I kneeled in front of her and, as I bent my forehead to her knees, I saw she held something between her fingers. A splinter of light. A fragment of pearlescent shell.

I stared at it as Flügel began his sermon behind me.

Don't forget me.

It was real. The shell was real.

As the pastor preached about God's earthly gift of marital attachment and its teachings of restraint and love, I held Thea's face in my palms and I spoke over him. I filled her ears with my own breathless pleading.

'Don't forget me,' I said. I was breaking apart. 'Thea, do not cast me out of your heart. Listen, listen, I know the word of God. "Set me as a seal upon thine heart, as a seal upon thine arm: for love is as strong as death."' I drew myself closer to her, I brought my voice to her ear. '"Jealousy is as cruel as the grave."'

'And so, as we celebrate these two young –'

'"The coals thereof are coals of fire."' I buried my face in her neck, cried into the cloth that had been meant for my own wedding. 'Thea, listen to me. Please hear me. "Many waters cannot quench love, neither can the floods drown it . . ."' I brought my mouth close to hers. '"Thy love is better than wine. Honey and milk are under thy tongue."'

'Dorothea Anna Eichenwald . . .'

'"Set me as a seal upon thine heart, upon thine arm."'

'Hans Reinhardt Pasche . . .'

'"Love is as strong as death."' I kissed the shell between her fingers as she rose and tucked it into her palm. '"Love is as strong as death."' Heard the ocean issue from it as she was married. Eternal. Ancient.

'"Love is as strong as death." Remember, Thea. Remember me.'

She was ever my song of songs.

As Thea and Hans returned down the aisle, I was bled dry of all feeling. My vision swam. Some part of me was aware of the congregation leaning over each other to congratulate Hans, jubilant, laughing and shaking his hand. Thea smiled as the women bent towards her. The sound of voices lifting and falling washed over me in a discordant cadence and I closed my eyes to try to centre myself, to summon one single clear thought.

Let her go.

I could not move. I sank back on my heels, aware of Flügel shepherding everyone out into the soft morning light. His robes brushed past me. I closed my eyes and waited until silence descended and the church was finally empty. Then I laid down in the aisle.

'Dear Lord, into your hands I commit my soul.'

No summons upon my spirit.

I looked up at the celestial body painted on the strung bedsheet above me.

No heavenly host. Only a long-limbed spider scurrying along, worrying the stretch of stars with frantic silhouette.

I left.

I did not keep the same direction. The sun was at once above me, now dawning to my right, now setting in the same place. Days and nights passed and though I kept moving – compulsively, urged on by some sense that I must place as much distance as possible between myself and Thea – I dwelled almost wholly within myself. I woke some nights and saw that the moon had changed and realised that it had waxed bold since its husking light the previous evening, and then I understood that I had forgotten the rhythm of days and they had bled by unnoticed. There was no handbell rung by Elder Pasche or Pastor Flügel to mark the time of day. No devotional services to begin the week. I felt neither chill nor sun, hunger nor thirst. My mind ran to a different measure; it forgot the steady turning of the earth.

I saw things. I saw the two Tiersmen kissing in their cabin. The cave of ochre and the shore that took the Ramindjeri woman home. I saw things that sickened me and aged me and made me weary of ongoing, but I continued. I didn't know what else to do.

I thought of Thea and bled into trees. I did not care if they fell. I became birds so that I might explode with song and fill hollow bones with longing, and woke in sunshine, their feather-light bodies in my fingers. I crawled into a dingo for the satisfaction of blood on my tongue, when blood was all there was to meet my grief: holy beat of marsupial heart crunching into silence beneath my teeth. I blacked out in iron-rich ecstasies of woe and hunger, woke back into this world with blood on my chin and ears furred. I stroked them at night till they faded and I became once again myself, unbeating heart, unbreathing lungs. Just shadow quickening with love and memory of pale head bending to me, lips pressing her seal in the molten wax of my being.

Distance and time affected nothing upon my heart.

Years passed. I believed I had seen her for the last time. I thought our story was done.

And then. And then.

THE
THIRD
DAY

THEN

incarnations

Thea, in all incarnations, wherever my soul has resided, I have loved you, am loving you, will love you. If the earth one day burns out its charge, you will find me in the ash. If the sea dries, find me in its sand. Fingers forever writing your name in ash, in sand, over and over in a love-patterned wasteland.

tributary

It is nearly dawn now. The hour of the first birds and their summoning of light and warmth. I feel the night leaving over the edge of the world, like a tablecloth slipping to the ground.

I am nearly finished. This will be the third morning I have seen the sun rise in the east. Here it comes. It rises so golden the world seems an altar to its glory. Here it comes.

My voice is held by the wind. Let me write my story on the air, and when it rains, let it pool upon the earth so that the valley may drink of it. Let this testament return to soil. Bones in the water. Voice on the land.

When I am gone, these things will remain.

My thoughts circled Thea, always.

But one evening as I lay on a slab of rock in stony high country, feeling the warmth of the day within it, my mind saw her face and my ears heard her voice in such a way that I sat up. I had spent so much time committing her to memory, and now memory unmade me. In my mind I saw again her lips, the curve of her chin, the sun on her eyelashes, fringing her gaze with light. The evening sky became the looming softness of pines.

'Hanne.'

I heard her. My skin prickled.

'*Ersurgant mortui, et ad me veniunt.*' Her voice, again. I felt her leaning above me, eyes moving upon me, and when I reached into the dark to touch her face, I felt fire.

Thea, alight, my flame swimming in the dark. Calling me. Summoning me.

The warmth of the stone deepened and grew warmer, until it was so hot I had to stand.

'Hanne!' Her voice was there again, but this time it carried distance. Thea was calling me from some place far away. It was not in my mind, it was not imagined. I could hear my name thrown again and again into the air, miles away, but it reached me. I heard her.

I did not imagine it. It was not the work of a broken heart. She was calling me.

And so I left to find her.

I walked all night, following the sound of my name. I didn't know where I was headed, only that I must keep going. Dawn rose red and violent; the sky was on fire. I was compelled. The day widened into a glory of sunlight. And then I heard children's voices calling in German and, looking up, saw that I stood at the upper shelf of a valley at once strange and familiar to me.

It took me some moments to assure myself that I had returned to Heiligendorf. It had changed since I had left it, and the realisation was like a blow to the heart. I had not understood just how much time had passed; I had fallen out of pace with the steady footfall of the world.

The slopes surrounding the village had been cleared of remaining bushland in my time of absence, the wheat crops extended. As I walked down into the cluster of houses, I saw that most had been replaced or improved beyond recognition. Thatch was now straw, not kangaroo grass, and I could see none of that bronze grass anywhere, nor the yellow flowers of the yam daisies I remembered from that first summer. Every available space had been given over to farming and pasture for sheep and cattle. Houses had been built right to the road to allow more space for vegetable gardens; orchards were now in full blossom behind. All had outbuildings of silvered red gum slab with haylofts, horse tack and wagons, hand ploughs and harrows beneath. Piles of manure beside pig sties. There were squat chimneys on pitched roofs, barns made of sapling rail, outdoor bake ovens.

They have recreated Kay, I thought. All this way and they have disfigured the land back into Prussia.

The only marked difference came from the gum trees still dotting the settlement. Yet these were fewer than I remembered, and I found myself unsure of exactly where I was without their old, familiar bearings. Adding to my sense of disorientation were the animals everywhere, the noise of them loud and unrelenting. The milking cows were more than I could count, and as the children herded them past me, their voices sweet with laughter, I could hear a background chorus of triumphant crowing, goose gabble against the higher sweetness of singing magpies.

The afternoon was full of spring haze. Everything growing was young green but the song of the place was different. Muted, somehow. Only the red gums and the occasional untouched acacia chanted deeper, older notes. Then the sound of hammer on anvil rang out and spoiled it all.

'Hanne.'

Her voice again. A sudden riptide of need dragged through me. Somewhere in this valley of rough gables and neat gardens was Thea. I said her name out loud and it was a prayer filling my body, already moving me closer to her.

*

The Pasches' farm teemed with activity. I could see Hermann and Georg in the yard with Christian, the brothers now older than Hans had been at his wedding. They were strong, upright men, and I noticed Georg pause to speak to a woman I did not recognise but who seemed to be his wife. I watched her raise a hand as he left, then duck her head under the door to a lean-to.

I hesitated then. I had envisioned walking to that lean-to and finding Thea there, stepping out of its shadow into the sunlight, but as I waited, only Georg's wife emerged, a wailing newborn over her shoulder.

I approached the homestead. The lean-to was empty. Inside the house, Rosina was cooking, a girl of five or six waiting next to her.

'Bertha, go and see what Frieda is doing,' she said, sweeping peelings from the table into a bucket.

'The baby woke. I heard him crying,' Bertha replied.

'Give all this to the pigs then.'

I passed Rosina and stepped into the room coming off the kitchen. It was a bedroom, a wooden cross above the narrow bed. Empty. Through that room lay another, with two more beds pushed together. Thea was nowhere to be seen.

I returned to the kitchen, unsure of what to do. Rosina was pouring water into a pot on the fire.

'Mama, they're back!' From the back door came the clatter of a bucket being dropped on the ground.

'Where, Bertha?'

'In the potatoes.'

Rosina wiped her hands on her apron, then ran out the back door. I followed her, somehow thinking the child had meant Thea and Hans, already picturing the two of them walking through the potato ground. But outside I saw, instead, several Peramangk men and women on their knees, digging up the new potatoes and dropping them into net bags.

'Get on with you,' Rosina shouted, running towards them, flapping her hands. 'Thieves!'

The women looked up but did not stop. Rosina motioned to Bertha, who was staring open-mouthed from the doorway. 'Go and get your father.'

Before she could do so, however, Georg's wife came running over with a stockwhip. She was red-faced, furious. I watched, horrified, as she ran at the women, cracking the whip and catching one of the older women on the face. The woman screamed, dropping the potatoes and bringing her hands to her eyes, as the others rose to their feet and, pulling her along with them, ran, woven bags held tightly in their fists, soles of their feet flashing. The men followed, shouting angrily at Georg's wife over their shoulders.

Rosina watched them leave, hands on her hips, breathing heavily. 'Thank you, Frieda.'

Frieda tossed the whip on the ground and sat down beside it, wiping the sweat from her face and neck. 'That is how my father did it in Neu Klemzig,' she said.

'In broad daylight, too.'

Bertha's voice came from the house behind them, full of warning. 'Mama . . .'

I looked up as Rosina did, saw a man stepping back through the potato field, spear in hand. He lifted his free palm and I saw that it was covered in blood.

'Frieda . . .' Rosina pulled the younger woman to her feet. Frieda paused, bending for the stockwhip, then thought better of it and ran with Rosina to the house, slamming the door shut after her.

I watched the spear pierce the air. The throw was so liquid, so sure, it seemed the spear was not only an extension of the man's arm, but a pure, darting exhalation of his anger and contempt. It was a ribboning of power and frustration. An act of assertion.

The wood licked knife-hot through the air, splitting the afternoon light.

The spear hit the centre of the door with a small wooden thud. It quivered against its buried point, shaking still, it seemed, with the man's disgust.

I turned to see his reaction, but he had already turned away and was walking back to his family on the periphery of the village, all of them silent except for the wailing of the woman whom Frieda had blinded with her whip.

Thea is not here, I thought to myself. And then I turned and saw Anna Maria beyond the farm border, one hand on her hip, the other held over her mouth.

'Hanne.'

Thea's voice came to me again, filled with distance and yet, so close, so urgent, my knees went weak with anticipation.

I stumbled towards the Eichenwalds' cottage, body-soft with hope.

Anna Maria was alone, setting out earthenware jars on her wooden table. The air smelled of dried herbs and liniments. I took in the empty house, then watched her work, strong hands wrapping beeswax in a cloth. She raised a mallet to break it into pieces, but something stopped her. She stood there for a moment, hammer raised, eyes lifting slowly from her work of salves.

'It's only me,' I told her. 'Hanne. I've come back.'

I felt her hesitate, felt the air prickle with the intensity of her listening.

'I've come for Thea,' I said. I touched her hand. Her bare forearms rose in gooseflesh.

Anna Maria put the mallet down on the table. Her voice, when she spoke, was a whisper. 'What do you want?'

'Thea,' I said. 'She's calling for me.' I reached out to touch her again but the Wend drew back and looked around the room. I brought my mouth to her ear. 'Where is Thea?'

Hair rose on the back of Anna Maria's neck. She breathed in sharply and, placing a hand over her heart, closed her eyes.

I paused, then asked the question again.

The Wend brought the tips of her fingers to her lips. 'She's not here,' she murmured, and in that instant I heard the strange words again.

'*Ersurgant mortui, et ad me veniunt.*'

A summoning from outside the cottage, from somewhere in the grey-green throat of bush beyond the village.

Anna Maria opened her eyes as I left the room. Before I stepped out the door, I saw her pick up her mallet and hold it to her chest, a shadow of a smile on her lips.

I could smell new-baked bread and frying bacon on the afternoon air, and as I hurried back onto the lane I saw it was coming from Gottfried Volkmann's place. Gottfried himself was outside, standing next to a sign written in English, *The German Arms*, talking with a fellow with his back to me. I could see several men inside through the open window, smiling at a woman offering a coffee pot.

The door opened and Elizabeth Volkmann stuck her head out, waiting for a lull in the conversation to summon her father inside.

'There's a man with a question about the mail cart,' she said. She had grown out of her baby face and looked like a thinner, quieter version of Henriette.

At that moment the man turned and my heart rose up into my throat. The man was Matthias. He was black-bearded now, stockier than I remembered, but his gap-toothed smile was the same. He held a baby in his arms and called out to a boy who suddenly ran from the front door of the Volkmanns' place into the laneway, chasing a puppy. Wilhelm, I thought, looking at the baby, and then, heart in mouth, realised that, no, Wilhelm must be the child with the dog. Life had flown on, unstemmed: Wilhelm held the measure of seven or eight years in his body. I stared at him, overwhelmed by the way children kept time and the realisation that the baby in my brother's arms was my niece or nephew.

I felt Thea's call on me like a hand around my heart, but I wanted to see my brother. I could hardly believe it was him. I followed Matthias as he rounded the side of a small, wood-shingled house, Wilhelm and the dog running in front of him. And as I followed my brother into his garden, I saw two little boys, no more than four years old, collecting eggs and placing them carefully in a basket held by Augusta, and something broke in me, for the boys carried Matthias's and Gottlob's faces as I had known them in my own childhood. Dark-haired, small.

'Papa, this one is broken,' said one of the boys, lifting an egg.

'Is it spoiled?' Matthias asked.

The boy lifted the egg to his brother's nose, laughed when he recoiled in disgust. 'Can I throw it?'

My brother nodded, smiling at Augusta as the two boys turned and ran through the small orchard beyond the vegetable garden and fowl house. Wilhelm followed after them, the puppy at his heels.

You're a papa now, I thought. Matthias, you are a father.

'Shall I take her?' Augusta asked, setting the basket of eggs on the ground and extending her arms for the baby.

My brother shook his head. 'She's sleeping.'

'You're soft on her,' Augusta said.

Matthias carefully lowered himself down onto the grassy verge of the vegetable garden, tucking the swaddling around his daughter, still nestled in his elbow.

Augusta picked up the egg basket. 'Call me if she cries,' she said, and went into the cottage.

I sat down next to my brother and rested my chin on his shoulder, looking down at his daughter. He smelled the same as he always had, and for a moment we were almost children again, sitting outside in Kay. It was as though nothing had happened. We were both alive, undivided. 'She's beautiful,' I said softly.

The baby wrinkled her nose, purled lips pouting as she blinked awake.

Matthias smiled at his daughter. I watched him lift a rough finger and gently trace the fine brown hair on her skull.

'Hello, Esther,' Matthias said softly. 'It's your papa.'

'Esther,' I whispered. The baby looked at me and smiled.

Matthias laughed. 'Augusta!' he called. 'Augusta, come and see!'

'What is it, Papa?' Wilhelm jogged back from the orchard, dog in his arms.

Matthias extended a hand and Wilhelm went to him, leaning into my brother's chest. 'Look, she's smiling,' he said.

Wilhelm grinned. 'What's she looking at?'

Matthias placed a hand on the boy's head. 'Who knows,' he replied softly. 'Who knows.'

The wind was rising. Out beyond the trees the wheat crop blew green waves across the slope. I did not know how to bear the passing of time.

'I have to go,' I told Matthias. I bent my mouth to his shoulder and kissed it. 'Don't forget me.'

I left my brother's house. The sun was setting; the sky was washed with violet. I was ready to see Thea. I was ready. But as I continued out of the village, past a new-planted spring garden and a one-roomed house, I heard my father's voice.

I stopped. Through the cottage's uncovered window I could see my father praying at the head of the table with his Bible open, Mama with her hair covered and eyes closed beside him. Facing her was a fine-boned, dark-haired girl.

Hermine.

I hardly recognised my sister. The irritable, easily upset baby was now this watchful, quiet child praying with my parents, sucking her upper lip. My mother's image.

How many nights had I been that daughter sitting at the table, bowing my head while my stomach twisted in hunger? The scene was so familiar to me that for a moment I imagined I, too, was about to join my parents at the table, about to be reprimanded for staying out, for not helping Mama prepare the *Abendbrot*. Part of me almost went inside to take up a seat, to pretend that nothing had happened.

You do not belong there anymore, I told myself. You've been claimed by different tides.

'I am glad you're happy,' I murmured against the glass. 'I am glad you have the daughter you needed.'

Love and hope turned me to liquid. I walked on beyond Heiligendorf, into the evening.

At midnight, I turned off the dwindling track from the village and followed a fence out towards the deep blue of the bush. I could see a solitary light blinking against a shadowed rise behind.

Thea's home, I thought. I knew it in the way I knew my own name.

'Hanne.'

Something was happening. I could feel the fibres and tendons of my body resonate with sound; I was a struck chord. There was a tremble at work within me and, heady with music, I grasped for the nearest fence post to steady myself and knocked something to the ground.

A stone.

I picked it up, weighed it in my hand. It was smooth and rounded with water, and I could hear the river like a skin upon it.

I looked back up to the light and stepped forwards, and when I placed my hand on the next post there was a stone there, too. Another on the next, and the next. Every post had been crowned.

I ran towards the light then. The earth held each falling foot, pushed me towards her, towards the cottage now visible in the darkness, to the glowing window, to her.

Thea.

And there she was. Lit in light from a lamp burning on the table in a one-roomed house, bending over the Book of Moses with a hand over her mouth and her eyes wet.

I was that eagle again, holding up the sky. Rapture rolled through me like blood.

She was older, more beautiful, more flawed. Her teeth still snagged on her lip but she was thinner, aged by sun and time. Hair escaped from her braids and wisped along her neck as it always had.

'Thea.'

She stilled, then. As though she had heard me.

I said her name again.

She stood suddenly. 'Hanne?' Her voice was a whisper.

I went to Thea and placed my arms around her. I rested my head against hers and she leaned into me, face turning towards mine, as though I had weight, as though she felt me there.

She started crying then. I felt the shudder of her against my rib cage and it was too much; tears ran down my face.

I unfolded myself from her. 'The stones,' I said. 'I saw the stones.'

'Hanne, if I dream, will you come to me?'

'Thea?'

A man's voice, quiet and sleepy, from the corner of the room.

I turned and saw Hans sitting up in bed, squinting in the lamplight. 'You're crying. What happened?'

'Nothing,' Thea said, turning to him. 'Go back to sleep.'

Hans got out of bed and stepped to her, pausing when he saw the Book of Moses open on the table. 'What are you doing?'

Thea wiped her eyes with the back of her hand. 'Nothing.' She started to laugh. 'I don't know what is happening to me. I'm . . . I'm seeing things.'

I told myself I must not, that to do so would be to harm him, but I walked towards Hans even as my hands reached for the table to hold myself back. My fingers slid over the wood. They did not grip it; there was no will in them. I stood behind him, so close that my lips almost touched the warmth of his bare skin. I saw the fine golden hairs on his neck. I closed my eyes, brushed my lips against his spine.

Is this what she does? I wondered.

'Thea.' Hans's voice was husky. He was breathing quickly. 'Who is here?'

From his shoulder I saw her look up.

She looked at me. She saw me. 'Hanne,' she said softly.

Hans turned and for one moment we regarded each other. For one brief moment he saw me and his eyes were wide and soft with recognition, and Thea smiled through her tears and brought her hands to her mouth. I felt my bones turning in the ocean, felt my mouth fill with sea water. Salt salt salt.

And then it passed. I was blanketed by the air, and I saw Hans search the darkness, heard the sob hook in Thea's throat.

I knew they had seen me. Hans's drowsiness was gone.

'Was she . . .?'

Thea was looking for me. 'She's still here,' she whispered. She sat down on their bed. 'Hanne, stay.'

She was luminous. Pearl in the water. Moon in the night. Hans kneeled down before her.

'What did you do?' he whispered.

Thea's eyes flicked to the open book on the table. 'I called her here.'

Hans gazed up at her, full of wonder. 'Is this a dream?'

I felt the sight of her quicken through him like wind over water. As it did me. As it always had.

Thea slowly shook her head.

I stepped forwards and placed a hand on Hans's shoulder, and I felt his lust, so different from my lust, which was a deeper love, which was the ache of years, the weight of waiting.

Don't, I thought. And then I did. The hunger of my heart led me. It was as easy as slipping into water.

We kissed her. I thought I would die from the force of life I felt, from the softness of her mouth on ours, which was the same softness I had remembered, had thought of every day since I had first felt it. Then I felt her tongue against ours, and then her hands around our neck, fingers pulling us into fire. I felt the need of her for me. I knew that she felt me there beside him, with him. And I knew he felt me too: in the us of our body, I felt him accommodate me, felt him pull me with him in his desire, then felt him relinquish his self to me so that I might act on mine. We were in the forest again. The blanket desiccated beneath us into pine needles, the thatch peeled back to stars.

Thea pulled us back down onto the bed, she pulled us against her, and I felt the slow roll of her hips against us, and I gave myself over to feeling. She sat up to undress, her eyes closed, and we looked at her, the unfathomable hidden beauty of her, perfection of rib and breast and navel, of hip and thigh and neck. Rapture swept through us like a wave until we could not bear it. I could not bear my own desire for her. It was sharper than Hans's. It carried a different sound.

Holy nail, to crucify me to such a cross.

And Hans closed his eyes, which were also my eyes, and I felt that I was in my own body, that she felt me as myself. We shed the clothes upon us and when I felt her skin against our own, I knew she felt me, was seeing me there with Hans, felt my warmth as she had imagined it. We ran our lips over her body, heard her breathing hard in our ear, felt her wet and sweet under our fingers, smelled sap, soil. We touched her again and again; we were inside her. My heart was yearning like a root ball for water, and she was tributary, she was river, and when she came, she called for me by name.

I woke later. I kept my eyes closed; I could not bear to feel myself away from her once more. But as I lay there, I felt Thea move next to us. I had not yet been thinned out of life, although I could feel it coming. I felt the darkness approach. I felt Hans sleeping and myself awake within him, Thea's bare arm curved around our waist, her head resting on our shoulder. I felt the press of her lips against the ear that was not my ear but might have been.

I could not speak. But I kissed her hair, and I brought her fingers to our lips.

'Don't go,' she whispered. She was half in sleep. 'Don't leave me. Not again.'

I did not know what to do. I could feel the pulling outwards from the intensity of life. But I wanted her to know I had been there, that they could both trust the memory of the night and find assurance that it had happened amidst its unreality.

As I felt again the gathering momentum of leaving, I placed Thea's hand over the initials on her pillow cover. H and T, entwined. She opened her eyes and saw them there, and stared back at me, and she saw me. Hans was asleep in the bed next to her, his hand over hers, and I was standing beside the bed, and she knew I was there.

Her eyes found mine. 'Don't go,' she whispered.

It was as much as I could do to walk three paces before I felt darkness close around me and was thrown up into it and knew no more.

walnuts

I woke suddenly in the scritch and call of the bush at midday, needles of she-oak beneath me. For one moment I did not know where I was, what had happened. And then I remembered the feel of Thea's hands on my skin, the lift of her neck under my mouth, and my body thrummed so hard in memory I had to bite down on my hand.

What had I done?

What had we done?

Cold stones groaned memories of liquid heat. The song of the soil was loud about me.

My hands were shaking, and when I looked down I saw that they bore unfamiliar knuckles. The nails were dark with dirt I had not worked. The lines upon my palms were not my own.

'Hans,' I said. 'Oh my God. Hans.'

The relief I felt when I found Hans alive, sitting opposite Thea at their table, was so overwhelming I felt scoured by it. He was not dead. I had not killed him.

'I know it happened,' Hans was saying quietly. The noon meal was on the table between them, but neither Hans nor Thea were eating and I saw, next to the untouched bread on their plates, the white-worked pillow cover I had left under Thea's sleeping hand.

Thea was still. A waiting pyre. I could see it in her limbs, in the set of her chin. Her fingers twitched against the surface of the table.

'I know it happened,' Hans continued. 'But I don't understand how.'

Thea opened the book and flipped to the third page. There, in gothic text, I saw '*Gespräche mit Toten zu führen*'. She turned it around and pushed the book towards him.

Hans read, face growing pale. 'To converse with the dead? Thea...' He looked up at her, then carefully closed the book and passed it back to her. 'You told me you only used the seventh book. The herbal cures. This seems...' He shook his head.

'I know.'

'You summoned her?'

Thea nodded. 'Three nights ago. When you were sleeping. I thought it didn't work. I was going to try again, last night, when she came.' Her hands were shaking. 'I saw her.'

Hans pushed the bread out of the way and leaned over the table, taking Thea's hands in his. 'I saw her too,' he said, and then he laughed in a frightened way. 'I felt her.'

Thea bent forwards and rested her forehead on their entwined hands. 'Please don't tell anyone.'

'I don't know how or why you did it, Thea, but' – he hesitated – 'there was no evil in it.' He attempted a smile. 'Not if it was Hanne.'

Thea lifted her head and looked up at him. 'You truly do not know why I did it?'

Hans seemed to falter. 'You miss her. You were friends.'

Thea sat up. Brought a hand against the back of her neck. 'I loved her,' she said eventually. Her voice was moss underfoot. Was a palm against a skin of water. I could not take my eyes off her.

Hans looked at her and said nothing.

'I still love her.' Thea's eyes were intemperate blue. The heart of a candle flame. 'Did you know such a thing was possible?'

Hans went very still. 'Did I know that love was possible?'

Thea bit her lip and sat back in her chair. 'I don't mean to hurt you,' she said.

'Thea . . .' Hans suddenly reached for her again. 'How can I make you happy?'

'I don't know,' she said. 'I don't know what is real anymore. I feel . . .' She took a shuddering breath. 'I feel as though I am burning down all the time.'

'What do you mean?'

She shook her head. 'Like I am being consumed by the depth of my feeling for her.'

'I miss her too.'

Thea took a deep breath and glanced up at the ceiling. 'Not like I do.'

Hans told her the story he remembered best about me then. Thea began to cry and laugh at the same time, nodding as Hans told her about the argument, me on my hands, searching for the source of the song I claimed to hear, the well all those years later.

'Yes,' she said. 'Yes, that was Hanne. She heard those songs. She sang them to me.'

Hans wiped the tears from Thea's cheeks. 'I'm sorry,' he said. 'I'm sorry she died.'

'I'm sorry too.' She kept crying. She could not stop.

'I have something.' Hans suddenly pushed back his chair and crossed the room. He pulled a small case out from under the bed in the corner, opened it, and took out a small cloth bag. 'Here,' he said, and placed it gently down on the table in front of Thea.

Thea opened the bag and looked inside. When she glanced back up at Hans, she looked like she might cry again. 'Walnuts.'

'Do you remember the tree in the Nussbaums' orchard?'

Thea nodded, tears running down her cheeks. 'You took them?'

'For her.' Hans rubbed a hand over his face. 'Oh, this is a strange conversation to be having.'

Thea laughed, eyes wet. 'We are strange people.'

Hans smiled. 'I wanted to marry her.' He gestured to the walnuts. 'These were going to be a wedding present. So she could plant her daughters here.'

Thea stood up. 'Let's plant them now.'

'Now?'

'Let's plant them for us. For Hanne.'

Thea and Hans planted the walnuts in their little orchard, creamy flowers already spasming on fruit trees. I climbed into the branches of a nearby stringybark, lay my cheek on its peeling surface and looked down on Thea and Hans, not knowing what to feel; feeling everything, Thea's assertion that she loved me illuminating me like a flame within a glass.

Perhaps the mystery is deeper than I know, I thought. Perhaps, the mystery is not to be unravelled. A fathom not to be plumbed. Perhaps there is still grace for me, I wondered, and the thought was a raindrop on my forehead, a finger down my spine, snow on my tongue.

'Hans?' Thea's voice called out below, concerned.

I looked down. Hans was still, leaning hard on his spade. He spat into the dirt.

'What is it?'

'Nothing,' Hans said, straightening. But then he vomited, and I could see, as I slid down the tree and started towards them, that it was salt water. As Thea helped him back to the house, I could smell it. The ocean, brackish against the gathering wind, blowing over the crops, slate clouds scudding low.

*

Hans was bed-bound by evening, groaning from a great pressure in his head, unable to eat. He complained of loose bones, of sand under his tongue. As Thea flipped pages in the Book of Moses, I sat on the edge of the bed and urged Hans to recover. Thea placed a cold compress on his brow and he cried out that his skull was a chalice of sea water, that there was a darkness coming for him.

'Time curves upon itself,' he moaned. 'The hole in the heart of God.'

'Hans,' Thea said, holding the compress in place with one hand and the book with the other. 'Hans, lie still. Try to rest.'

He spluttered and sea water fell upon his chest. 'I can't breathe,' he said. 'I'm drowning.'

Oh God, I thought to myself. I did this. I have killed him.

Thea paused in her turning of pages and abruptly got up. I watched her as she found their Bible and tore a page from the endpapers, muttering, 'Almighty Lord, forgive me,' then proceeded to write something down. I got up and stood over her shoulder and read: 'So says the Lord: I will look for what is lost again, bind what is wounded, replace what is weak for what is firm and strong. I shall protect thee.'

Thea smoked the paper before sunrise for seven mornings, and each dawn rose upon a grimmer picture than the last. The fever mounted until Hans could not speak at all, his nightclothes ringed with tide-ebbings of salt. Water ran from his ears. Thea tucked the paper under his clothes, upon his chest. It was damp from the ocean rising in him. Still, she persisted, and after the seventh day, she buried the smoked, stained paper a little distance from the planted walnuts.

For weeks I watched her work their farm alone while Hans lay in bed. After lighting the kitchen fire, Thea went outside to feed and milk their cow, driving it down the track for the shepherd to take to pasture, then spent the morning setting milk in pans and collecting water from the creek for the animals, garden, fruit trees and vines. She chopped firewood, boiled, scrubbed and wrung Hans's salted, evil-smelling clothes, and, once, screamed into the empty air when the washing line toppled and the laundry fell into the dirt.

Thea turned herself to work, and as wretched as I was at bearing fault for Hans's suffering, I could not help but marvel at how the yoke, the axe, the pans, the scythe, the spade became extensions of herself. So much time had passed since I had carried weight, I had forgotten what it was to work with my whole body. Thea appeared to me as a wonder. Silver, silent miracle of vigour and determination.

Then, seven weeks after the burial of the smoked paper, as summer stretched itself over the valley in a skein of pale heat, Hans recovered. One day he was lying in bed, tongue dry with sand, and the next he rose and ate a little *Schlippermilch*. The following day he did not return to bed until nightfall, and soon there was nothing about him to indicate he had been so long unwell, apart from a lean frame and a persistent smell of tidal water.

'You seem better,' Thea said that night. She watched as he wiped his plate clean with bread.

Hans smiled at her. 'Do you think so?'

'I do.'

'I feel better. I feel as though it was all a bad dream.' He shook his head. 'A nightmare.'

'You see now, about the book. Its power.'

Hans drank deeply from his mug of wine, looking at her over the brim, eyes crinkled. 'I always believed you. It is not for me to judge the ways the Almighty works upon the world.' He wiped his mouth. 'You're not eating.'

'No.' Thea pushed her plate across the table towards him. 'Here.'

'You need to eat too.' He kept looking at her, head to one side, hand wrapped around his wine.

Thea looked pale. She stared at the two plates slick with animal fat.

'What is it?' Hans put down his mug. 'Thea?'

'Please, eat,' she murmured, pushing her chair back. 'Eat.' And she rushed from the room, hands over her mouth.

Hans found her by the outhouse, on her hands and knees. Thea stirred as he approached and I could tell she did not want him to see the mess she had made.

Hans's voice was soft. He helped her to her feet, placed her arm around his shoulders, and lifted her.

As they passed me in the doorway, I placed my hand on Thea's chest and followed them inside. I let Hans place her on their bed, remove her outer things and pull the blanket over her.

'I'll get you some water,' he said.

'It's empty,' she croaked.

'I'll go to the creek.'

As soon as he left the room I crawled in next to Thea, buried my face in her neck, and wrapped my arms around her stomach. Her heart was beating quickly. And there was something else there too. Beyond the strong knocking in her chest, a steady patter. Another heart, another body in her body. I listened to them pulse, letting the sound surround me until it felt like a rip pulling me out into a dark sea, thrumming with its own energy. Inescapable.

Days turned. Exhaustion and nausea left Thea bone-tired in the summer warmth. She hauled herself through the day's washing and cooking, red-knuckled. Some days, when Hans was out in the fields, she undressed and quietly examined the changes in her body, touching the hard roundness of her stomach with open palms, filled with awe. On hot days she sat by the creek and placed her feet in the water to soothe her swollen ankles, leaning against the bank with eyes closed against the sun.

The wind came, and then the rain, and the ground offered up mushrooms that Thea collected, sitting on her heels, no longer able to bend to the ground. She was out there one morning, knife in hand, when Anna Maria came walking along the fence line, waving her arms wildly in the air at her daughter who, on seeing her mother, shouted with delight, then sat back on the ground and sobbed.

'Oh, Thea!' Anna Maria laughed, running towards her. 'Oh, Thea. Look at the size of you now!'

Thea lifted up her arms like a child. 'My mama.'

'Oh, my girl,' Anna Maria said, hoisting Thea to her feet. She stepped back, placed her hands on the round lift of her daughter's apron. 'Yes. A boy. Where is Hans?'

'Adelaide. Buying leather to resole his boots.'

'Here, I can pick those up,' said Anna Maria, bending to collect the scattered mushrooms. 'Let's go inside, shall we? We have so much to say.'

Inside, Anna Maria made Thea sit while she made coffee for them both and told her the news of Heiligendorf. 'Your father wanted to come, of course, but he has a great deal of work now, it wasn't possible.' She placed a cup in front of Thea and kissed her on the head. 'He will come to meet his grandson, when he arrives.'

'When do you think that will be?' asked Thea, blowing on her coffee.

Anna Maria smiled. 'Soon.'

'You feel it?'

'I know it.'

Thea smiled. 'How do you know that you know things?'

Anna Maria reached into her basket and brought out a slab of something wrapped in a cloth. 'I brought you *Streuselkuchen*.' She picked up a knife and cut her daughter a slice.

'I mean it,' Thea said gently. She gave her mother a searching look. 'How do you know for sure?'

Anna Maria placed a hand over her stomach. 'I feel it here. I know it here.'

'I summoned Hanne.'

Anna Maria put her cake back down on the table and stared at Thea. 'You summoned her.'

'With the sixth book.'

'And she came?'

'Yes. Hans saw her too. She was with us.'

Anna Maria picked up Thea's folded hands. 'Thea, was this a dream? Did she come to you in a dream?'

'Not in a dream. I was awake,' Thea whispered. 'She looked older. My age. She was standing just there. And then I couldn't see her anymore, but I could feel her.'

'I wondered . . .'

'What?'

'I felt a presence one night. A searching. A searching for you.' Anna Maria placed her hand over Thea's stomach. 'You felt her here?'

Thea shook her head. 'I felt her everywhere.' She began to laugh, fingers over her mouth. 'The next day I thought I had gone mad. I had been so lonely, I wondered if I had dreamed her.'

'Does it matter if you did?'

'Yes! Yes, I need to know it happened. I need to know that she's with me. Like you once said she might be.'

'What does it matter to your life, Thea?' asked Anna Maria gently. She gestured to Thea's stomach. 'What would it change?'

Thea placed a hand over her heart. 'Everything.'

Thea went into labour three nights later, just as a storm arrived with torrential rain that sank the yard into mud and a wind that threatened to lift the thatch. By the time she was leaning over the bed, eyes scrunched tight each time the pain moved through her, thunder was booming so loudly I felt it in my lungs.

Anna Maria was laughing to herself. 'What a night this child has picked.'

Hans nailed cloth over the little window to keep out most of the wet, and then sat in front of the fire, pale and anxious, piling log after log onto the flames.

'Hans, this isn't a fever,' said Anna Maria. 'You can't sweat a baby out.'

'I'll go,' he said, standing up. 'Check on the animals.'

There was a flicker of lightning outside. A flash under the door.

'Don't be stupid,' Thea gasped. 'You'll drown in this.' Another contraction seized her and she groaned and pushed her face into the mattress.

Anna Maria rubbed Thea's back. 'Let him go make himself busy. You'll be a little while yet.'

Thea turned around, wide-eyed. 'Is something wrong?'

Her mother smiled. 'Not at all, my daughter.'

The night passed in an endless outpouring of sound. Hans returned, drenched through, and reluctantly fell asleep by the fire after Anna Maria assured him all was as it should be. I marvelled that the relentless drumming of rain did not wake him. At some point in the near-dawn, as Thea was telling her mother she could not do this, that she would not, I went outside, and it seemed to me that the sky was the sea, that the world had swung upside down and the oceans, now above us in smoky, steeled darkness, were falling upon the earth in revelations of water.

I tilted my face to the sky and opened my mouth, and the sea was upon my tongue.

He was perfect. I watched from the doorway as the baby, his voice all tender vibration of need, was lifted onto Thea's chest. As she nursed him, Hans and Anna Maria sat on the bed beside her and offered up gratitude to God, each word holding their relief and joy.

'Johann,' Thea said, as they lifted their heads from prayer. 'His name is Johann.'

The rain stopped as he was born, as though it had served only to herald his coming.

I waited until they were all asleep before I stepped to the little wooden bassinet beside the bed.

I was in awe of him. So soon come from the place of creation, he seemed to shiver with the mystery of life. I brought my face to his, heard the strange noises he made, his small, light, rapid breathing.

I placed my palm on his chest, noticed the eyelashes not yet unfurled.

In his sleep the child mouthed at his blanket and, finding no sustenance there, crumpled into a kittenish cry. I stood and saw that Thea was already pulling herself out of bed, hands already reaching for his body. She pulled at her nightgown and brought him to her breast, arms crossed beneath him, eyes half closed, as he set to nursing with little grunts.

I marvelled at him and, in that moment, knew him as my own.

ordinary divinity

The winter passed in milk and love, wet cloths strung before the fire, sleep broken-backed. News travelled to Heiligendorf, and the women of the congregation walked to the cottage with food and gifts and clothing. Anna Maria visited as often she was able, knocking on the door and sweeping in with salves and food and offers to hold the baby so that Thea might sleep. Mother and daughter spent nights going through the Seventh Book of Moses, Anna Maria telling Thea which cures she had found best when Thea was a child. 'You should plant an oak tree,' she told Thea. 'A young oak will be good for broken bones.'

I sat within the cottage, content to behold Johann as he grew, to make sure of his grip on the world. I was overwhelmed by the possibilities of his life. What he might do, how he might die. I could not help but hope that he would be a good man, would be good to women and men and himself, would know how to be silent and when to speak. At nights, I sat by his cradle and wished for him all things that might make a life beautiful. A love of growing things, a noticing of the overlooked. A sturdy, soft heart ever open to ordinary divinity: a ripe apricot half upon the tongue; the nape of a lover's neck; the sound of a duck landing on water from flight. And I wished that he would see enough sunrises that his last would not be tragic. The hours could never fit all the things I wished for him.

*

Spring suggested itself to the wind and the valley was splendour-bright in sunlight, a consolation for the fractured nights of feeding and crying and settling. The orchard creeped with green and eddies of wattle blossom from the bush behind the cottage ringed dried puddles in the yard. Johann's cloths gathered yellow dust on the line. The air was warm.

One afternoon I was sitting cross-legged on the floor, next to Johann in his cradle. He had been screaming for most of the day and Thea was bent over, rocking him with her eyes half-closed, brow creased in frustration. When a knocking came at the cottage door, Thea, exhausted, called out for Anna Maria to come in and did not turn around. It wasn't until I heard the visitor clear her throat that I looked up and saw Christiana Radtke standing in the doorway.

Thea glanced over her shoulder, then stood up, startled. 'Oh. Christiana. I wasn't expecting you.'

'Congratulations,' Christiana said, attempting a thin sort of smile. 'I'm sorry I didn't come sooner.' She pointed at the crying baby. 'Johann, isn't it?'

Thea picked him up, and his cries finally eased into a shuddering hiccup. 'He's teething, I think,' she said. 'None of us are getting much sleep. Oh, Christiana, have a seat. Sorry, here.' She pulled out a chair from the table with her free hand.

Christiana sat down stiffly, eyes moving over the inside of the little cottage, taking in the bed in the corner, the chair by the fire, the little carved animals lined up on the windowsill. 'Where is Hans?' she asked.

'In Heiligendorf,' Thea said, easing herself down into the chair opposite. 'At the blacksmith's. I expect he'll be back tonight.'

Christiana said nothing but brought a fingertip to the table and traced the marks left by the adze. 'I meant to come earlier,' she said. 'With Mama.'

'That's all right,' Thea said, voice gentle. 'You must be busy.'

'Yes. Laundering for the English.' She hesitated. 'Henriette is engaged. Pastor Flügel will read the banns this Sunday.'

'Oh, that's lovely news.'

Christiana glanced up, nodding, but did not share Thea's smile. 'To Rudolph Simmel.'

Thea opened her mouth to comment, but Christiana continued, 'Anyway, I've brought you something. For Johann. Although he might already be too big.' She reached down and picked up the basket she had brought, setting it on her lap.

'Thank you, Christiana. That's kind –'

'It's just gathering dust at home.' Christiana took out a neatly folded baby slip, embroidered at the neck. 'I have another that I shall give to Henriette. When the time is right.' She placed it on the table and put the basket back on the floor.

Thea lifted Johann to her other shoulder so that she could look more closely at the dress. 'It is beautiful,' she said. 'Won't you need it for yourself, though?'

Christiana raised her chin into the air. 'I'm not married.'

'You might be. One day.'

'One day . . .' Christiana gave Thea a dark look. 'You take pleasure from my misfortune.'

Thea's face fell. 'Not at all.'

'But you agree that I am unfortunate.'

Thea frowned, puzzled. 'No, Christiana, you misunderstand me.'

'You know about Georg, I suppose.'

'What?'

Christiana stood up suddenly. 'He had no choice. She was already pregnant.'

Thea pushed back her chair and stretched out an arm to Christiana. 'Here, why don't you hold Johann? I didn't mean to upset you. It's a lovely gift – truly, it is.'

Christiana stopped abruptly, eyes fixed on the hearth. 'What is that?' she whispered. I turned and saw what had caught her attention. Two unmortared bricks sitting side by side. I watched as she looked up and saw, above a low fire, the uncovered keeping hole.

The colour drained from Thea's face. 'It's nothing,' she said. Johann began to cry again.

Christiana held up a hand, staring at Thea. A moment passed between them, and then Christiana rushed to the hearth, grabbing Thea's shoulder to block her as she lunged to the fireplace. I moved too, scrambling to my feet as though I could stop her, as though I had the power to protect Thea from Christiana and her outrage. But I could do nothing. Christiana extended her free arm through my protesting body and pulled out the Book of Moses from the keep hole.

'Christiana,' Thea began. 'It's not –'

Christiana, one hand still gripped around the fabric of Thea's blouse, looked up, face lit with a look of triumph and horror. 'You lied. You did all those things.'

'I didn't.'

Christiana hesitated, chin trembling, then let go of Thea and flicked to the title page. She read it, and then flung the book furiously into the fire. A cloud of ash rose as it landed, embers scattering into the room.

Thea jumped back from the flurry of sparks, one hand wrapped around her mouth, the other holding Johann to her shoulder. She was shaking.

No, I thought. No, no, no. I stooped to the fire and tried to pull out the book. My fingers raked through the coals without so much as stirring the ash.

No, she needs this. She needs it.

'Your mother is a liar and so are you.'

Thea moved to take the book from the embers but Christiana

grabbed her again, pushing her away. She levelled a finger at Thea's mouth. 'You bewitched him.'

'What?' Thea murmured, hands around her son. She was white.

Christiana stared at her. 'Hans,' she said, voice suddenly small and plaintive and broken. Then, as the book began to smoulder on the coals, she turned on her heel and strode out the door.

Thea placed Johann in his crib and rushed to the fire just as dark, acrid smoke began billowing from the hearth. She reached for the book but as she gripped the leather and pulled, the pages fell out and immediately blackened on the coals. They curled into ash before my eyes.

Thea sank to the floor, binding in hand. She was too late. Johann's crying turned to insistent, choked screams.

I kneeled next to her. The paper was not catching properly, it was darkening, charring into ash without the reassurance of a hot, bright flame, dissolving into a noxious smoke, now pouring from the hearth. Thea closed her eyes against the sting of it.

'It's gone,' I said quietly. As if she heard me, Thea threw the cover back into the fire with a sob.

She began to cough. Already the room was hazy with fumes. Thea placed her arm over her nose and mouth and slowly pushed herself up to standing. Johann was coughing now, too. I watched her look around for wood, for kindling, for anything to build the fire with and stop its low smouldering. Finding nothing, she picked Johann up from his crib and walked out the open door of the cottage. I followed her as she stumbled to the woodpile beside the fowl house, lungs racking. She lowered herself to the chopping block and wiped her streaming eyes with her sleeve. The baby was breathing quickly, eyes scrunched shut. Behind us, black smoke was issuing through the open door and out of the chimney, reeking of pigskin and something dark and fatty and spoiled, like marrow burning in the bone.

Sawn branches were piled high against the side of the fowl house. Settling Johann against one shoulder, Thea placed the hem of her apron between her teeth and started filling it with kindling, reaching into the heap for the driest wood.

There was a low, eerie growl nearby.

I turned my head as Thea did, saw the same feral black cat staring at the woodpile. Her back arched, tail on end, tipped in white. She yowled again, and then, spitting, streaked off into the bush behind the cottage.

Thea's eyes widened in surprise.

'Hans's cat,' I whispered to myself, and then I heard Thea suddenly, sharply, inhale. The apron hem fell from her mouth, the kindling tumbled to the ground. She staggered backwards in a quiet, urgent scramble, one hand still tight around Johann.

I saw it then.

A sheened coil within the wood heap, a small brown head swaying.

Thea brought her struck hand to her heart, staring at the brown snake that was already sliding from the stacked kindling, was already winding into the landscape, absorbed into it.

Oh God, I thought. Oh God, what has happened?

The moment Thea returned to the cottage, the book smouldering on the coals burst into flame. The air inside, thick and poisonous, began to clear.

Thea was pale. Her hair was unwinding from her braids. She paced the room, taking her hand from Johann's back to examine the strike marks on the flesh of her palm. Then, as if deciding, she set Johann back in his cradle and washed the wound in water from the jug on the table. Johann continued to cry, quivering fists above his head, as though he knew what had happened and was already railing against it.

I could do nothing but watch. Thea gingerly dabbed her hand dry with her apron and then wrapped it in the dress Christiana had brought as the fire roared with burning paper. The flames cast a weird glow against the cottage walls. The air was thickly gauzed with smoke.

Thea stumbled then, and I felt cold fear. I was back inside the ship, in the darkness, terrified at the cant of the floor, and the water coming to drown us. For a moment she was motionless. Then she stooped to pick up Johann again and it was as though the floor had tilted, as though the world had forsaken its axis and nothing was sure, nothing was steady. The ocean was here. It was hungry. She staggered sideways.

I could do nothing.

Thea left Johann in his cradle and, instead, tried to drag it to the side of the bed in the corner of the room, holding a hand to her head as though it pained her. She fell again. I saw dark water pooling on the floor. Leaving the cradle in the middle of the room, she stumbled to the bed alone.

I climbed in with her. I wanted her in my arms. I wanted to guard her from what was happening, the terrible waters rising.

Thea lay on her side, her injured hand tucked under her chin and her free arm dangling over the edge, fingers waving at Johann.

'Shh,' she was saying. 'You are safe. You are loved.'

I placed my mouth over the bite on her hand and felt her pulse jump against my lip. Her wrist was warm and soft and there was the suggestion of vein and artery and tiny bones lying hidden beneath the skin, and I touched my tongue to the punctures and tasted something oddly sweet, a little sharp. I sucked at it in a wild hope that it would do something, that I might help her. There was no bitterness.

'You are safe,' Thea was still saying to Johann. Her voice had become strained. 'You are loved.' She said it again and again until Johann stopped crying. She said it until she could not form words, until it sounded as though she were talking underwater, as though she had moved beyond language, as though her tongue had lost its way. I could hear the roar of the sea taking back the bush, filling the valleys and the high country, taking the air from the room.

Thea's breathing changed, then. I heard her heart fall out of time with every hymn I had ever composed to its syncopation. Her chest began to rise and fall, too fast. I was no longer certain she was taking in air. Her body shook.

I wanted so badly to pray, but my tongue had forgotten the taste of the Lord, and so I sang. As her eyes closed and her face became slack, as her breathing became strangled, I sang. I sang against the rushing of the tide. Her fingers trembled, but there was no intention in them, and then they were hanging, and she was still, and my song had become a cry. The ocean rose up around the bed and I asked the trees and the earth and the burning fire in the hearth to do something. It was not enough that they might move and turn as though nothing was happening; they must stop what was happening because I could not. I could not do a thing.

Oh God in your Kingdom, oh Thea. Thea. Open your eyes.

I was holding her. I was bearing it, bearing her. I was not letting go of her.

The waves rose and we were underwater, and, suddenly, there was a stillness and a silence.

I held her. She died as I held her.

Hans came home later that night. He came into the house holding a lamp aloft, braced against the dark, and in its light I could see the concern and fear on his face at Johann, screaming in his cradle, his swaddling unravelled and his face red and tight with tears, at the fire dead in the hearth. I had listened to the baby choke on his own cries for hours by then, but I couldn't move. I was afraid to let go of Thea.

Hans set the lantern on the table and picked up Johann. I watched him take in the cold ashes, the absence of Thea's usual candle casting a glow in her corner by the fire, by the seat he had made her. He rubbed Johann's back, soothing him.

'Thea?' Hans's voice seemed too loud for such a small space. I could hear the fear in it and guessed at his thoughts. She has run for help. She is trapped outside somewhere. Someone has taken her. A well. A fire. A fall. Then he turned to the bed and saw that she was in it.

Hans took up the lantern again, his other arm holding Johann, already shuddered into sleep, exhausted, relieved to be held finally.

'Thea?'

She did not move and he said her name again.

And then he set the lantern on the floor so that he could touch her.

I saw the touch confirm for him what he must have feared the moment he stepped into the house and heard the screams of his son. I saw him understand that his wife was gone.

Still, he gently lay Johann on the bed between Thea's body and the wall, and leaned over to kiss her. Then he sat and, for a long time, looked at her. I wondered if he knew what had happened.

Eventually, in that silence of deep night, he stood and put on his coat, then picked his son up and wrapped him in a blanket, before leaving, lantern in hand.

All that long night I hoped that Thea would remain as I have. I held her body and remembered the albatross, and wondered whether Thea, too, might find herself outside the cottage by the fig tree, listening to the rare sound of a magpie singing the midnight hour, wondering at angels. Even as I held her body, I listened for her footfall, and there was a moment, when the birdsong summoned the dawn and I heard voices, that I thought I might see her again. But the grey light brought with it only Hans, Flügel and Anna Maria, cradling Johann in her arms.

The pastor found the strike marks and fit his lips around prayer and condolence. Anna Maria broke down and cried with such undisguised grief that Hans left the cottage. Flügel reached for Johann, but Anna Maria would not relinquish the boy, and the child and the woman cried together, over the pastor's assertion of grace. When Flügel stepped outside to give her a moment with her daughter, I watched the Wend wipe her eyes and go to the cold fireplace. She was still when she saw the bricks upon the hearth, the keeping hole uncovered and empty. I watched her kneel and extend a hand over the ashes, then slowly, as though it were still alight, pick out a small, charred fragment of paper. She brought it to her chest and howled.

I left, then.

I kissed Thea's forehead through the sheet that had been pulled up over it, and without knowing quite what I was doing, knowing only that I must leave, must go, I walked outside, past Flügel waiting by the door, past Hans hurling stones at the sky, and climbed up to this ridge. I sat and watched the sun rise over the world. I felt surrender approaching.

And then I felt within me the urge to speak.

NOW

heart-shimmer, heart-shiver

Thea died three days ago, and since then I have felt a change within me. Even this sunlight on my skin feels strange, as though it pours through me, as though it cannot settle its warmth upon my body. I sense time at work too, when for so long I have felt adrift on endlessness. My bones feel as though they have been kneaded by years. I think, perhaps, I am finally waiting for a folding-up. Dissolution.

I think back to the darkness that held me after the whale song on the *Kristi*, and it no longer seems like an abstract memory, but a promise. That great benevolence. That suspension of nothing and everything. Something coming. A happening.

This will all end soon.

And so I have spoken. These passing days I have described what has happened to me, and what I felt, and what I continue to feel. Gathered up and thrown on the wind to be wound on the air. To stir leaves and gutter candles and fill the sails of ships. I am unthreaded of it. I am the empty eye of the needle.

That two girls might meet and already know each other. Might already love each other.

One hand finding the other.

I thought that if I placed my palm against the rush of quickened wind and swore to our love, made myself an apostle of it, wondered at the miracle of it, I might inure myself to the pain of severance. I wanted to bear witness but perhaps, too, I was searching for a way to understand that it is all over. I wanted to say goodbye to her. Testimony as farewell.

Down in the valley the bell is tolling, and not for the hour.

The bell only rings at this time for the dead. It rings in the day's labour and it knells its close. It summons the faithful and disperses them. Warns of bushfire, flood. And when someone dies, it announces each year of life blessed to them, tolls in steady, slow rhythm until the age of death is reached.

Twenty-one. Twenty-two.

Each strike of the bell is a year of seasons, sorrow and joy. Of meals eaten and prayers offered. Leaf burst and flourish and fall and rot.

Twenty-five. Twenty-six. Twenty-seven.

There. It has stopped. The deep echo floods the valley floor for a moment before fading. There, the span of a life wrung out in sound.

They will bury Thea now.

I will go and I will see her lowered into this earth, and then I will know she is gone. There will be no reason to stay and I will wait for timelessness to come for me. I imagine it already lapping at each hour.

Down and down and down into the valley. There is the scar line of fence posts, emptied now of her stones, her promises of together, and as I follow them to the house I see the mourners in black gathering outside in the yard.

Hans is one of six bearers holding the coffin on the funeral bier, Matthias behind him, an arm on the shoulder of his friend. Augusta and Matthias's eldest boy leads the procession to the graveside, carrying his black wooden cross with such solemnity that I would smile if it were not Thea dead, Thea in the coffin, Thea no longer here, gone where everyone else has gone.

Sweet, absorbing darkness.

I want to wear black too. I want to take a moonless night and make a shroud of it, I want to wrap it about my head and cry into that night of no moon. I will take the black of a well and dress myself in its dark, hidden water until it fills my mouth and drowns me, and I may be where she is.

The cemetery is still a corner of gentle soil. I am glad that Thea has a hand of good earth to hold her bones. The grave has been dug east to west, and as the coffin is lowered into it, the pastor talks of trumpets sounding on Judgement Day. As he speaks, I imagine Thea lifting out of soil to a rising sun. Never not miraculous, a seed in the earth.

'Dorothea passes from our community of believers into the company of those who need faith no longer, but see God face to face,' says the pastor, and he nods at Hans, who takes a handful of dirt and casts it onto the coffin.

Thea's body is committed to the earth.

Johann sleeps in my brother's arms. I watch Matthias kiss his pale head.

*

I stand alone as '*Mitten wir im Leben sind mit dem Tod umfangen*' is sung by the mourners. All the voices rise in natural, long-familiar harmonies, and I tremble at the melding of deep and high. In my mind I see Thea at her first service in the pine forest, nudged by her mother and turning to me. Thea, looking back, eyes meeting my own.

I sing, then. For the first time since the ship, I sing a hymn. It swells inside me like a wave and I hear my own voice like a bell, holding the last note for a moment longer, unwilling to let it end.

The endless song, I think, as the mourners turn from the grave and walk away. I want to sing the endless song.

And then I am alone. Devoted still.

'Your voice is a gift.'

I turn. I am turning, I am the world in orbit turning heartsore to the sun, and she is there, she is shining, she is golden. Thea, my love, my whole heart-shimmer, heart-shiver. Curtain torn. Seed splitting. Light pouring through an open window and blazing holy upon me.

'Hanne,' she cries, and her hands are on my cheeks, fingertips on my mouth, palms holding my crying face, holding me up in light, in love.

I fall to my knees and she kneels with me. Thea, Thea in front of me, both of us kneeling under a cathedral of sky.

Love runs through her like a seam of gold. It runs through me, too, and we are illuminated.

the song is endless

We are golden here. The light makes us so.

If the grapes are sweet, it is because we sleep under the gnarled hands that offer them. If the water tastes of salt, it is because the rain makes its way through our hair, it is because we let it pour over our skin and so bless it.

If you kindle a fire, we will warm ourselves by it. We will warm ourselves at every fire you light. Pour your wine and let us drink and hold communion with the world that made it. That made us, and you. Small miracles of life.

If you ever feel pain that comes from a deep knowing that it will not last, that it cannot last, it will pass, it is passing, know that some things remain.

The song is endless.

We will wait for you, and then we will go together.

author's note

Hanne, like all other characters in this novel, is fictional, but those familiar with South Australian colonial history may recognise real-life parallels between her community and others. In writing this book I have leaned hard on the 1838 voyage of the *Zebra* from Altona to Adelaide, as well as the experiences of the Old Lutherans who, after arriving in South Australia, formed the town of Hahndorf (Bukartilla) on Peramangk land.

In writing this book I do not seek to glorify, simplify or sentimentalise the colonisation of Australia. The land 'settled' by the Old Lutherans who established Hahndorf and other villages in the Adelaide Hills had been inhabited for millennia by the original custodians of the land, the Peramangk people. Few violent encounters were recorded as occurring between the Old Lutherans and the Peramangk at Hahndorf – the latter almost certainly saved the former from starvation by teaching them how to source food in the months after their arrival – but the ongoing effects of colonialisation continue to this day, and no treaty has been made with any Aboriginal peoples.

I urge those who wish to offer support to look up the following:
ANTaR – antar.org.au
Healing Foundation – healingfoundation.org.au
Indigenous Literacy Foundation – indigenousliteracyfoundation.
org.au

acknowledgements

I am so grateful to those who have cheered on the writing of this book over the past five years. There is no way *Devotion* would have been written without your encouragement.

Thank you to Pippa Masson for your faith in me, your honesty and warmth, and for always being in my corner. I am so very lucky to have you as my agent, along with the rest of the brilliant team at Curtis Brown Australia. Thank you to Gordon Wise and Kate Cooper and the team at Curtis Brown UK. Your support and enthusiasm are so appreciated, and I am honoured to have representation with you. To Dan Lazar at Writers House, thank you for your kind, considerate suggestions, and for your positive attitude. To Jerry Kalajian at Intellectual Property Group, thank you for your patience and passion.

To Cate Paterson, for your calm and steady encouragement, thank you. It is a privilege to be published with Picador. Thank you to Mathilda Imlah for being so generous with your time and genius, even when you really had much better and more important things to do. Thank you to Ali Lavau, superstar, for your considered edit. Thank you to Tracey Cheetham (deadset legend), Danielle Walker, and all the incredible people at Pan Macmillan Australia for the passion you bring, and the myriad ways you have helped this book on its way. I'd give you all a hug if I could.

To Sophie Jonathan, thank you for knowing when to dig deeper, and for your superb, intelligent mind. Thank you to Kate Green and the wonderful team at Picador UK for loving books the way you do. I am eternally thrilled to be one of your authors.

To Elder Mandy Brown, I am deeply grateful for your time, insights, and conversation. Thank you for speaking with me and sharing your knowledge. Our chats had a profound impact on me.

Thank you to Anni Luur Fox for your stories about Hahndorf and enthusiasm for its history. Thank you to Annette Humphries for all of your kind assistance.

To Kristie Hedley, thank you for so generously supporting the #authorsforfireys charitable auction in early 2020. (I hope you forgive me for using the Latin origin of your name.)

Thank you to Margot McGovern and Lisa Bennett for reassuring me that a Lutheran ghost was a good idea, and for all our writers' coven nights. To my friends who continue to get in touch with me even when I don't reply for weeks, and who somehow still forgive me for disappearing, thank you. Thank you to Gail and David for your support. Thank you to Pam, Alan, Briony and Owen for your unconditional love and for reminding me that I always get there eventually.

To my children (who were born during the writing of this book), I love you both so much. Anouk, thank you for every sweet interruption, every picture drawn on my research papers. Rory, thank you for your ready laugh, and for all the snuggles.

And finally, thank you to Heidi, my love. Thank you for the pram chats, the picnic lunches on the floor, wrangling children so I could have another hour to write. But most of all, thank you for your belief in me and this story. *Devotion* is for you.